SCOOBY-DOO

WHERE ARE YOU?

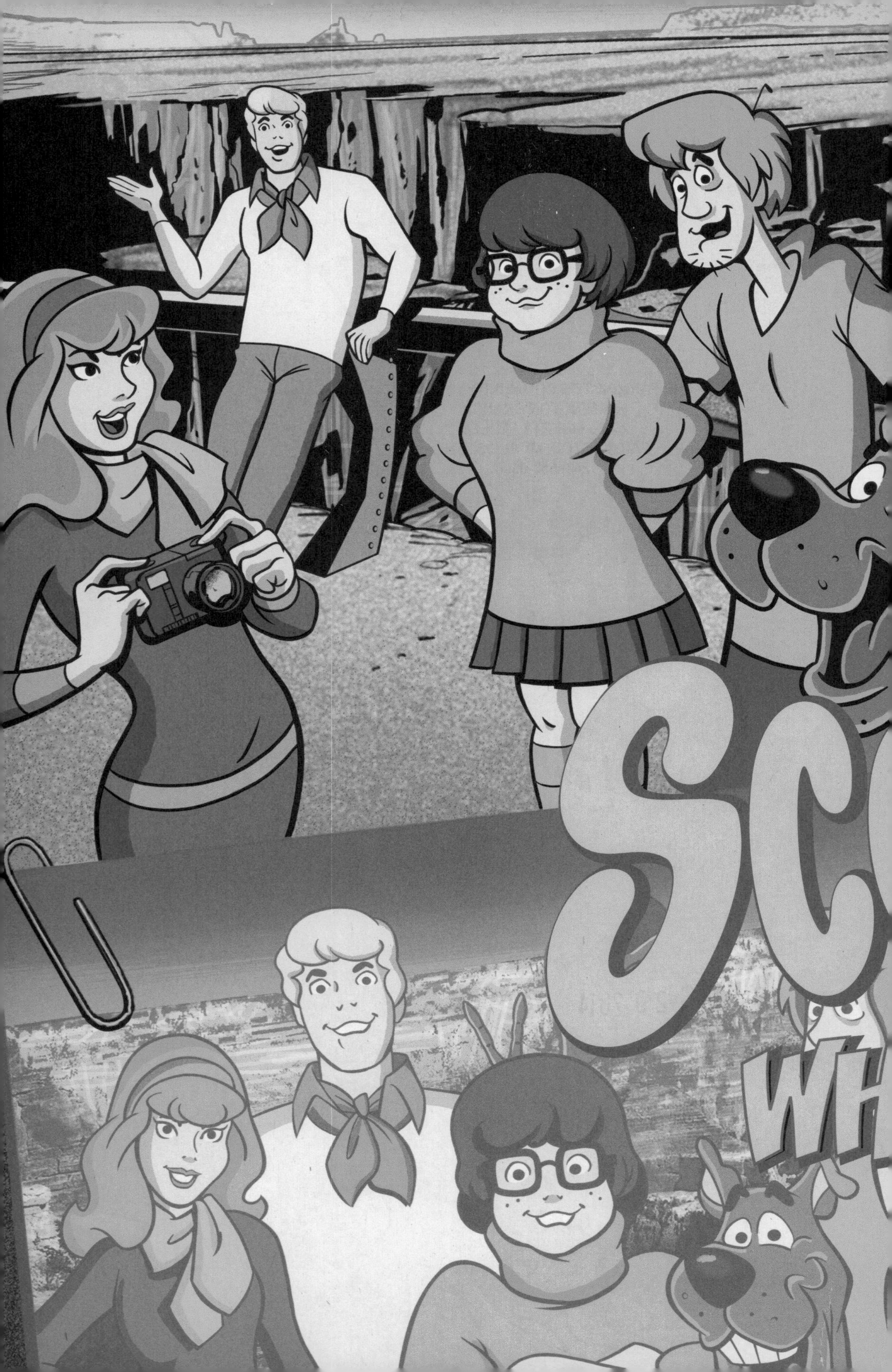

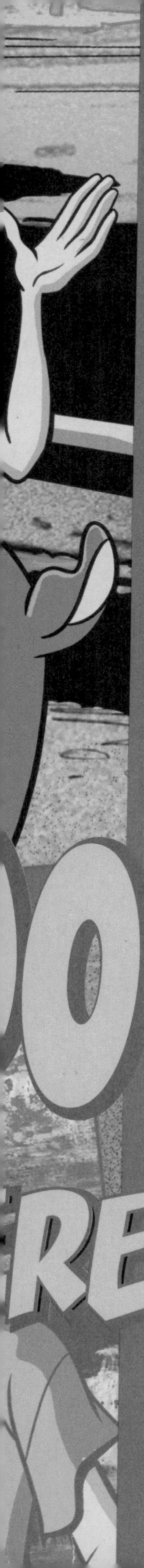

Scott Gross
Chris Duffy
Sam Henderson
John Rozum
Terrance Griep Jr.
Scott Beatty
Robert Greenberger
Writers

Scott Gross
Tim Harkins
Manny Galan
Mike DeCarlo
Joe Staton
Andrew Pepoy
Scott Neely
Fabio Laguna
Bill Alger
Bob Smith
Artists

WildStorm FX
Patricia Mulvihill
David Rodriguez
Paul Becton
David Rodriguez
Heroic Age
Colorists

Nick J. Napolitano
Tim Harkins
Travis Lanham
John Costanza
Albert DeGuzman
Phil Felix
Letterers

Scott Gross
Collection Cover

OOBY-DOO
RE ARE YOU?

Scott Peterson **Bronwyn Taggart** **Dana Kurtin** **Chuck Kim** Editors – Original Series
Chynna Clugston Flores Assistant Editor – Original Series
Robin Wildman Editor
Robbin Brosterman Design Director – Books

Bob Harras VP – Editor-in-Chief

Diane Nelson President
Dan DiDio and **Jim Lee** Co-Publishers
Geoff Johns Chief Creative Officer
John Rood Executive VP – Sales, Marketing and Business Development
Amy Genkins Senior VP – Business and Legal Affairs
Nairi Gardiner Senior VP – Finance
Jeff Boison VP – Publishing Operations
Mark Chiarello VP – Art Direction and Design
John Cunningham VP – Marketing
Terri Cunningham VP – Talent Relations and Services
Alison Gill Senior VP – Manufacturing and Operations
Hank Kanalz Senior VP – Digital
Jay Kogan VP – Business and Legal Affairs, Publishing
Jack Mahan VP – Business Affairs, Talent
Nick Napolitano VP – Manufacturing Administration
Sue Pohja VP – Book Sales
Courtney Simmons Senior VP – Publicity
Bob Wayne Senior VP – Sales

SCOOBY-DOO, WHERE ARE YOU?

DC Comics, 1700 Broadway, New York, NY 10019
A Warner Bros. Entertainment Company.
Printed by RR Donnelley, Willard, OH, USA. 10/12/12. Second Printing.
ISBN: 978-1-4012-3358-7

SUSTAINABLE FORESTRY INITIATIVE
Certified Chain of Custody
Promoting Sustainable Forestry
www.sfiprogram.org
SFI-01042
APPLIES TO TEXT STOCK ONLY

Library of Congress Cataloging-in-Publication Data

Scooby-Doo, where are you? / Scott Gross, Chris Duffy ... [et al.], writers ; Scott Gross, Tim
Harkins ... [et al.], artists.
p. cm.
"Originally published in single magazine form in Scooby-Doo Where Are You #1-6."
ISBN 978-1-4012-3358-7
1. Graphic novels. I. Gross, Scott. II. Duffy, Chris (Comic book writer) III. Harkins, Tim.
PN6728.S37S39 2012
741.5'973–dc23

2012030476

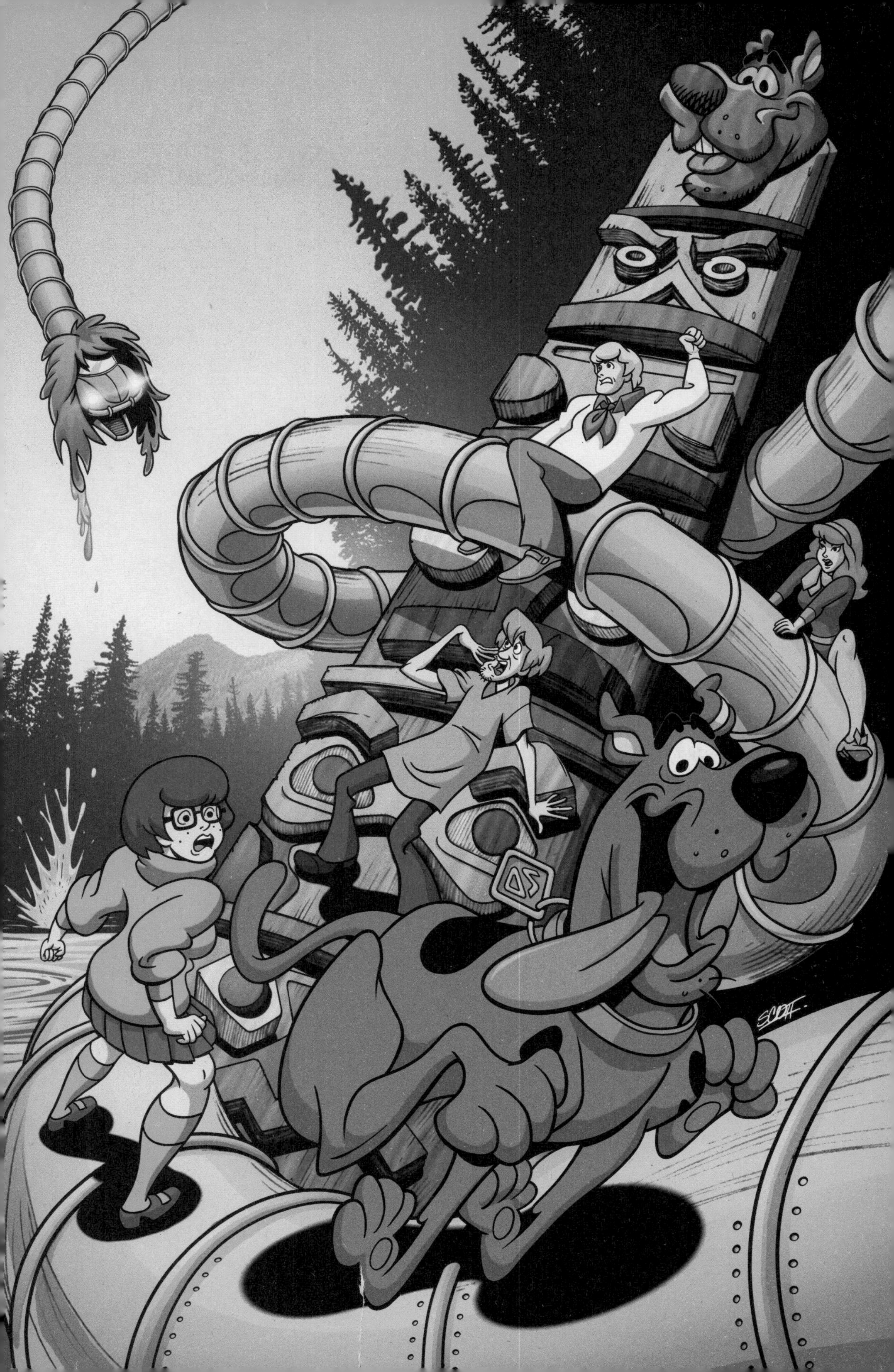

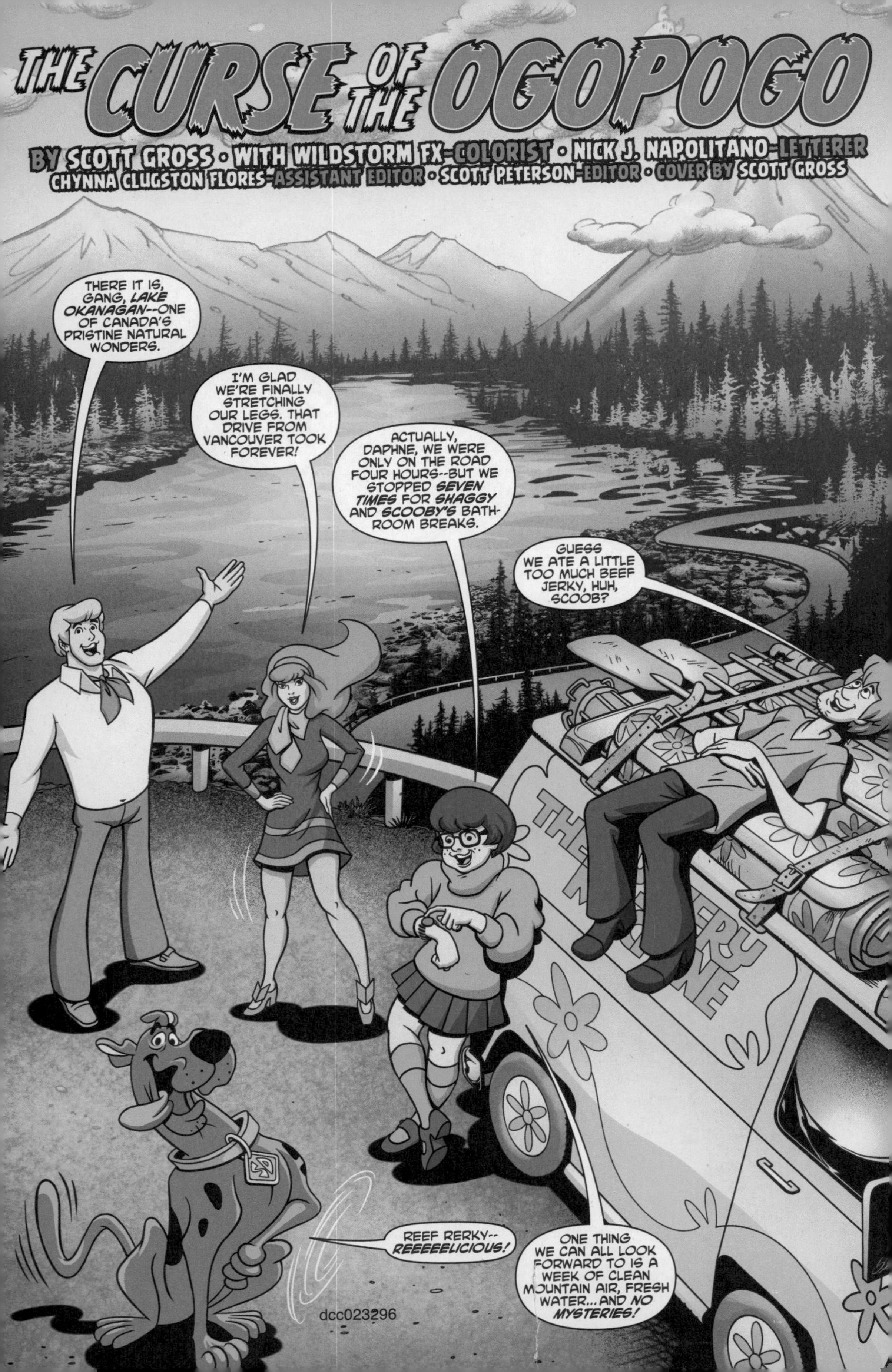
THE CURSE OF THE OGOPOGO
BY SCOTT GROSS • WITH WILDSTORM FX-COLORIST • NICK J. NAPOLITANO-LETTERER
CHYNNA CLUGSTON FLORES-ASSISTANT EDITOR • SCOTT PETERSON-EDITOR • COVER BY SCOTT GROSS
THERE IT IS, GANG, LAKE OKANAGAN--ONE OF CANADA'S PRISTINE NATURAL WONDERS.
I'M GLAD WE'RE FINALLY STRETCHING OUR LEGS. THAT DRIVE FROM VANCOUVER TOOK FOREVER!
ACTUALLY, DAPHNE, WE WERE ONLY ON THE ROAD FOUR HOURS--BUT WE STOPPED SEVEN TIMES FOR SHAGGY AND SCOOBY'S BATHROOM BREAKS.
GUESS WE ATE A LITTLE TOO MUCH BEEF JERKY, HUH, SCOOB?
REEF RERKY--REEEEELICIOUS!
ONE THING WE CAN ALL LOOK FORWARD TO IS A WEEK OF CLEAN MOUNTAIN AIR, FRESH WATER...AND NO MYSTERIES!
THE MYSTERY MACHINE
dcc023296

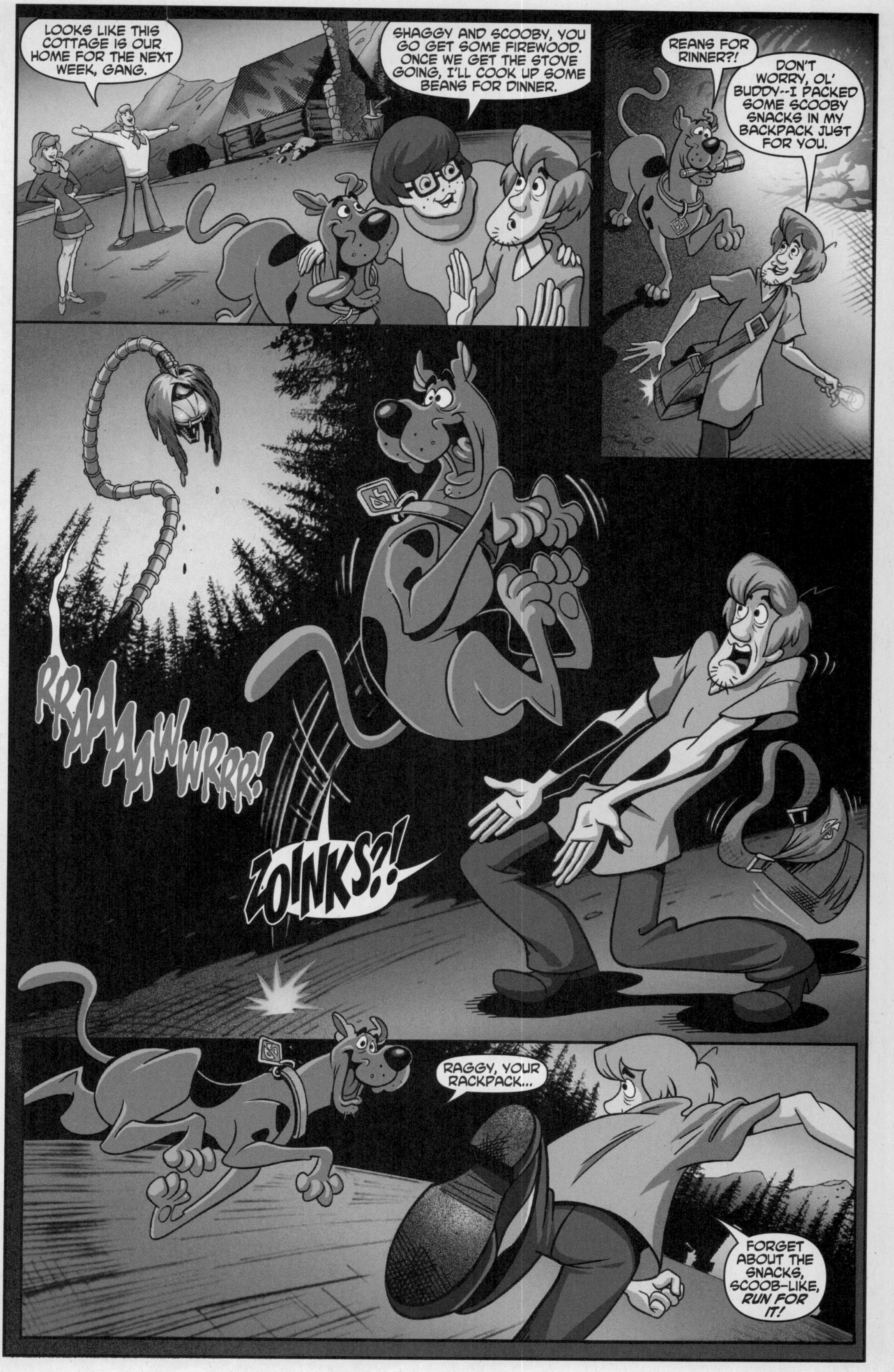

LOOKS LIKE THIS COTTAGE IS OUR HOME FOR THE NEXT WEEK, GANG.
SHAGGY AND SCOOBY, YOU GO GET SOME FIREWOOD. ONCE WE GET THE STOVE GOING, I'LL COOK UP SOME BEANS FOR DINNER.
REANS FOR RINNER?!
DON'T WORRY, OL' BUDDY--I PACKED SOME SCOOBY SNACKS IN MY BACKPACK JUST FOR YOU.
RRAAAAAWWRRR!
ZOINKS?!
RAGGY, YOUR RACKPACK...
FORGET ABOUT THE SNACKS, SCOOB--LIKE, *RUN FOR IT!*

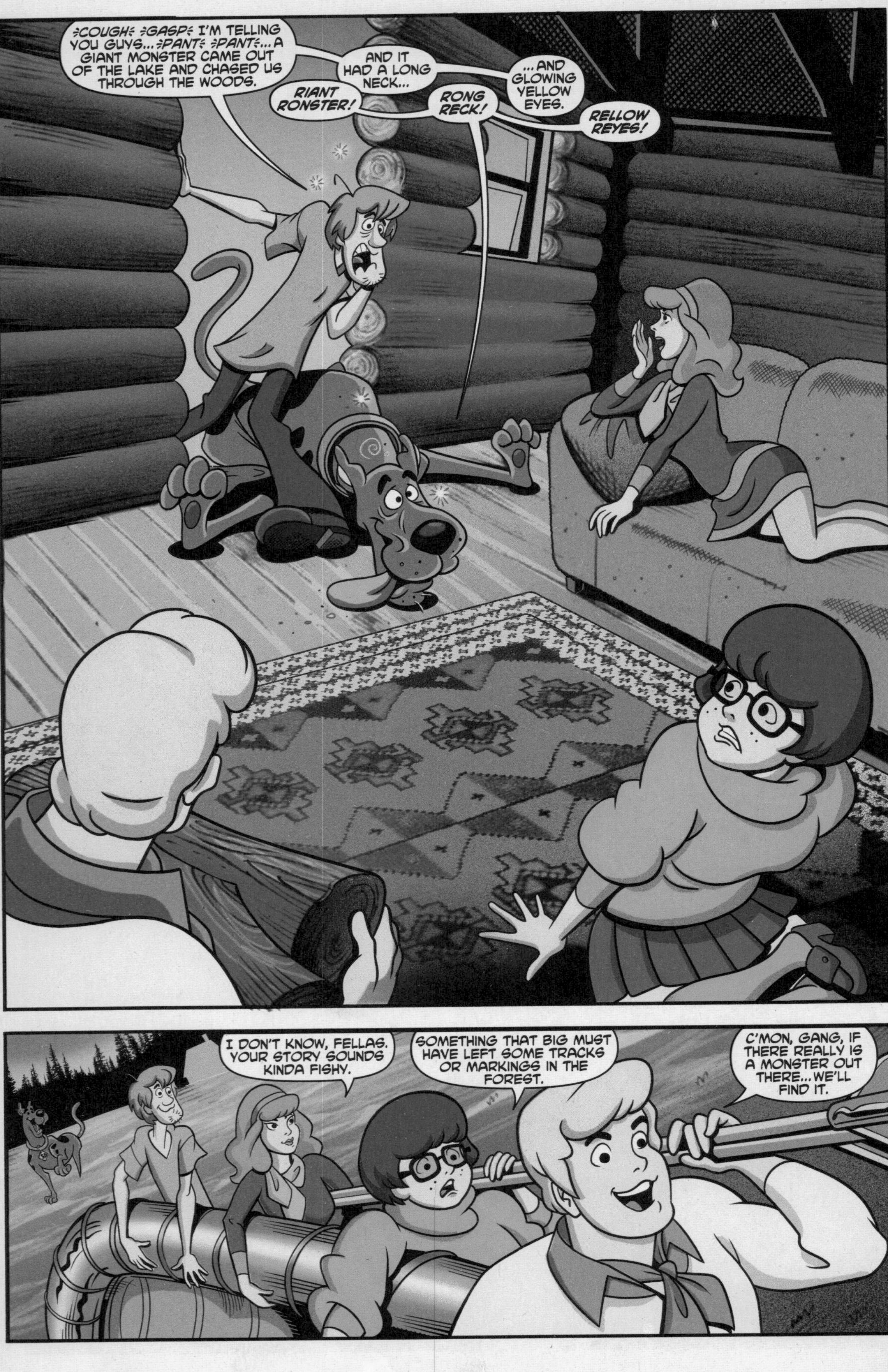
COUGH *GASP* I'M TELLING YOU GUYS... *PANT* *PANT*... A GIANT MONSTER CAME OUT OF THE LAKE AND CHASED US THROUGH THE WOODS.
RIANT RONSTER!
AND IT HAD A LONG NECK...
RONG RECK!
...AND GLOWING YELLOW EYES.
RELLOW REYES!
I DON'T KNOW, FELLAS. YOUR STORY SOUNDS KINDA FISHY.
SOMETHING THAT BIG MUST HAVE LEFT SOME TRACKS OR MARKINGS IN THE FOREST.
C'MON, GANG, IF THERE REALLY IS A MONSTER OUT THERE... WE'LL FIND IT.

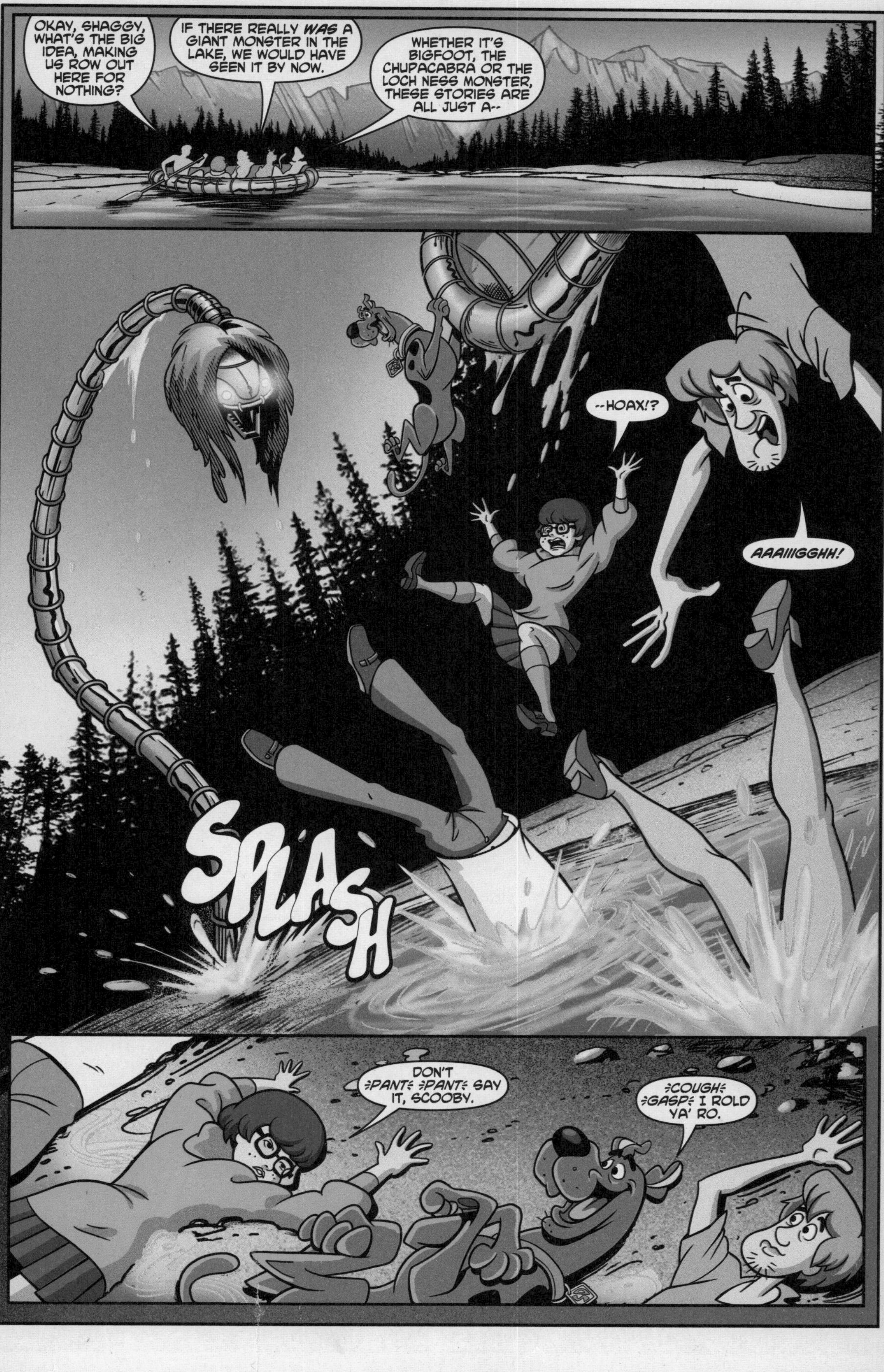
OKAY, SHAGGY, WHAT'S THE BIG IDEA, MAKING US ROW OUT HERE FOR NOTHING?
IF THERE REALLY *WAS* A GIANT MONSTER IN THE LAKE, WE WOULD HAVE SEEN IT BY NOW.
WHETHER IT'S BIGFOOT, THE CHUPACABRA OR THE LOCH NESS MONSTER, THESE STORIES ARE ALL JUST A--
--HOAX!?
AAAIIIGGHH!
SPLASH
DON'T *PANT* *PANT* SAY IT, SCOOBY.
COUGH *GASP* I ROLD YA' RO.

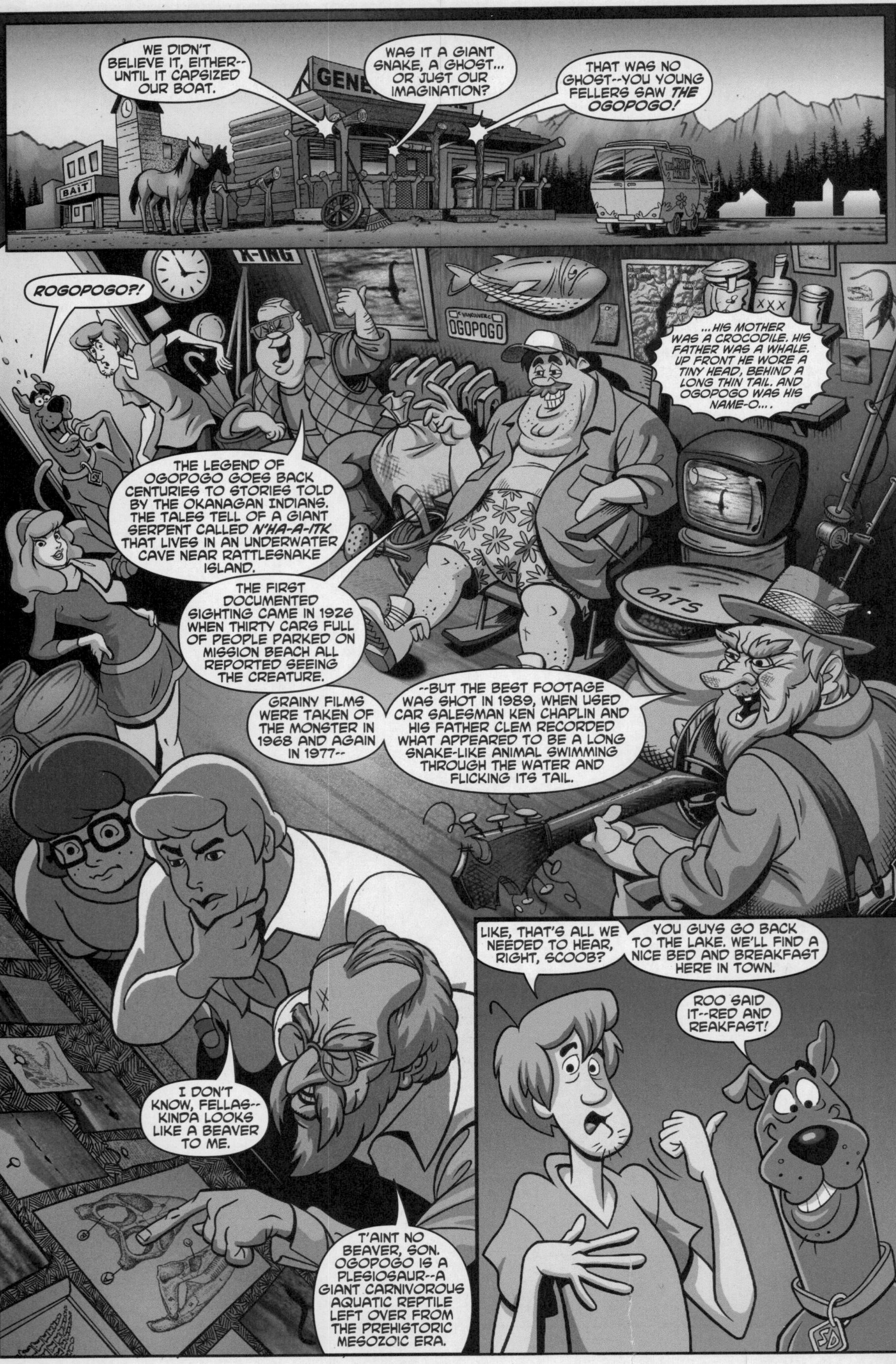
WE DIDN'T BELIEVE IT, EITHER--UNTIL IT CAPSIZED OUR BOAT.
WAS IT A GIANT SNAKE, A GHOST... OR JUST OUR IMAGINATION?
THAT WAS NO GHOST--YOU YOUNG FELLERS SAW *THE OGOPOGO!*
BAIT
ROGOPOGO?!
X-ING
OGOPOGO
...HIS MOTHER WAS A CROCODILE. HIS FATHER WAS A WHALE. UP FRONT HE WORE A TINY HEAD, BEHIND A LONG THIN TAIL. AND OGOPOGO WAS HIS NAME-O....
THE LEGEND OF OGOPOGO GOES BACK CENTURIES TO STORIES TOLD BY THE OKANAGAN INDIANS. THE TALES TELL OF A GIANT SERPENT CALLED *N'HA-A-ITK* THAT LIVES IN AN UNDERWATER CAVE NEAR RATTLESNAKE ISLAND.
THE FIRST DOCUMENTED SIGHTING CAME IN 1926 WHEN THIRTY CARS FULL OF PEOPLE PARKED ON MISSION BEACH ALL REPORTED SEEING THE CREATURE.
OATS
GRAINY FILMS WERE TAKEN OF THE MONSTER IN 1968 AND AGAIN IN 1977--
--BUT THE BEST FOOTAGE WAS SHOT IN 1989, WHEN USED CAR SALESMAN KEN CHAPLIN AND HIS FATHER CLEM RECORDED WHAT APPEARED TO BE A LONG SNAKE-LIKE ANIMAL SWIMMING THROUGH THE WATER AND FLICKING ITS TAIL.
I DON'T KNOW, FELLAS--KINDA LOOKS LIKE A BEAVER TO ME.
T'AINT NO BEAVER, SON. OGOPOGO IS A PLESIOSAUR--A GIANT CARNIVOROUS AQUATIC REPTILE LEFT OVER FROM THE PREHISTORIC MESOZOIC ERA.
LIKE, THAT'S ALL WE NEEDED TO HEAR, RIGHT, SCOOB?
YOU GUYS GO BACK TO THE LAKE. WE'LL FIND A NICE BED AND BREAKFAST HERE IN TOWN.
ROO SAID IT--RED AND REAKFAST!

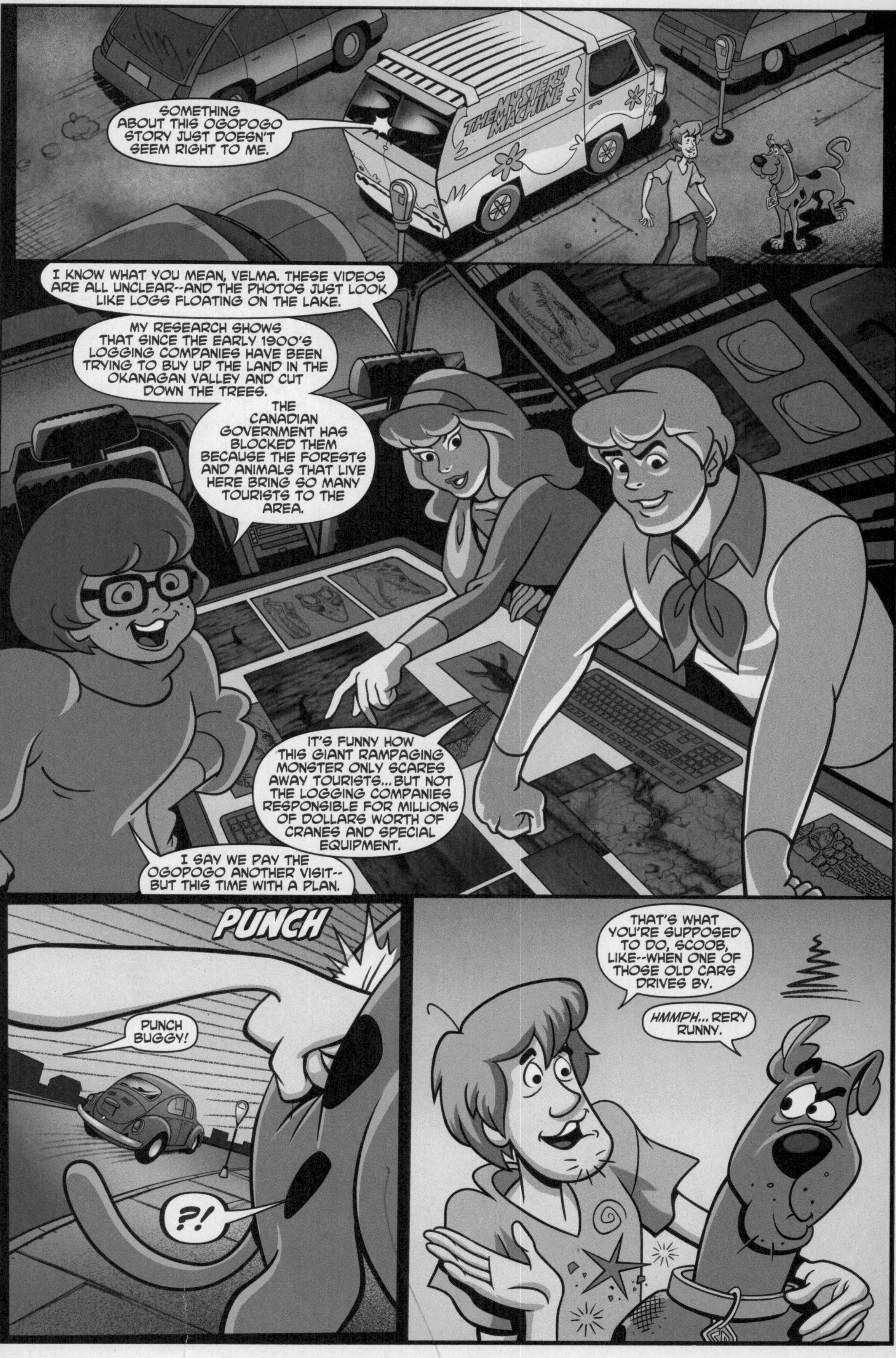
SOMETHING ABOUT THIS OGOPOGO STORY JUST DOESN'T SEEM RIGHT TO ME.
THE MYSTERY MACHINE
I KNOW WHAT YOU MEAN, VELMA. THESE VIDEOS ARE ALL UNCLEAR--AND THE PHOTOS JUST LOOK LIKE LOGS FLOATING ON THE LAKE.
MY RESEARCH SHOWS THAT SINCE THE EARLY 1900'S LOGGING COMPANIES HAVE BEEN TRYING TO BUY UP THE LAND IN THE OKANAGAN VALLEY AND CUT DOWN THE TREES.
THE CANADIAN GOVERNMENT HAS BLOCKED THEM BECAUSE THE FORESTS AND ANIMALS THAT LIVE HERE BRING SO MANY TOURISTS TO THE AREA.
IT'S FUNNY HOW THIS GIANT RAMPAGING MONSTER ONLY SCARES AWAY TOURISTS...BUT NOT THE LOGGING COMPANIES RESPONSIBLE FOR MILLIONS OF DOLLARS WORTH OF CRANES AND SPECIAL EQUIPMENT.
I SAY WE PAY THE OGOPOGO ANOTHER VISIT--BUT THIS TIME WITH A PLAN.
PUNCH
PUNCH BUGGY!
?!
THAT'S WHAT YOU'RE SUPPOSED TO DO, SCOOB, LIKE--WHEN ONE OF THOSE OLD CARS DRIVES BY.
HMMPH... RERY RUNNY.

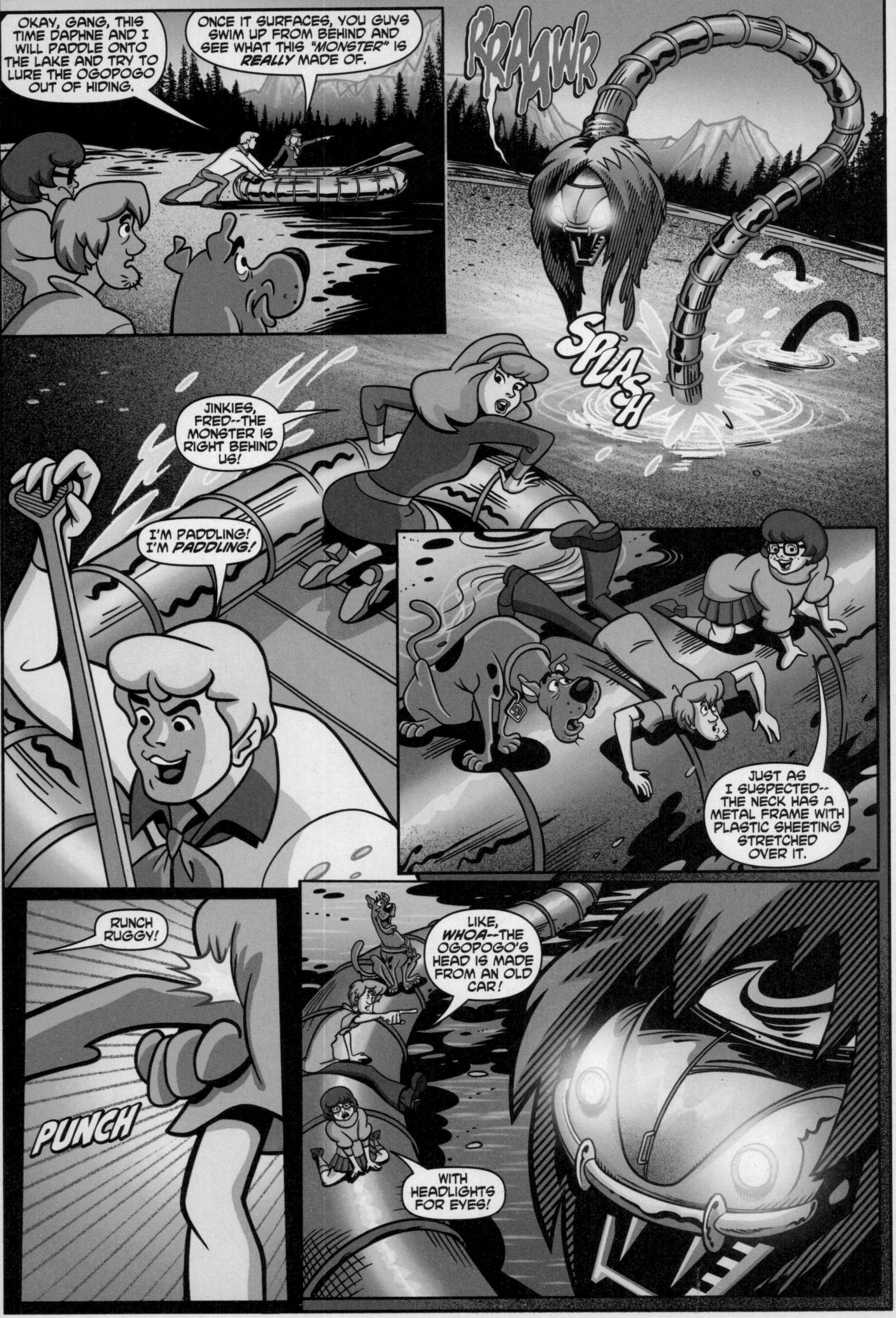
OKAY, GANG, THIS TIME DAPHNE AND I WILL PADDLE ONTO THE LAKE AND TRY TO LURE THE OGOPOGO OUT OF HIDING.
ONCE IT SURFACES, YOU GUYS SWIM UP FROM BEHIND AND SEE WHAT THIS "MONSTER" IS REALLY MADE OF.
RRAAAWR
SPLASH
JINKIES, FRED--THE MONSTER IS RIGHT BEHIND US!
I'M PADDLING! I'M PADDLING!
JUST AS I SUSPECTED--THE NECK HAS A METAL FRAME WITH PLASTIC SHEETING STRETCHED OVER IT.
RUNCH RUGGY!
PUNCH
LIKE, WHOA--THE OGOPOGO'S HEAD IS MADE FROM AN OLD CAR!
WITH HEADLIGHTS FOR EYES!

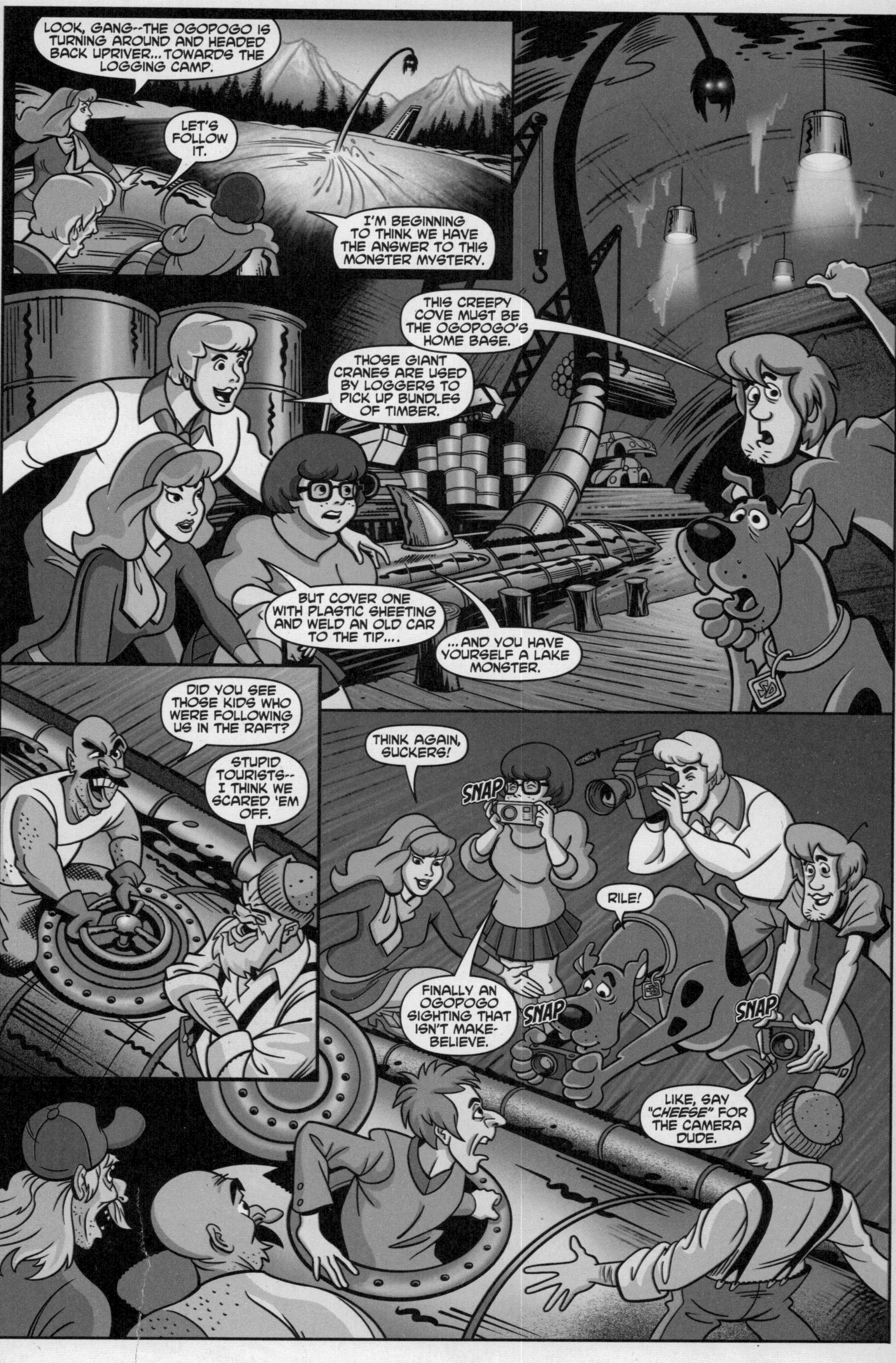
LOOK, GANG--THE OGOPOGO IS TURNING AROUND AND HEADED BACK UPRIVER... TOWARDS THE LOGGING CAMP.
LET'S FOLLOW IT.
I'M BEGINNING TO THINK WE HAVE THE ANSWER TO THIS MONSTER MYSTERY.
THIS CREEPY COVE MUST BE THE OGOPOGO'S HOME BASE.
THOSE GIANT CRANES ARE USED BY LOGGERS TO PICK UP BUNDLES OF TIMBER.
BUT COVER ONE WITH PLASTIC SHEETING AND WELD AN OLD CAR TO THE TIP....
...AND YOU HAVE YOURSELF A LAKE MONSTER.
DID YOU SEE THOSE KIDS WHO WERE FOLLOWING US IN THE RAFT?
STUPID TOURISTS-- I THINK WE SCARED 'EM OFF.
THINK AGAIN, SUCKERS!
SNAP
RILE!
FINALLY AN OGOPOGO SIGHTING THAT ISN'T MAKE-BELIEVE.
SNAP
SNAP
LIKE, SAY "CHEESE" FOR THE CAMERA DUDE.

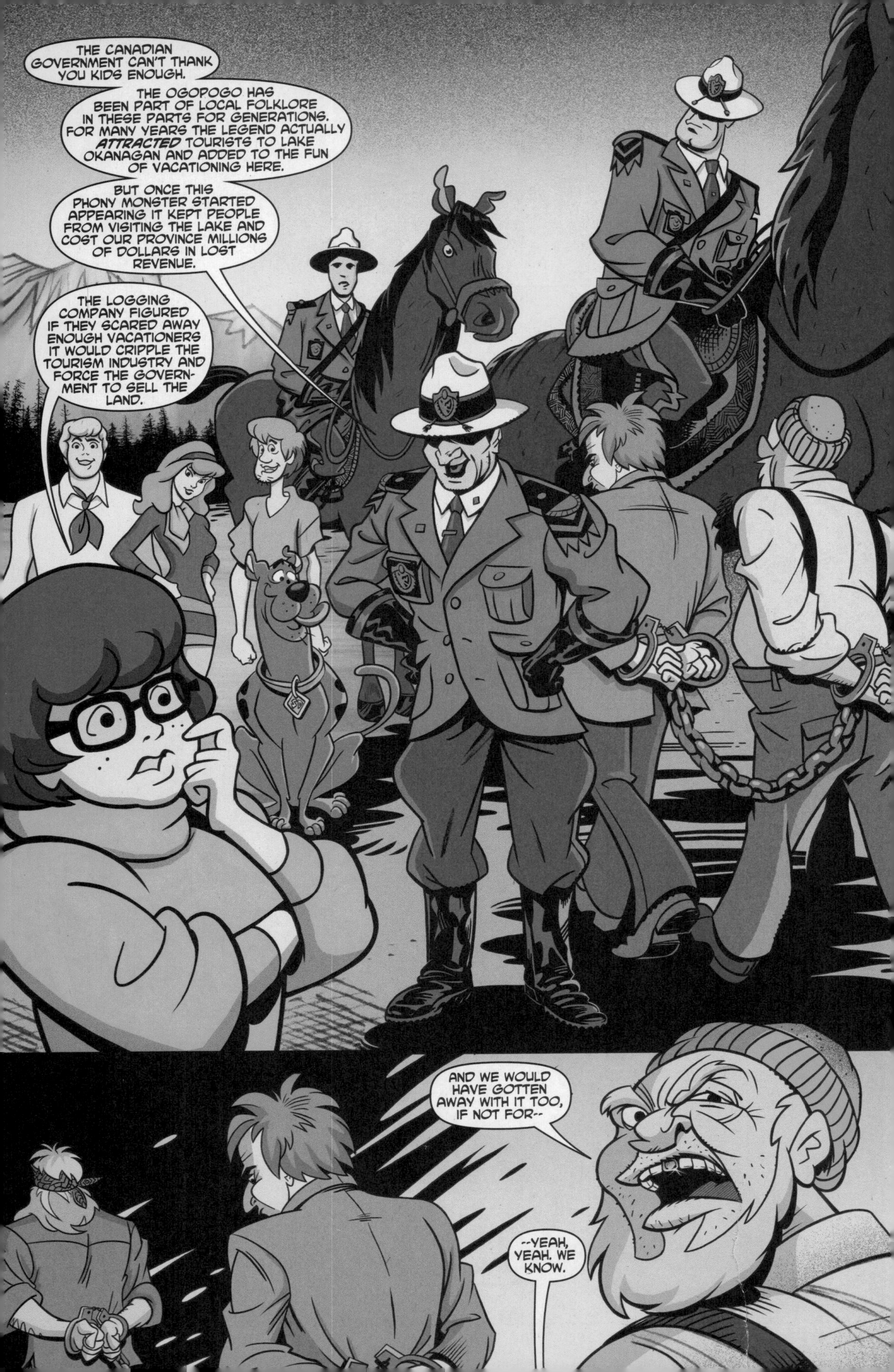
THE CANADIAN GOVERNMENT CAN'T THANK YOU KIDS ENOUGH.
THE OGOPOGO HAS BEEN PART OF LOCAL FOLKLORE IN THESE PARTS FOR GENERATIONS. FOR MANY YEARS THE LEGEND ACTUALLY *ATTRACTED* TOURISTS TO LAKE OKANAGAN AND ADDED TO THE FUN OF VACATIONING HERE.
BUT ONCE THIS PHONY MONSTER STARTED APPEARING IT KEPT PEOPLE FROM VISITING THE LAKE AND COST OUR PROVINCE MILLIONS OF DOLLARS IN LOST REVENUE.
THE LOGGING COMPANY FIGURED IF THEY SCARED AWAY ENOUGH VACATIONERS IT WOULD CRIPPLE THE TOURISM INDUSTRY AND FORCE THE GOVERNMENT TO SELL THE LAND.
AND WE WOULD HAVE GOTTEN AWAY WITH IT TOO, IF NOT FOR--
--YEAH, YEAH. WE KNOW.

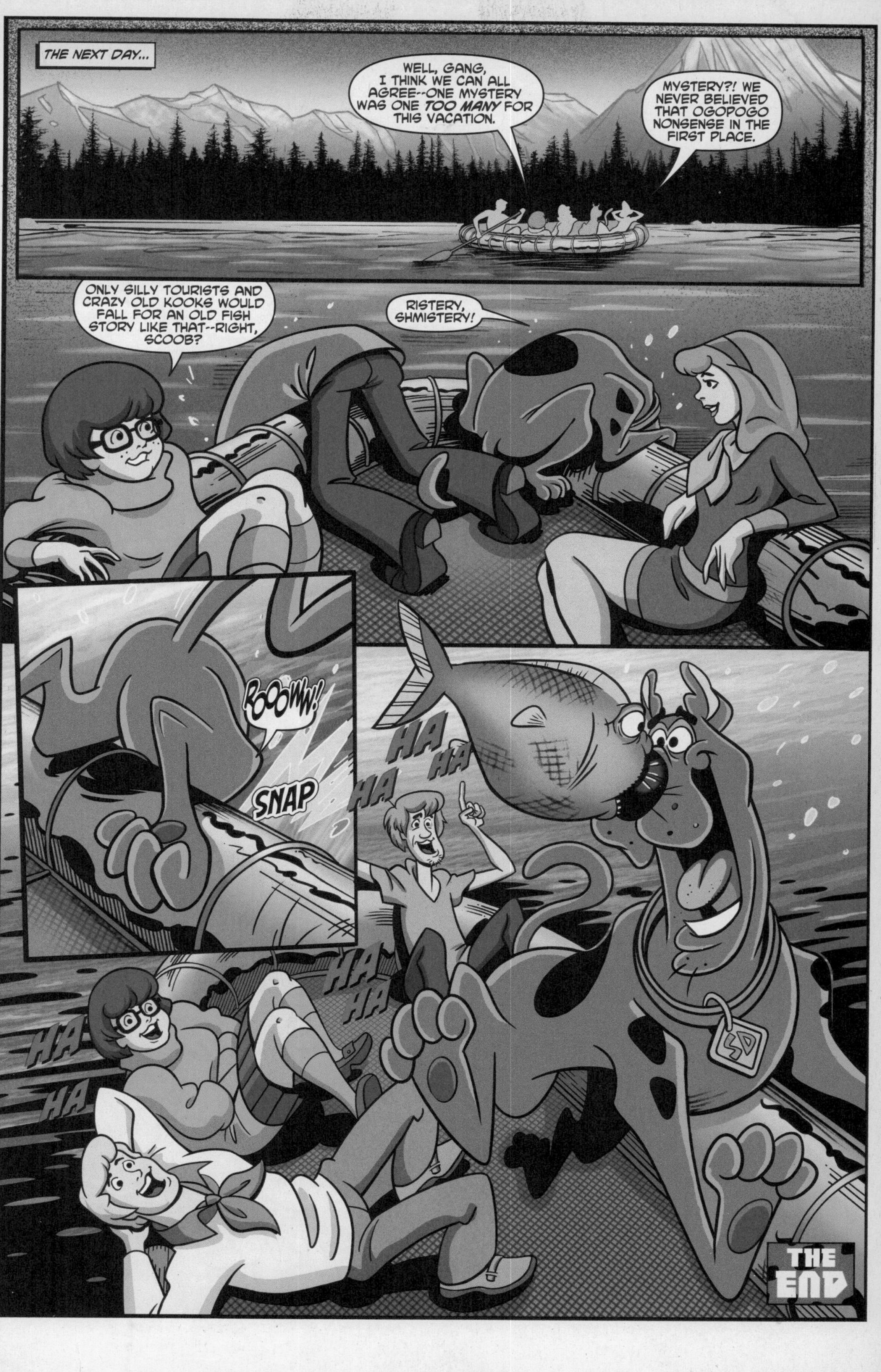
THE NEXT DAY...
WELL, GANG, I THINK WE CAN ALL AGREE--ONE MYSTERY WAS ONE TOO MANY FOR THIS VACATION.
MYSTERY?! WE NEVER BELIEVED THAT OGOPOGO NONSENSE IN THE FIRST PLACE.
ONLY SILLY TOURISTS AND CRAZY OLD KOOKS WOULD FALL FOR AN OLD FISH STORY LIKE THAT--RIGHT, SCOOB?
RISTERY, SHMISTERY!
ROOOWW!
SNAP
HA HA HA HA
HA HA
HA HA
THE END

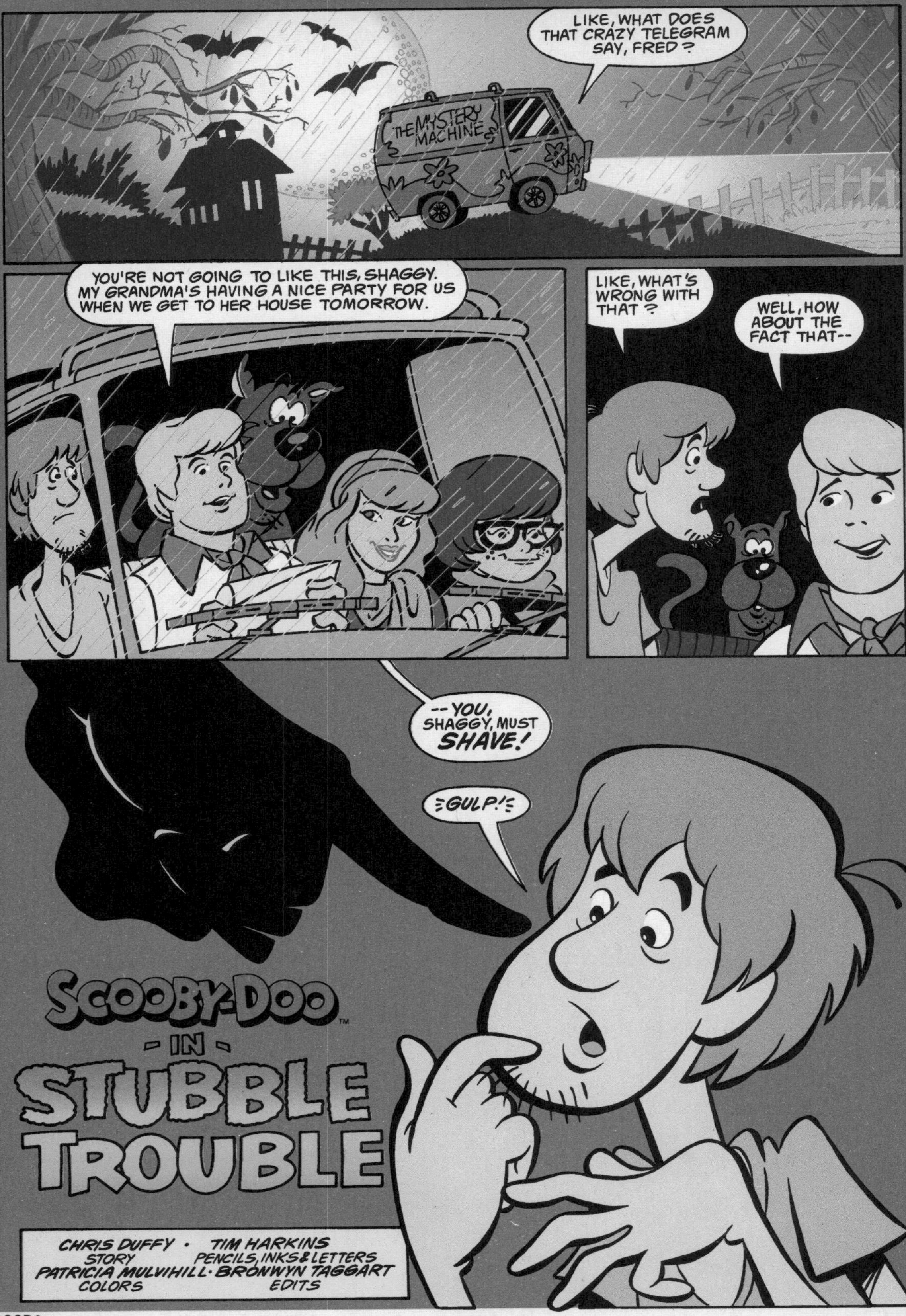
LIKE, WHAT DOES THAT CRAZY TELEGRAM SAY, FRED?
THE MYSTERY MACHINE
YOU'RE NOT GOING TO LIKE THIS, SHAGGY. MY GRANDMA'S HAVING A NICE PARTY FOR US WHEN WE GET TO HER HOUSE TOMORROW.
LIKE, WHAT'S WRONG WITH THAT?
WELL, HOW ABOUT THE FACT THAT--
--YOU, SHAGGY, MUST SHAVE!
GULP!
SCOOBY-DOO™
- IN -
STUBBLE TROUBLE
CHRIS DUFFY · TIM HARKINS
STORY PENCILS, INKS & LETTERS
PATRICIA MULVIHILL · BRONWYN TAGGART
COLORS EDITS

DCSD6

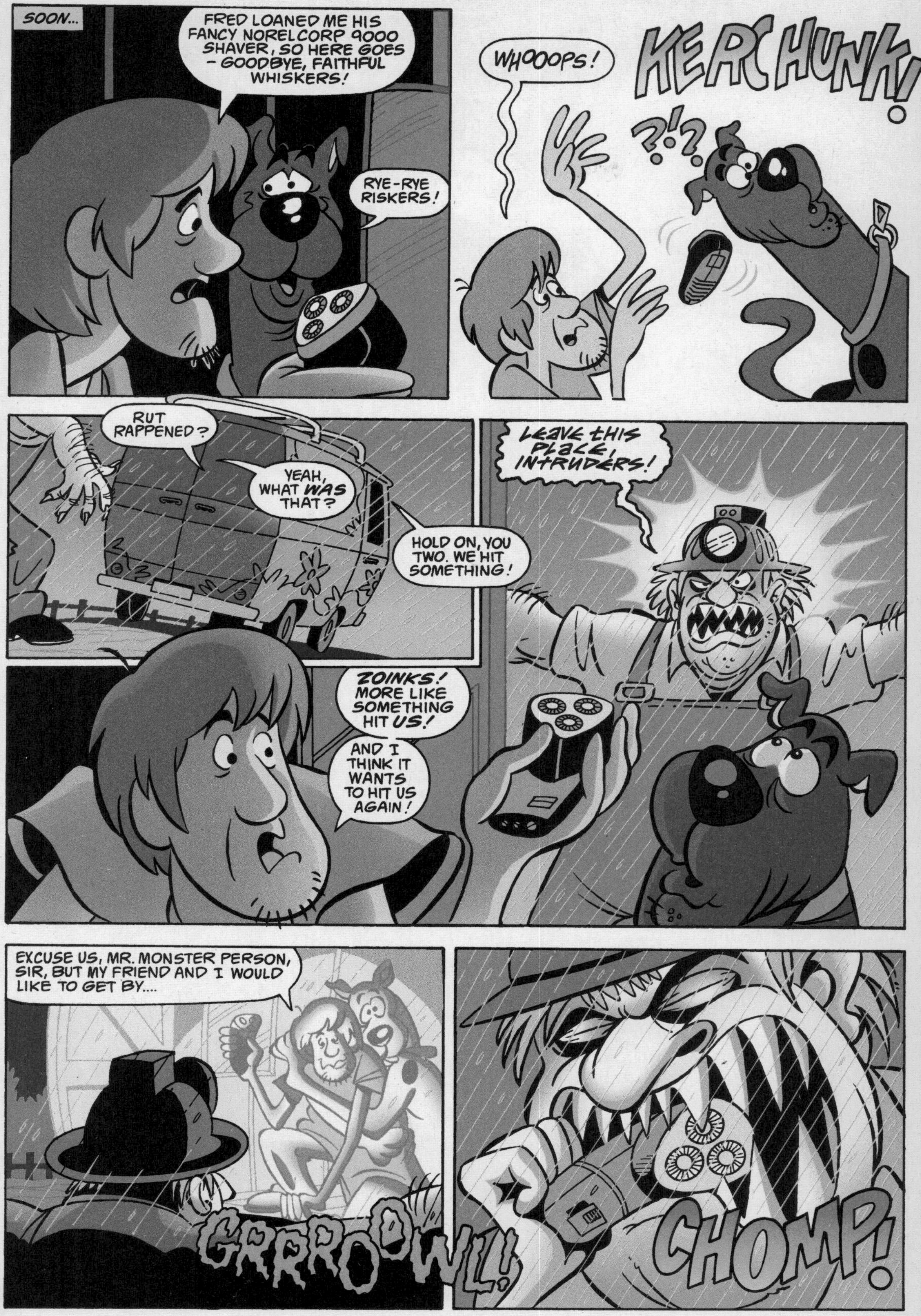
SOON...
FRED LOANED ME HIS FANCY NORELCORP 9000 SHAVER, SO HERE GOES – GOODBYE, FAITHFUL WHISKERS!
RYE-RYE RISKERS!
WHOOOPS!
KERCHUNK!
?!?
RUT RAPPENED?
YEAH, WHAT WAS THAT?
HOLD ON, YOU TWO. WE HIT SOMETHING!
LEAVE THIS PLACE, INTRUDERS!
ZOINKS! MORE LIKE SOMETHING HIT US!
AND I THINK IT WANTS TO HIT US AGAIN!
EXCUSE US, MR. MONSTER PERSON, SIR, BUT MY FRIEND AND I WOULD LIKE TO GET BY....
GRRROOWL!
CHOMP!

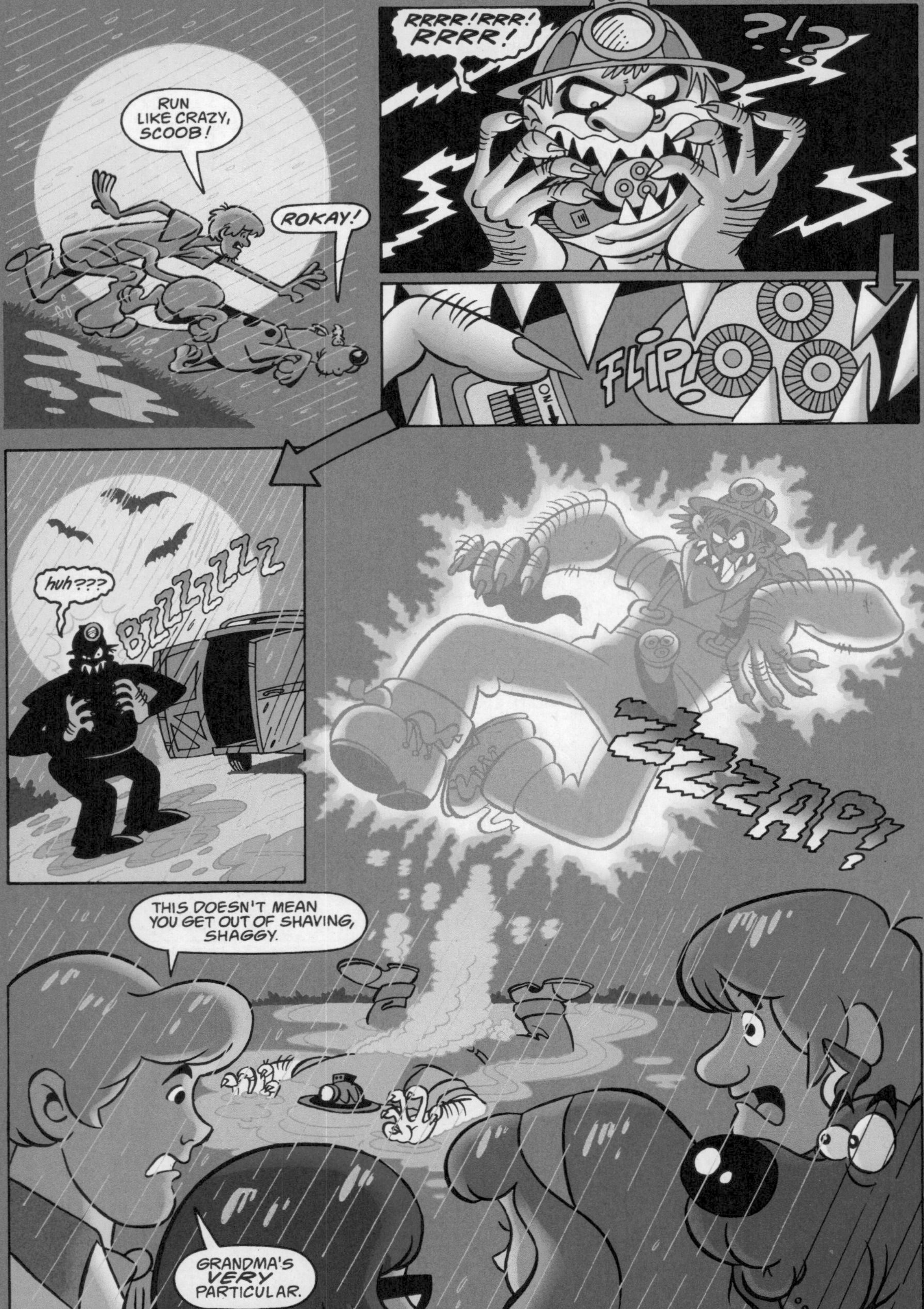
RUN LIKE CRAZY, SCOOB!
ROKAY!
RRRR! RRR! RRRR!
?!?
FLIP!
huh???
BZZZZZZ
ZZZZAP!!
THIS DOESN'T MEAN YOU GET OUT OF SHAVING, SHAGGY.
GRANDMA'S VERY PARTICULAR.

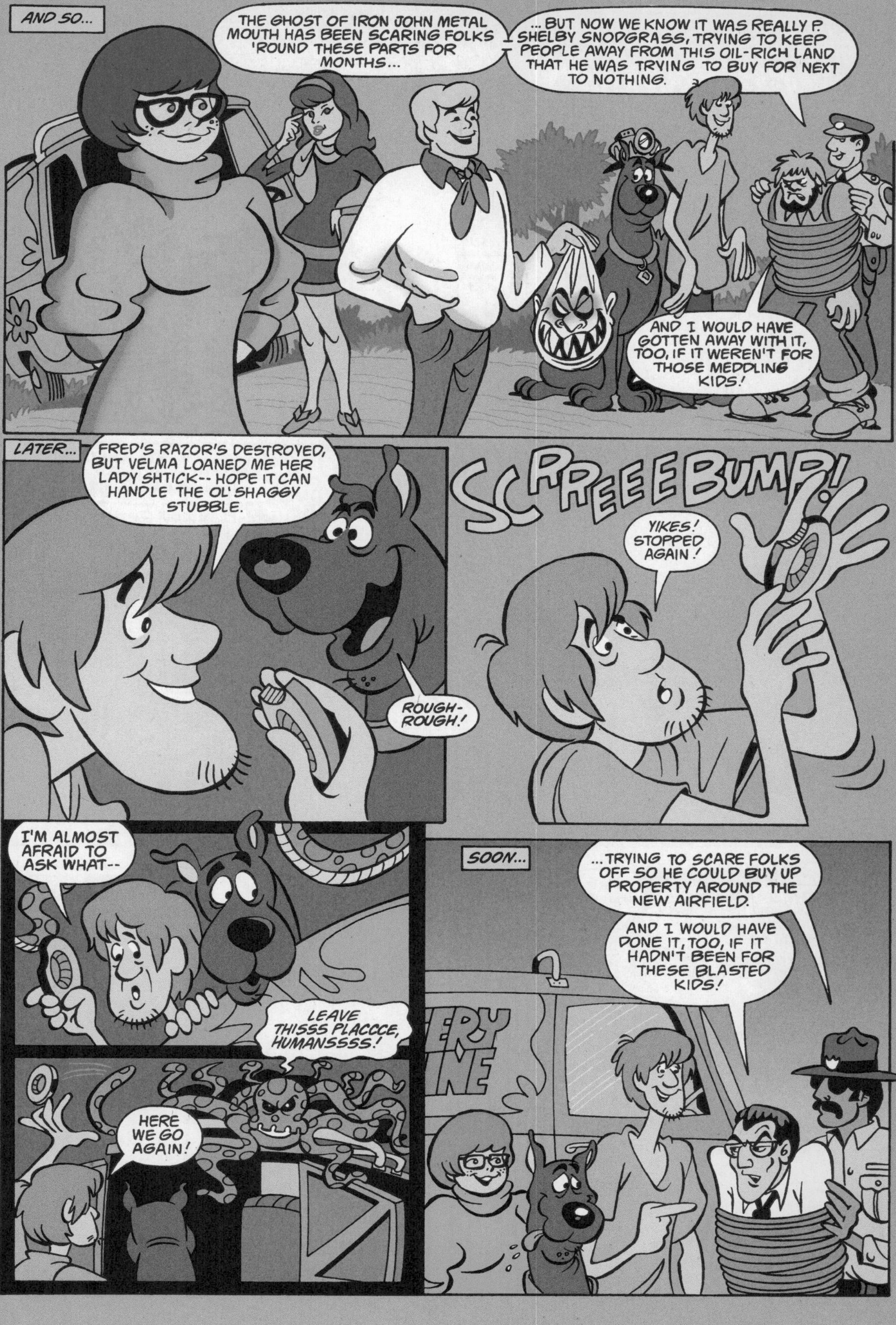
AND SO...
THE GHOST OF IRON JOHN METAL MOUTH HAS BEEN SCARING FOLKS 'ROUND THESE PARTS FOR MONTHS...
...BUT NOW WE KNOW IT WAS REALLY P. SHELBY SNODGRASS, TRYING TO KEEP PEOPLE AWAY FROM THIS OIL-RICH LAND THAT HE WAS TRYING TO BUY FOR NEXT TO NOTHING.
AND I WOULD HAVE GOTTEN AWAY WITH IT, TOO, IF IT WEREN'T FOR THOSE MEDDLING KIDS!
LATER...
FRED'S RAZOR'S DESTROYED, BUT VELMA LOANED ME HER LADY SHTICK-- HOPE IT CAN HANDLE THE OL' SHAGGY STUBBLE.
ROUGH-ROUGH!
SCRREEEEBUMP!
YIKES! STOPPED AGAIN!
I'M ALMOST AFRAID TO ASK WHAT--
LEAVE THISSS PLACCCE, HUMANSSSS!
HERE WE GO AGAIN!
SOON...
...TRYING TO SCARE FOLKS OFF SO HE COULD BUY UP PROPERTY AROUND THE NEW AIRFIELD.
AND I WOULD HAVE DONE IT, TOO, IF IT HADN'T BEEN FOR THESE BLASTED KIDS!

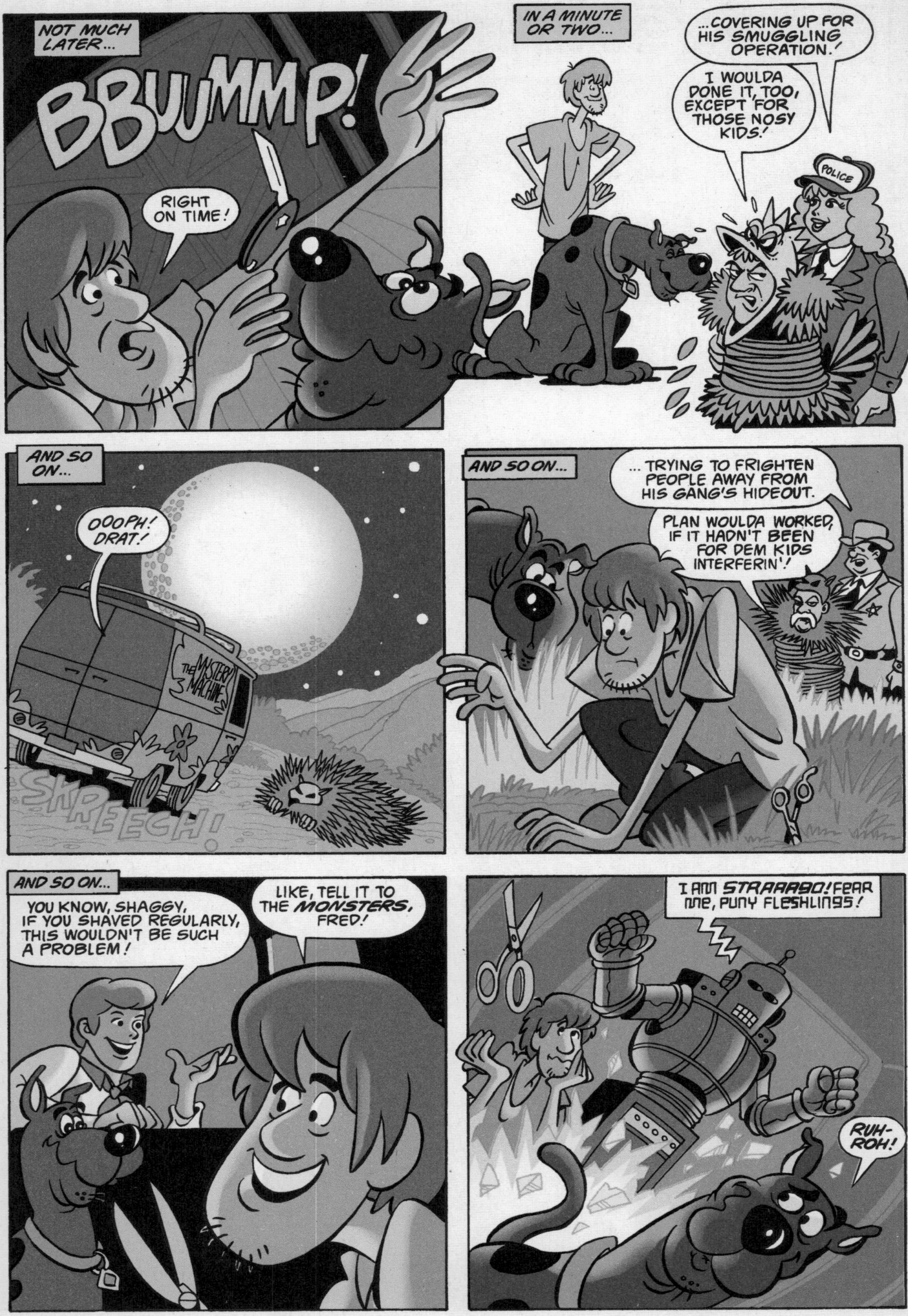

NOT MUCH LATER...
BBUUMMP!
RIGHT ON TIME!
IN A MINUTE OR TWO...
...COVERING UP FOR HIS SMUGGLING OPERATION.'
I WOULDA DONE IT, TOO, EXCEPT FOR THOSE NOSY KIDS!'
POLICE
AND SO ON...
OOOPH! DRAT!
THE MYSTERY MACHINE
SKREECH!
AND SO ON...
... TRYING TO FRIGHTEN PEOPLE AWAY FROM HIS GANG'S HIDEOUT.
PLAN WOULDA WORKED, IF IT HADN'T BEEN FOR DEM KIDS INTERFERIN'!
AND SO ON...
YOU KNOW, SHAGGY, IF YOU SHAVED REGULARLY, THIS WOULDN'T BE SUCH A PROBLEM!
LIKE, TELL IT TO THE MONSTERS, FRED!
I AM STRAAAGO! FEAR ME, PUNY FLESHLINGS!
RUH-ROH!

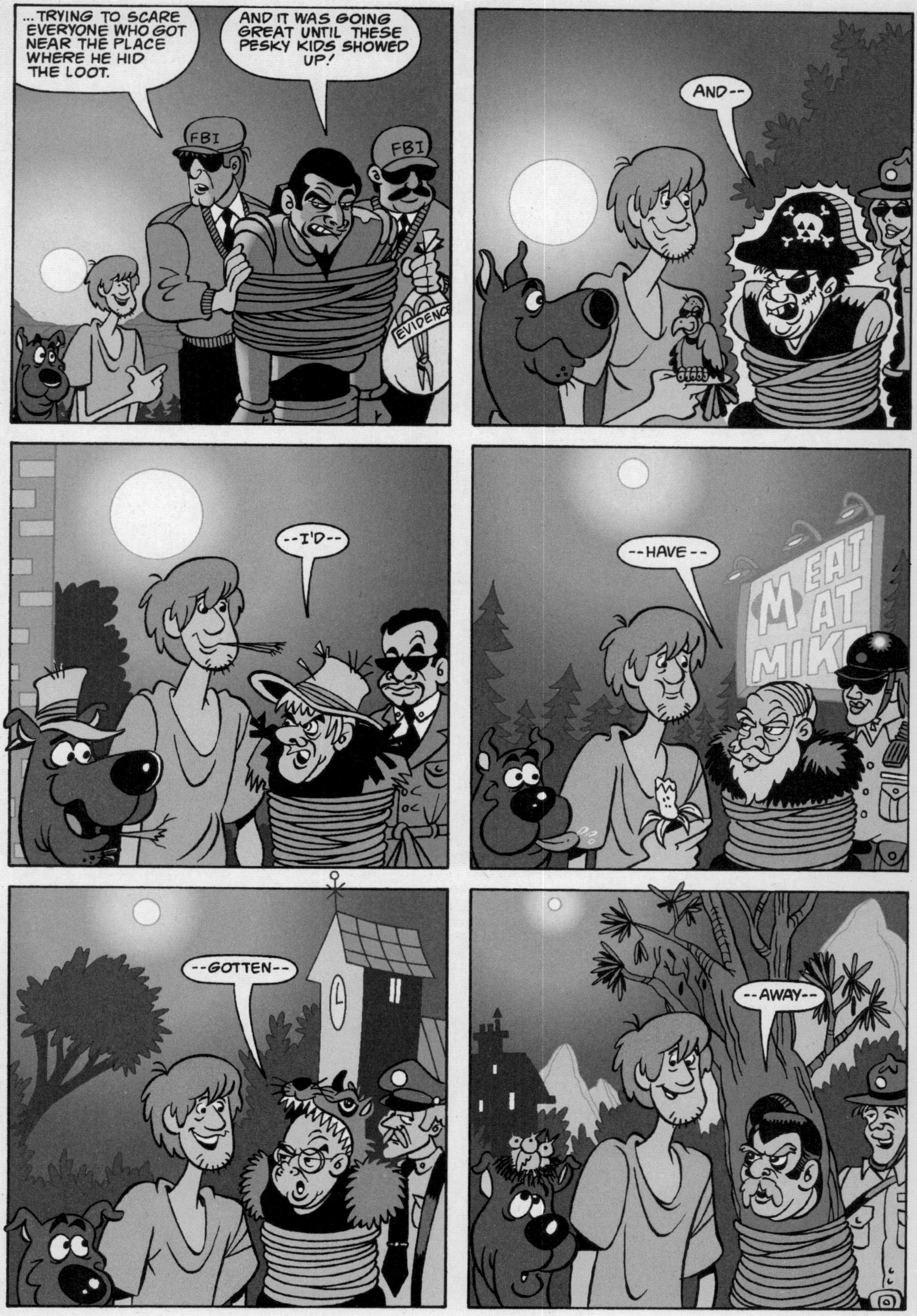
...TRYING TO SCARE EVERYONE WHO GOT NEAR THE PLACE WHERE HE HID THE LOOT.
AND IT WAS GOING GREAT UNTIL THESE PESKY KIDS SHOWED UP!
FBI
FBI
EVIDENCE
AND--
--I'D--
--HAVE--
MEAT AT MIKE
--GOTTEN--
--AWAY--

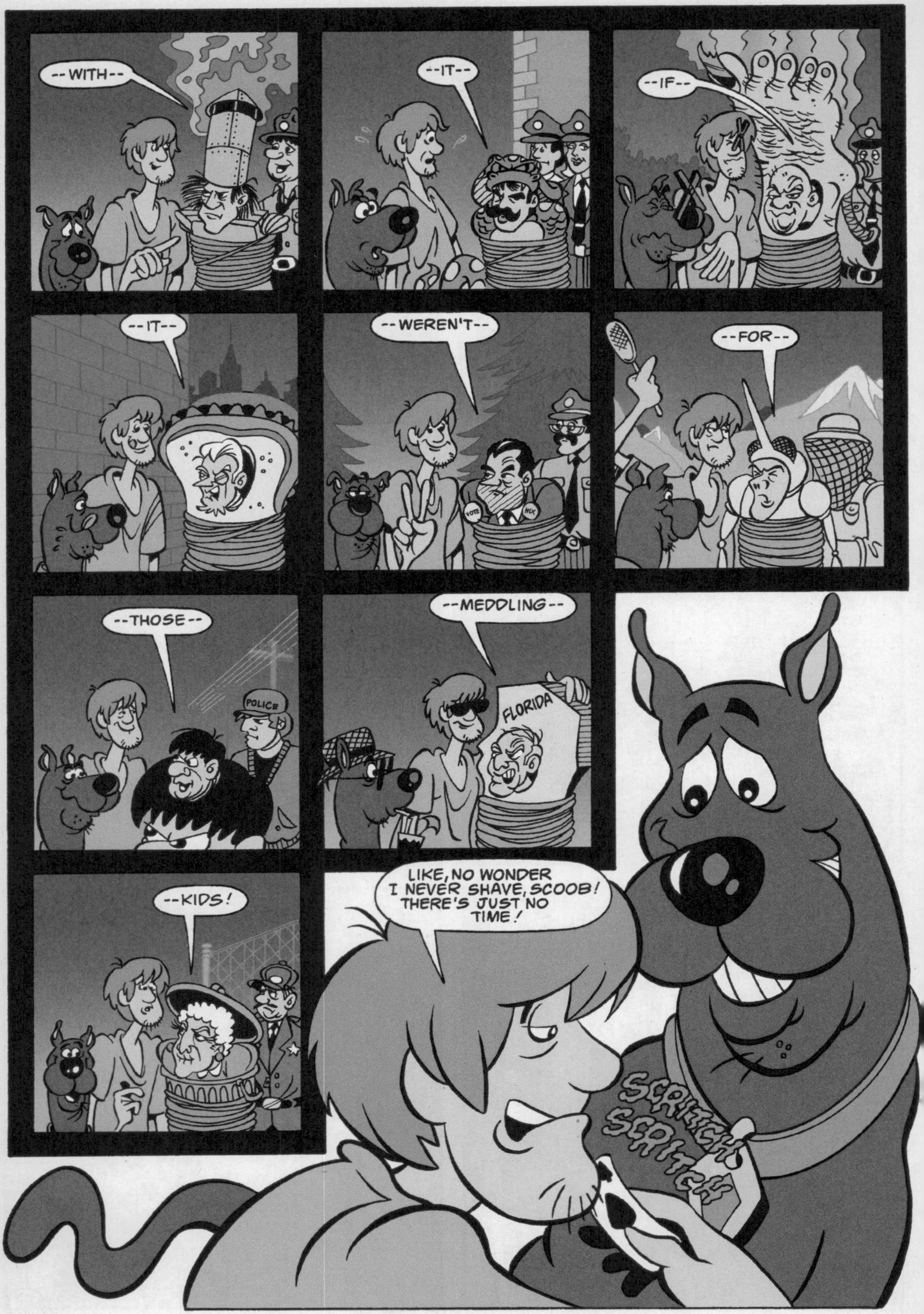
--WITH--
--IT--
--IF--
--IT--
--WEREN'T--
--FOR--
--THOSE--
POLICE
--MEDDLING--
FLORIDA
--KIDS!
LIKE, NO WONDER I NEVER SHAVE, SCOOB! THERE'S JUST NO TIME!
SCRITCH SCRITCH SCRITCH

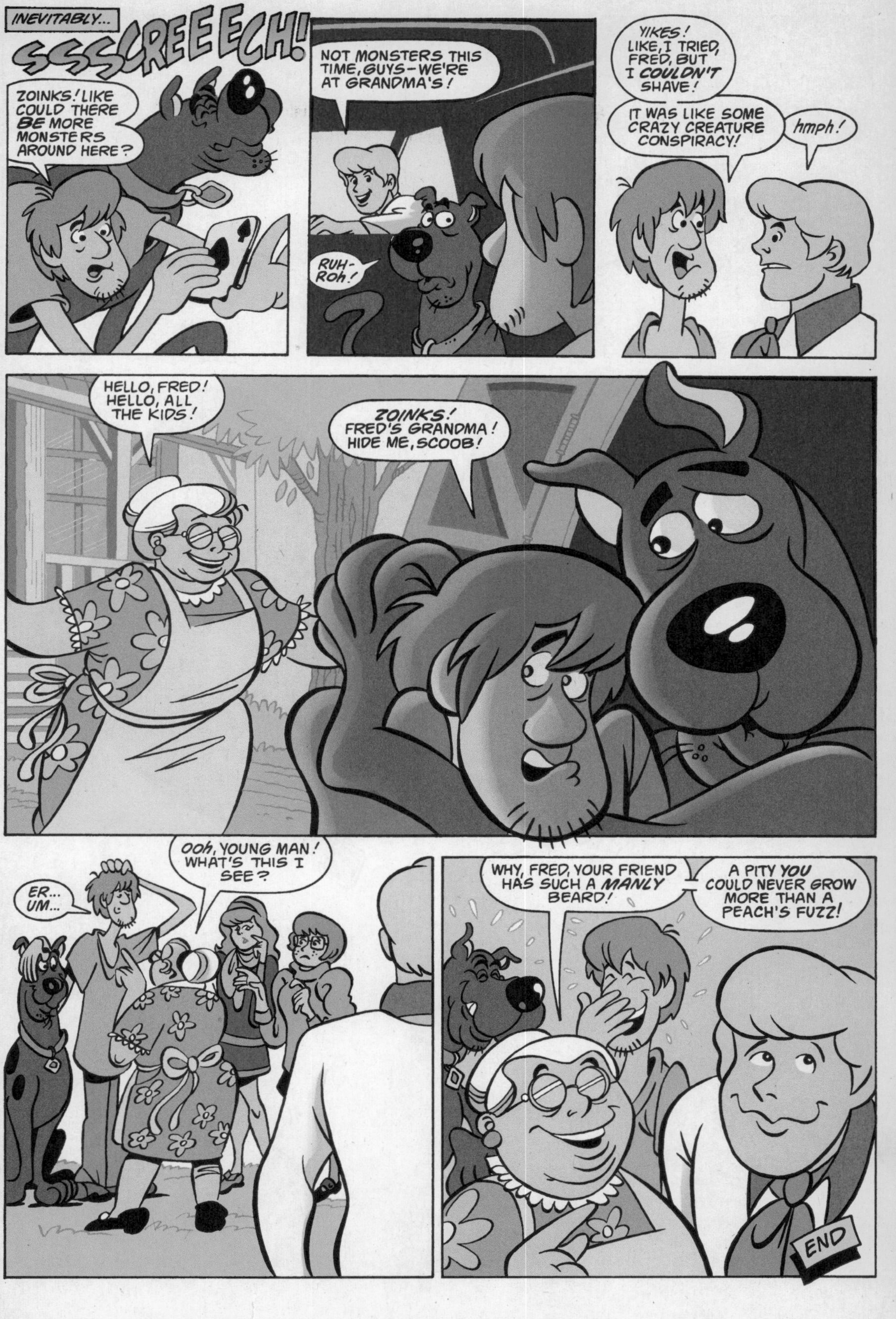
INEVITABLY...
SSSCREEEECH!
ZOINKS! LIKE COULD THERE BE MORE MONSTERS AROUND HERE?
NOT MONSTERS THIS TIME, GUYS—WE'RE AT GRANDMA'S!
RUH-ROH!
YIKES! LIKE, I TRIED, FRED, BUT I COULDN'T SHAVE!
IT WAS LIKE SOME CRAZY CREATURE CONSPIRACY!
hmph!
HELLO, FRED! HELLO, ALL THE KIDS!
ZOINKS! FRED'S GRANDMA! HIDE ME, SCOOB!
ER... UM...
Ooh, YOUNG MAN! WHAT'S THIS I SEE?
WHY, FRED, YOUR FRIEND HAS SUCH A MANLY BEARD!
A PITY YOU COULD NEVER GROW MORE THAN A PEACH'S FUZZ!
END

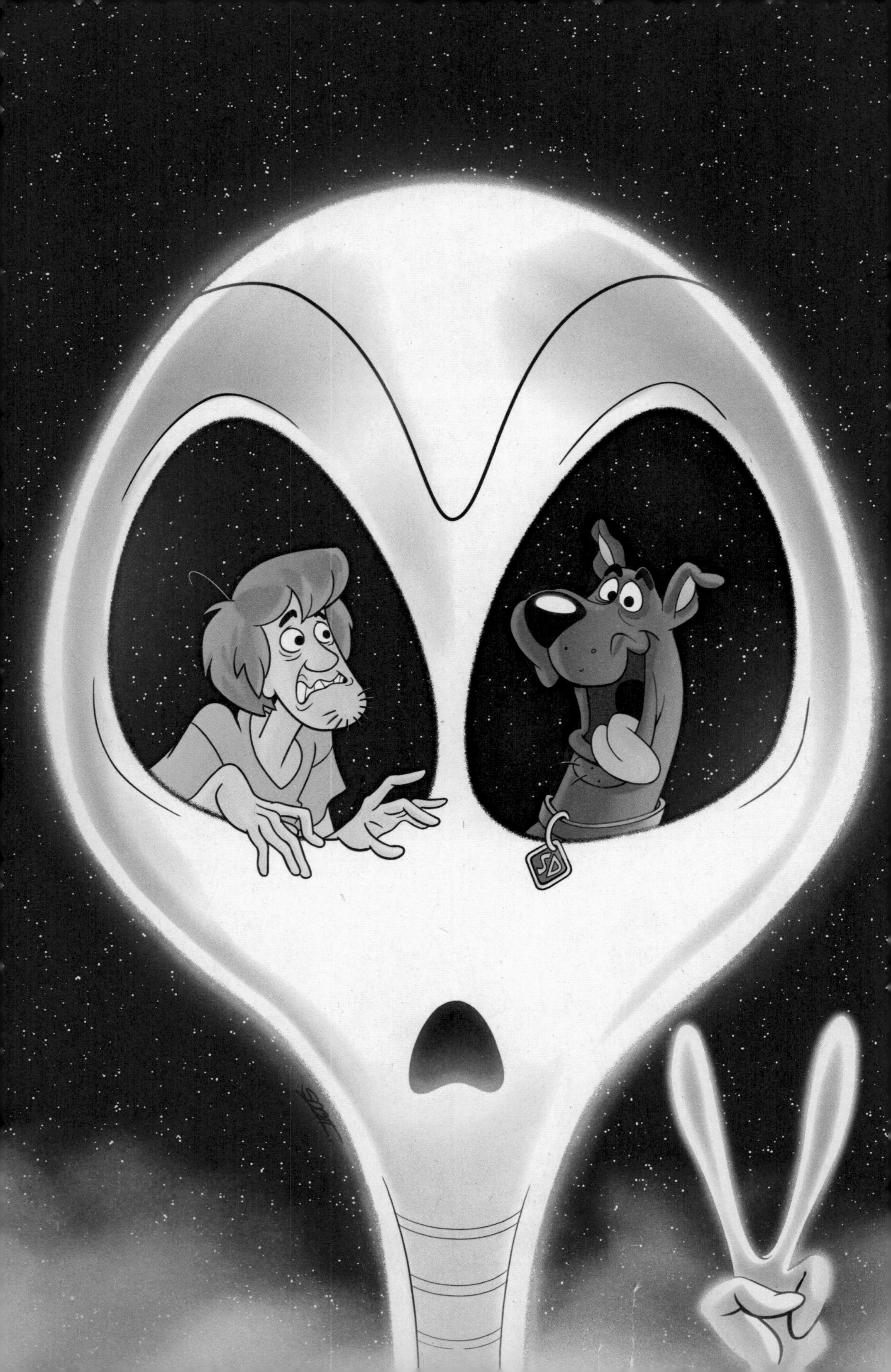

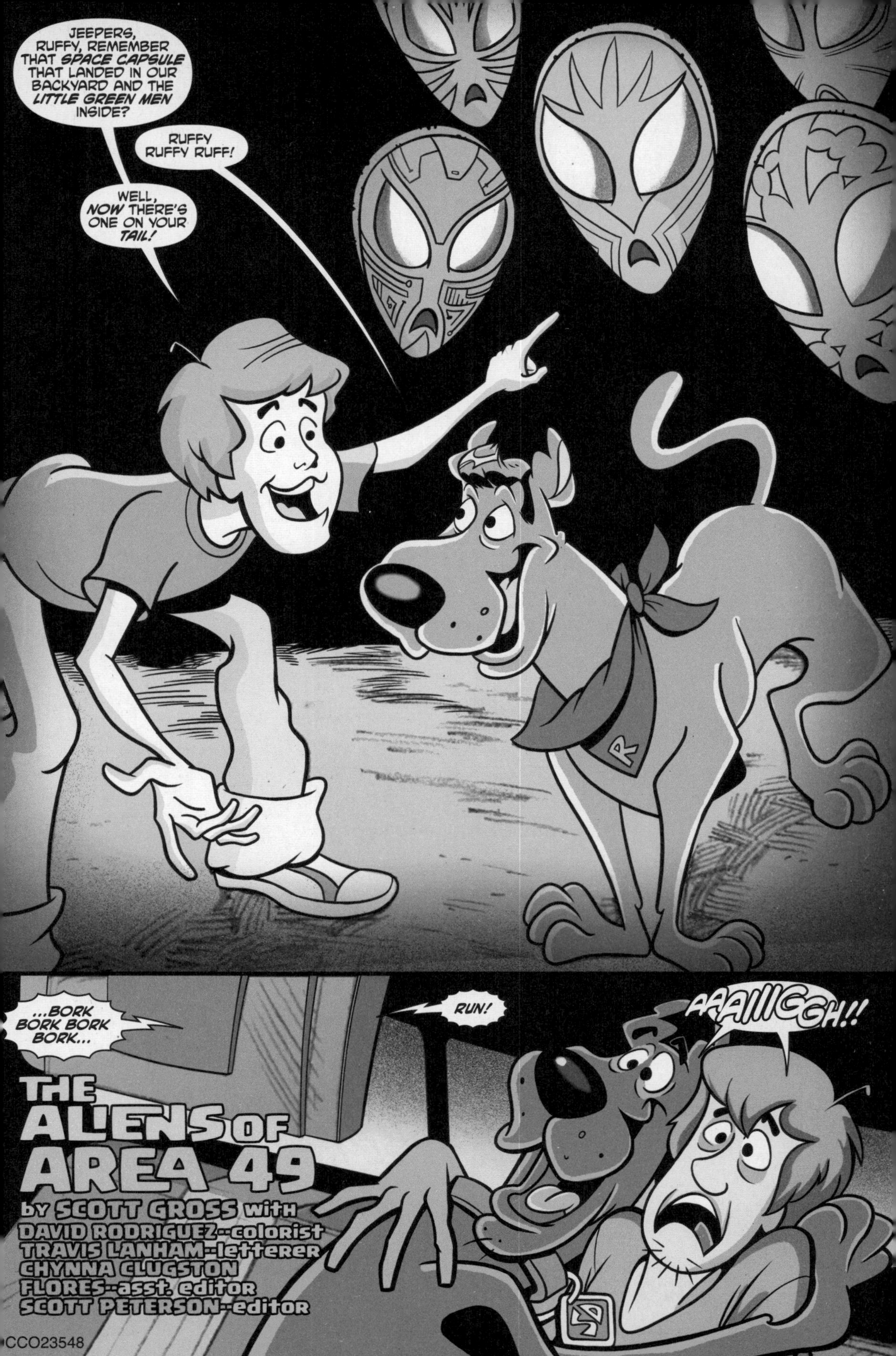
JEEPERS, RUFFY, REMEMBER THAT SPACE CAPSULE THAT LANDED IN OUR BACKYARD AND THE LITTLE GREEN MEN INSIDE?
RUFFY RUFFY RUFF!
WELL, NOW THERE'S ONE ON YOUR TAIL!
...BORK BORK BORK BORK BORK...
RUN!
AAAIIIGGH!!
THE ALIENS OF AREA 49
by SCOTT GROSS with
DAVID RODRIGUEZ--colorist
TRAVIS LANHAM--letterer
CHYNNA CLUGSTON FLORES--asst. editor
SCOTT PETERSON--editor

CCO23548

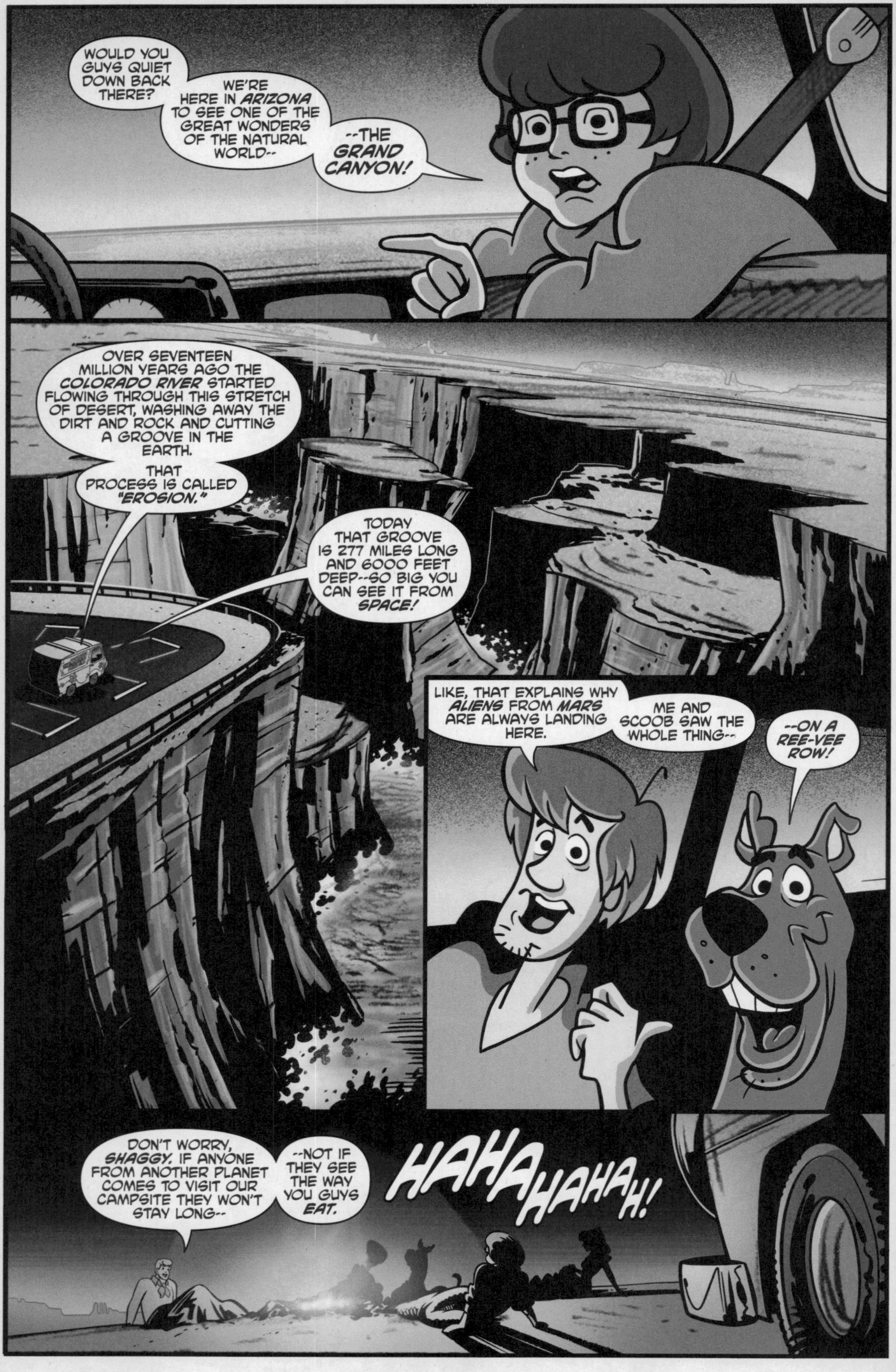
WOULD YOU GUYS QUIET DOWN BACK THERE?
WE'RE HERE IN ARIZONA TO SEE ONE OF THE GREAT WONDERS OF THE NATURAL WORLD--
--THE GRAND CANYON!
OVER SEVENTEEN MILLION YEARS AGO THE COLORADO RIVER STARTED FLOWING THROUGH THIS STRETCH OF DESERT, WASHING AWAY THE DIRT AND ROCK AND CUTTING A GROOVE IN THE EARTH.
THAT PROCESS IS CALLED "EROSION."
TODAY THAT GROOVE IS 277 MILES LONG AND 6000 FEET DEEP--SO BIG YOU CAN SEE IT FROM SPACE!
LIKE, THAT EXPLAINS WHY ALIENS FROM MARS ARE ALWAYS LANDING HERE.
ME AND SCOOB SAW THE WHOLE THING--
--ON A REE-VEE ROW!
DON'T WORRY, SHAGGY. IF ANYONE FROM ANOTHER PLANET COMES TO VISIT OUR CAMPSITE THEY WON'T STAY LONG--
--NOT IF THEY SEE THE WAY YOU GUYS EAT.
HAHAHAHAHAH!

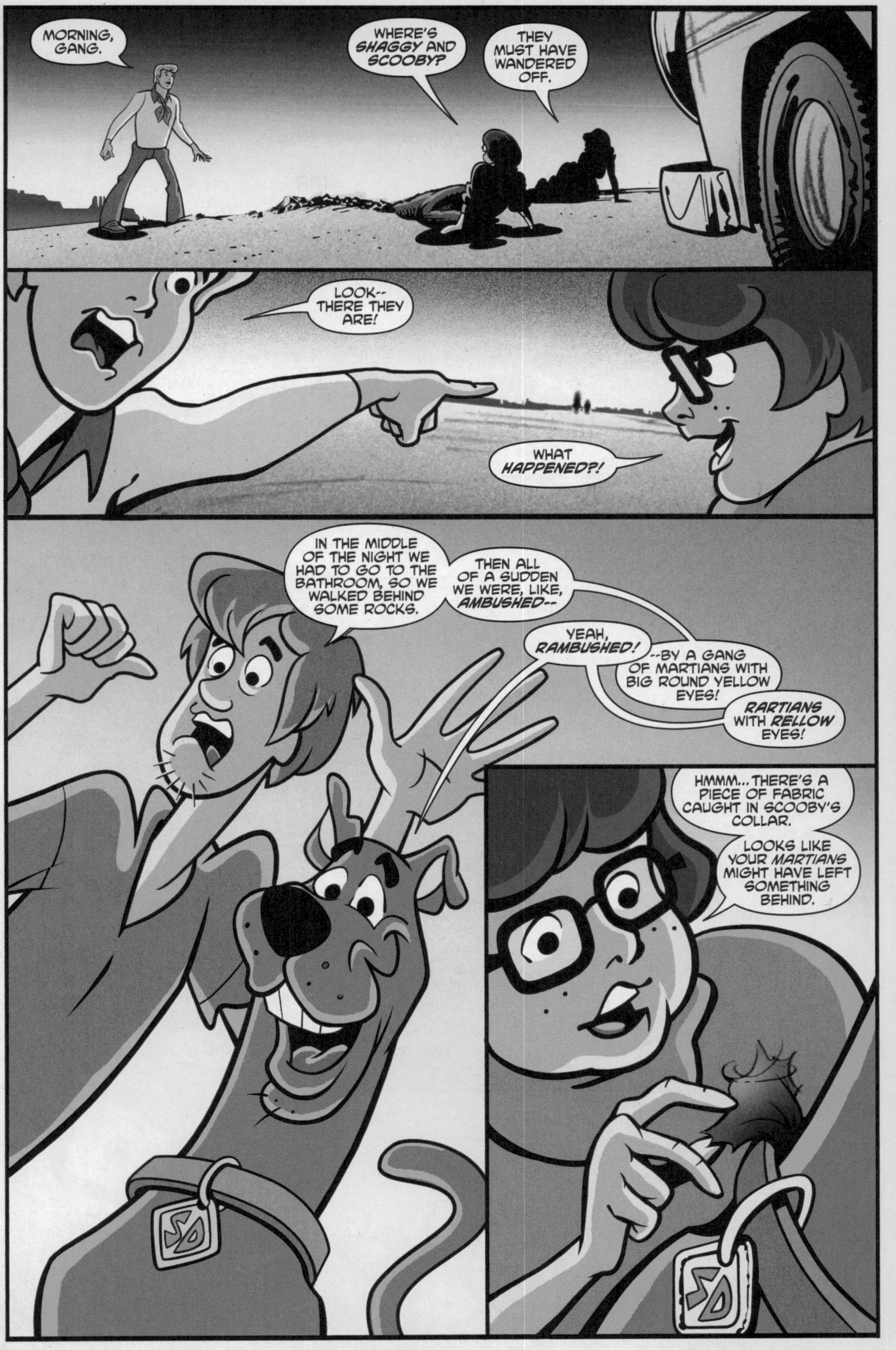
MORNING, GANG.
WHERE'S *SHAGGY* AND *SCOOBY?*
THEY MUST HAVE WANDERED OFF.
LOOK-- THERE THEY ARE!
WHAT *HAPPENED?!*
IN THE MIDDLE OF THE NIGHT WE HAD TO GO TO THE BATHROOM, SO WE WALKED BEHIND SOME ROCKS.
THEN ALL OF A SUDDEN WE WERE, LIKE, *AMBUSHED--*
YEAH, *RAMBUSHED!*
--BY A GANG OF MARTIANS WITH BIG ROUND YELLOW EYES!
RARTIANS WITH *RELLOW* EYES!
HMMM... THERE'S A PIECE OF FABRIC CAUGHT IN SCOOBY'S COLLAR.
LOOKS LIKE YOUR *MARTIANS* MIGHT HAVE LEFT SOMETHING BEHIND.

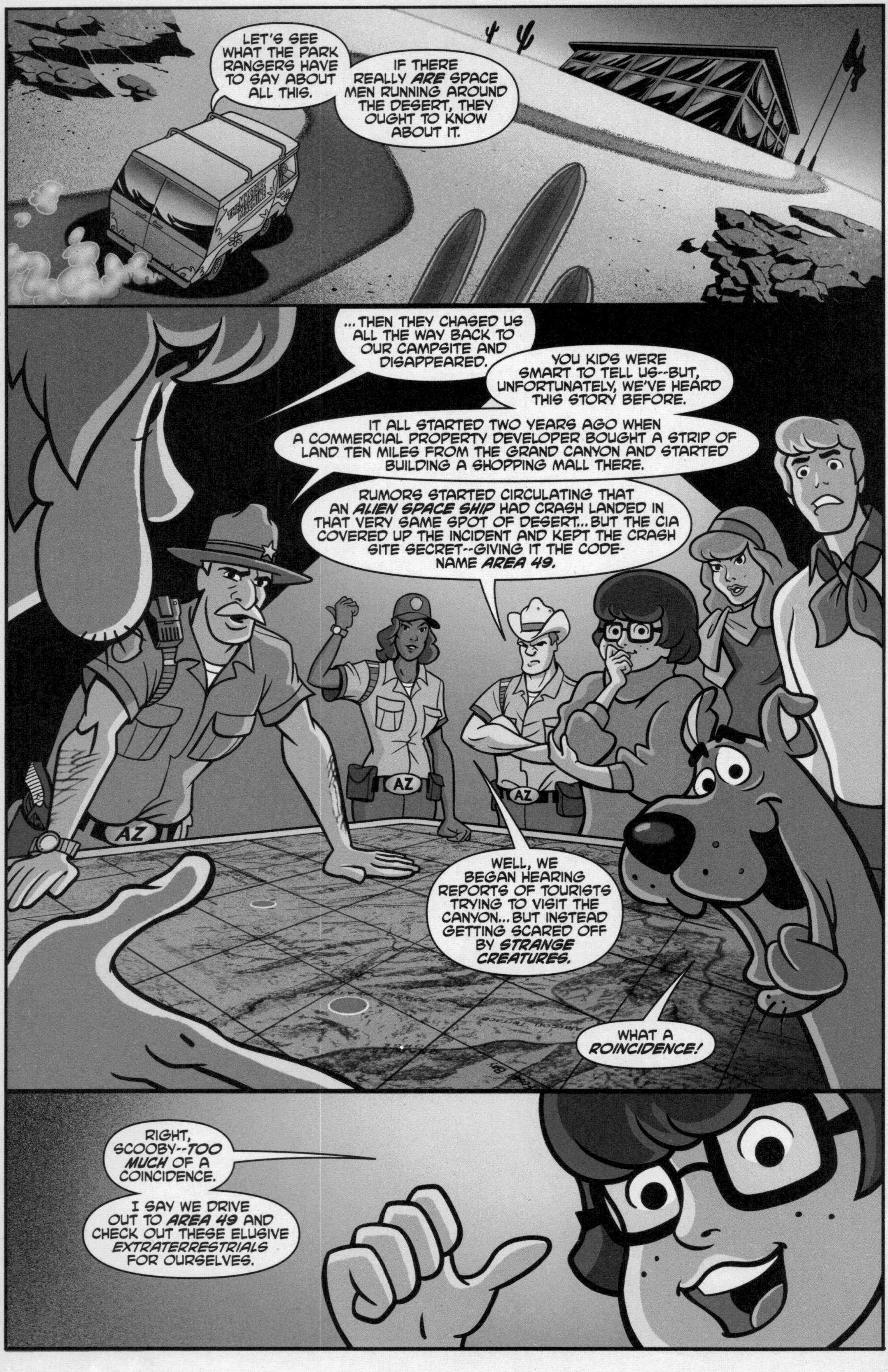

LET'S SEE WHAT THE PARK RANGERS HAVE TO SAY ABOUT ALL THIS.
IF THERE REALLY *ARE* SPACE MEN RUNNING AROUND THE DESERT, THEY OUGHT TO KNOW ABOUT IT.
THE MYSTERY MACHINE
...THEN THEY CHASED US ALL THE WAY BACK TO OUR CAMPSITE AND DISAPPEARED.
YOU KIDS WERE SMART TO TELL US--BUT, UNFORTUNATELY, WE'VE HEARD THIS STORY BEFORE.
IT ALL STARTED TWO YEARS AGO WHEN A COMMERCIAL PROPERTY DEVELOPER BOUGHT A STRIP OF LAND TEN MILES FROM THE GRAND CANYON AND STARTED BUILDING A SHOPPING MALL THERE.
RUMORS STARTED CIRCULATING THAT AN *ALIEN SPACE SHIP* HAD CRASH LANDED IN THAT VERY SAME SPOT OF DESERT... BUT THE CIA COVERED UP THE INCIDENT AND KEPT THE CRASH SITE SECRET--GIVING IT THE CODE-NAME *AREA 49.*
AZ
AZ
AZ
WELL, WE BEGAN HEARING REPORTS OF TOURISTS TRYING TO VISIT THE CANYON... BUT INSTEAD GETTING SCARED OFF BY *STRANGE CREATURES.*
WHAT A *ROINCIDENCE!*
RIGHT, SCOOBY--*TOO MUCH* OF A COINCIDENCE.
I SAY WE DRIVE OUT TO *AREA 49* AND CHECK OUT THESE ELUSIVE *EXTRATERRESTRIALS* FOR OURSELVES.

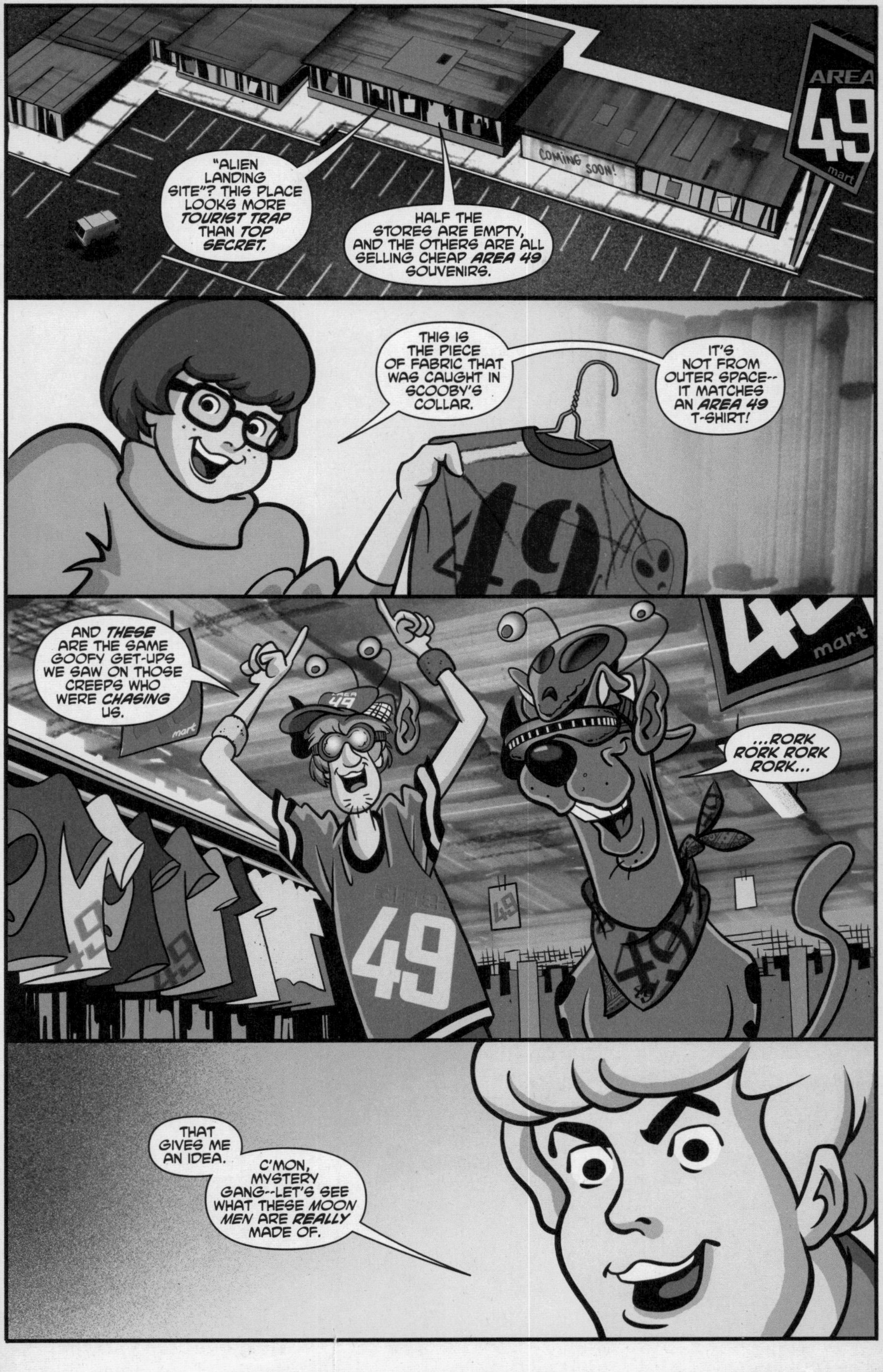
AREA 49 mart
COMING SOON!
"ALIEN LANDING SITE"? THIS PLACE LOOKS MORE TOURIST TRAP THAN TOP SECRET.
HALF THE STORES ARE EMPTY, AND THE OTHERS ARE ALL SELLING CHEAP AREA 49 SOUVENIRS.
THIS IS THE PIECE OF FABRIC THAT WAS CAUGHT IN SCOOBY'S COLLAR.
IT'S NOT FROM OUTER SPACE--IT MATCHES AN AREA 49 T-SHIRT!
AND THESE ARE THE SAME GOOFY GET-UPS WE SAW ON THOSE CREEPS WHO WERE CHASING US.
...RORK RORK RORK RORK...
THAT GIVES ME AN IDEA.
C'MON, MYSTERY GANG--LET'S SEE WHAT THESE MOON MEN ARE REALLY MADE OF.

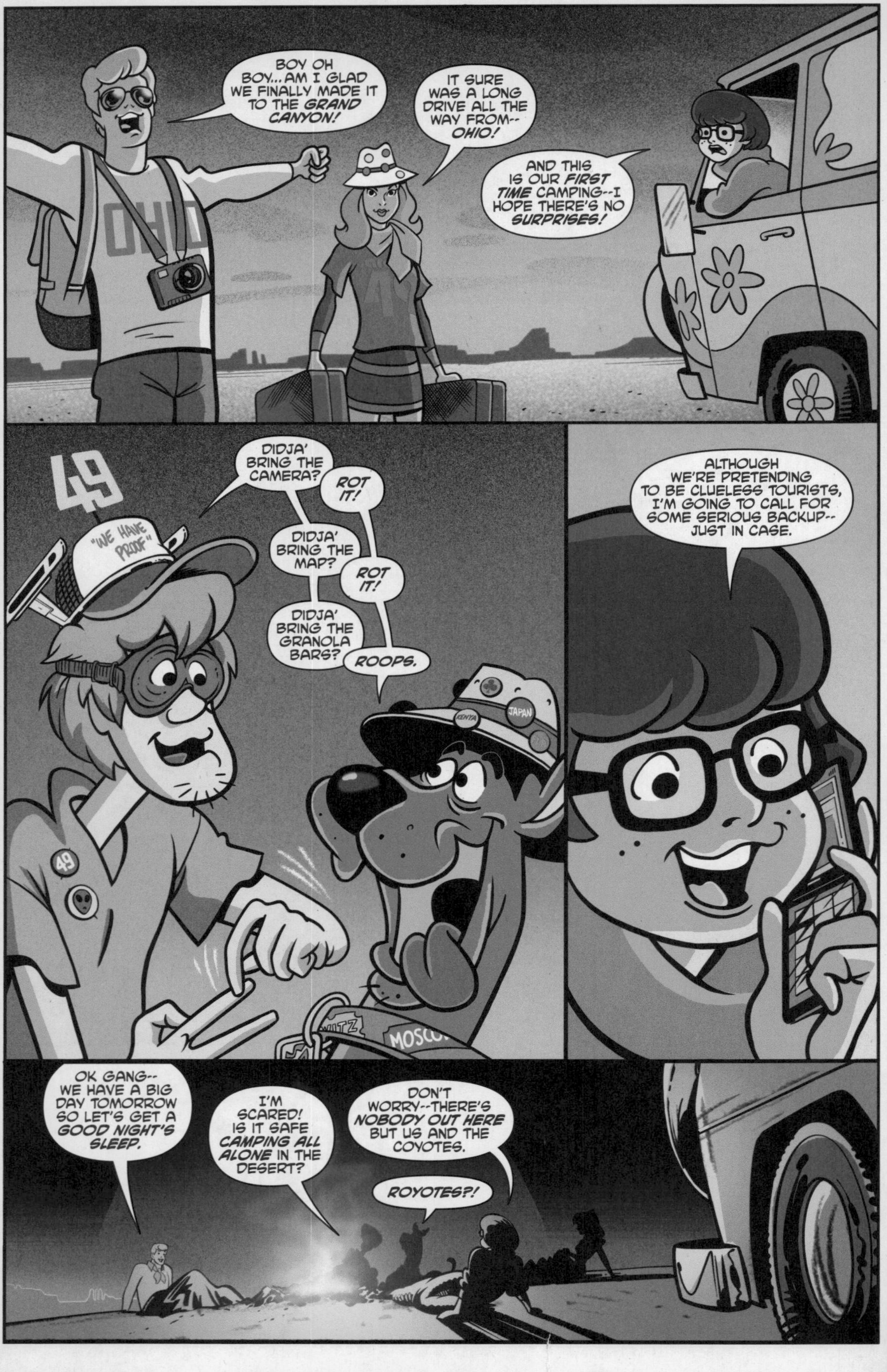
BOY OH BOY... AM I GLAD WE FINALLY MADE IT TO THE *GRAND CANYON!*
IT SURE WAS A LONG DRIVE ALL THE WAY FROM-- *OHIO!*
AND THIS IS OUR *FIRST TIME* CAMPING--I HOPE THERE'S NO *SURPRISES!*
OHIO
49
"WE HAVE PROOF"
DIDJA' BRING THE CAMERA?
ROT IT!
DIDJA' BRING THE MAP?
ROT IT!
DIDJA' BRING THE GRANOLA BARS?
ROOPS.
KENYA
JAPAN
49
MOSCO
ALTHOUGH WE'RE PRETENDING TO BE CLUELESS TOURISTS, I'M GOING TO CALL FOR SOME SERIOUS BACKUP-- JUST IN CASE.
OK GANG-- WE HAVE A BIG DAY TOMORROW SO LET'S GET A *GOOD NIGHT'S SLEEP.*
I'M SCARED! IS IT SAFE *CAMPING ALL ALONE* IN THE DESERT?
DON'T WORRY--THERE'S *NOBODY OUT HERE* BUT US AND THE COYOTES.
ROYOTES?!

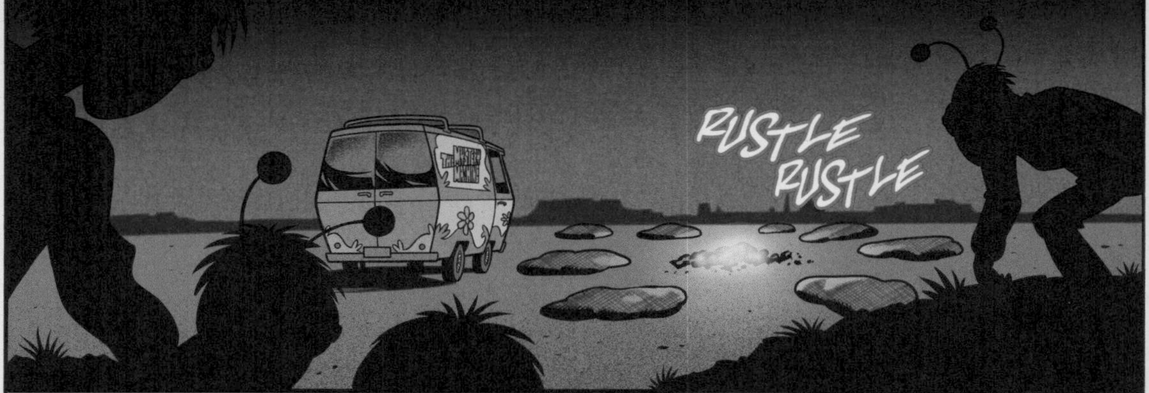
RUSTLE
RUSTLE

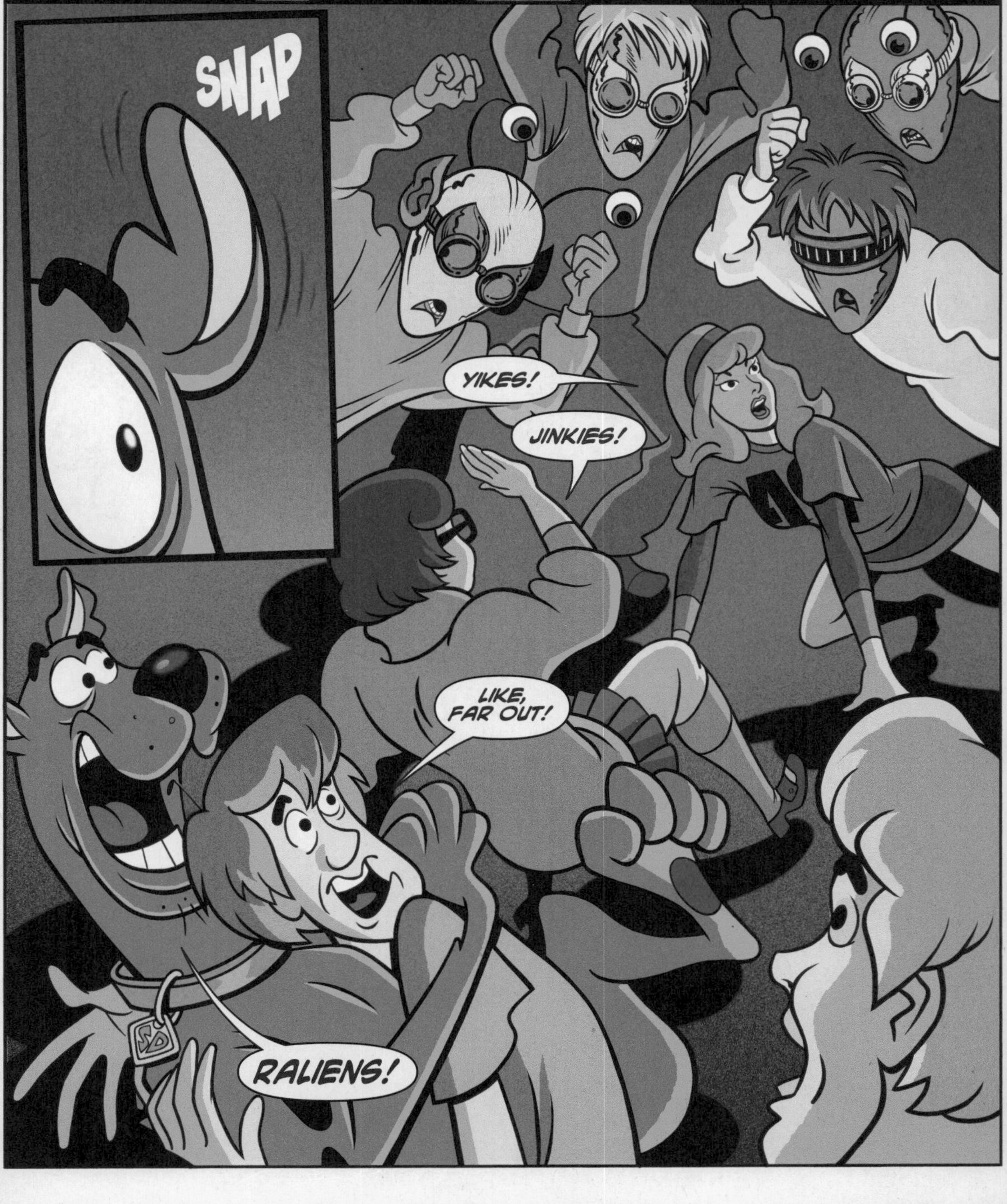
SNAP
YIKES!
JINKIES!
LIKE, FAR OUT!
RALIENS!

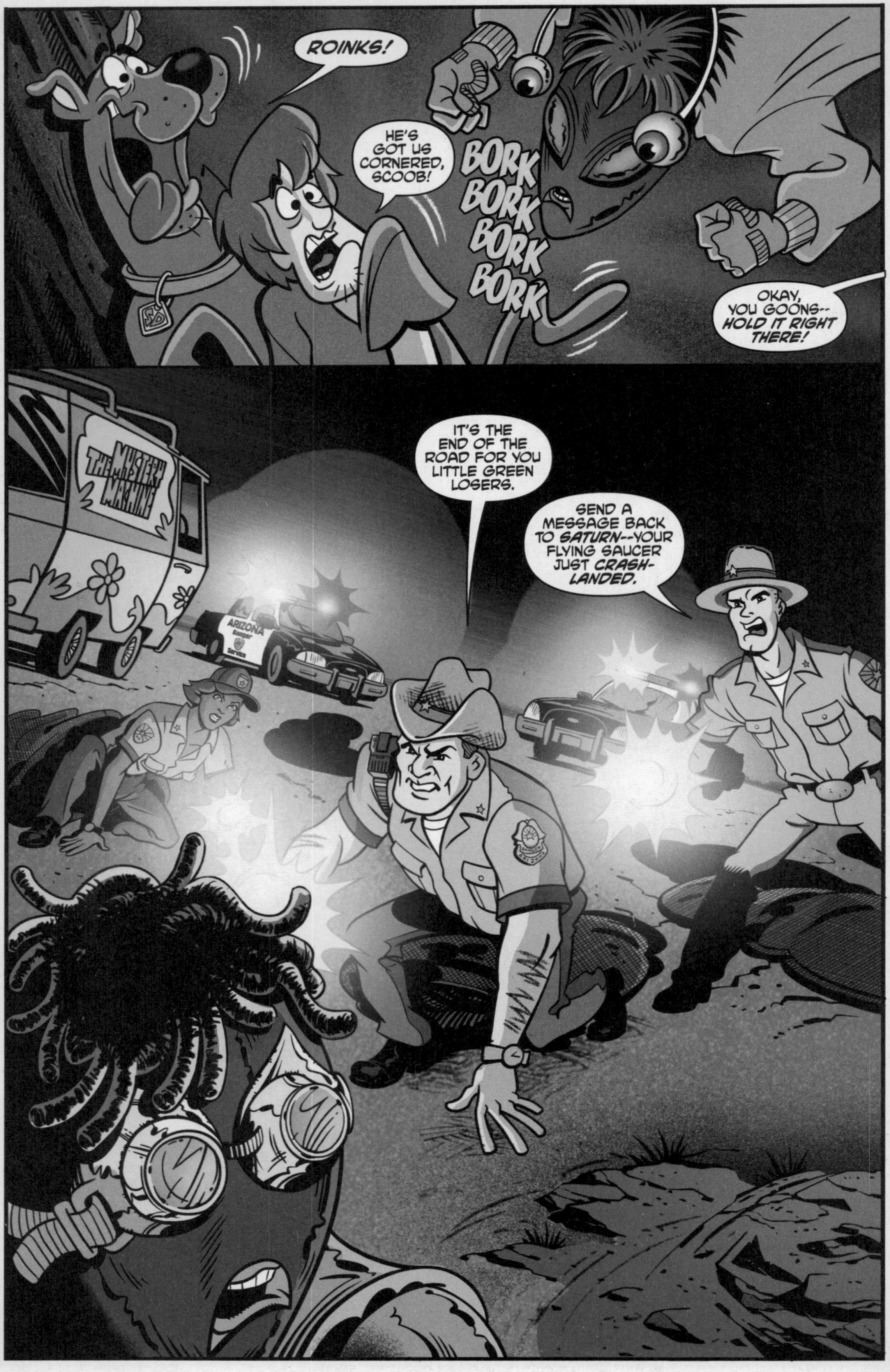
ROINKS!
HE'S GOT US CORNERED, SCOOB!
BORK BORK BORK BORK
OKAY, YOU GOONS-- HOLD IT RIGHT THERE!
THE MYSTERY MACHINE
ARIZONA Ranger Service
IT'S THE END OF THE ROAD FOR YOU LITTLE GREEN LOSERS.
SEND A MESSAGE BACK TO SATURN--YOUR FLYING SAUCER JUST CRASH-LANDED.

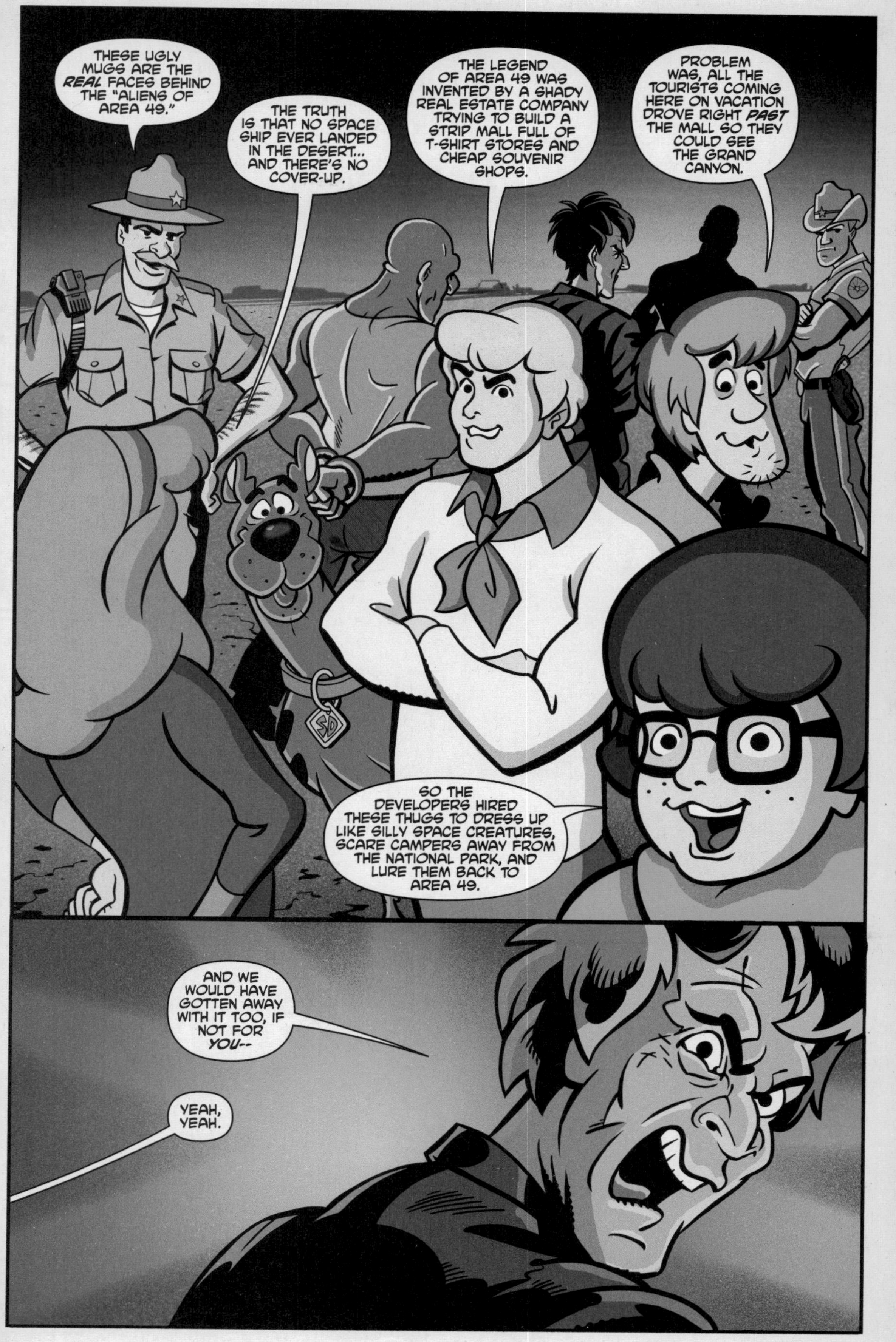

THESE UGLY MUGS ARE THE *REAL* FACES BEHIND THE "ALIENS OF AREA 49."
THE TRUTH IS THAT NO SPACE SHIP EVER LANDED IN THE DESERT... AND THERE'S NO COVER-UP.
THE LEGEND OF AREA 49 WAS INVENTED BY A SHADY REAL ESTATE COMPANY TRYING TO BUILD A STRIP MALL FULL OF T-SHIRT STORES AND CHEAP SOUVENIR SHOPS.
PROBLEM WAS, ALL THE TOURISTS COMING HERE ON VACATION DROVE RIGHT *PAST* THE MALL SO THEY COULD SEE THE GRAND CANYON.
SO THE DEVELOPERS HIRED THESE THUGS TO DRESS UP LIKE SILLY SPACE CREATURES, SCARE CAMPERS AWAY FROM THE NATIONAL PARK, AND LURE THEM BACK TO AREA 49.
AND WE WOULD HAVE GOTTEN AWAY WITH IT TOO, IF NOT FOR *YOU*--
YEAH, YEAH.

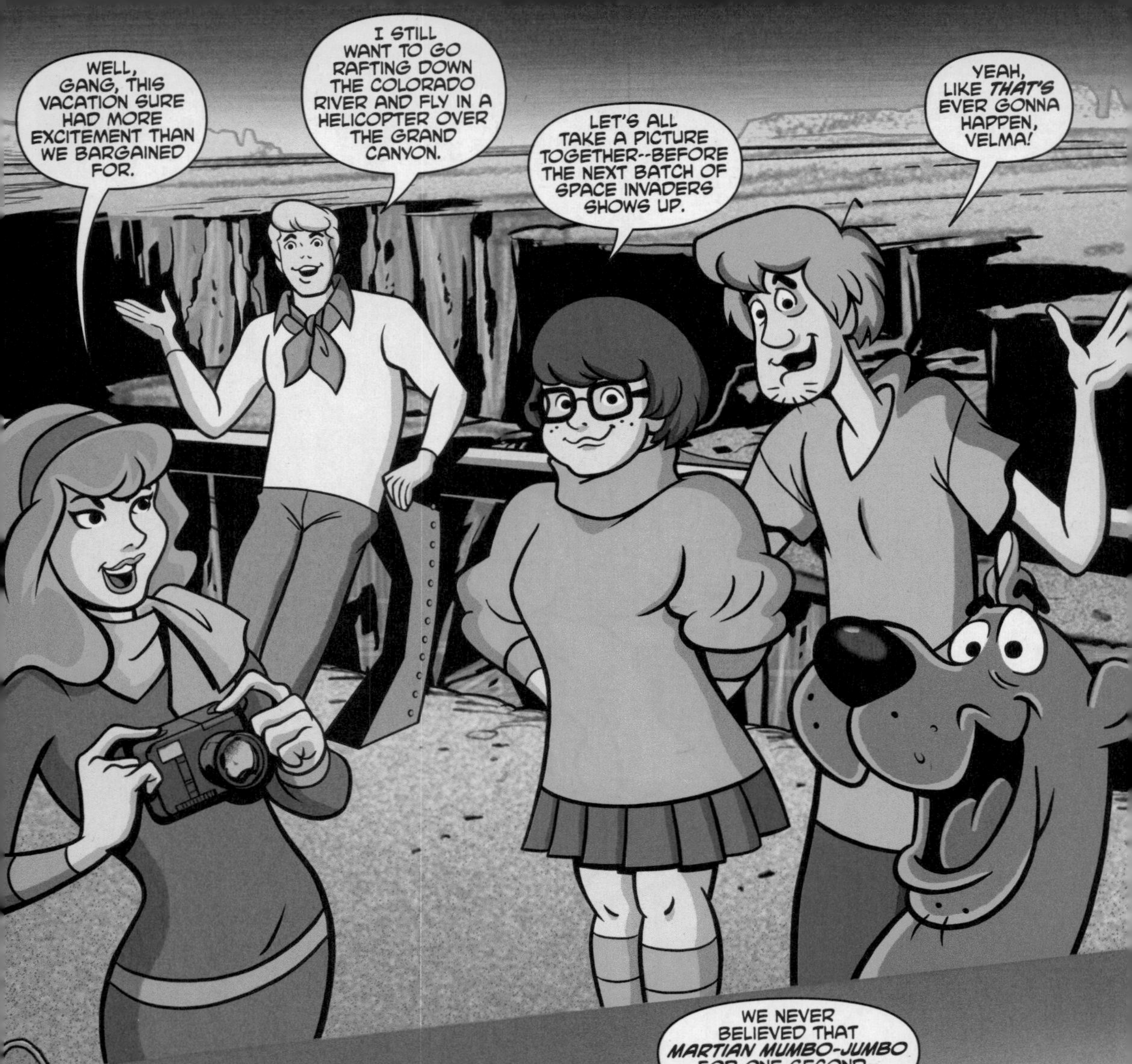
WELL, GANG, THIS VACATION SURE HAD MORE EXCITEMENT THAN WE BARGAINED FOR.
I STILL WANT TO GO RAFTING DOWN THE COLORADO RIVER AND FLY IN A HELICOPTER OVER THE GRAND CANYON.
LET'S ALL TAKE A PICTURE TOGETHER--BEFORE THE NEXT BATCH OF SPACE INVADERS SHOWS UP.
YEAH, LIKE *THAT'S* EVER GONNA HAPPEN, VELMA!

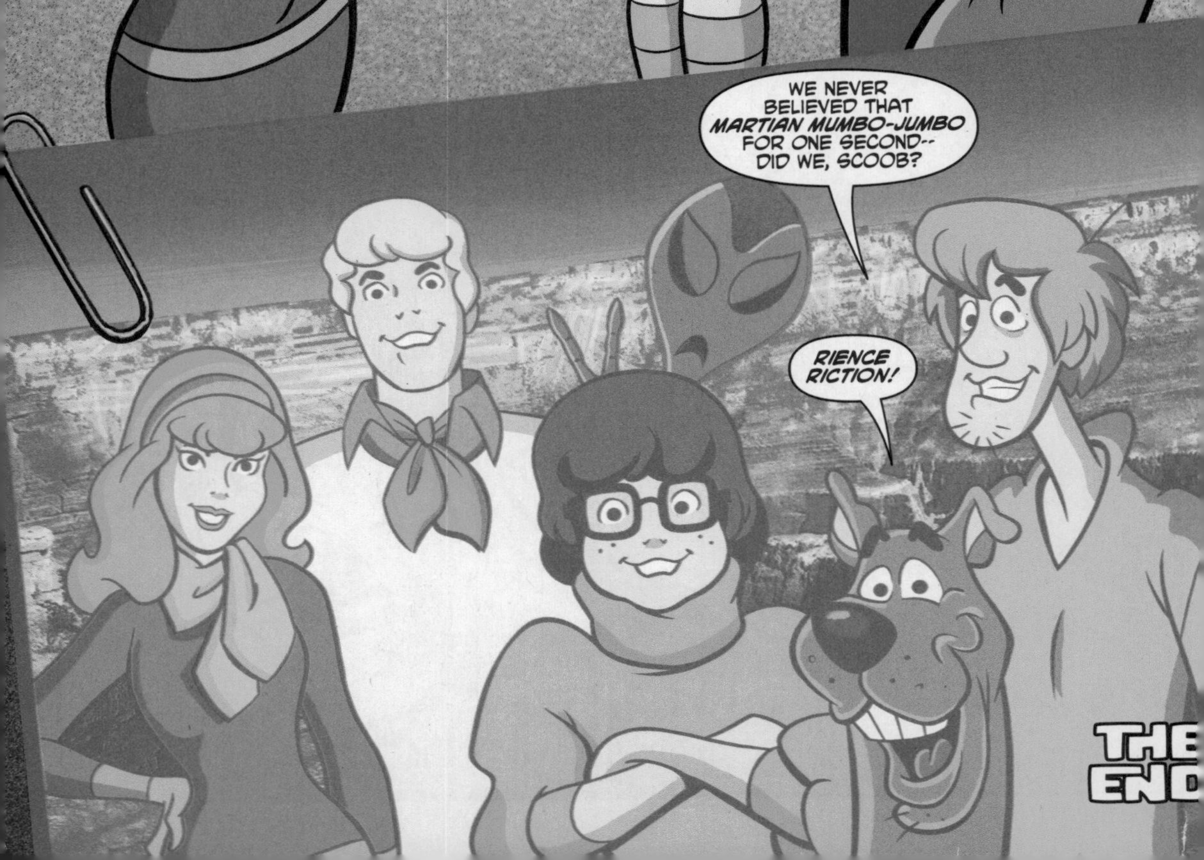
WE NEVER BELIEVED THAT *MARTIAN MUMBO-JUMBO* FOR ONE SECOND--DID WE, SCOOB?
RIENCE RICTION!
THE END

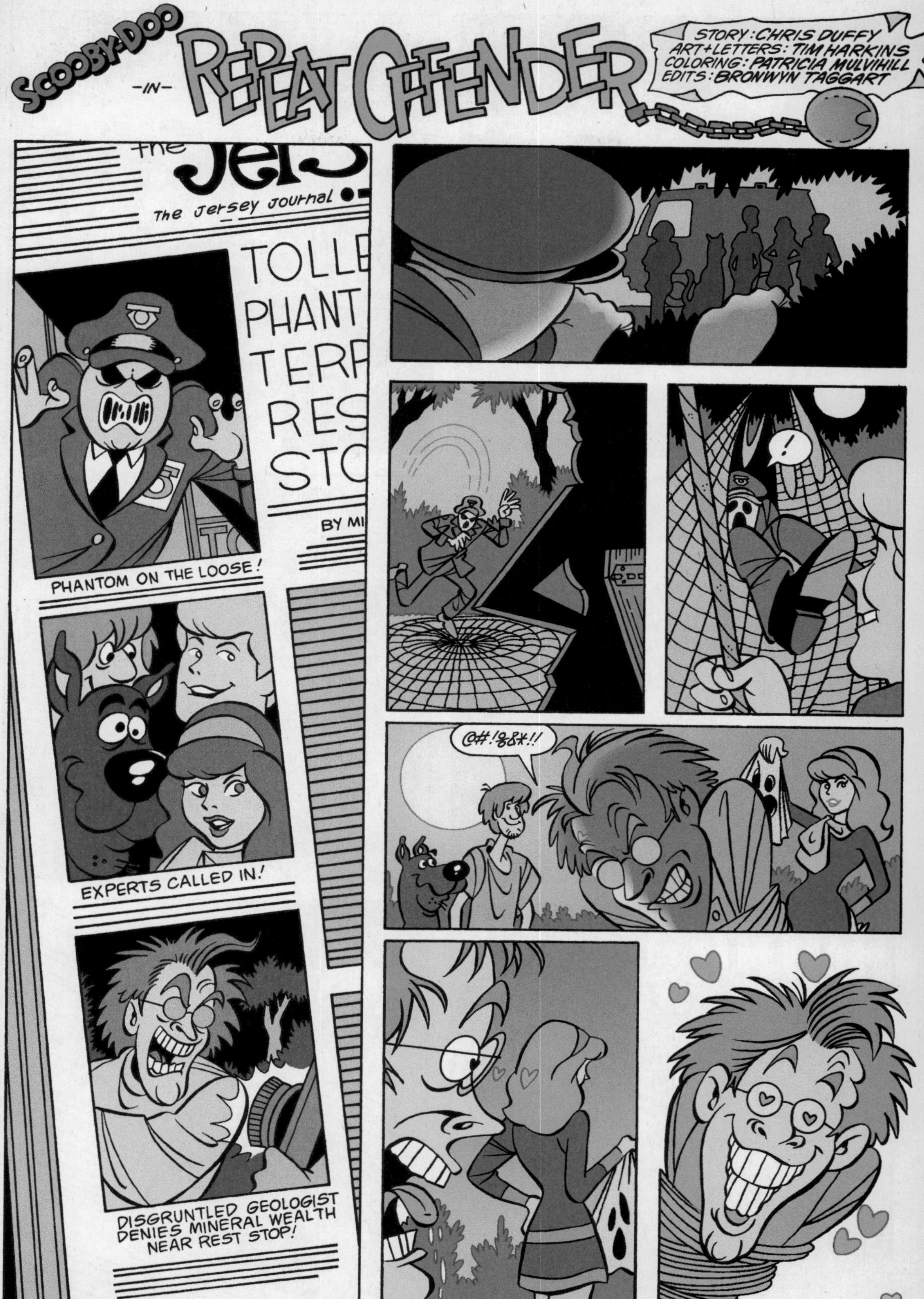
SCOOBY-DOO
-IN-
REPEAT OFFENDER
STORY: CHRIS DUFFY
ART+LETTERS: TIM HARKINS
COLORING: PATRICIA MULVIHILL
EDITS: BRONWYN TAGGART
the Jers
The Jersey Journal
TOLLE
PHANT
TERR
RES
STO
BY MI
PHANTOM ON THE LOOSE!
EXPERTS CALLED IN!
DISGRUNTLED GEOLOGIST DENIES MINERAL WEALTH NEAR REST STOP!
!
@#!&$*!!

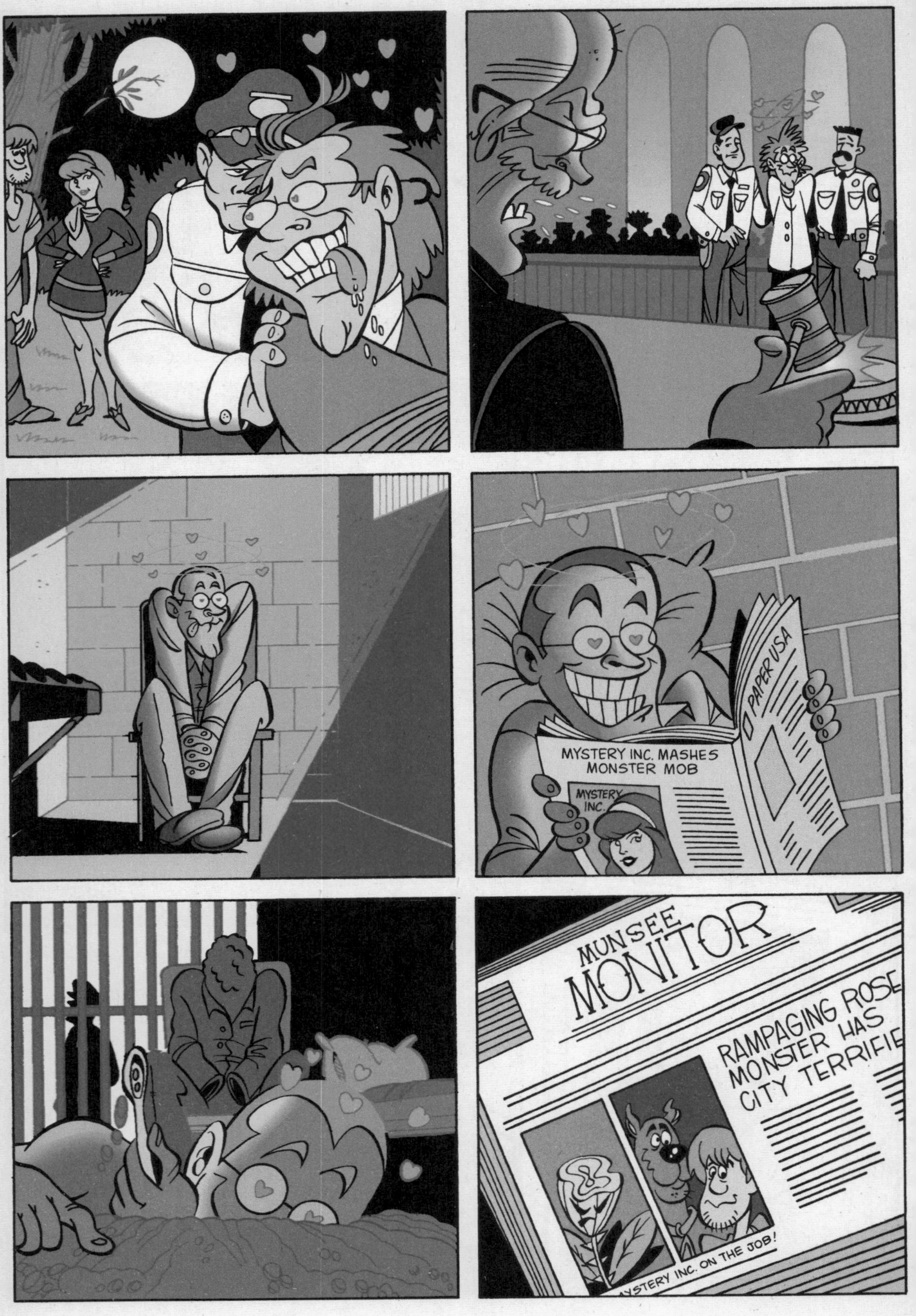
PAPER USA
MYSTERY INC. MASHES MONSTER MOB
MYSTERY INC.
MUNSEE MONITOR
RAMPAGING ROSE MONSTER HAS CITY TERRIFIE
MYSTERY INC. ON THE JOB!

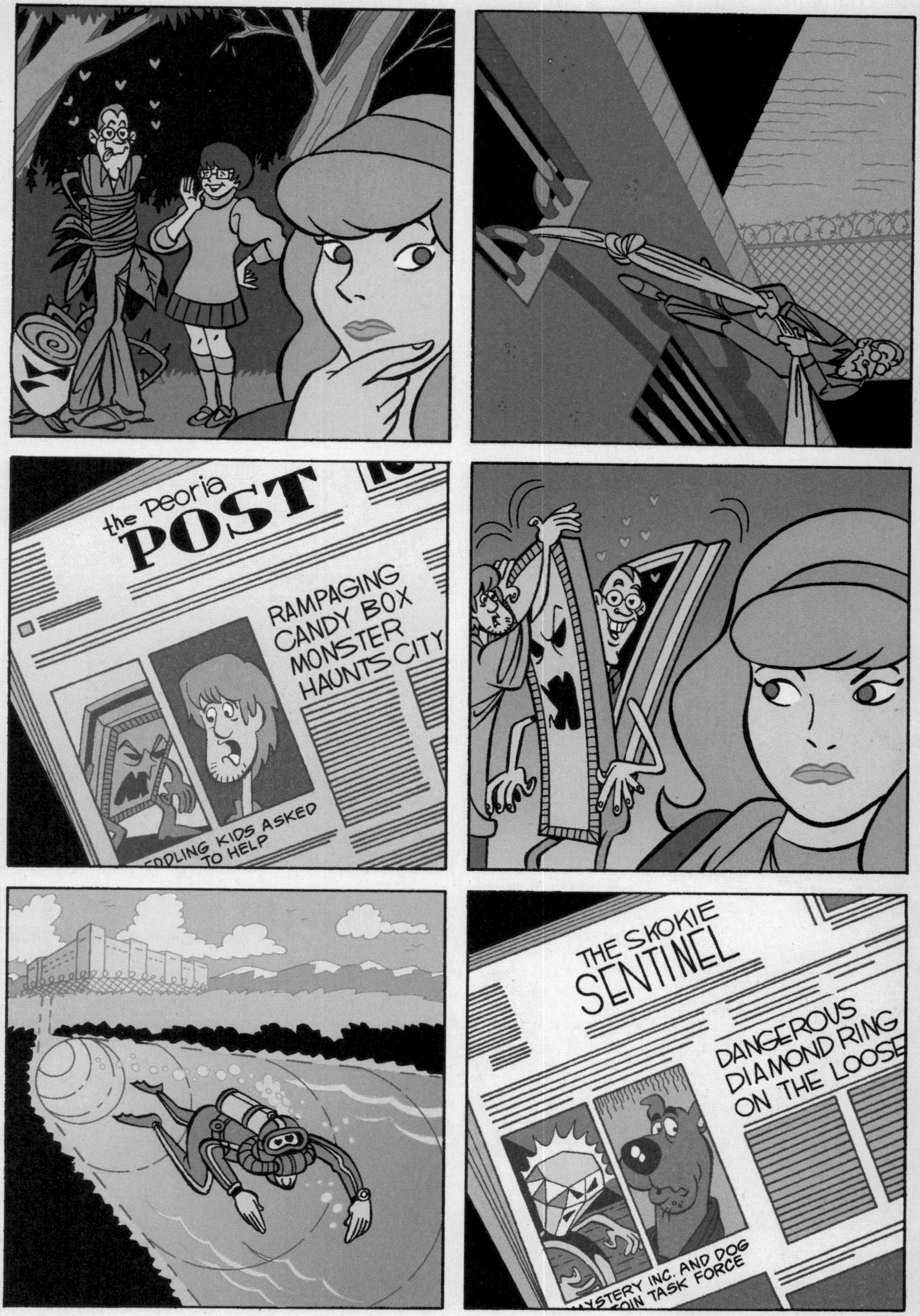
the Peoria POST
RAMPAGING CANDY BOX MONSTER HAUNTS CITY
EDDLING KIDS ASKED TO HELP
THE SKOKIE SENTINEL
DANGEROUS DIAMOND RING ON THE LOOSE
MYSTERY INC. AND DOG
TASK FORCE

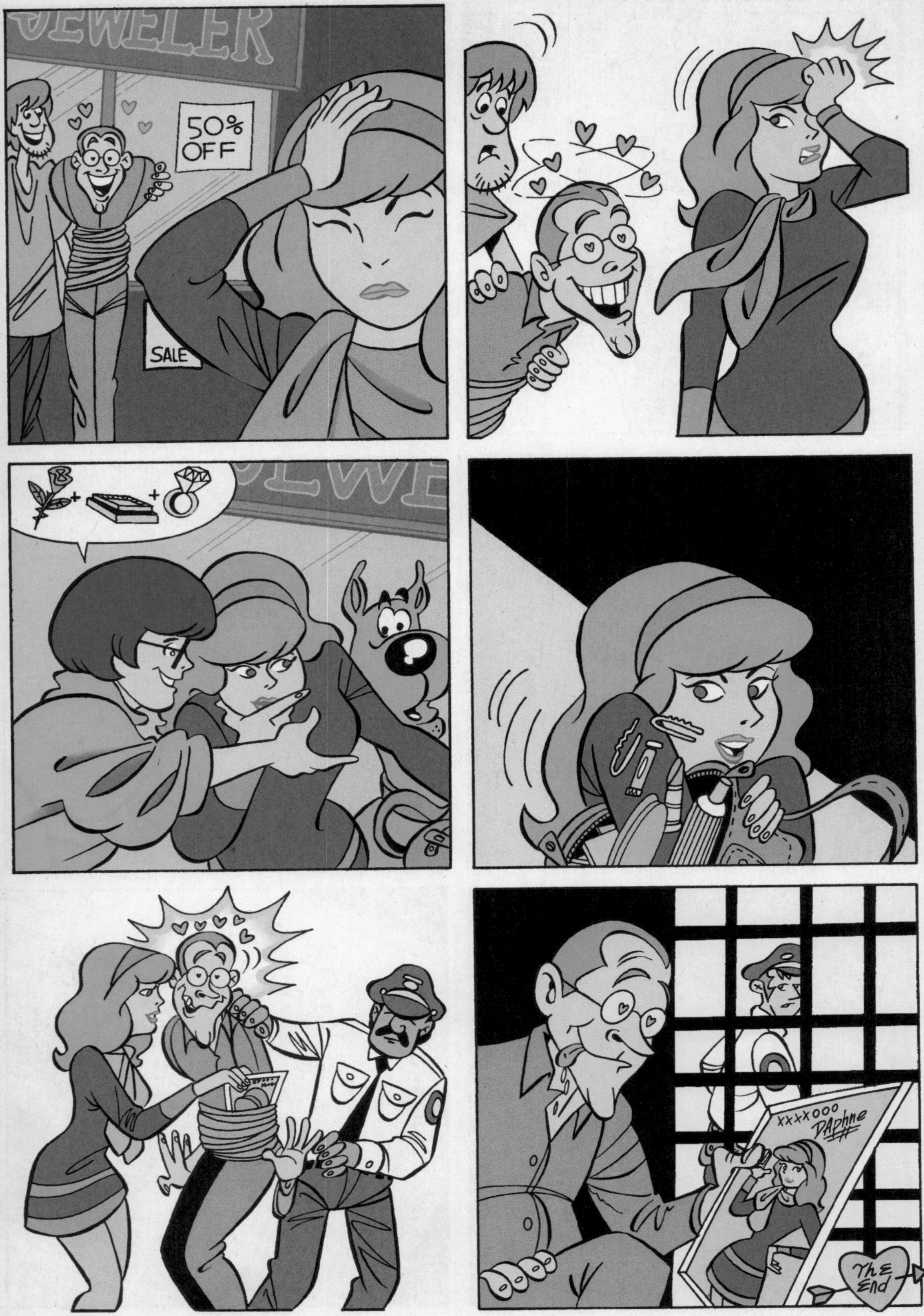
JEWELER
50% OFF
SALE
XXXXOOO
Daphne
The End

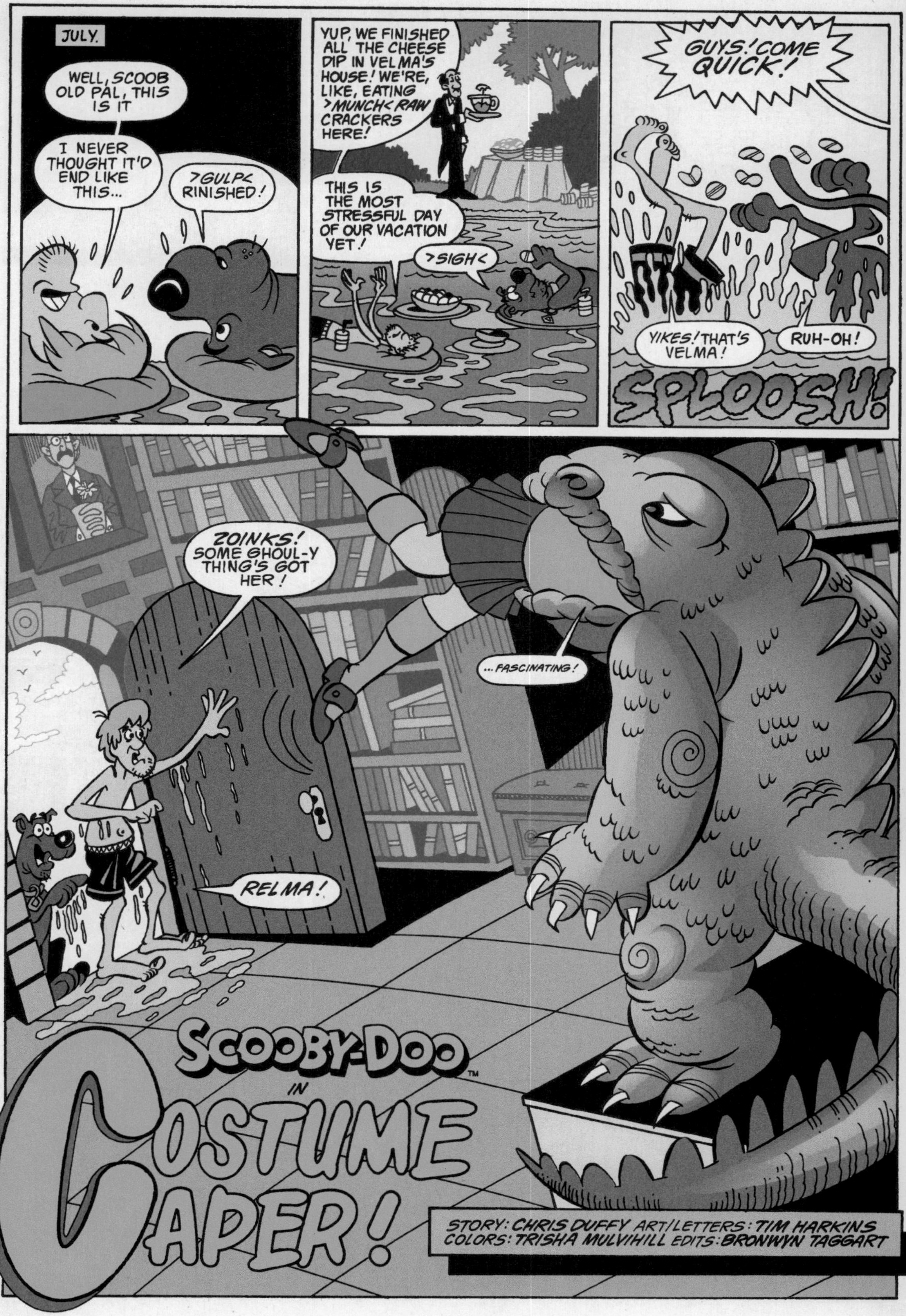
JULY.
WELL, SCOOB OLD PAL, THIS IS IT
I NEVER THOUGHT IT'D END LIKE THIS...
>GULP< RINISHED!
YUP, WE FINISHED ALL THE CHEESE DIP IN VELMA'S HOUSE! WE'RE, LIKE, EATING >MUNCH< RAW CRACKERS HERE!
THIS IS THE MOST STRESSFUL DAY OF OUR VACATION YET!
>SIGH<
GUYS! COME QUICK!
YIKES! THAT'S VELMA!
RUH-OH!
SPLOOSH!
ZOINKS! SOME GHOUL-Y THING'S GOT HER!
...FASCINATING!
RELMA!
SCOOBY-DOO™
IN
COSTUME CAPER!
STORY: CHRIS DUFFY ART/LETTERS: TIM HARKINS
COLORS: TRISHA MULVIHILL EDITS: BRONWYN TAGGART

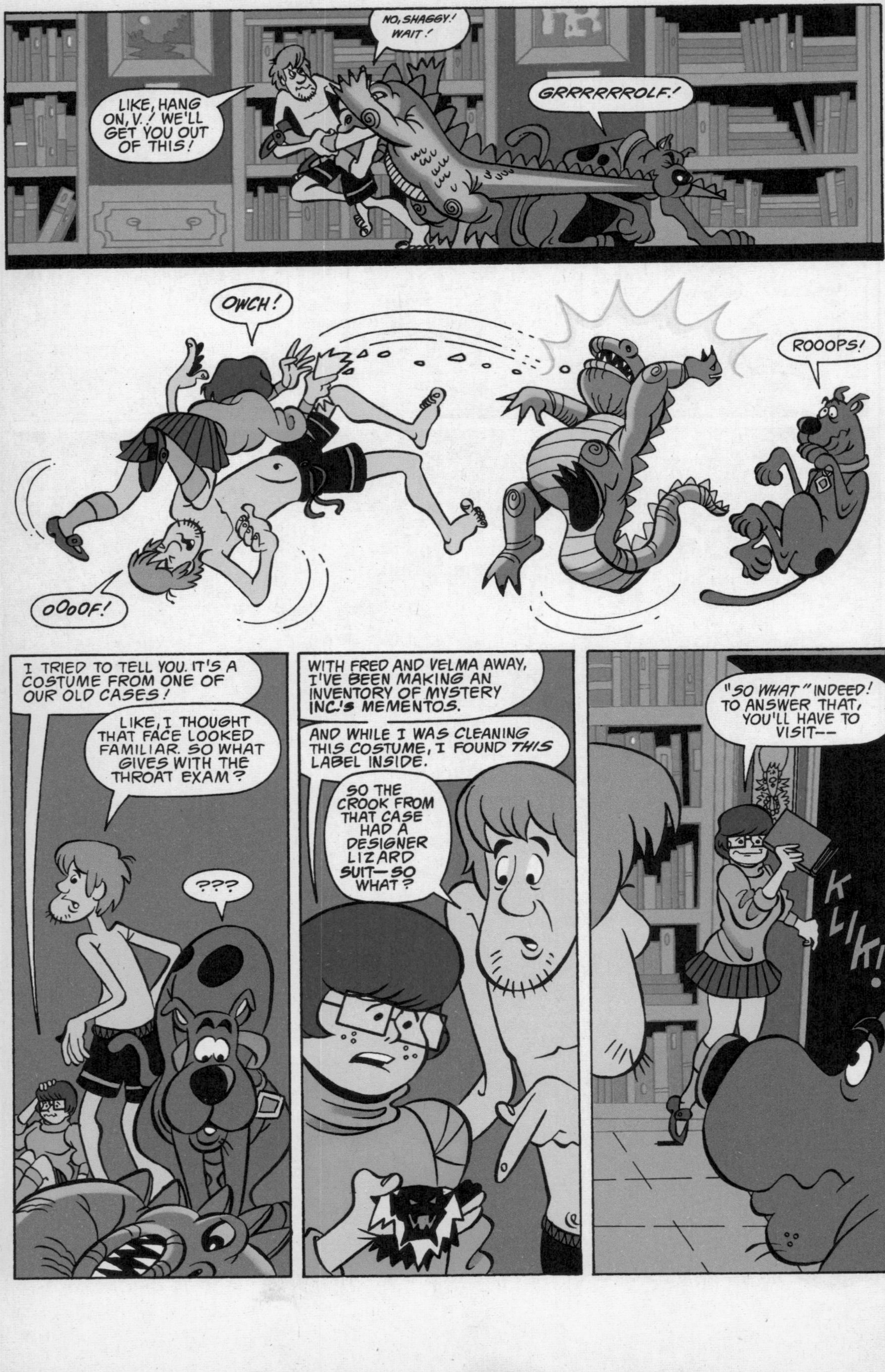
NO, SHAGGY! WAIT!
LIKE, HANG ON, V.! WE'LL GET YOU OUT OF THIS!
GRRRRRROLF!
OWCH!
ROOOPS!
OOOOF!
I TRIED TO TELL YOU. IT'S A COSTUME FROM ONE OF OUR OLD CASES!
LIKE, I THOUGHT THAT FACE LOOKED FAMILIAR. SO WHAT GIVES WITH THE THROAT EXAM?
???
WITH FRED AND VELMA AWAY, I'VE BEEN MAKING AN INVENTORY OF MYSTERY INC.'S MEMENTOS.
AND WHILE I WAS CLEANING THIS COSTUME, I FOUND THIS LABEL INSIDE.
SO THE CROOK FROM THAT CASE HAD A DESIGNER LIZARD SUIT—SO WHAT?
"SO WHAT" INDEED! TO ANSWER THAT, YOU'LL HAVE TO VISIT--
KLIK!

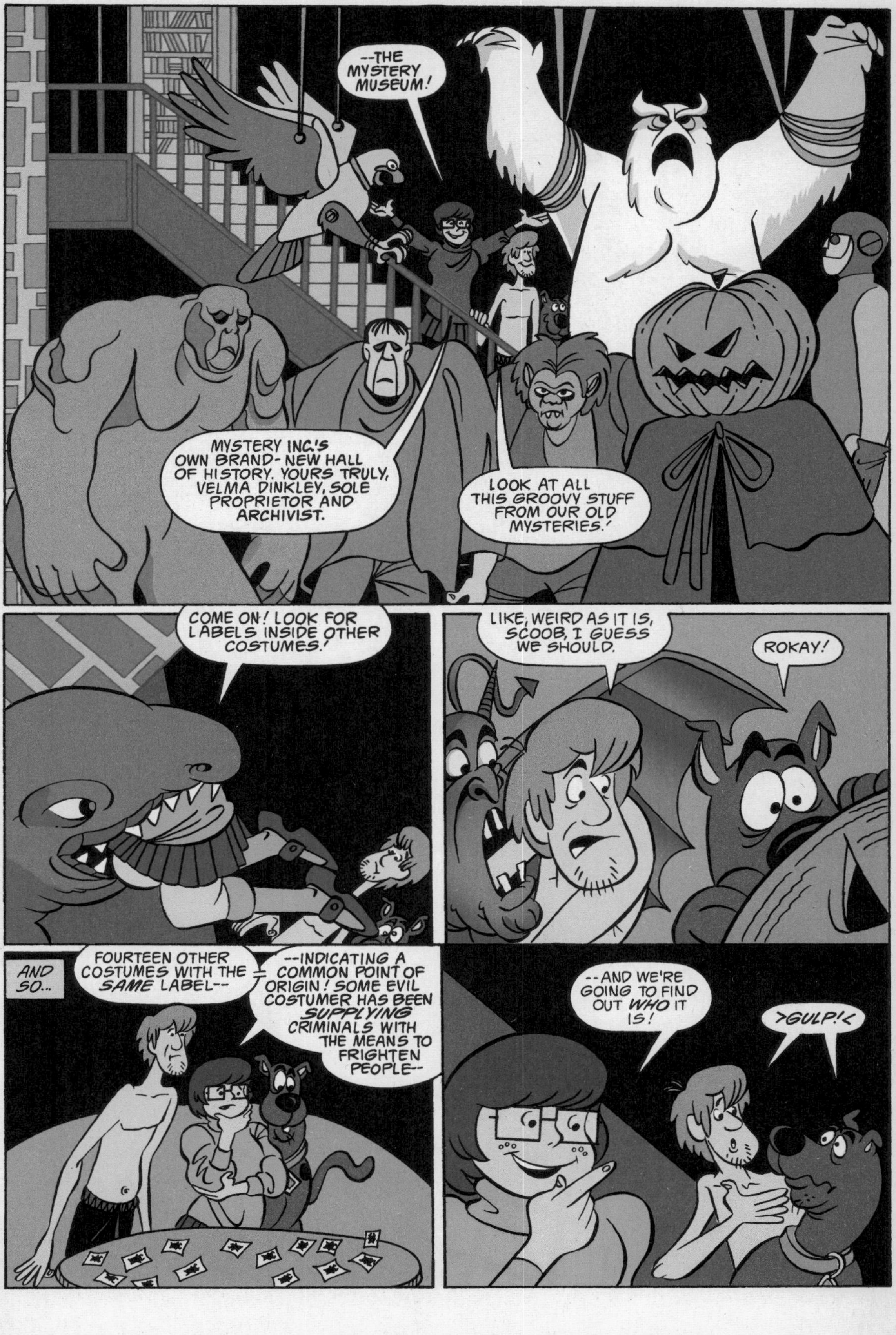
--THE MYSTERY MUSEUM!
MYSTERY INC.'S OWN BRAND-NEW HALL OF HISTORY. YOURS TRULY, VELMA DINKLEY, SOLE PROPRIETOR AND ARCHIVIST.
LOOK AT ALL THIS GROOVY STUFF FROM OUR OLD MYSTERIES!
COME ON! LOOK FOR LABELS INSIDE OTHER COSTUMES!
LIKE, WEIRD AS IT IS, SCOOB, I GUESS WE SHOULD.
ROKAY!
AND SO...
FOURTEEN OTHER COSTUMES WITH THE SAME LABEL--
--INDICATING A COMMON POINT OF ORIGIN! SOME EVIL COSTUMER HAS BEEN SUPPLYING CRIMINALS WITH THE MEANS TO FRIGHTEN PEOPLE--
--AND WE'RE GOING TO FIND OUT WHO IT IS!
>GULP!<

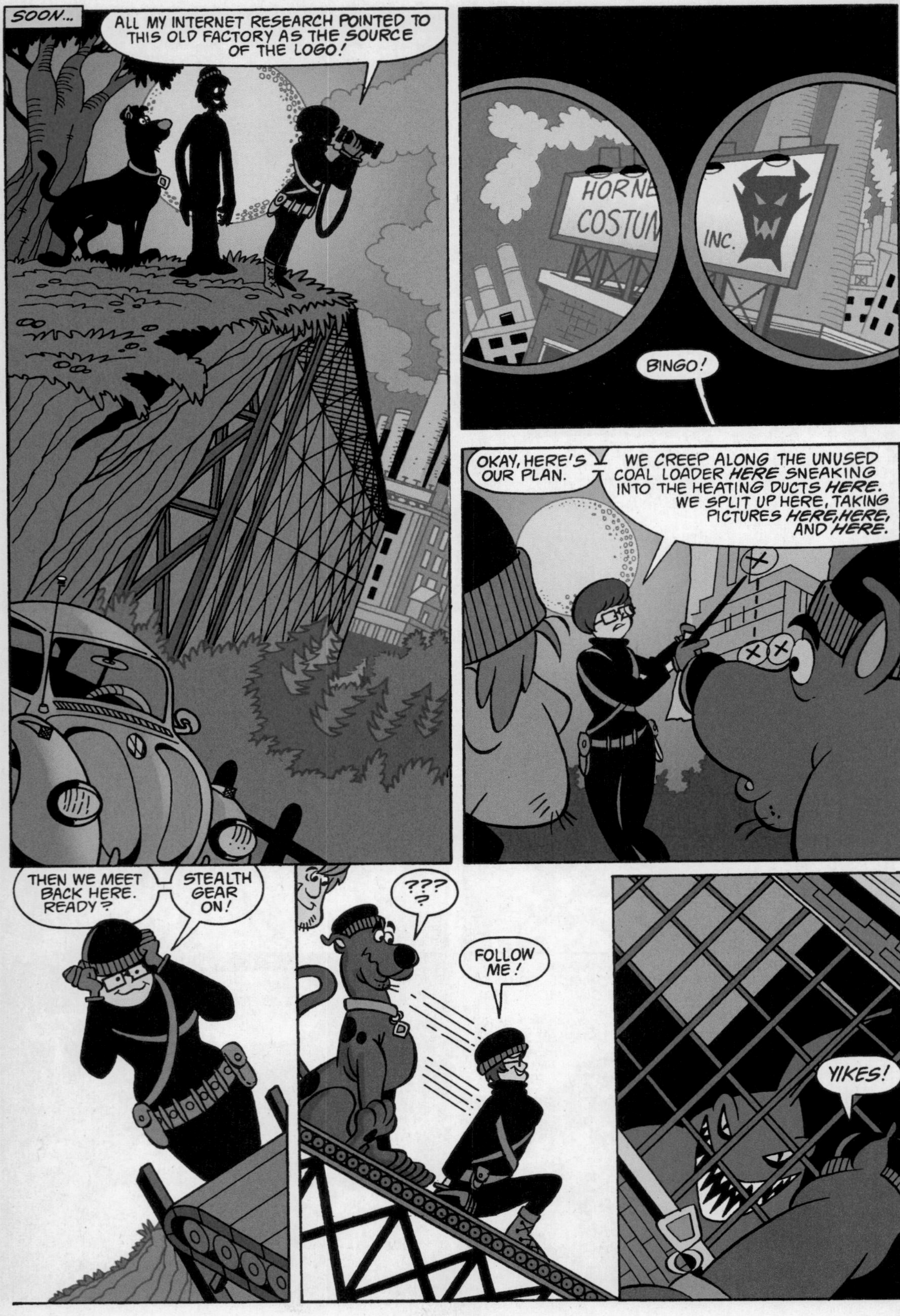
SOON...
ALL MY INTERNET RESEARCH POINTED TO THIS OLD FACTORY AS THE SOURCE OF THE LOGO!
HORNE
COSTUM
INC.
BINGO!
OKAY, HERE'S OUR PLAN.
WE CREEP ALONG THE UNUSED COAL LOADER HERE SNEAKING INTO THE HEATING DUCTS HERE. WE SPLIT UP HERE, TAKING PICTURES HERE, HERE, AND HERE.
THEN WE MEET BACK HERE. READY?
STEALTH GEAR ON!
???
FOLLOW ME!
YIKES!

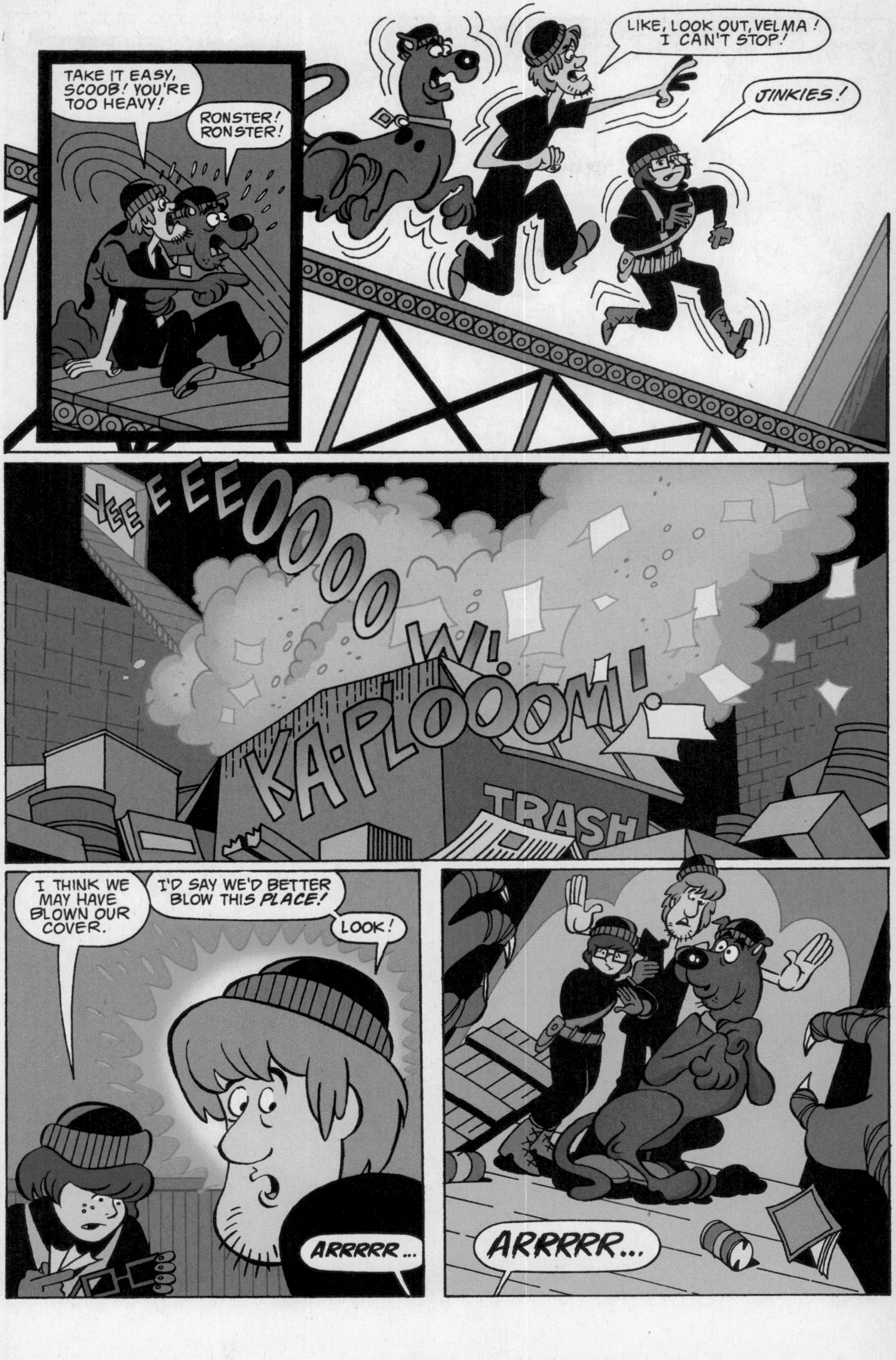
TAKE IT EASY, SCOOB! YOU'RE TOO HEAVY!
RONSTER! RONSTER!
LIKE, LOOK OUT, VELMA! I CAN'T STOP!
JINKIES!
YEEEEEOOOOOW!
KA-PLOOOOM!
TRASH
I THINK WE MAY HAVE BLOWN OUR COVER.
I'D SAY WE'D BETTER BLOW THIS *PLACE!*
LOOK!
ARRRRR...
ARRRRR...

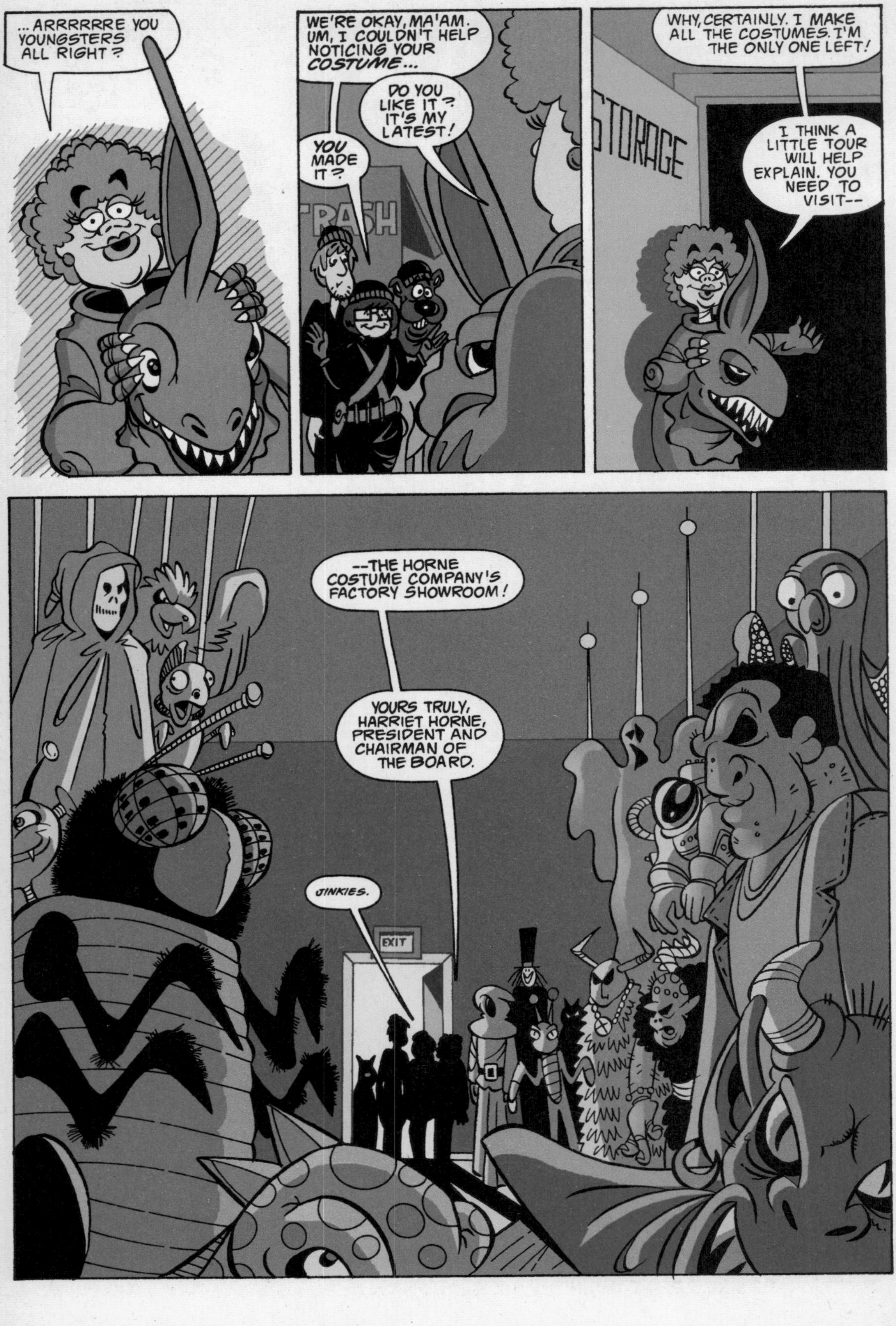
...ARRRRRRE YOU YOUNGSTERS ALL RIGHT?
WE'RE OKAY, MA'AM. UM, I COULDN'T HELP NOTICING YOUR COSTUME...
YOU MADE IT?
DO YOU LIKE IT? IT'S MY LATEST!
TRASH
WHY, CERTAINLY. I MAKE ALL THE COSTUMES. I'M THE ONLY ONE LEFT!
STORAGE
I THINK A LITTLE TOUR WILL HELP EXPLAIN. YOU NEED TO VISIT--
--THE HORNE COSTUME COMPANY'S FACTORY SHOWROOM!
YOURS TRULY, HARRIET HORNE, PRESIDENT AND CHAIRMAN OF THE BOARD.
JINKIES.
EXIT

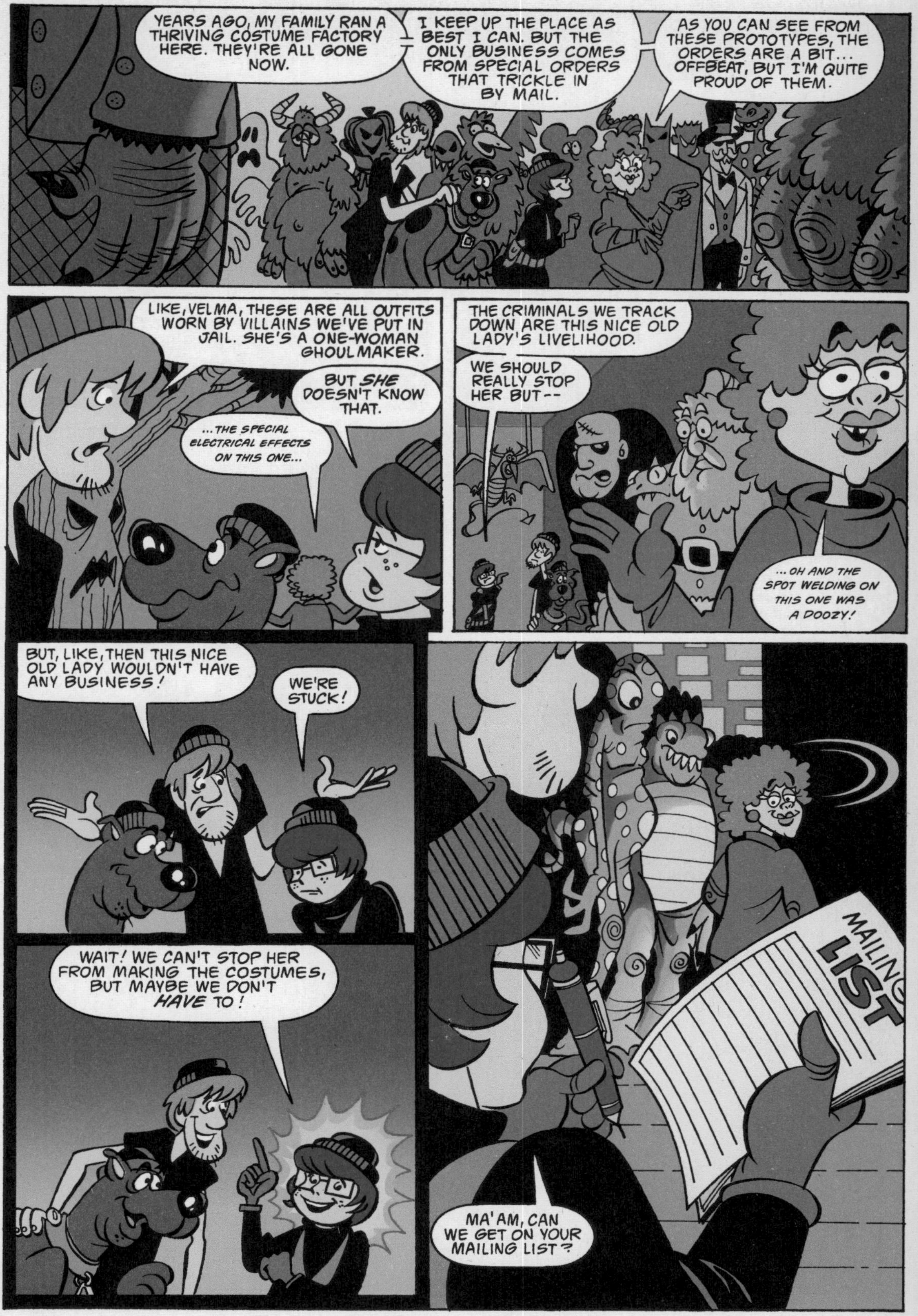
YEARS AGO, MY FAMILY RAN A THRIVING COSTUME FACTORY HERE. THEY'RE ALL GONE NOW.
I KEEP UP THE PLACE AS BEST I CAN. BUT THE ONLY BUSINESS COMES FROM SPECIAL ORDERS THAT TRICKLE IN BY MAIL.
AS YOU CAN SEE FROM THESE PROTOTYPES, THE ORDERS ARE A BIT... OFFBEAT, BUT I'M QUITE PROUD OF THEM.
LIKE, VELMA, THESE ARE ALL OUTFITS WORN BY VILLAINS WE'VE PUT IN JAIL. SHE'S A ONE-WOMAN GHOULMAKER.
BUT SHE DOESN'T KNOW THAT.
...THE SPECIAL ELECTRICAL EFFECTS ON THIS ONE...
THE CRIMINALS WE TRACK DOWN ARE THIS NICE OLD LADY'S LIVELIHOOD.
WE SHOULD REALLY STOP HER BUT--
...OH AND THE SPOT WELDING ON THIS ONE WAS A DOOZY!
BUT, LIKE, THEN THIS NICE OLD LADY WOULDN'T HAVE ANY BUSINESS!
WE'RE STUCK!
WAIT! WE CAN'T STOP HER FROM MAKING THE COSTUMES, BUT MAYBE WE DON'T HAVE TO!
MAILING LIST
MA'AM, CAN WE GET ON YOUR MAILING LIST?

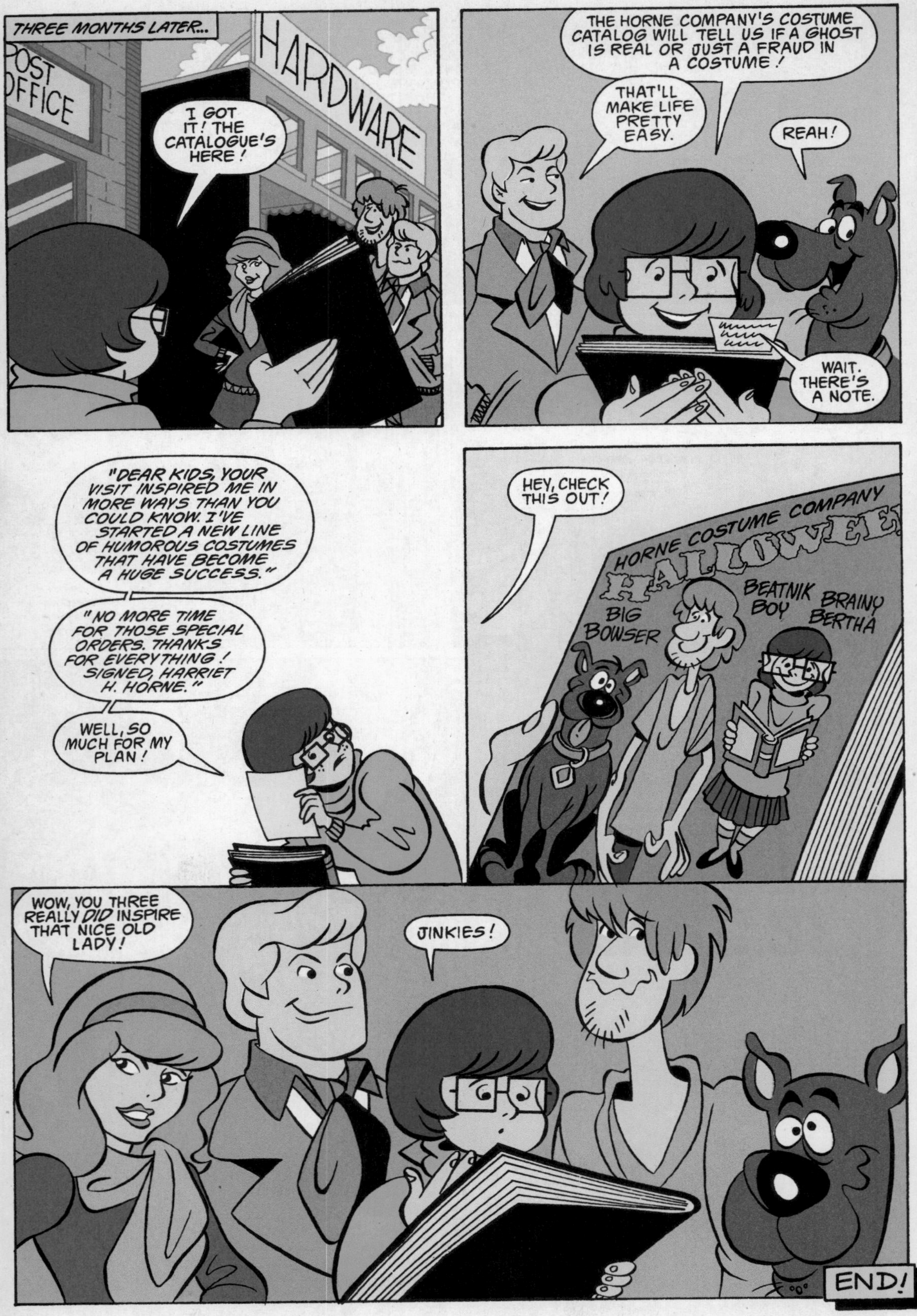
THREE MONTHS LATER...
POST OFFICE
HARDWARE
I GOT IT! THE CATALOGUE'S HERE!
THE HORNE COMPANY'S COSTUME CATALOG WILL TELL US IF A GHOST IS REAL OR JUST A FRAUD IN A COSTUME!
THAT'LL MAKE LIFE PRETTY EASY.
REAH!
WAIT. THERE'S A NOTE.
"DEAR KIDS, YOUR VISIT INSPIRED ME IN MORE WAYS THAN YOU COULD KNOW. I'VE STARTED A NEW LINE OF HUMOROUS COSTUMES THAT HAVE BECOME A HUGE SUCCESS."
"NO MORE TIME FOR THOSE SPECIAL ORDERS. THANKS FOR EVERYTHING! SIGNED, HARRIET H. HORNE."
WELL, SO MUCH FOR MY PLAN!
HEY, CHECK THIS OUT!
HORNE COSTUME COMPANY
HALLOWEEN
BIG BOWSER
BEATNIK BOY
BRAINY BERTHA
WOW, YOU THREE REALLY DID INSPIRE THAT NICE OLD LADY!
JINKIES!
END!

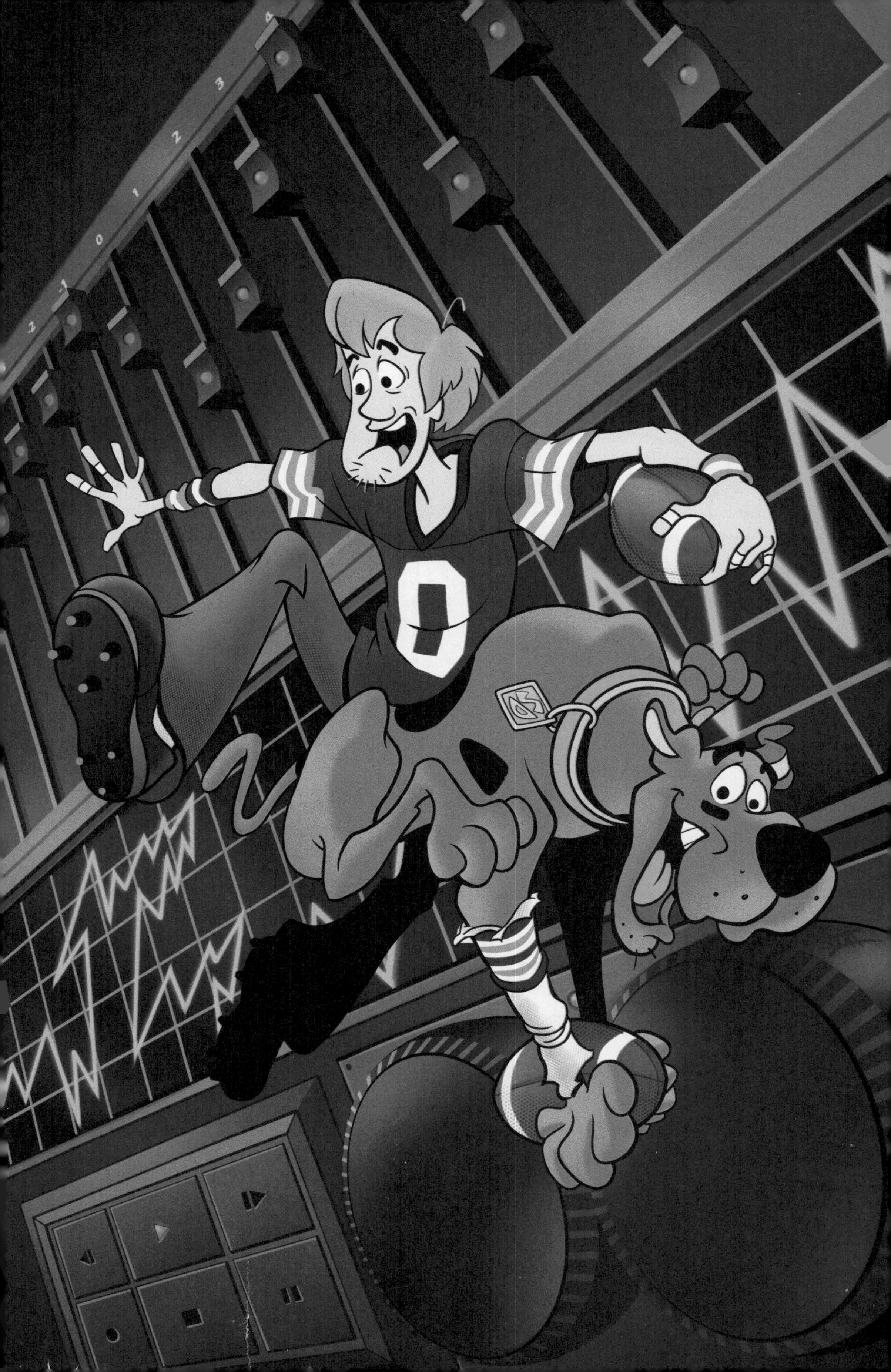

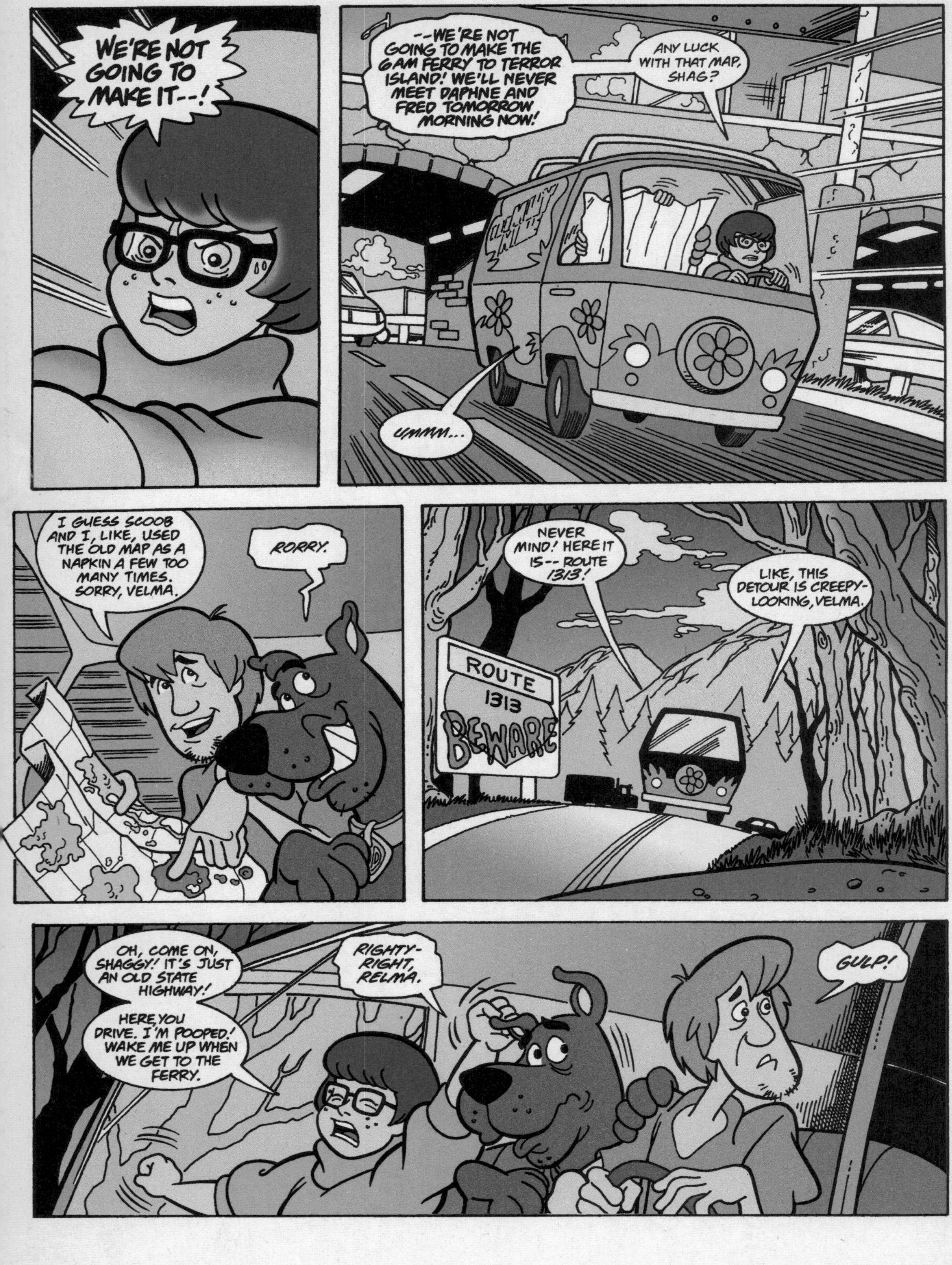
WE'RE NOT GOING TO MAKE IT--!
--WE'RE NOT GOING TO MAKE THE 6AM FERRY TO TERROR ISLAND! WE'LL NEVER MEET DAPHNE AND FRED TOMORROW MORNING NOW!
ANY LUCK WITH THAT MAP, SHAG?
UMMM...
I GUESS SCOOB AND I, LIKE, USED THE OLD MAP AS A NAPKIN A FEW TOO MANY TIMES. SORRY, VELMA.
RORRY.
NEVER MIND! HERE IT IS-- ROUTE 1313!
LIKE, THIS DETOUR IS CREEPY-LOOKING, VELMA.
ROUTE 1313
BEWARE
OH, COME ON, SHAGGY! IT'S JUST AN OLD STATE HIGHWAY!
HERE, YOU DRIVE. I'M POOPED! WAKE ME UP WHEN WE GET TO THE FERRY.
RIGHTY-RIGHT, RELMA.
GULP!

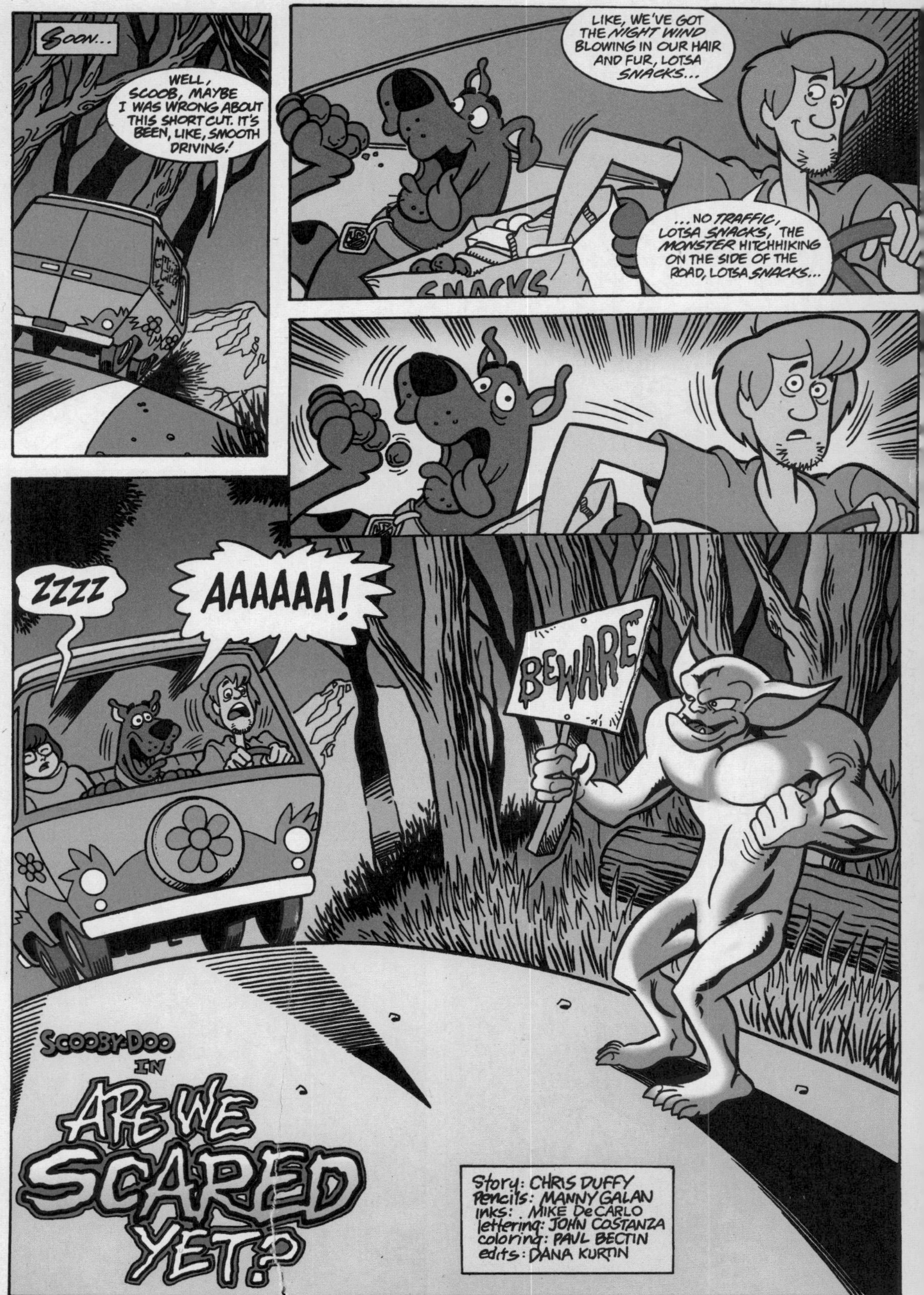
SOON...
WELL, SCOOB, MAYBE I WAS WRONG ABOUT THIS SHORT CUT. IT'S BEEN, LIKE, SMOOTH DRIVING!
LIKE, WE'VE GOT THE NIGHT WIND BLOWING IN OUR HAIR AND FUR, LOTSA SNACKS...
...NO TRAFFIC, LOTSA SNACKS, THE MONSTER HITCHHIKING ON THE SIDE OF THE ROAD, LOTSA SNACKS...
SNACKS
ZZZZ
AAAAAA!
BEWARE
SCOOBY-DOO IN
ARE WE SCARED YET?
Story: CHRIS DUFFY
Pencils: MANNY GALAN
inks: MIKE DeCARLO
lettering: JOHN COSTANZA
coloring: PAUL BECTIN
edits: DANA KURTIN

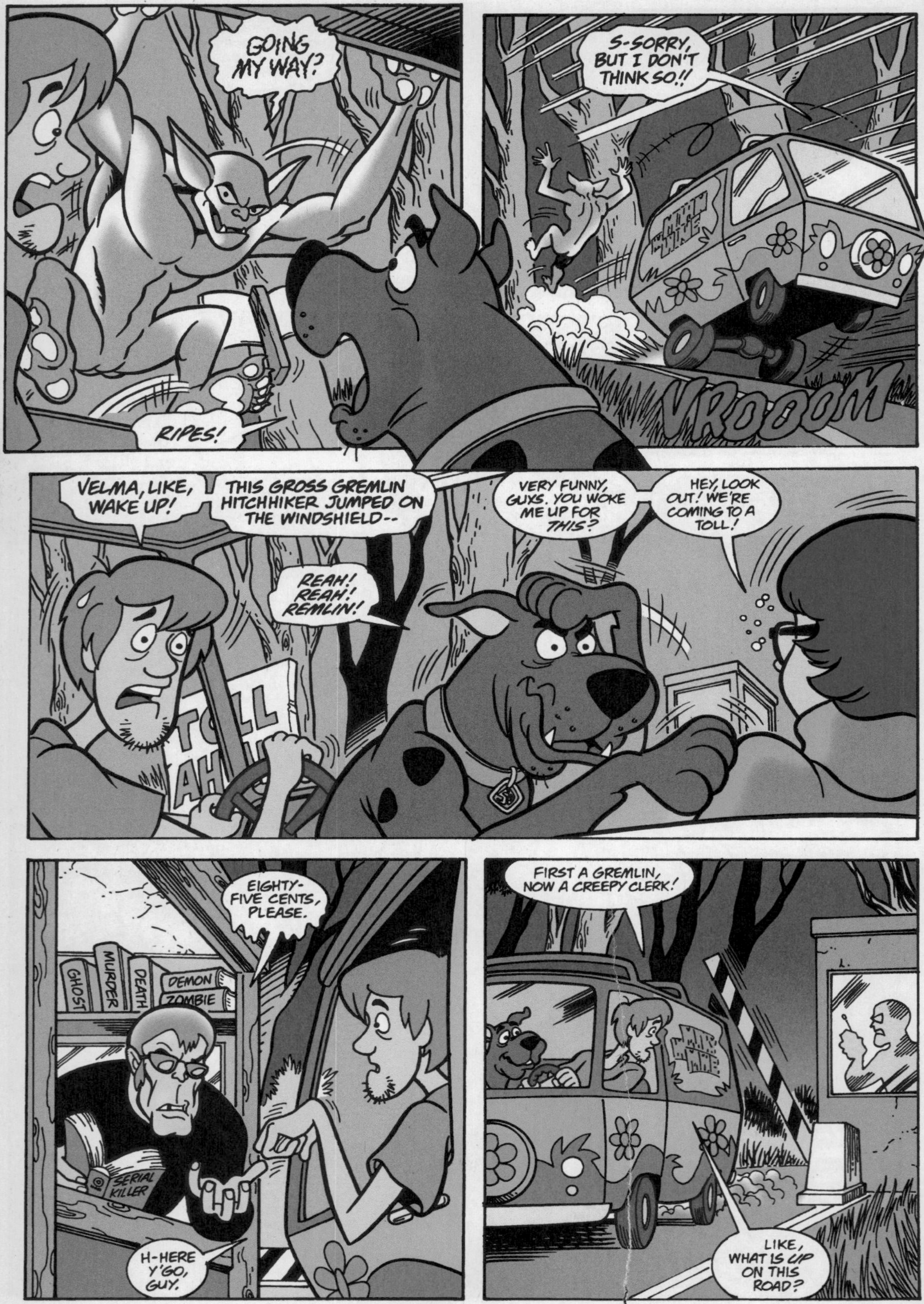
GOING MY WAY?
RIPES!
S-SORRY, BUT I DON'T THINK SO!!
VROOOM
VELMA, LIKE, WAKE UP!
THIS GROSS GREMLIN HITCHHIKER JUMPED ON THE WINDSHIELD--
REAH! REAH! REMLIN!
VERY FUNNY, GUYS. YOU WOKE ME UP FOR THIS?
HEY, LOOK OUT! WE'RE COMING TO A TOLL!
TOLL
EIGHTY-FIVE CENTS, PLEASE.
GHOST
MURDER
DEATH
DEMON
ZOMBIE
SERIAL KILLER
H-HERE Y'GO, GUY.
FIRST A GREMLIN, NOW A CREEPY CLERK!
LIKE, WHAT IS UP ON THIS ROAD?

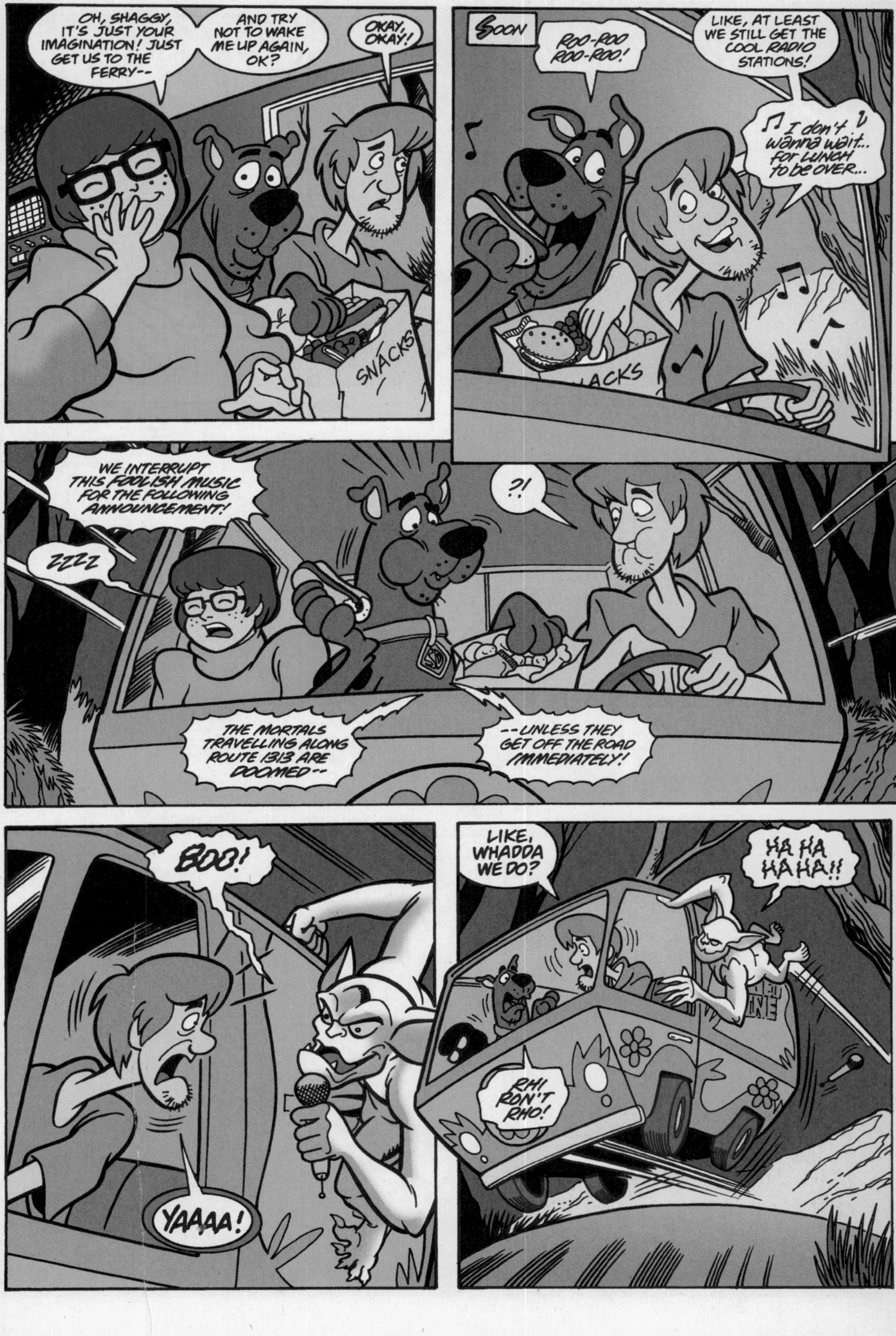
OH, SHAGGY, IT'S JUST YOUR IMAGINATION! JUST GET US TO THE FERRY--
AND TRY NOT TO WAKE ME UP AGAIN, OK?
OKAY, OKAY!
SOON
ROO-ROO ROO-ROO!
LIKE, AT LEAST WE STILL GET THE COOL RADIO STATIONS!
I don't wanna wait... for lunch to be over...
SNACKS
WE INTERRUPT THIS FOOLISH MUSIC FOR THE FOLLOWING ANNOUNCEMENT!
?!
ZZZZ
THE MORTALS TRAVELLING ALONG ROUTE 1313 ARE DOOMED--
--UNLESS THEY GET OFF THE ROAD IMMEDIATELY!
BOO!
YAAAA!
LIKE, WHADDA WE DO?
HA HA HA HA!!
RHI RON'T RHO!

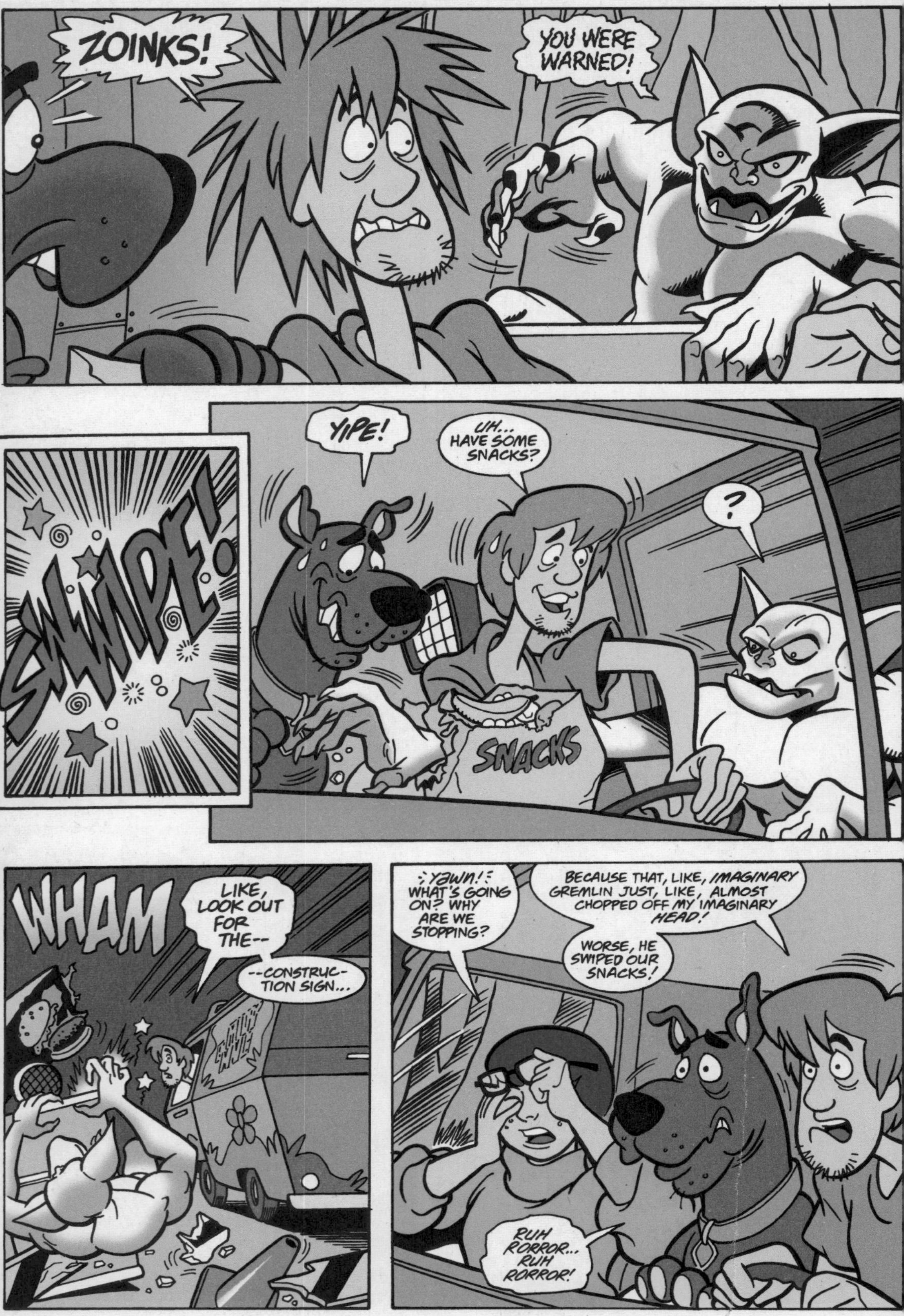
ZOINKS!
YOU WERE WARNED!
SWIPE!
YIPE!
UH... HAVE SOME SNACKS?
?
SNACKS
WHAM
LIKE, LOOK OUT FOR THE--
--CONSTRUCTION SIGN...
YAWN! WHAT'S GOING ON? WHY ARE WE STOPPING?
BECAUSE THAT, LIKE, IMAGINARY GREMLIN JUST, LIKE, ALMOST CHOPPED OFF MY IMAGINARY HEAD!
WORSE, HE SWIPED OUR SNACKS!
RUH RORROR... RUH RORROR!

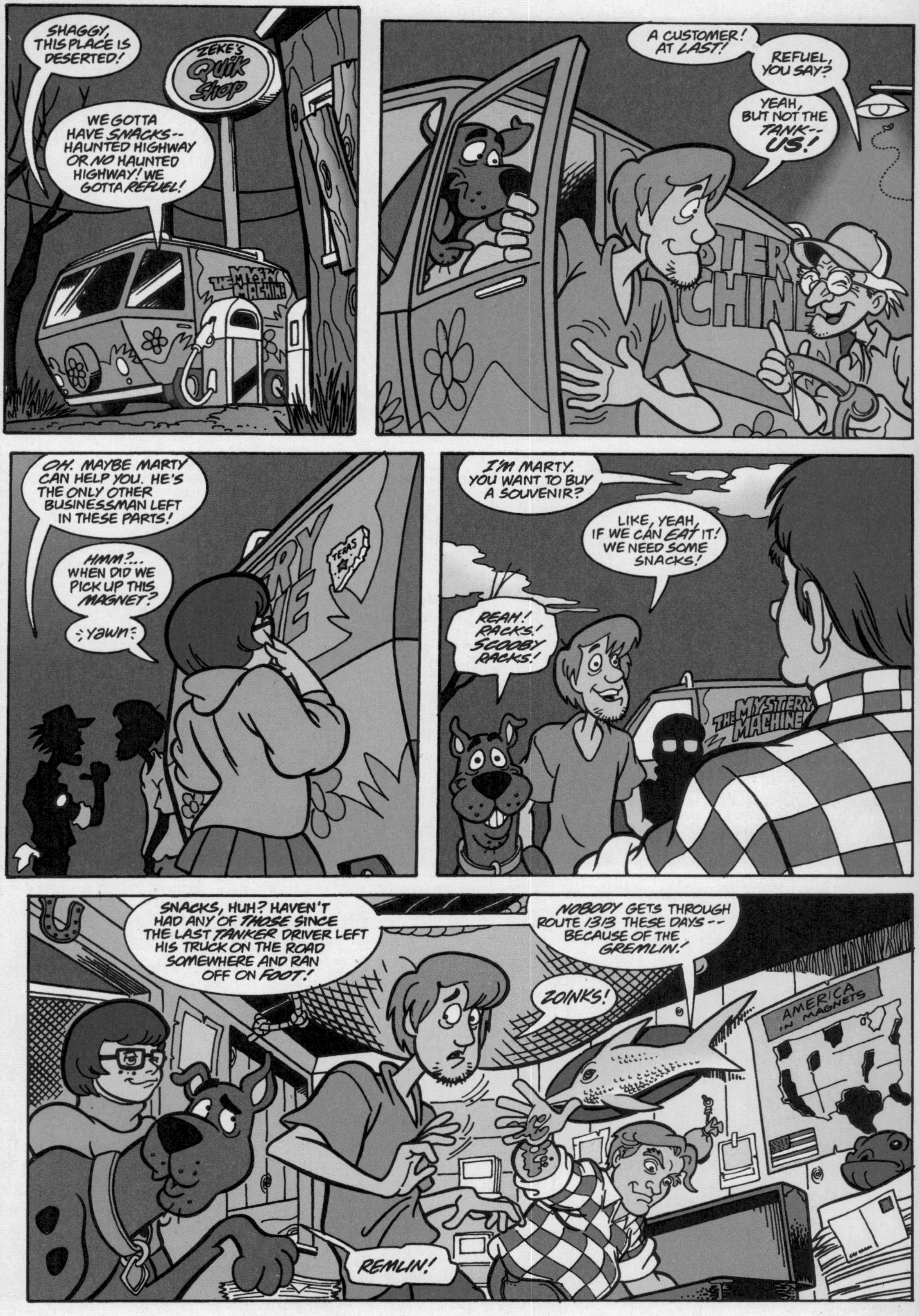
SHAGGY, THIS PLACE IS DESERTED!
ZEKE'S Quik Shop
WE GOTTA HAVE SNACKS-- HAUNTED HIGHWAY OR NO HAUNTED HIGHWAY! WE GOTTA REFUEL!
A CUSTOMER! AT LAST!
REFUEL, YOU SAY?
YEAH, BUT NOT THE TANK-- US!
OH. MAYBE MARTY CAN HELP YOU. HE'S THE ONLY OTHER BUSINESSMAN LEFT IN THESE PARTS!
HMM?... WHEN DID WE PICK UP THIS MAGNET?
TEXAS
YAWN
I'M MARTY. YOU WANT TO BUY A SOUVENIR?
LIKE, YEAH, IF WE CAN EAT IT! WE NEED SOME SNACKS!
REAH! RACKS! SCOOBY RACKS!
THE MYSTERY MACHINE
SNACKS, HUH? HAVEN'T HAD ANY OF THOSE SINCE THE LAST TANKER DRIVER LEFT HIS TRUCK ON THE ROAD SOMEWHERE AND RAN OFF ON FOOT!
NOBODY GETS THROUGH ROUTE 1313 THESE DAYS -- BECAUSE OF THE GREMLIN!
ZOINKS!
AMERICA IN MAGNETS
REMLIN!

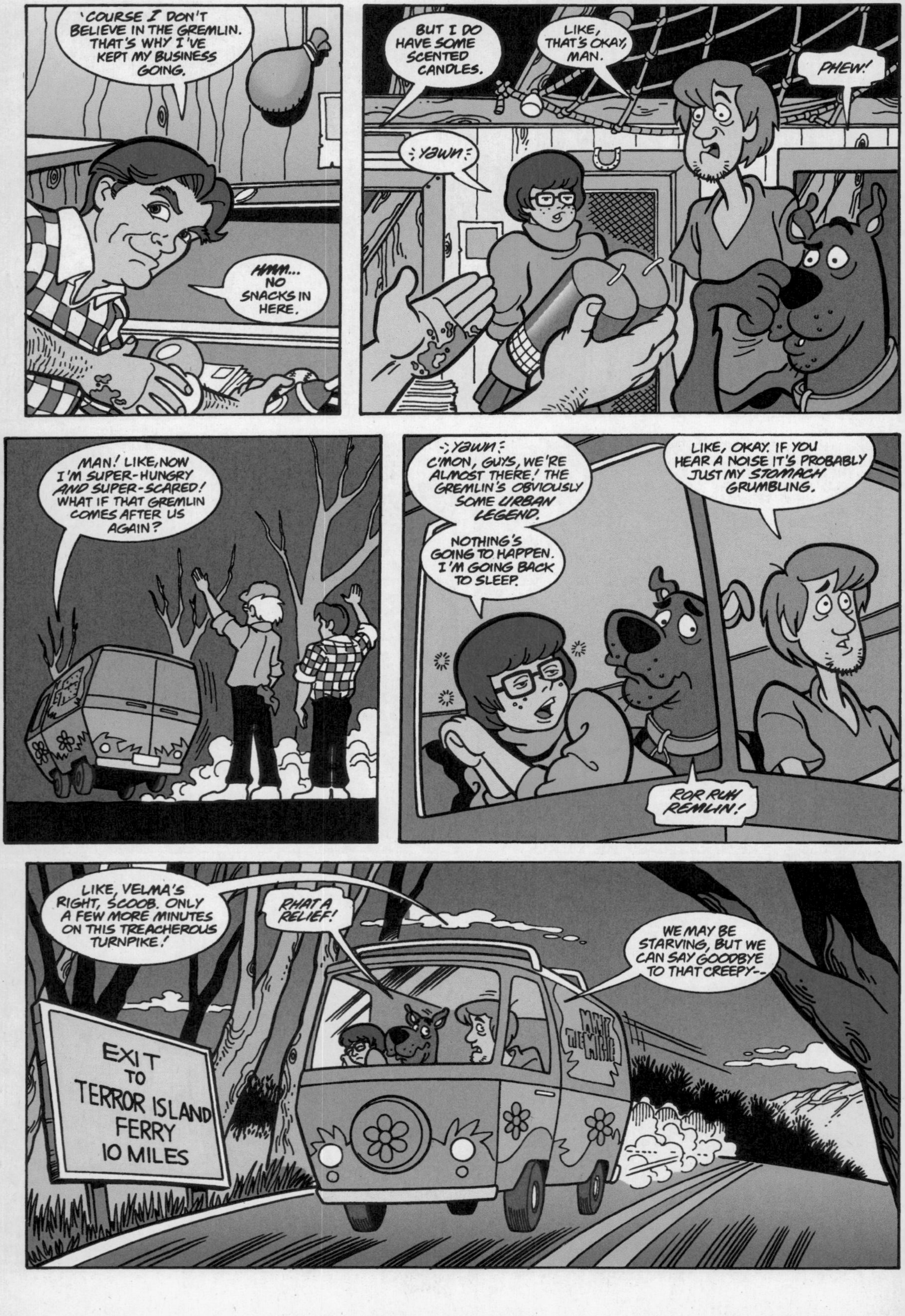
'COURSE I DON'T BELIEVE IN THE GREMLIN. THAT'S WHY I'VE KEPT MY BUSINESS GOING.
HMM... NO SNACKS IN HERE.
BUT I DO HAVE SOME SCENTED CANDLES.
LIKE, THAT'S OKAY, MAN.
PHEW!
YAWN
MAN! LIKE, NOW I'M SUPER-HUNGRY AND SUPER-SCARED! WHAT IF THAT GREMLIN COMES AFTER US AGAIN?
YAWN C'MON, GUYS, WE'RE ALMOST THERE! THE GREMLIN'S OBVIOUSLY SOME URBAN LEGEND.
NOTHING'S GOING TO HAPPEN. I'M GOING BACK TO SLEEP.
LIKE, OKAY. IF YOU HEAR A NOISE IT'S PROBABLY JUST MY STOMACH GRUMBLING.
ROR RUH REMLIN!
LIKE, VELMA'S RIGHT, SCOOB. ONLY A FEW MORE MINUTES ON THIS TREACHEROUS TURNPIKE!
RHAT A RELIEF!
WE MAY BE STARVING, BUT WE CAN SAY GOODBYE TO THAT CREEPY--
EXIT TO TERROR ISLAND FERRY 10 MILES

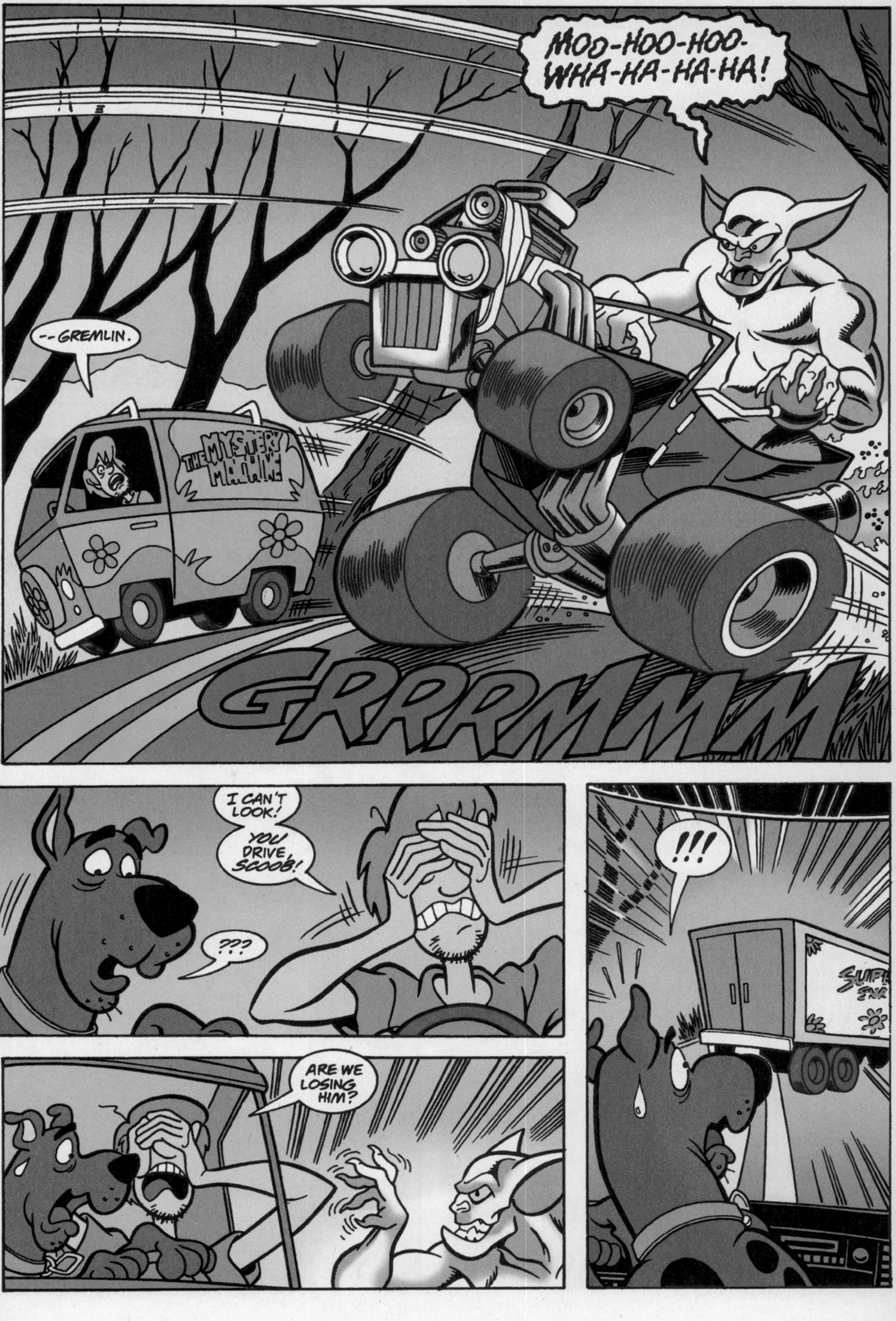
--GREMLIN.
MOO-HOO-HOO-WHA-HA-HA-HA!
THE MYSTERY MACHINE
GRRRMMMM
I CAN'T LOOK!
YOU DRIVE, SCOOB!
???
ARE WE LOSING HIM?
!!!

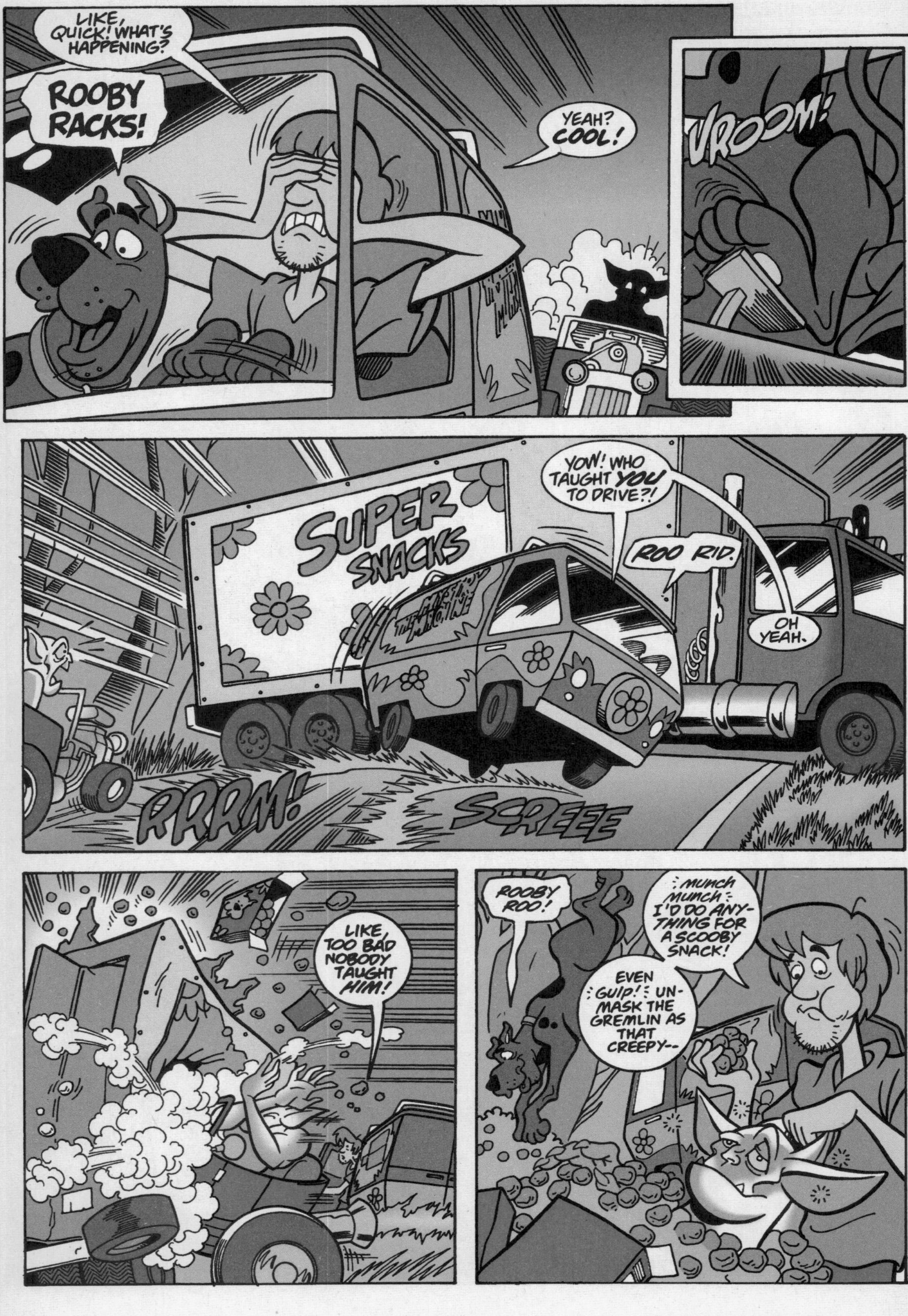

LIKE, QUICK! WHAT'S HAPPENING?
ROOBY RACKS!
YEAH? COOL!
VROOM!
YOW! WHO TAUGHT YOU TO DRIVE?!
ROO RID.
OH YEAH.
SUPER SNACKS
RRRM!
SCREEE
LIKE, TOO BAD NOBODY TAUGHT HIM!
ROOBY ROO!
munch munch I'D DO ANYTHING FOR A SCOOBY SNACK!
EVEN gulp! UNMASK THE GREMLIN AS THAT CREEPY--

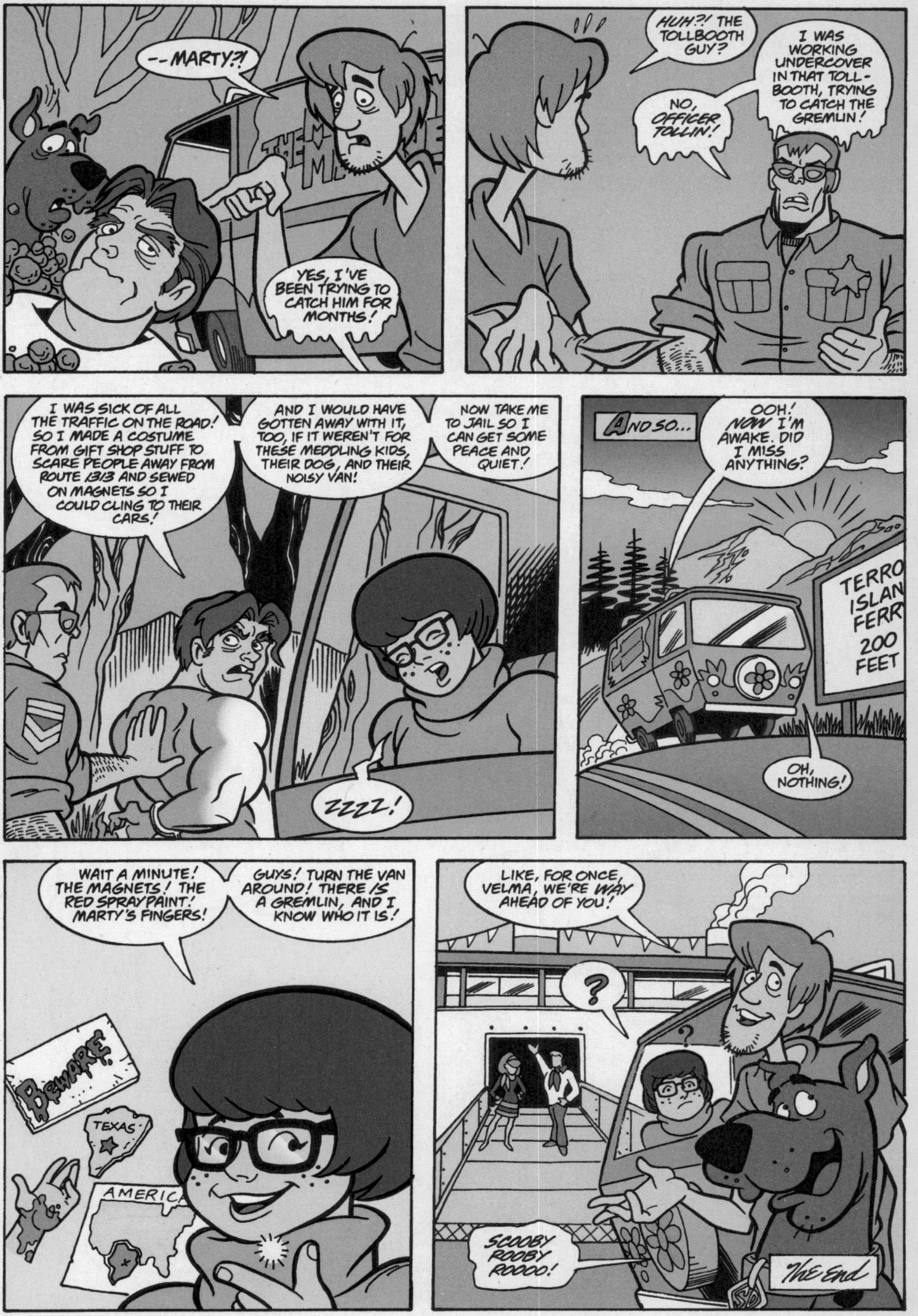
--MARTY?!
YES, I'VE BEEN TRYING TO CATCH HIM FOR MONTHS!
HUH?! THE TOLLBOOTH GUY?
NO, OFFICER TOLLIN!
I WAS WORKING UNDERCOVER IN THAT TOLL-BOOTH, TRYING TO CATCH THE GREMLIN!
I WAS SICK OF ALL THE TRAFFIC ON THE ROAD! SO I MADE A COSTUME FROM GIFT SHOP STUFF TO SCARE PEOPLE AWAY FROM ROUTE 1313 AND SEWED ON MAGNETS SO I COULD CLING TO THEIR CARS!
AND I WOULD HAVE GOTTEN AWAY WITH IT, TOO, IF IT WEREN'T FOR THESE MEDDLING KIDS, THEIR DOG, AND THEIR NOISY VAN!
NOW TAKE ME TO JAIL SO I CAN GET SOME PEACE AND QUIET!
ZZZZ!
AND SO...
OOH! NOW I'M AWAKE. DID I MISS ANYTHING?
TERRO ISLAN FERRY 200 FEET
OH, NOTHING!
WAIT A MINUTE! THE MAGNETS! THE RED SPRAY PAINT! MARTY'S FINGERS!
GUYS! TURN THE VAN AROUND! THERE IS A GREMLIN, AND I KNOW WHO IT IS!
BEWARE
TEXAS
AMERICA
LIKE, FOR ONCE, VELMA, WE'RE WAY AHEAD OF YOU!
?
?
SCOOBY ROOBY ROOOO!
The End

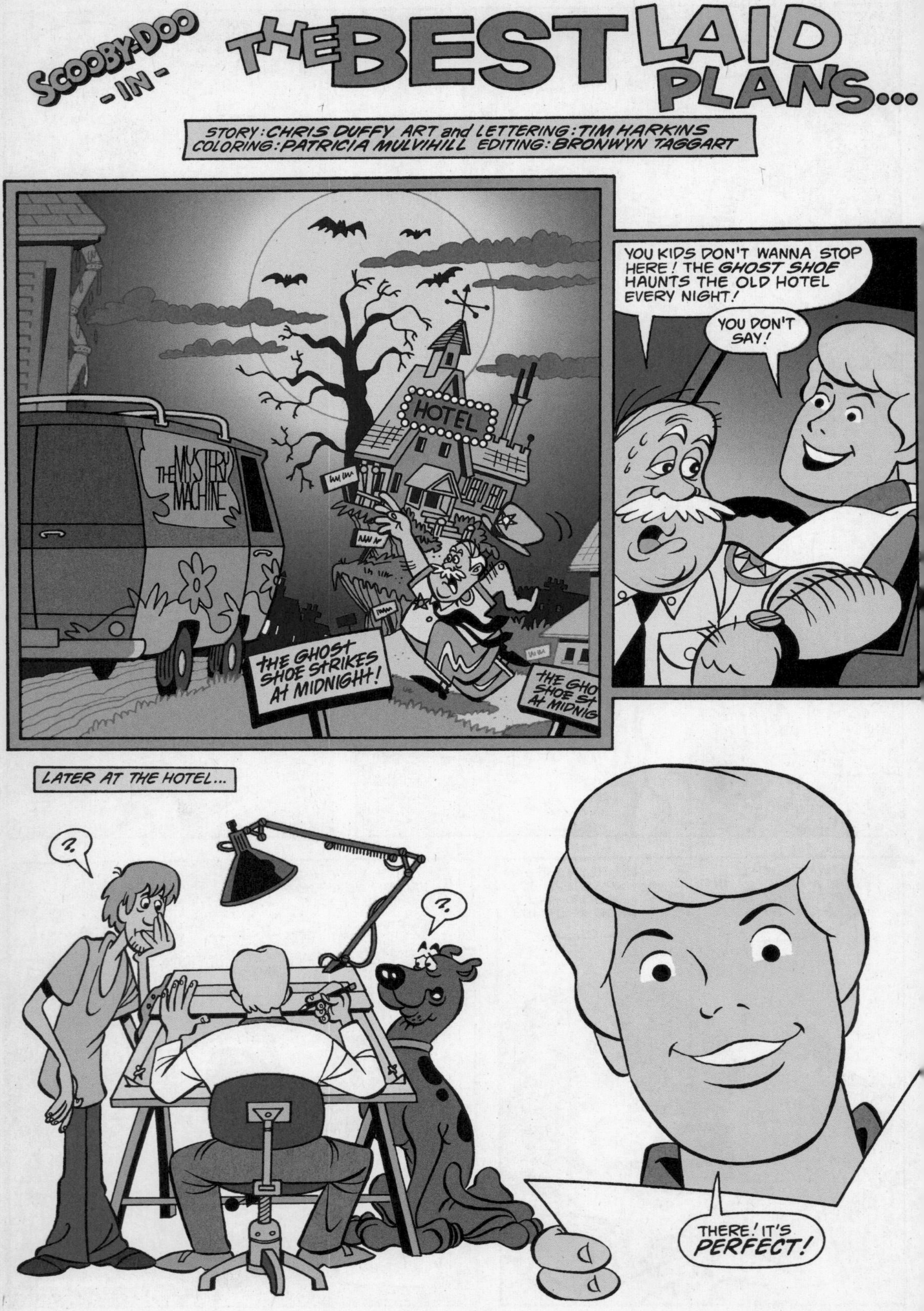
SCOOBY-DOO -IN-
THE BEST LAID PLANS...
STORY: CHRIS DUFFY ART and LETTERING: TIM HARKINS
COLORING: PATRICIA MULVIHILL EDITING: BRONWYN TAGGART
HOTEL
THE MYSTERY MACHINE
THE GHOST SHOE STRIKES AT MIDNIGHT!
YOU KIDS DON'T WANNA STOP HERE! THE GHOST SHOE HAUNTS THE OLD HOTEL EVERY NIGHT!
YOU DON'T SAY!
LATER AT THE HOTEL...
?
?
THERE! IT'S PERFECT!

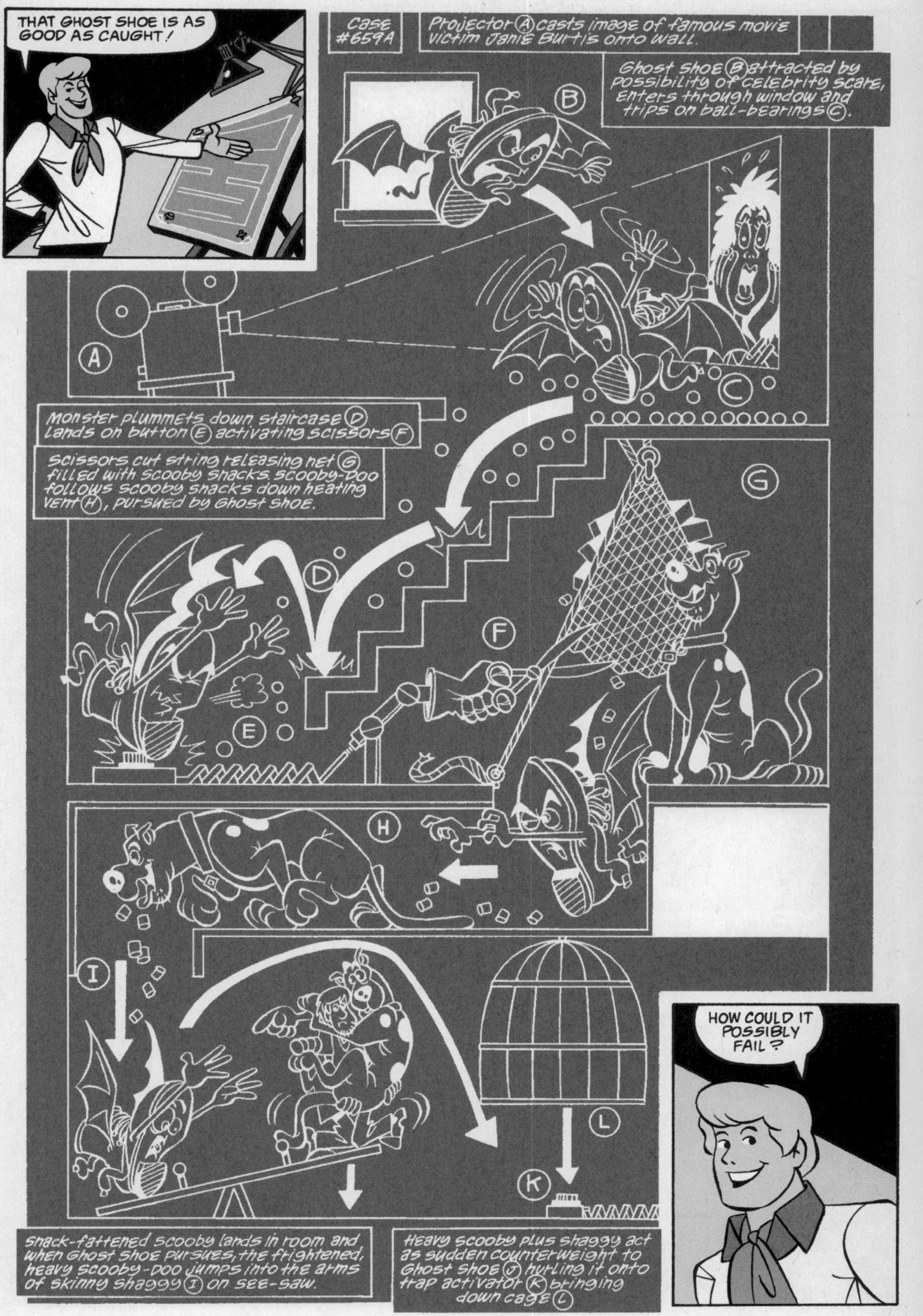
THAT GHOST SHOE IS AS GOOD AS CAUGHT!
CASE #659A
Projector (A) casts image of famous movie victim Janie Burtis onto wall.
Ghost Shoe (B) attracted by possibility of celebrity scare, enters through window and trips on ball-bearings (C).
Monster plummets down staircase (D) lands on button (E) activating scissors (F)
Scissors cut string releasing net (G) filled with Scooby Snacks. Scooby-Doo follows Scooby Snacks down heating vent (H), pursued by Ghost Shoe.
Snack-fattened Scooby lands in room and when Ghost Shoe pursues, the frightened, heavy Scooby-Doo jumps into the arms of skinny Shaggy (I) on see-saw.
Heavy Scooby plus Shaggy act as sudden counterweight to Ghost Shoe (J) hurling it onto trap activator (K) bringing down cage (L)
HOW COULD IT POSSIBLY FAIL?

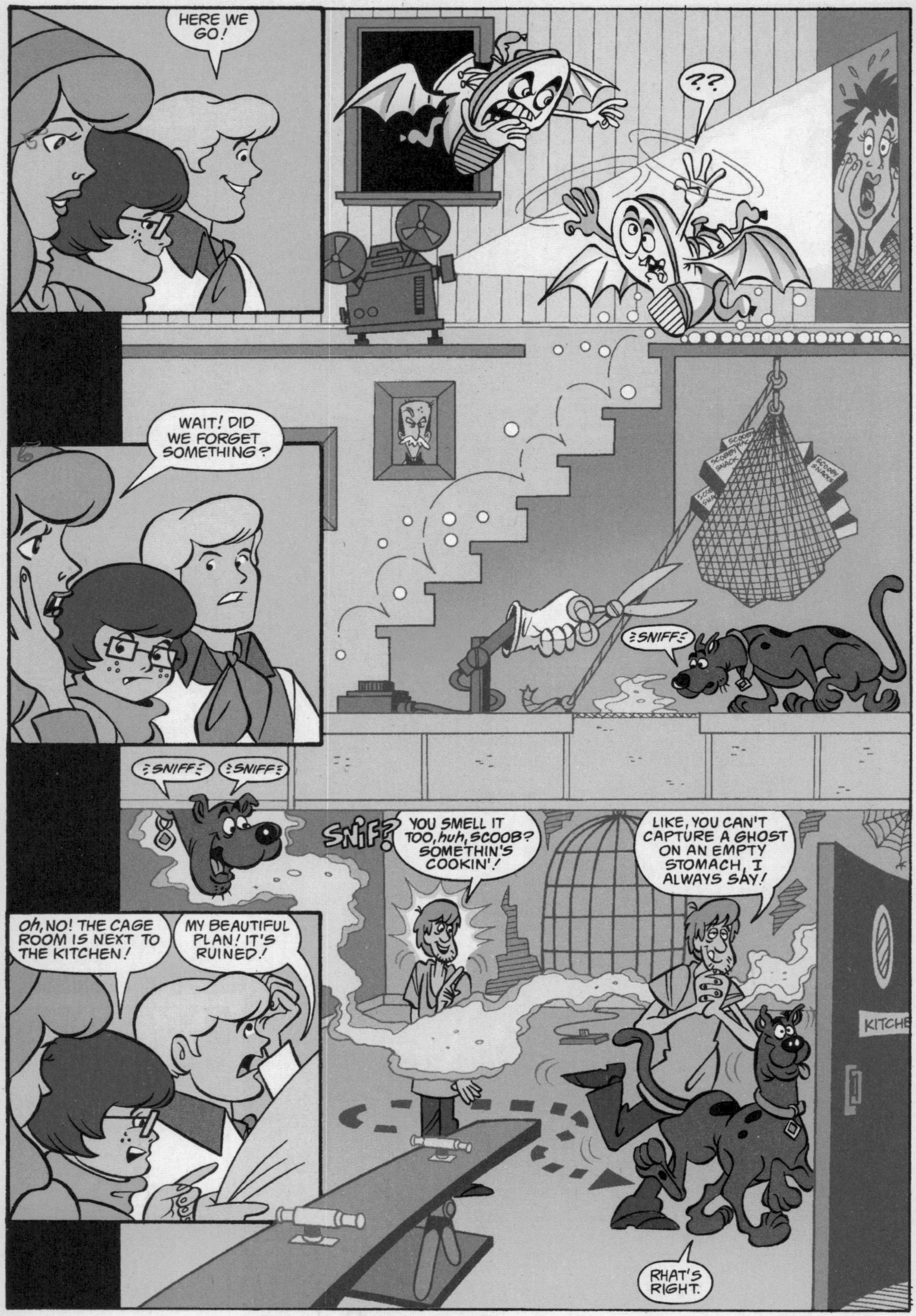
HERE WE GO!
??
WAIT! DID WE FORGET SOMETHING?
SCOOBY SNACK
SNIFF
SNIFF
SNIFF
SNIF?
YOU SMELL IT TOO, huh, SCOOB? SOMETHIN'S COOKIN'!
LIKE, YOU CAN'T CAPTURE A GHOST ON AN EMPTY STOMACH, I ALWAYS SAY!
Oh, NO! THE CAGE ROOM IS NEXT TO THE KITCHEN!
MY BEAUTIFUL PLAN! IT'S RUINED!
KITCHE
RHAT'S RIGHT.

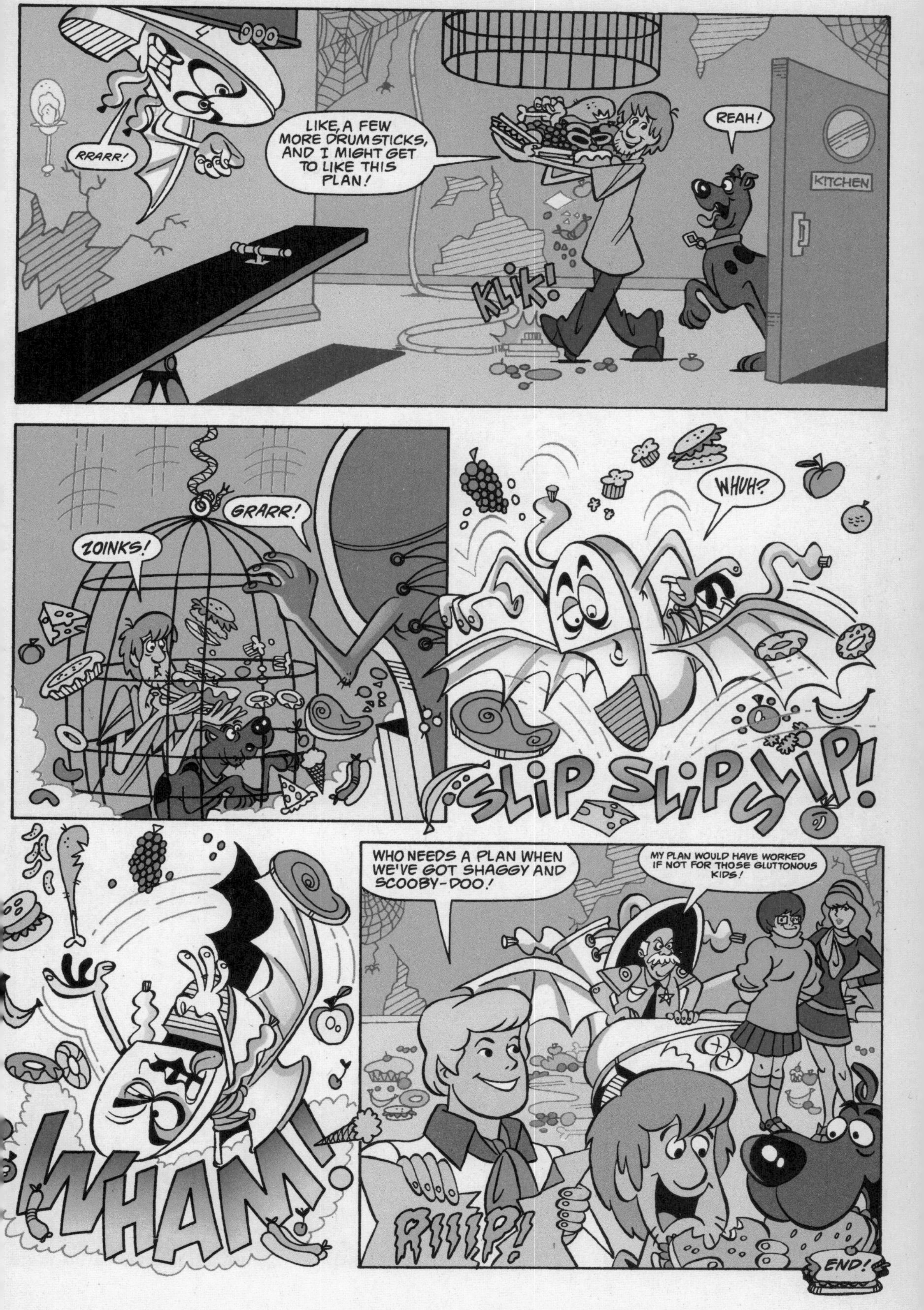
RRARR!
LIKE, A FEW MORE DRUMSTICKS, AND I MIGHT GET TO LIKE THIS PLAN!
REAH!
KITCHEN
KLIK!
GRARR!
ZOINKS!
WHUH?
SLIP SLIP SLIP!
WHAM!
WHO NEEDS A PLAN WHEN WE'VE GOT SHAGGY AND SCOOBY-DOO!
MY PLAN WOULD HAVE WORKED IF NOT FOR THOSE GLUTTONOUS KIDS!
RIIIP!
END!

SCOOBY-DOO

IN "HOW I SPENT MY WINTER BREAK"

GOODNIGHT, SHAGGY AND SCOOBY.

GOOD NIGHT, MOM!

JACKULA

SON OF HANKENSTEIN

SAM HENDERSON
STORY
TIM HARKINS
PENCILS, LETTERS
and INKS
TRISH MULVIHILL
COLORS
BRONWYN TAGGART
EDITOR
THANKS TO
MIKE BRISBOIS

ah, IT'S GOOD TO GET SOME REST AND RELAXATION.....

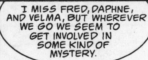

I MISS FRED, DAPHNE, AND VELMA, BUT WHEREVER WE GO WE SEEM TO GET INVOLVED IN SOME KIND OF MYSTERY.

THERE'LL BE NO MYSTERIES FOR US THIS WEEKEND!

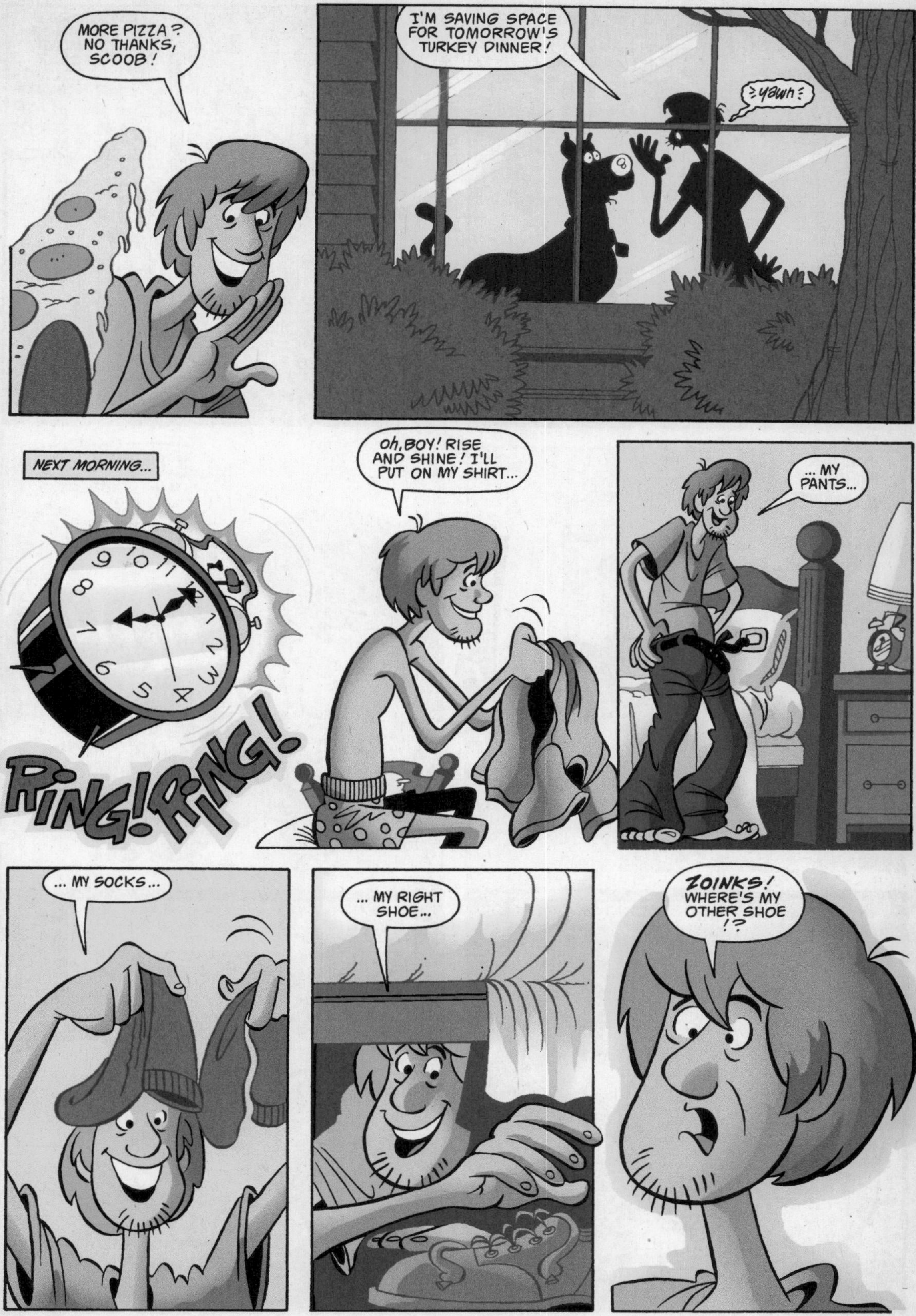
MORE PIZZA? NO THANKS, SCOOB!
I'M SAVING SPACE FOR TOMORROW'S TURKEY DINNER!
yawn
NEXT MORNING...
RING! RING!
Oh, BOY! RISE AND SHINE! I'LL PUT ON MY SHIRT...
... MY PANTS...
... MY SOCKS...
... MY RIGHT SHOE...
ZOINKS! WHERE'S MY OTHER SHOE !?

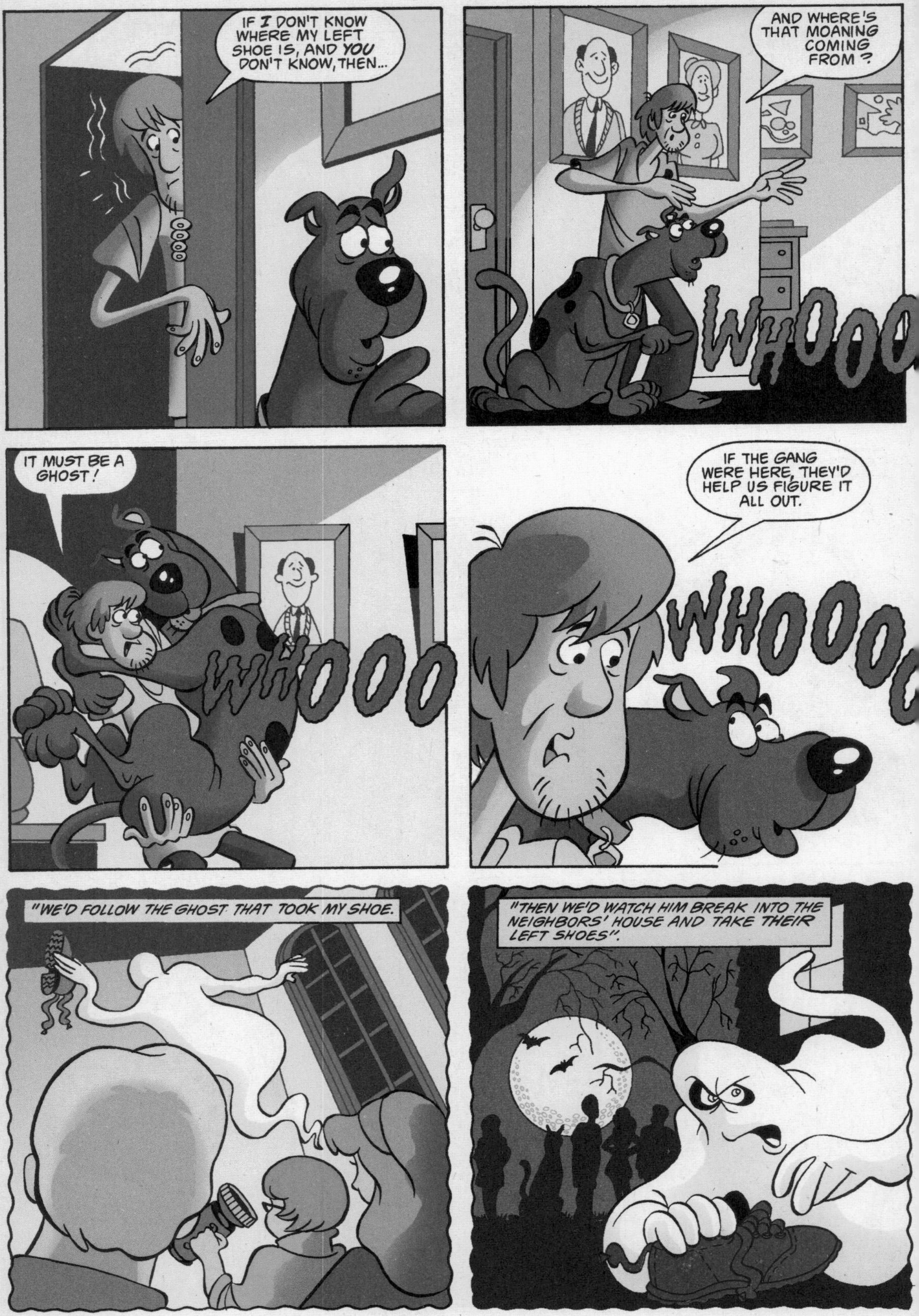

IF I DON'T KNOW WHERE MY LEFT SHOE IS, AND YOU DON'T KNOW, THEN...
AND WHERE'S THAT MOANING COMING FROM ?
WHOOOO
IT MUST BE A GHOST!
WHOOOO
IF THE GANG WERE HERE, THEY'D HELP US FIGURE IT ALL OUT.
WHOOOO
"WE'D FOLLOW THE GHOST THAT TOOK MY SHOE.
"THEN WE'D WATCH HIM BREAK INTO THE NEIGHBORS' HOUSE AND TAKE THEIR LEFT SHOES".

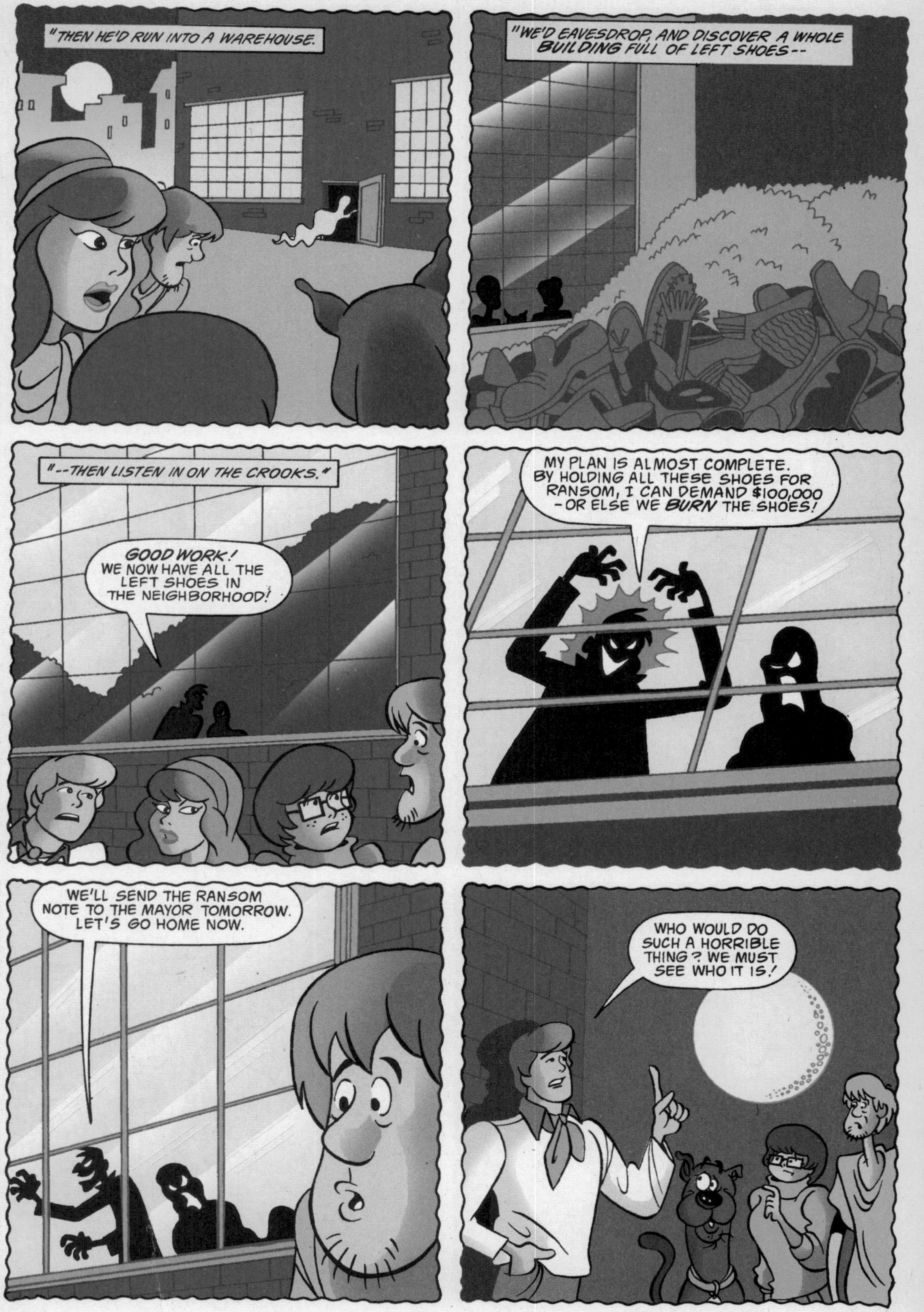
"THEN HE'D RUN INTO A WAREHOUSE.
"WE'D EAVESDROP, AND DISCOVER A WHOLE BUILDING FULL OF LEFT SHOES--
"--THEN LISTEN IN ON THE CROOKS."
GOOD WORK! WE NOW HAVE ALL THE LEFT SHOES IN THE NEIGHBORHOOD!
MY PLAN IS ALMOST COMPLETE. BY HOLDING ALL THESE SHOES FOR RANSOM, I CAN DEMAND $100,000 -OR ELSE WE BURN THE SHOES!
WE'LL SEND THE RANSOM NOTE TO THE MAYOR TOMORROW. LET'S GO HOME NOW.
WHO WOULD DO SUCH A HORRIBLE THING? WE MUST SEE WHO IT IS!

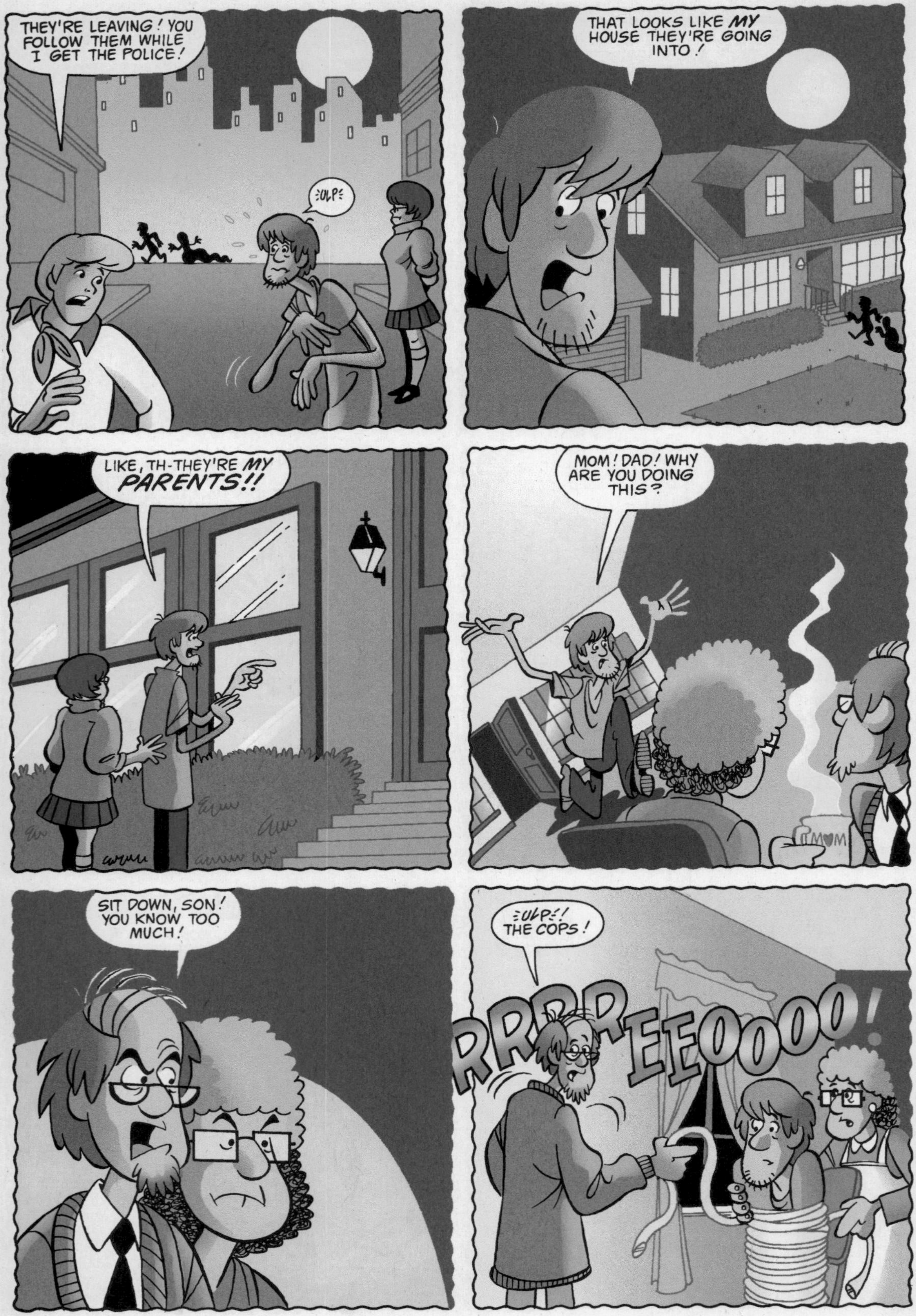
THEY'RE LEAVING! YOU FOLLOW THEM WHILE I GET THE POLICE!
ULP
THAT LOOKS LIKE MY HOUSE THEY'RE GOING INTO!
LIKE, TH-THEY'RE MY PARENTS!!
MOM! DAD! WHY ARE YOU DOING THIS?
MOM
SIT DOWN, SON! YOU KNOW TOO MUCH!
ULP! THE COPS!
RRRREEOOOOO!

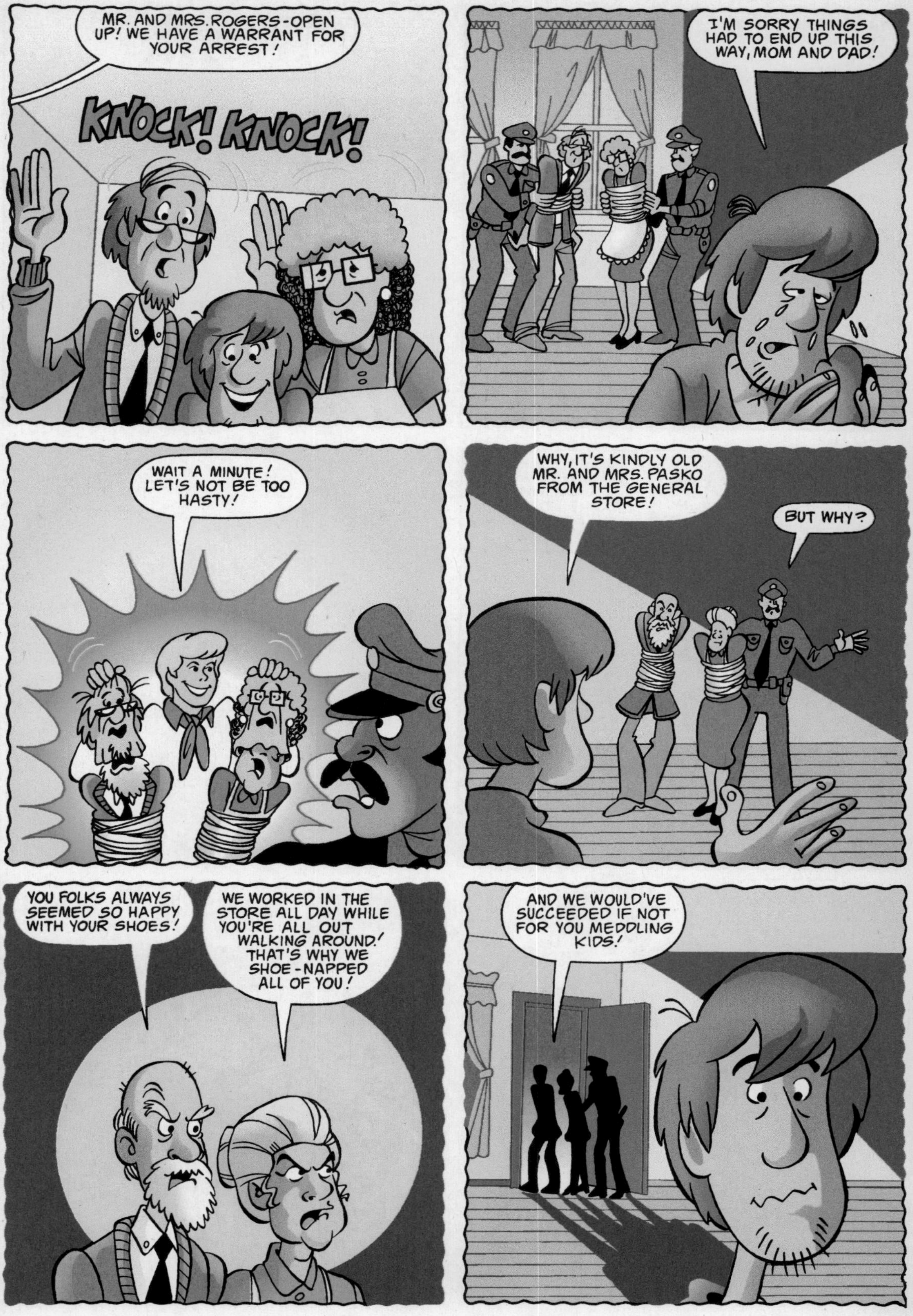
MR. AND MRS. ROGERS-OPEN UP! WE HAVE A WARRANT FOR YOUR ARREST!
KNOCK! KNOCK!
I'M SORRY THINGS HAD TO END UP THIS WAY, MOM AND DAD!
WAIT A MINUTE! LET'S NOT BE TOO HASTY!
WHY, IT'S KINDLY OLD MR. AND MRS. PASKO FROM THE GENERAL STORE!
BUT WHY?
YOU FOLKS ALWAYS SEEMED SO HAPPY WITH YOUR SHOES!
WE WORKED IN THE STORE ALL DAY WHILE YOU'RE ALL OUT WALKING AROUND! THAT'S WHY WE SHOE-NAPPED ALL OF YOU!
AND WE WOULD'VE SUCCEEDED IF NOT FOR YOU MEDDLING KIDS!

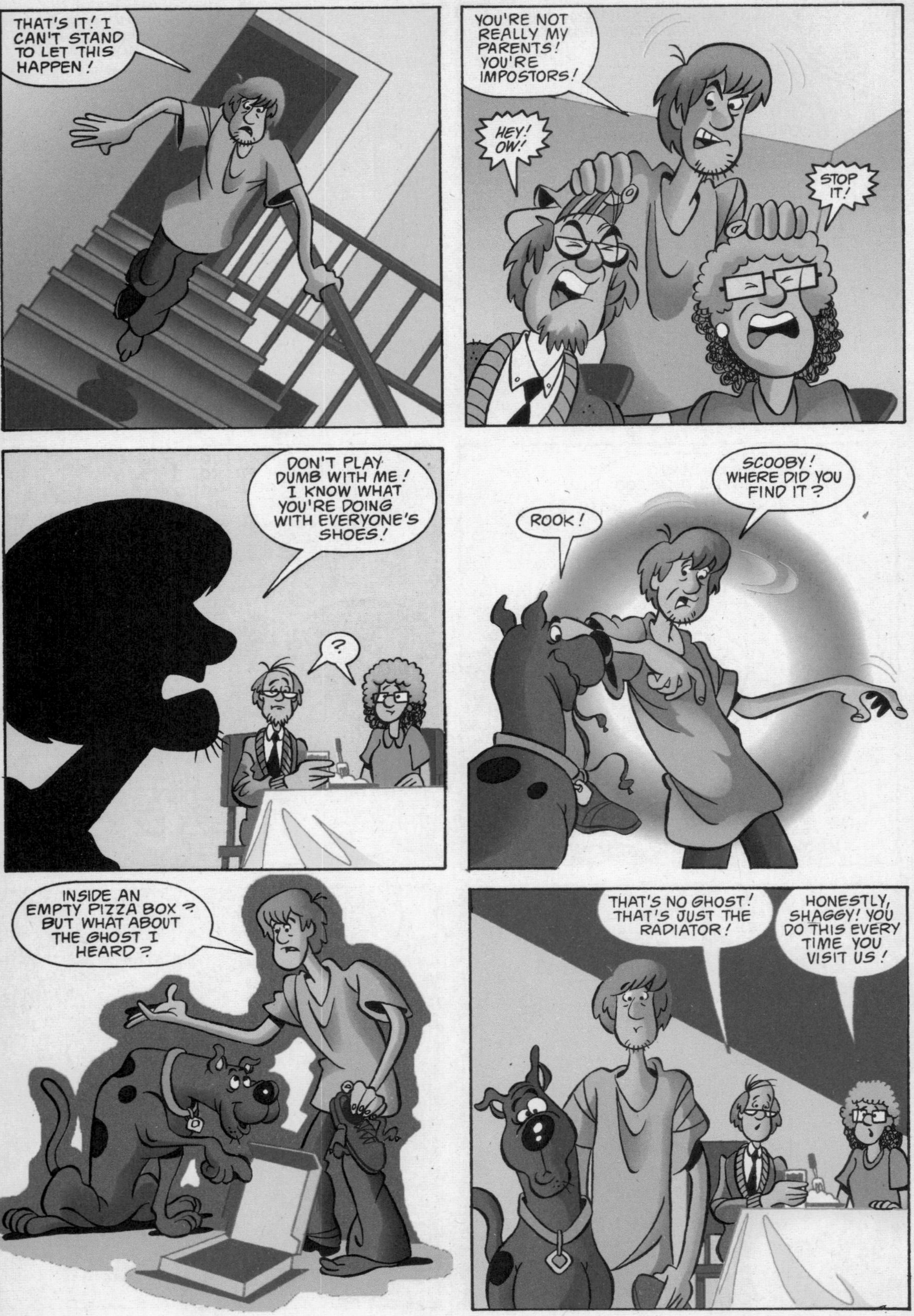
THAT'S IT! I CAN'T STAND TO LET THIS HAPPEN!
YOU'RE NOT REALLY MY PARENTS! YOU'RE IMPOSTORS!
HEY! OW!
STOP IT!
DON'T PLAY DUMB WITH ME! I KNOW WHAT YOU'RE DOING WITH EVERYONE'S SHOES!
?
SCOOBY! WHERE DID YOU FIND IT?
ROOK!
INSIDE AN EMPTY PIZZA BOX? BUT WHAT ABOUT THE GHOST I HEARD?
THAT'S NO GHOST! THAT'S JUST THE RADIATOR!
HONESTLY, SHAGGY! YOU DO THIS EVERY TIME YOU VISIT US!

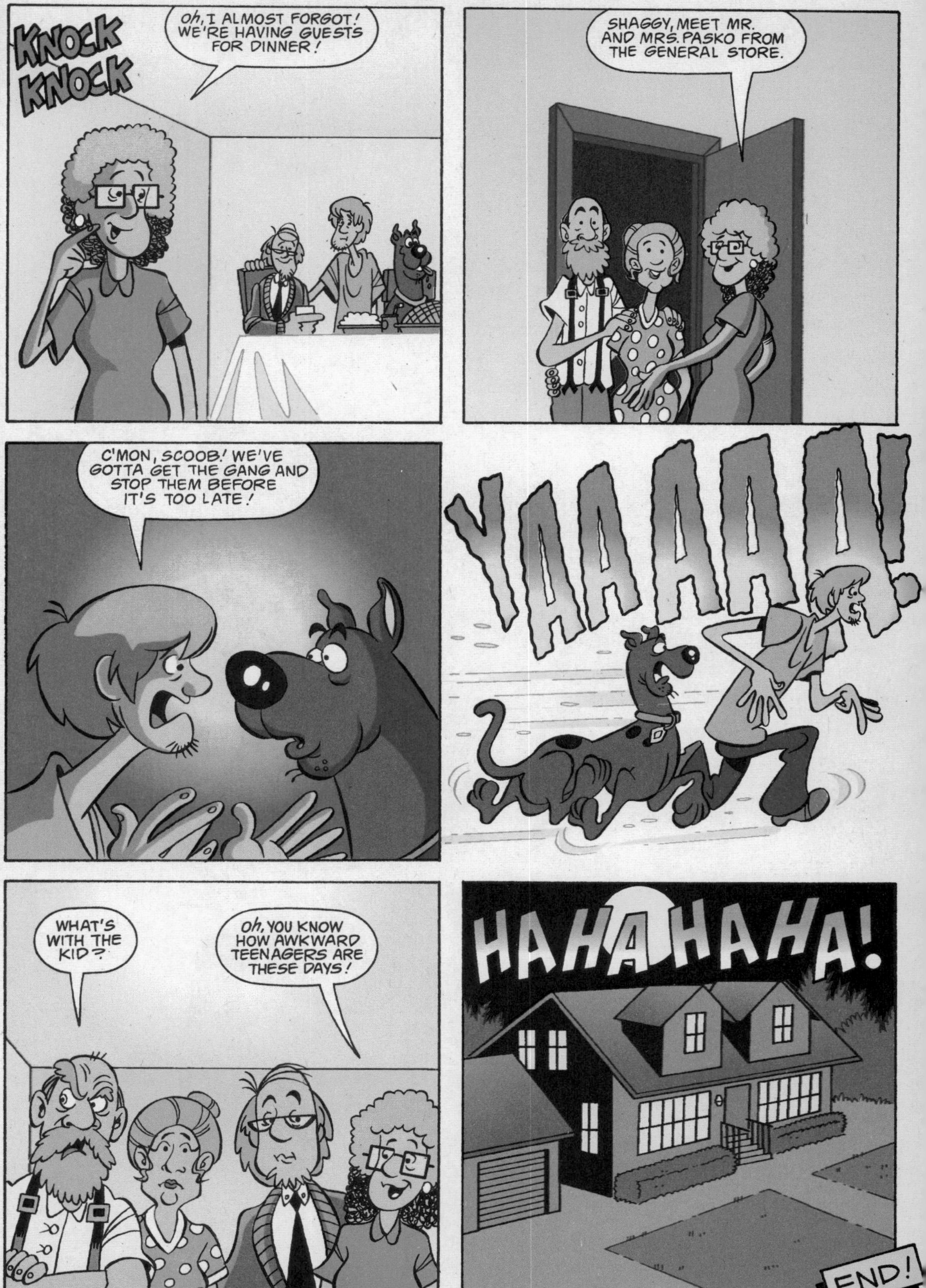
KNOCK KNOCK
Oh, I ALMOST FORGOT! WE'RE HAVING GUESTS FOR DINNER!
SHAGGY, MEET MR. AND MRS. PASKO FROM THE GENERAL STORE.
C'MON, SCOOB! WE'VE GOTTA GET THE GANG AND STOP THEM BEFORE IT'S TOO LATE!
YAAAAA!
WHAT'S WITH THE KID?
Oh, YOU KNOW HOW AWKWARD TEENAGERS ARE THESE DAYS!
HAHAHAHA!
END!

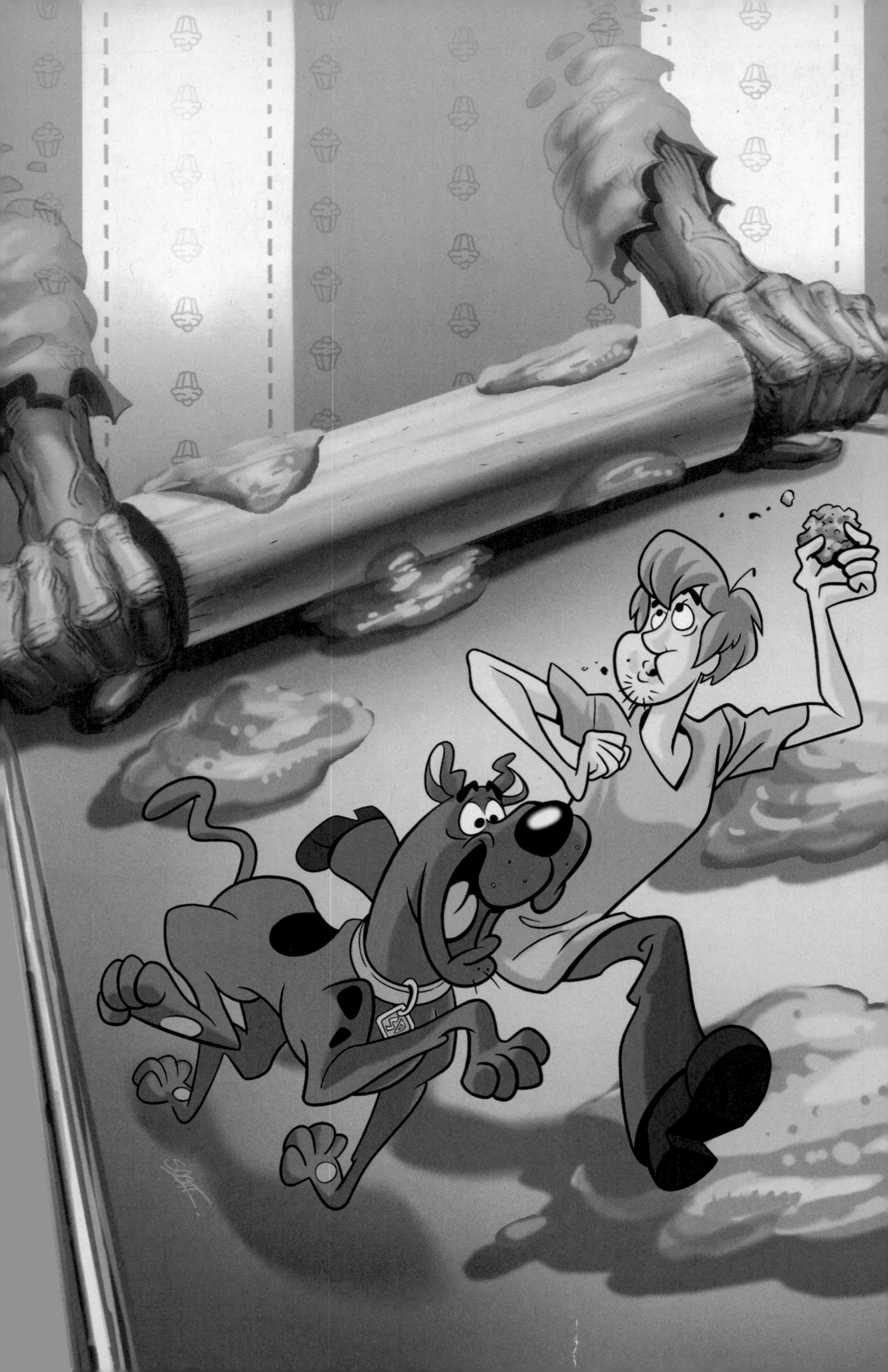

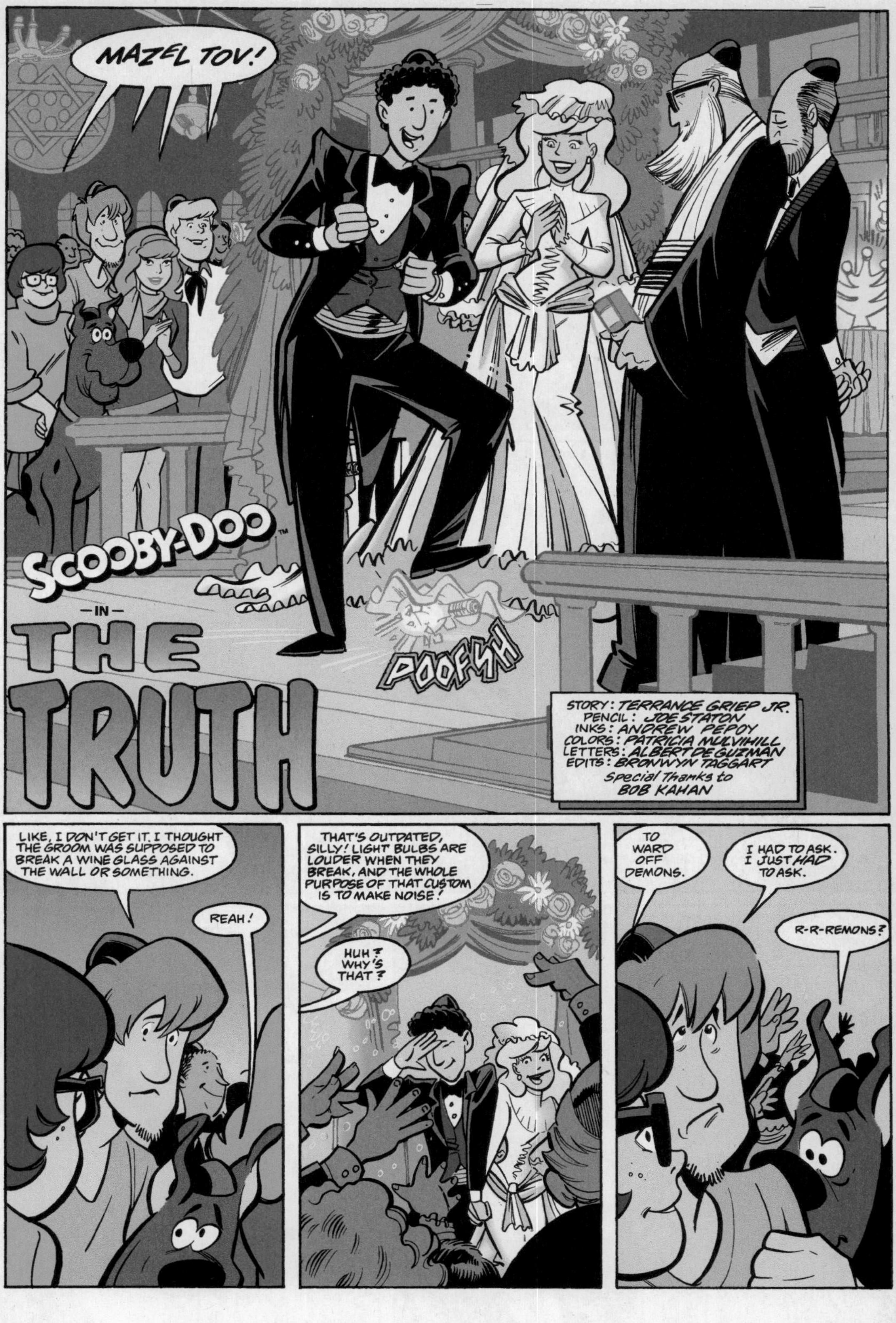
MAZEL TOV!
SCOOBY-DOO™
-IN-
THE TRUTH
POOFSH
STORY: TERRANCE GRIEP JR.
PENCIL: JOE STATON
INKS: ANDREW PEPOY
COLORS: PATRICIA MULVIHILL
LETTERS: ALBERT DE GUZMAN
EDITS: BRONWYN TAGGART
Special Thanks to
BOB KAHAN
LIKE, I DON'T GET IT. I THOUGHT THE GROOM WAS SUPPOSED TO BREAK A WINE GLASS AGAINST THE WALL OR SOMETHING.
REAH!
THAT'S OUTDATED, SILLY! LIGHT BULBS ARE LOUDER WHEN THEY BREAK, AND THE WHOLE PURPOSE OF THAT CUSTOM IS TO MAKE NOISE!
HUH? WHY'S THAT?
TO WARD OFF DEMONS.
I HAD TO ASK. I JUST HAD TO ASK.
R-R-REMONS?

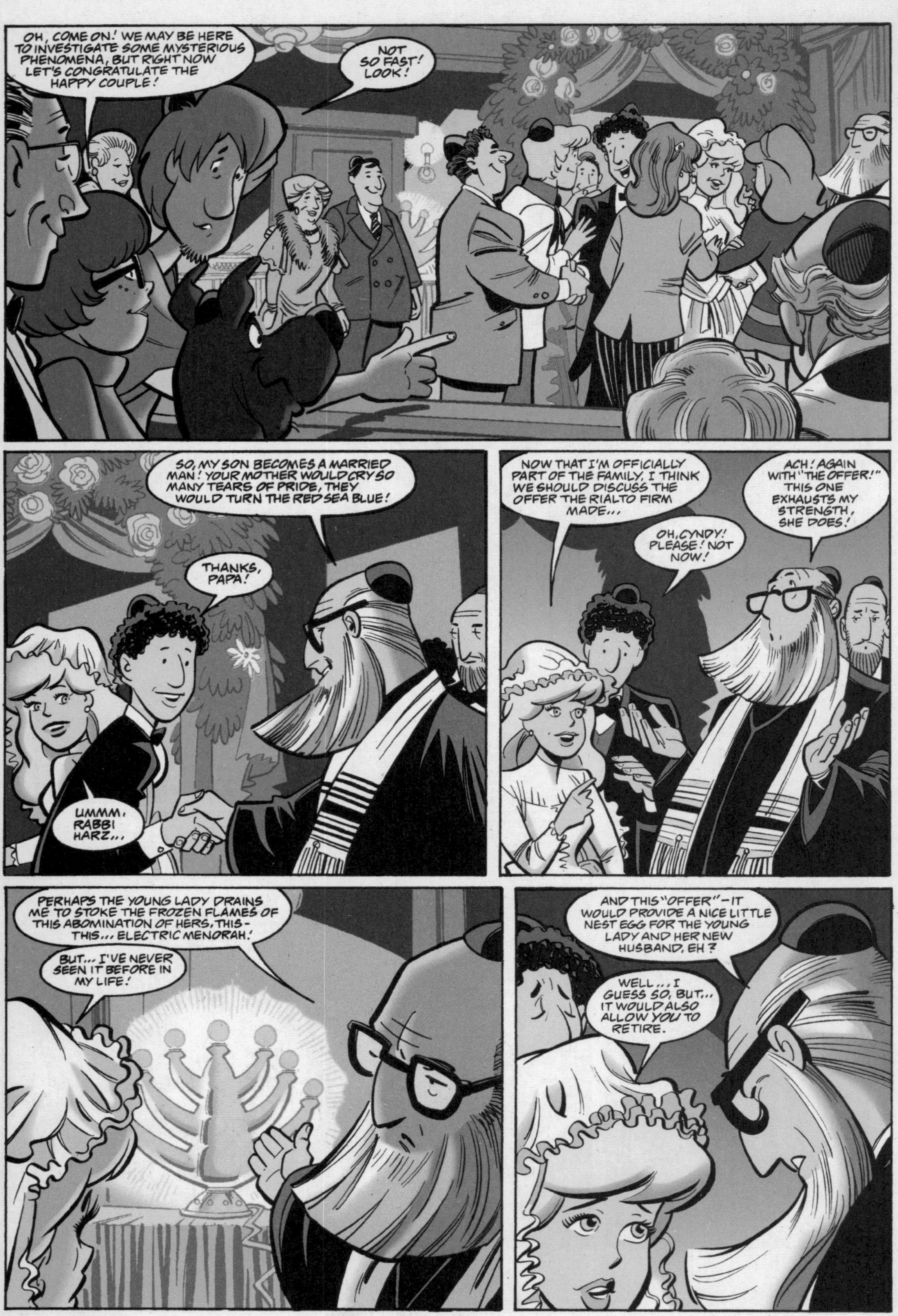
OH, COME ON! WE MAY BE HERE TO INVESTIGATE SOME MYSTERIOUS PHENOMENA, BUT RIGHT NOW LET'S CONGRATULATE THE HAPPY COUPLE!
NOT SO FAST! LOOK!
SO, MY SON BECOMES A MARRIED MAN! YOUR MOTHER WOULD CRY SO MANY TEARS OF PRIDE, THEY WOULD TURN THE RED SEA BLUE!
THANKS, PAPA!
UMMM, RABBI HARZ...
NOW THAT I'M OFFICIALLY PART OF THE FAMILY, I THINK WE SHOULD DISCUSS THE OFFER THE RIALTO FIRM MADE...
OH, CYNDY! PLEASE! NOT NOW!
ACH! AGAIN WITH "THE OFFER!" THIS ONE EXHAUSTS MY STRENGTH, SHE DOES!
PERHAPS THE YOUNG LADY DRAINS ME TO STOKE THE FROZEN FLAMES OF THIS ABOMINATION OF HERS, THIS-THIS... ELECTRIC MENORAH!
BUT... I'VE NEVER SEEN IT BEFORE IN MY LIFE!
AND THIS "OFFER"—IT WOULD PROVIDE A NICE LITTLE NEST EGG FOR THE YOUNG LADY AND HER NEW HUSBAND, EH?
WELL... I GUESS SO, BUT... IT WOULD ALSO ALLOW YOU TO RETIRE.

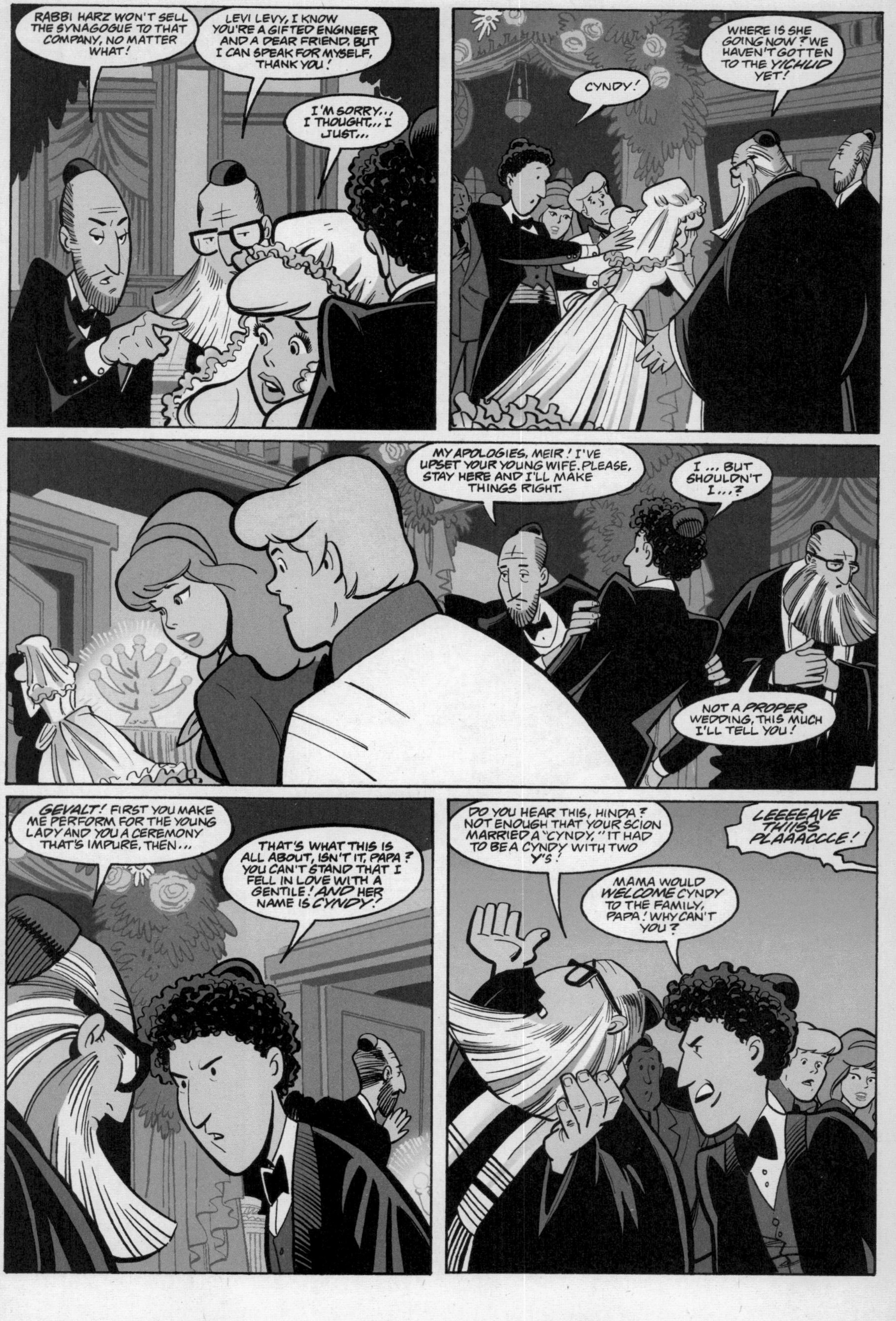
RABBI HARZ WON'T SELL THE SYNAGOGUE TO THAT COMPANY, NO MATTER WHAT!
LEVI LEVY, I KNOW YOU'RE A GIFTED ENGINEER AND A DEAR FRIEND, BUT I CAN SPEAK FOR MYSELF, THANK YOU!
I'M SORRY... I THOUGHT... I JUST...
CYNDY!
WHERE IS SHE GOING NOW? WE HAVEN'T GOTTEN TO THE YICHUD YET!
MY APOLOGIES, MEIR! I'VE UPSET YOUR YOUNG WIFE. PLEASE, STAY HERE AND I'LL MAKE THINGS RIGHT.
I ... BUT SHOULDN'T I...?
NOT A PROPER WEDDING, THIS MUCH I'LL TELL YOU!
GEVALT! FIRST YOU MAKE ME PERFORM FOR THE YOUNG LADY AND YOU A CEREMONY THAT'S IMPURE, THEN...
THAT'S WHAT THIS IS ALL ABOUT, ISN'T IT, PAPA? YOU CAN'T STAND THAT I FELL IN LOVE WITH A GENTILE! AND HER NAME IS CYNDY!
DO YOU HEAR THIS, HINDA? NOT ENOUGH THAT YOUR SCION MARRIED A "CYNDY," IT HAD TO BE A CYNDY WITH TWO Y'S!
MAMA WOULD WELCOME CYNDY TO THE FAMILY, PAPA! WHY CAN'T YOU?
LEEEEAVE THIIISS PLAAACCCE!

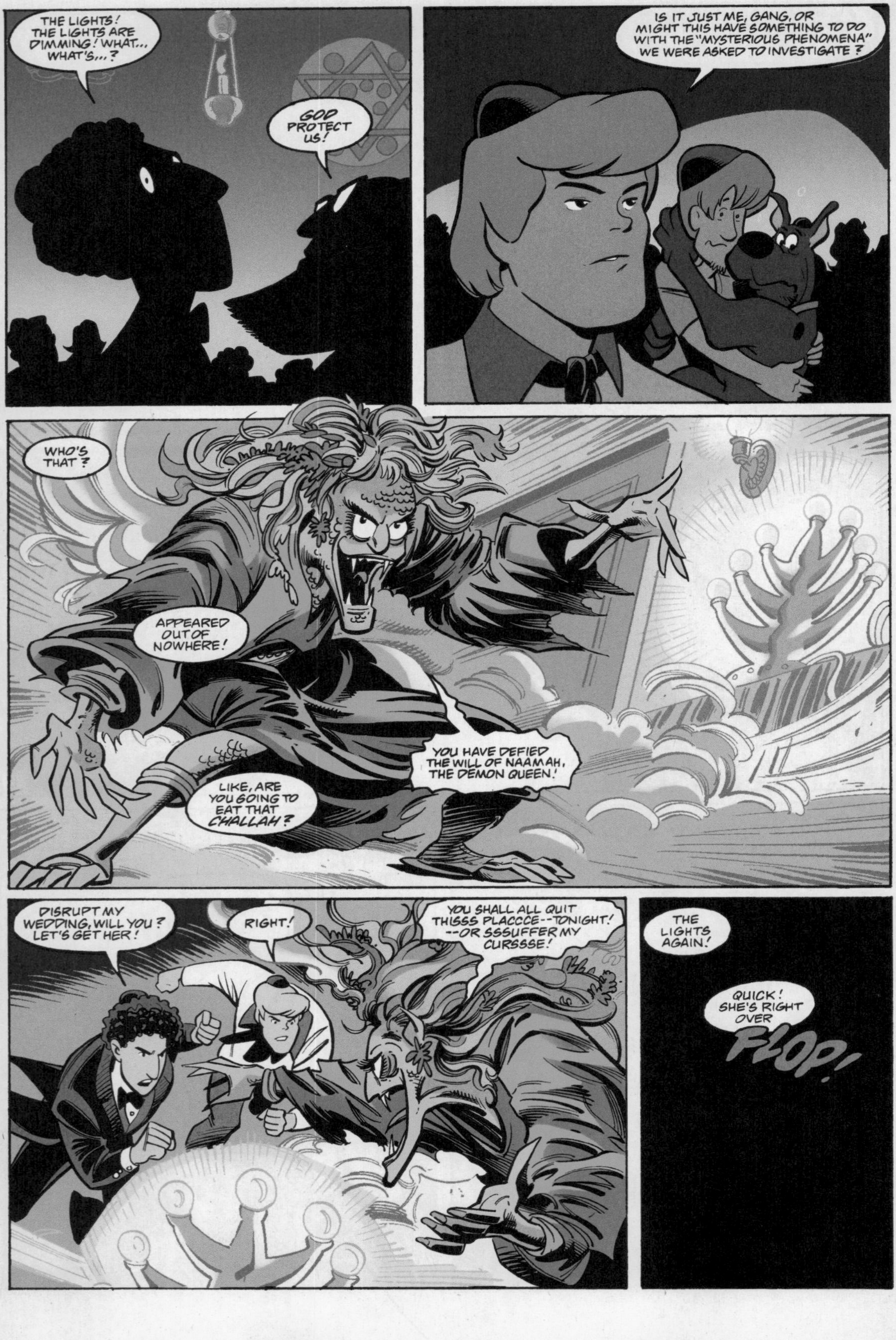
THE LIGHTS! THE LIGHTS ARE DIMMING! WHAT... WHAT'S...?
GOD PROTECT US!
IS IT JUST ME, GANG, OR MIGHT THIS HAVE SOMETHING TO DO WITH THE "MYSTERIOUS PHENOMENA" WE WERE ASKED TO INVESTIGATE?
WHO'S THAT?
APPEARED OUT OF NOWHERE!
YOU HAVE DEFIED THE WILL OF NAAMAH, THE DEMON QUEEN!
LIKE, ARE YOU GOING TO EAT THAT CHALLAH?
DISRUPT MY WEDDING, WILL YOU? LET'S GET HER!
RIGHT!
YOU SHALL ALL QUIT THISSS PLACCCE--TONIGHT! --OR SSSUFFER MY CURSSSE!
THE LIGHTS AGAIN!
QUICK! SHE'S RIGHT OVER
FLOP!

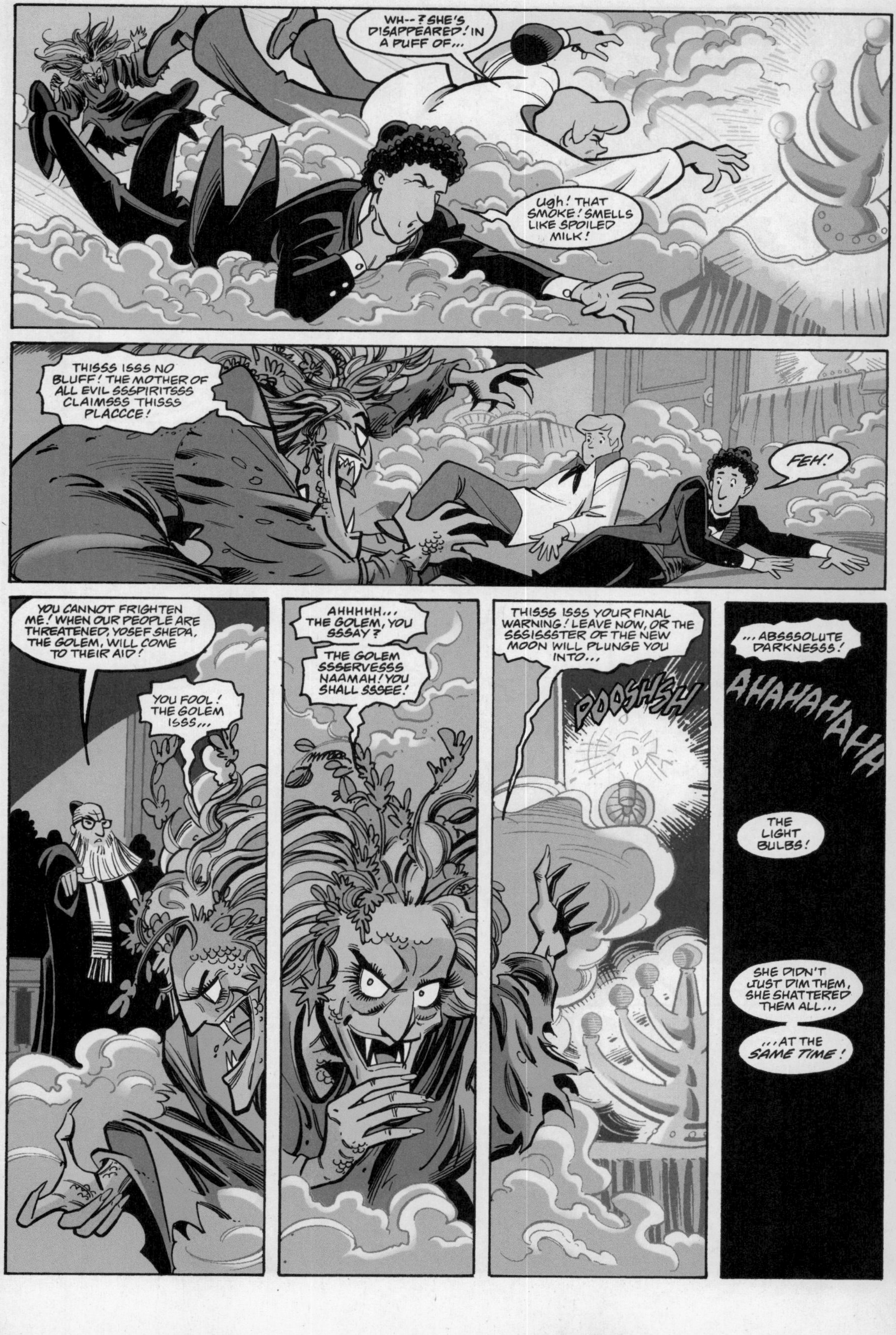
WH--? SHE'S DISAPPEARED! IN A PUFF OF...
Ugh! THAT SMOKE! SMELLS LIKE SPOILED MILK!
THISSS ISSS NO BLUFF! THE MOTHER OF ALL EVIL SSSPIRITSSS CLAIMSSS THISSS PLACCCE!
FEH!
YOU CANNOT FRIGHTEN ME! WHEN OUR PEOPLE ARE THREATENED, YOSEF SHEDA, THE GOLEM, WILL COME TO THEIR AID!
YOU FOOL! THE GOLEM ISSS...
AHHHHH... THE GOLEM, YOU SSSAY?
THE GOLEM SSSERVESSS NAAMAH! YOU SHALL SSSEE!
THISSS ISSS YOUR FINAL WARNING! LEAVE NOW, OR THE SSSISSSTER OF THE NEW MOON WILL PLUNGE YOU INTO...
POOSHSH
...ABSSSOLUTE DARKNESSS!
AHAHAHAHAHAHH
THE LIGHT BULBS!
SHE DIDN'T JUST DIM THEM, SHE SHATTERED THEM ALL...
...AT THE SAME TIME!

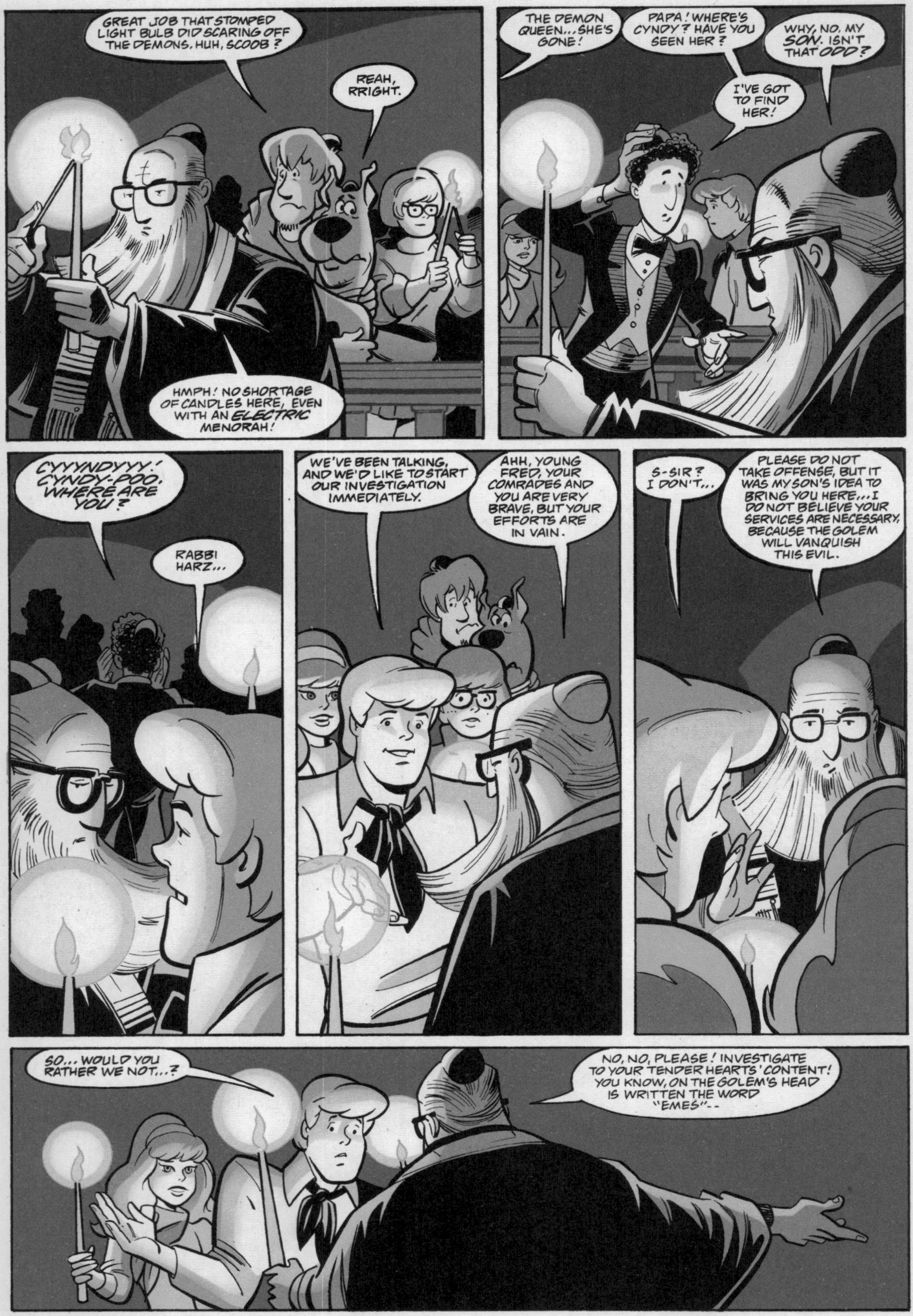
GREAT JOB THAT STOMPED LIGHT BULB DID SCARING OFF THE DEMONS, HUH, SCOOB?
REAH, RRIGHT.
HMPH! NO SHORTAGE OF CANDLES HERE, EVEN WITH AN ELECTRIC MENORAH!
THE DEMON QUEEN... SHE'S GONE!
PAPA! WHERE'S CYNDY? HAVE YOU SEEN HER?
I'VE GOT TO FIND HER!
WHY, NO, MY SON. ISN'T THAT ODD?
CYYYNDYYY! CYNDY-POO, WHERE ARE YOU?
RABBI HARZ...
WE'VE BEEN TALKING, AND WE'D LIKE TO START OUR INVESTIGATION IMMEDIATELY.
AHH, YOUNG FRED, YOUR COMRADES AND YOU ARE VERY BRAVE, BUT YOUR EFFORTS ARE IN VAIN.
S-SIR? I DON'T...
PLEASE DO NOT TAKE OFFENSE, BUT IT WAS MY SON'S IDEA TO BRING YOU HERE... I DO NOT BELIEVE YOUR SERVICES ARE NECESSARY, BECAUSE THE GOLEM WILL VANQUISH THIS EVIL.
SO... WOULD YOU RATHER WE NOT...?
NO, NO, PLEASE! INVESTIGATE TO YOUR TENDER HEARTS' CONTENT! YOU KNOW, ON THE GOLEM'S HEAD IS WRITTEN THE WORD "EMES"--

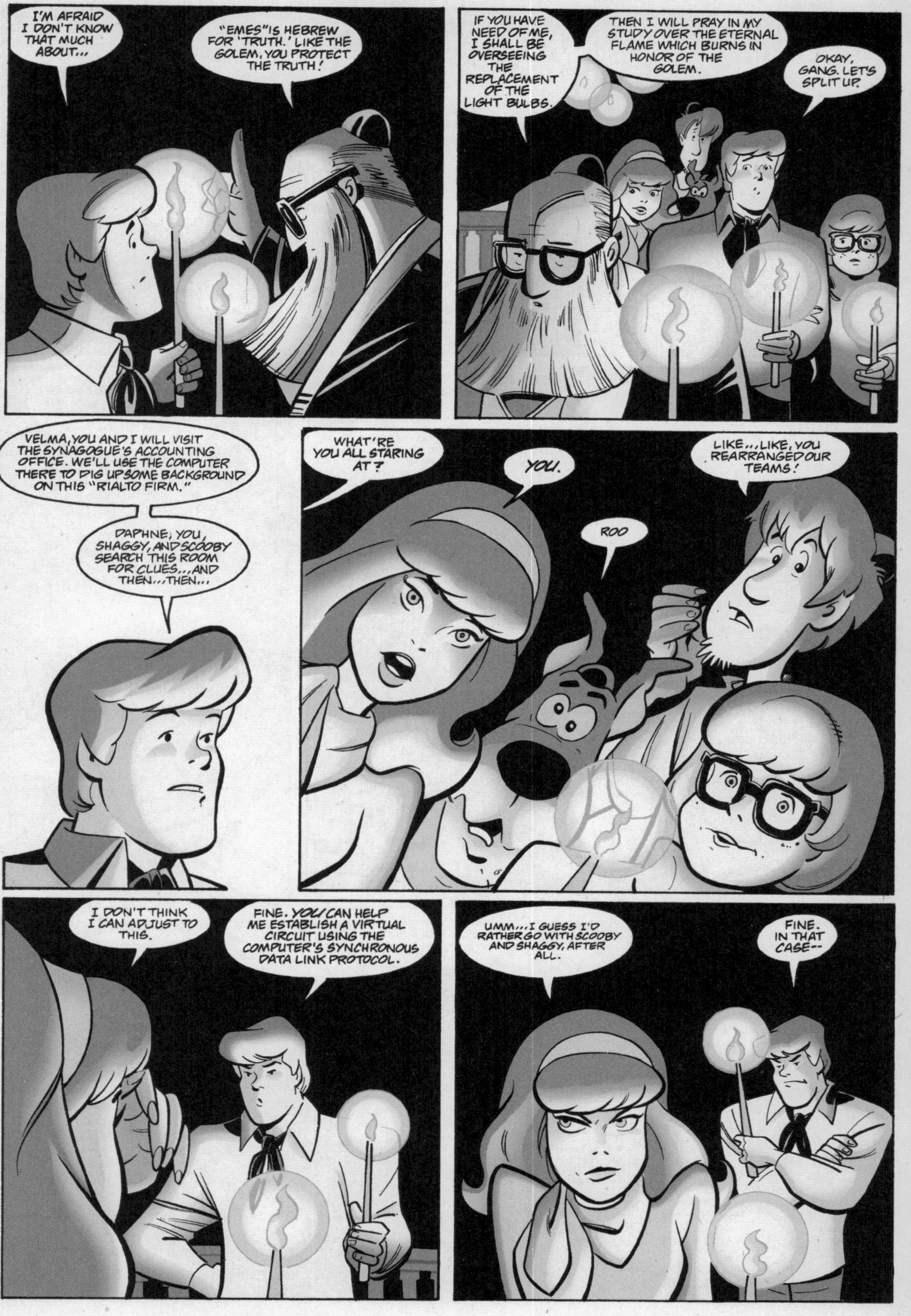

I'M AFRAID I DON'T KNOW THAT MUCH ABOUT...
"EMES" IS HEBREW FOR 'TRUTH.' LIKE THE GOLEM, YOU PROTECT THE TRUTH!
IF YOU HAVE NEED OF ME, I SHALL BE OVERSEEING THE REPLACEMENT OF THE LIGHT BULBS.
THEN I WILL PRAY IN MY STUDY OVER THE ETERNAL FLAME WHICH BURNS IN HONOR OF THE GOLEM.
OKAY, GANG. LET'S SPLIT UP.
VELMA, YOU AND I WILL VISIT THE SYNAGOGUE'S ACCOUNTING OFFICE. WE'LL USE THE COMPUTER THERE TO DIG UP SOME BACKGROUND ON THIS "RIALTO FIRM."
DAPHNE, YOU, SHAGGY, AND SCOOBY SEARCH THIS ROOM FOR CLUES...AND THEN...THEN...
WHAT'RE YOU ALL STARING AT?
YOU.
ROO
LIKE...LIKE, YOU REARRANGED OUR TEAMS!
I DON'T THINK I CAN ADJUST TO THIS.
FINE. YOU CAN HELP ME ESTABLISH A VIRTUAL CIRCUIT USING THE COMPUTER'S SYNCHRONOUS DATA LINK PROTOCOL.
UMM...I GUESS I'D RATHER GO WITH SCOOBY AND SHAGGY, AFTER ALL.
FINE. IN THAT CASE--

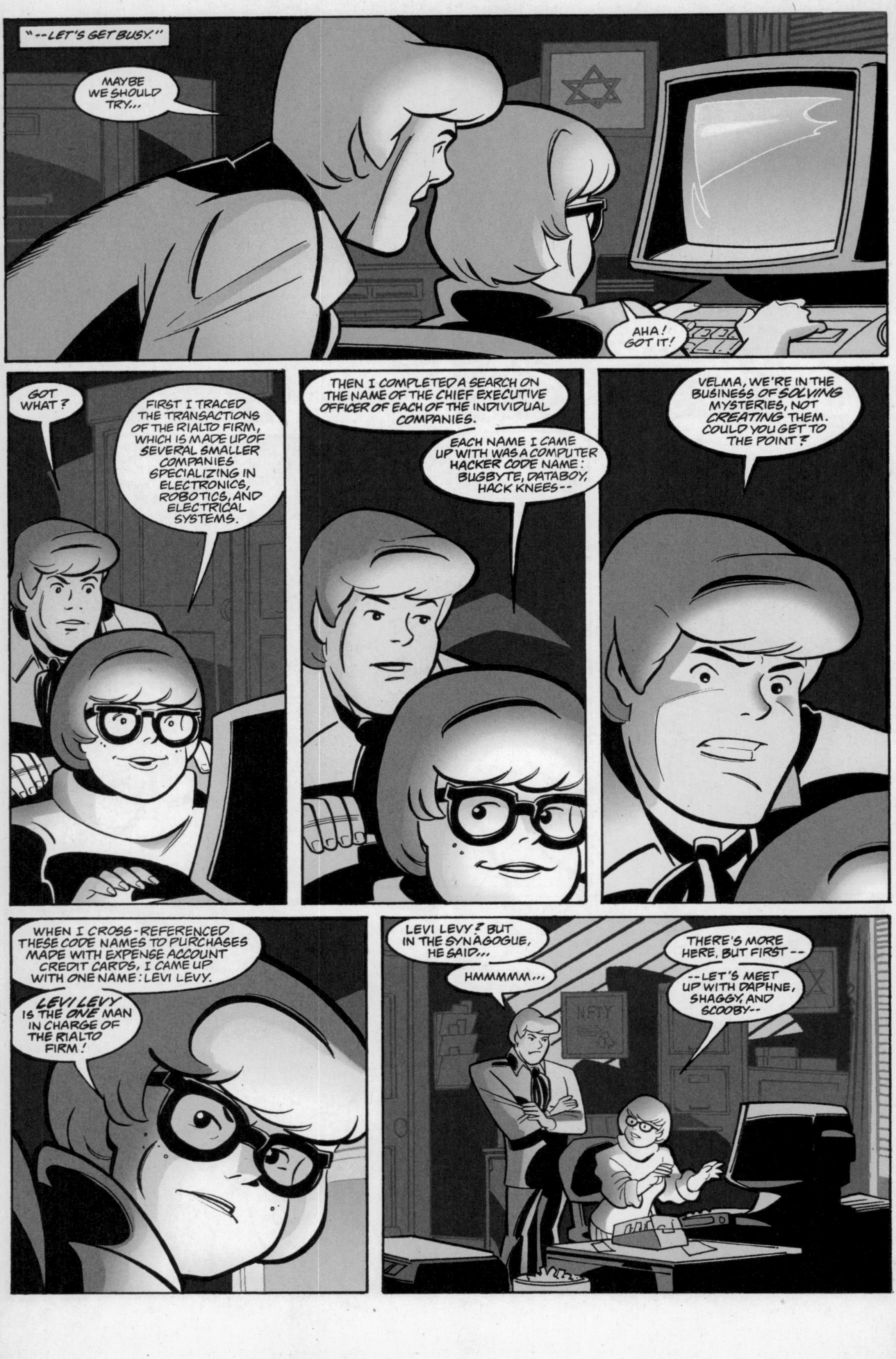
"--LET'S GET BUSY."
MAYBE WE SHOULD TRY...
AHA! GOT IT!
GOT WHAT?
FIRST I TRACED THE TRANSACTIONS OF THE RIALTO FIRM, WHICH IS MADE UP OF SEVERAL SMALLER COMPANIES SPECIALIZING IN ELECTRONICS, ROBOTICS, AND ELECTRICAL SYSTEMS.
THEN I COMPLETED A SEARCH ON THE NAME OF THE CHIEF EXECUTIVE OFFICER OF EACH OF THE INDIVIDUAL COMPANIES.
EACH NAME I CAME UP WITH WAS A COMPUTER HACKER CODE NAME: BUGBYTE, DATABOY, HACK KNEES--
VELMA, WE'RE IN THE BUSINESS OF SOLVING MYSTERIES, NOT CREATING THEM. COULD YOU GET TO THE POINT?
WHEN I CROSS-REFERENCED THESE CODE NAMES TO PURCHASES MADE WITH EXPENSE ACCOUNT CREDIT CARDS, I CAME UP WITH ONE NAME: LEVI LEVY.
LEVI LEVY IS THE ONE MAN IN CHARGE OF THE RIALTO FIRM!
LEVI LEVY? BUT IN THE SYNAGOGUE, HE SAID...
HMMMMM...
THERE'S MORE HERE, BUT FIRST--
--LET'S MEET UP WITH DAPHNE, SHAGGY, AND SCOOBY--
NFTY

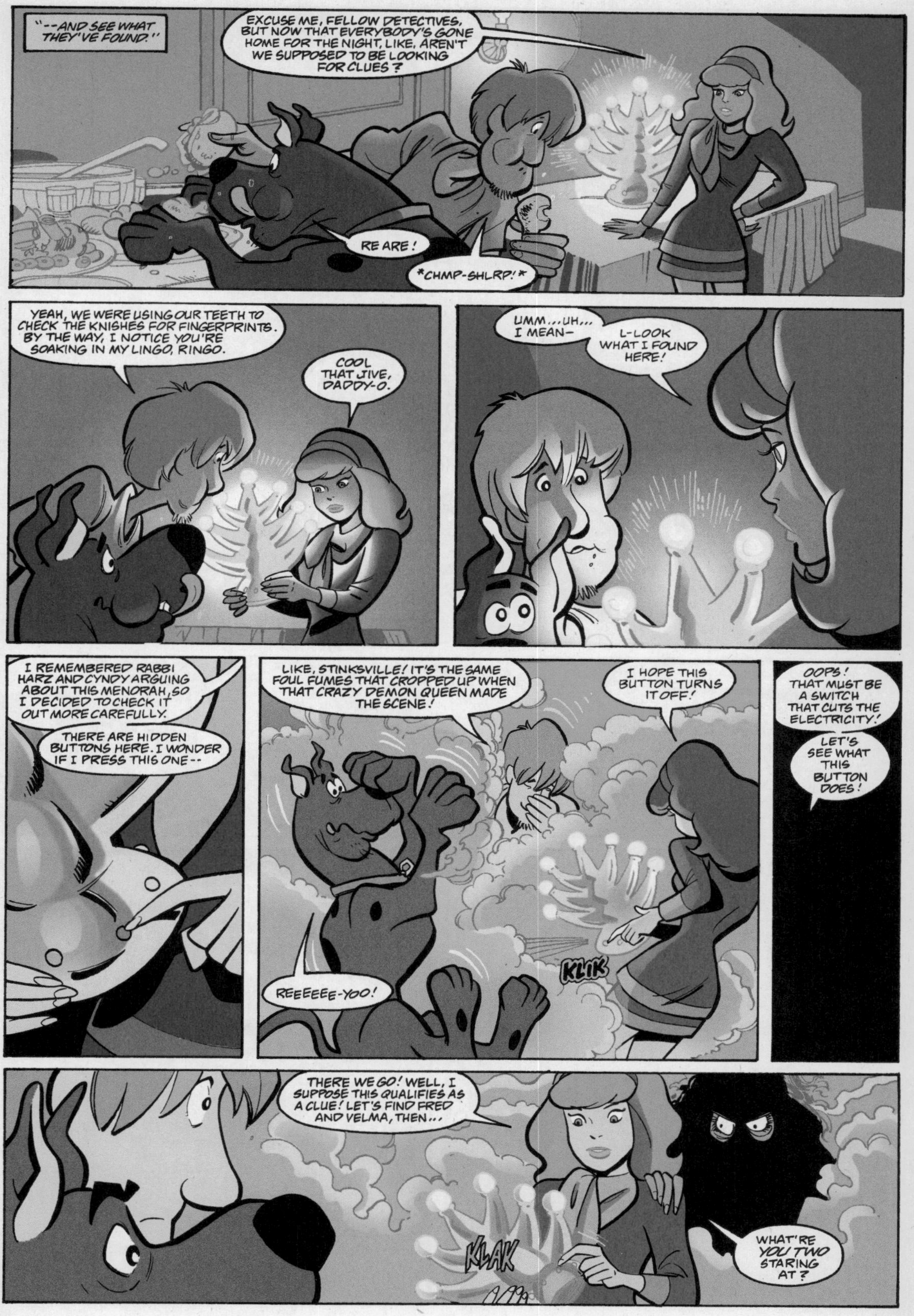
"--AND SEE WHAT THEY'VE FOUND."
EXCUSE ME, FELLOW DETECTIVES, BUT NOW THAT EVERYBODY'S GONE HOME FOR THE NIGHT, LIKE, AREN'T WE SUPPOSED TO BE LOOKING FOR CLUES?
RE ARE!
CHMP-SHLRP!
YEAH, WE WERE USING OUR TEETH TO CHECK THE KNISHES FOR FINGERPRINTS. BY THE WAY, I NOTICE YOU'RE SOAKING IN MY LINGO, RINGO.
COOL THAT JIVE, DADDY-O.
UMM...UH... I MEAN-
L-LOOK WHAT I FOUND HERE!
I REMEMBERED RABBI HARZ AND CYNDY ARGUING ABOUT THIS MENORAH, SO I DECIDED TO CHECK IT OUT MORE CAREFULLY.
THERE ARE HIDDEN BUTTONS HERE. I WONDER IF I PRESS THIS ONE--
LIKE, STINKSVILLE! IT'S THE SAME FOUL FUMES THAT CROPPED UP WHEN THAT CRAZY DEMON QUEEN MADE THE SCENE!
I HOPE THIS BUTTON TURNS IT OFF!
KLIK
REEEEEE-YOO!
OOPS! THAT MUST BE A SWITCH THAT CUTS THE ELECTRICITY!
LET'S SEE WHAT THIS BUTTON DOES!
THERE WE GO! WELL, I SUPPOSE THIS QUALIFIES AS A CLUE! LET'S FIND FRED AND VELMA, THEN...
KLAK
WHAT'RE YOU TWO STARING AT?

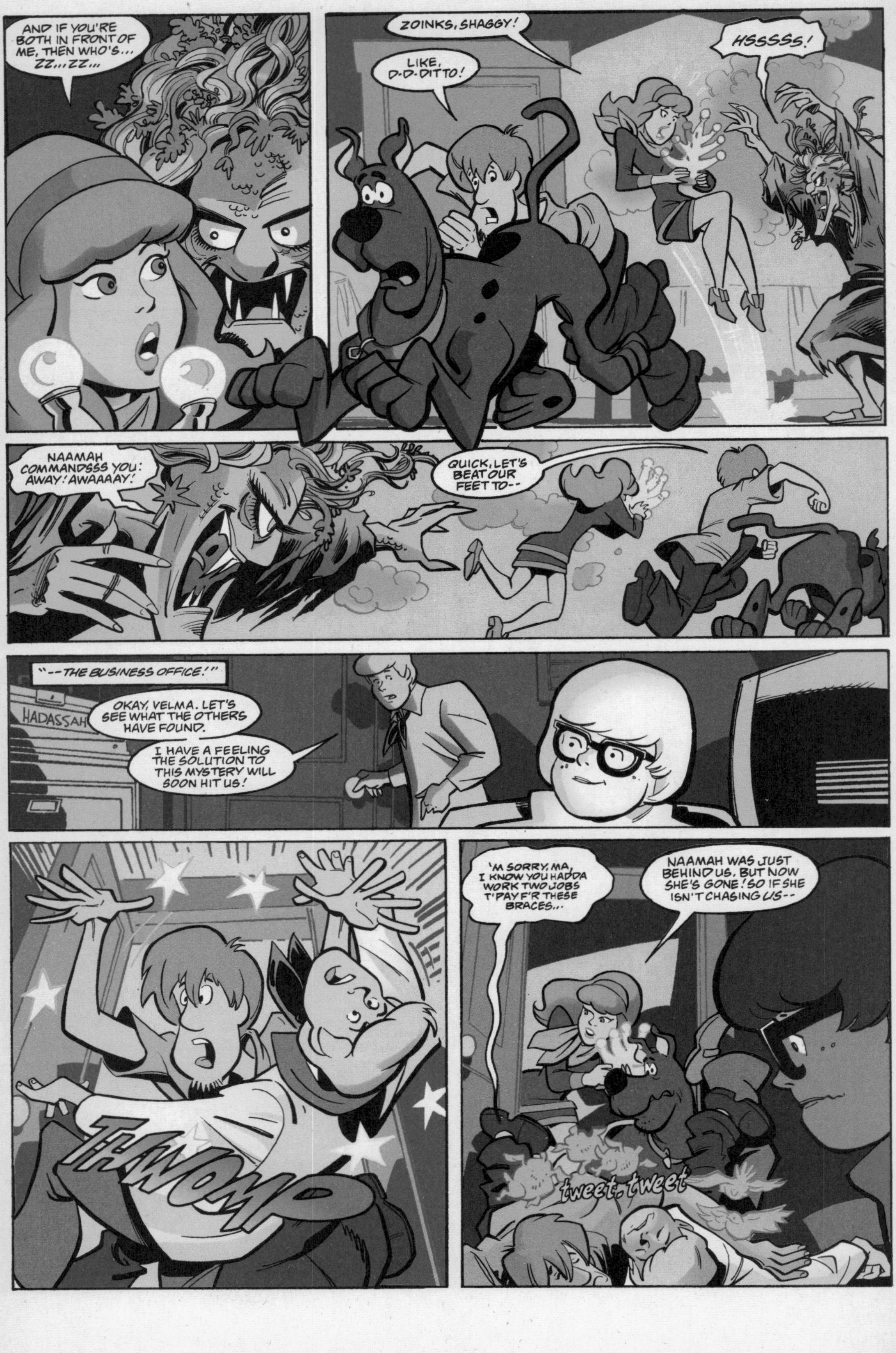
AND IF YOU'RE BOTH IN FRONT OF ME, THEN WHO'S... ZZ...ZZ...
ZOINKS, SHAGGY!
LIKE, D-D-DITTO!
HSSSSS!
NAAMAH COMMANDSSS YOU: AWAY! AWAAAAY!
QUICK, LET'S BEAT OUR FEET TO--
"--THE BUSINESS OFFICE!"
HADASSAH
OKAY, VELMA. LET'S SEE WHAT THE OTHERS HAVE FOUND.
I HAVE A FEELING THE SOLUTION TO THIS MYSTERY WILL SOON HIT US!
THWOMP
'M SORRY, MA, I KNOW YOU HADDA WORK TWO JOBS T'PAY F'R THESE BRACES...
NAAMAH WAS JUST BEHIND US. BUT NOW SHE'S GONE! SO IF SHE ISN'T CHASING US--
tweet. tweet

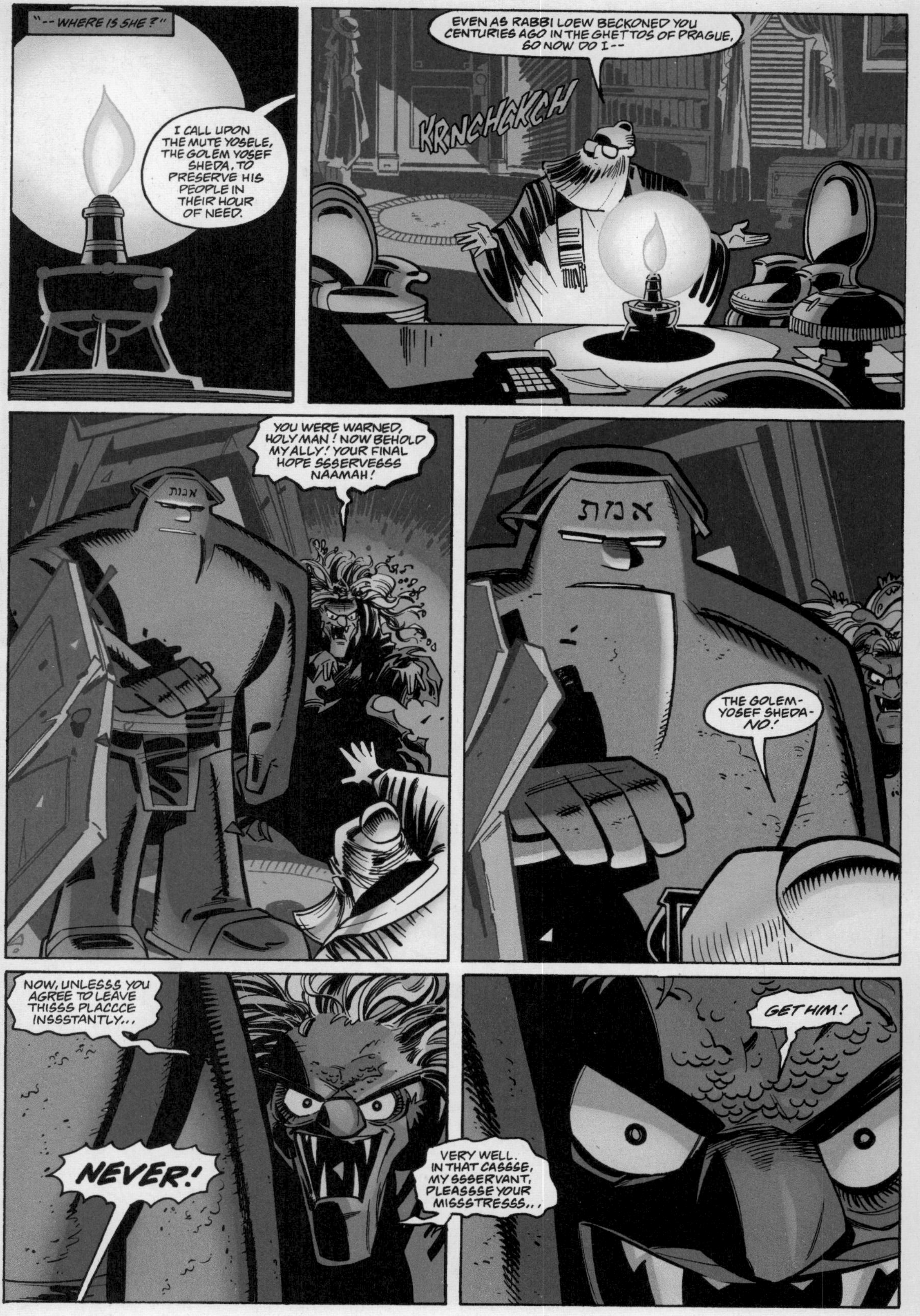
"--WHERE IS SHE?"
I CALL UPON THE MUTE YOSELE, THE GOLEM YOSEF SHEDA, TO PRESERVE HIS PEOPLE IN THEIR HOUR OF NEED.
EVEN AS RABBI LOEW BECKONED YOU CENTURIES AGO IN THE GHETTOS OF PRAGUE, SO NOW DO I--
KRNCHCKCH
YOU WERE WARNED, HOLY MAN! NOW BEHOLD MY ALLY! YOUR FINAL HOPE SSSERVESSS NAAMAH!
אמת
THE GOLEM-YOSEF SHEDA-NO!
NOW, UNLESSS YOU AGREE TO LEAVE THISSS PLACCCE INSSSTANTLY...
NEVER!
VERY WELL. IN THAT CASSSE, MY SSSERVANT, PLEASSSE YOUR MISSSTRESSS...
GET HIM!

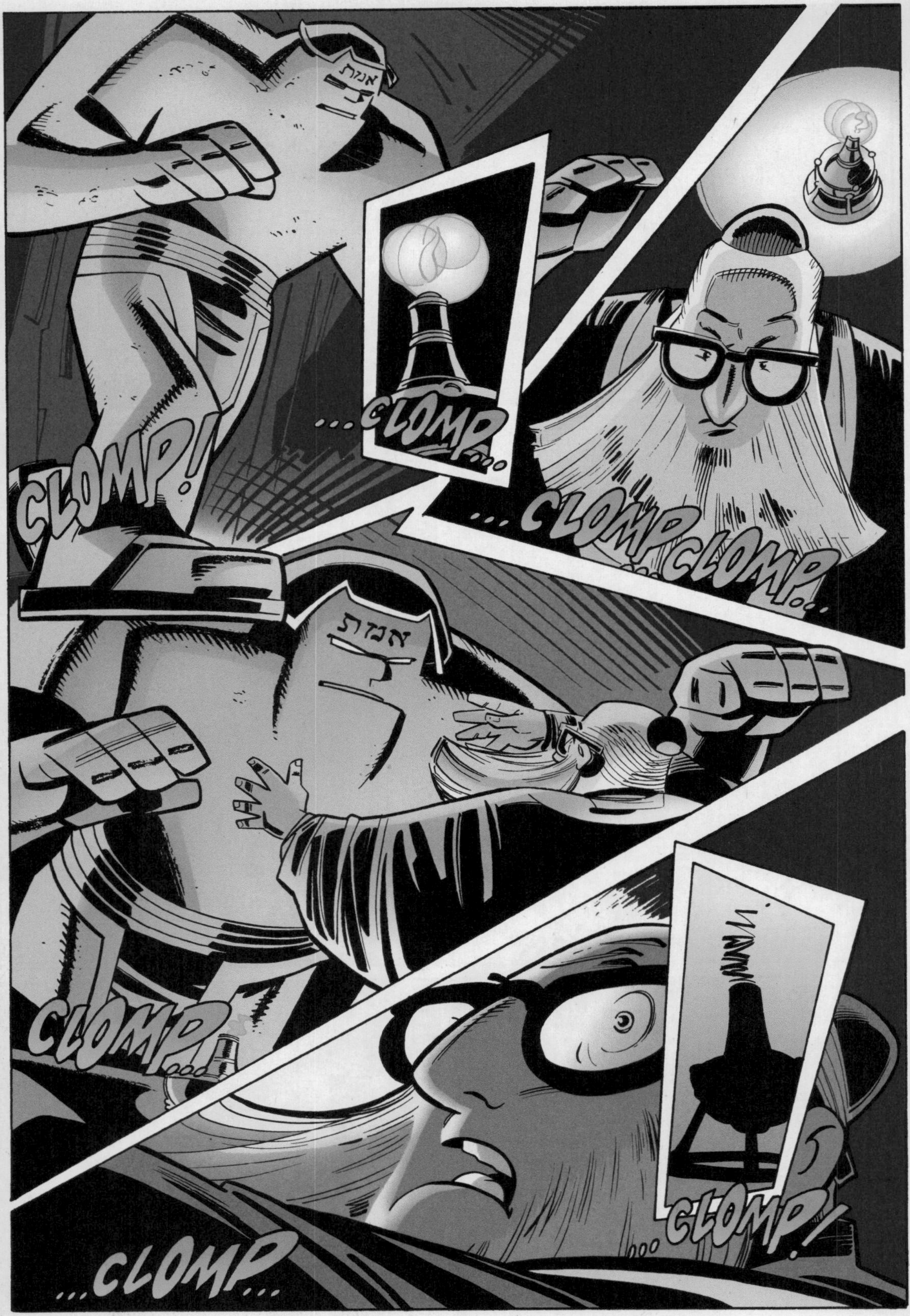
CLOMP!
...CLOMP...
...CLOMP
CLOMP...
CLOMP...
...CLOMP!
...CLOMP...

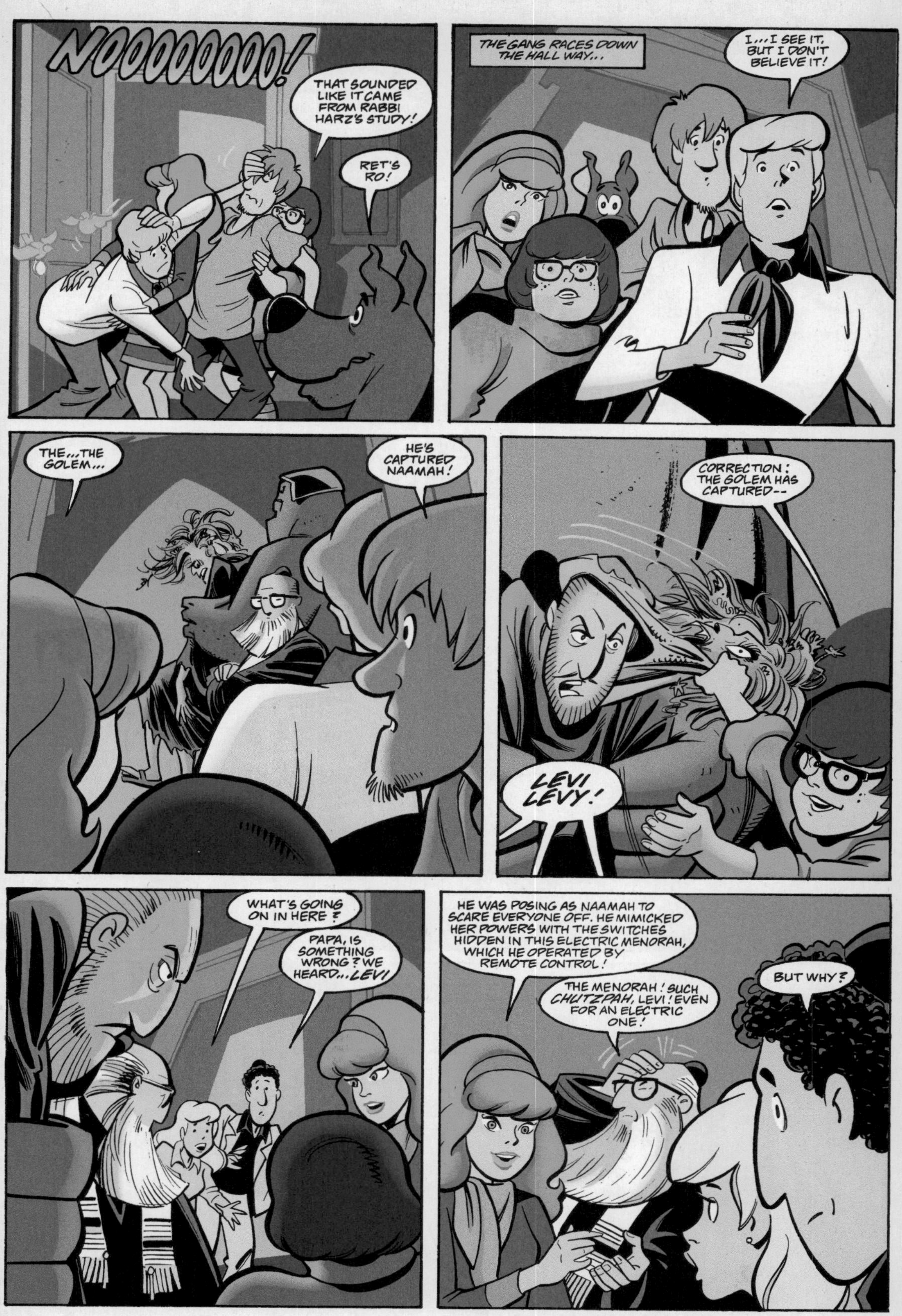
NOOOOOOOO!
THAT SOUNDED LIKE IT CAME FROM RABBI HARZ'S STUDY!
RET'S RO!
THE GANG RACES DOWN THE HALL WAY...
I...I SEE IT, BUT I DON'T BELIEVE IT!
THE...THE GOLEM...
HE'S CAPTURED NAAMAH!
CORRECTION: THE GOLEM HAS CAPTURED--
LEVI LEVY!
WHAT'S GOING ON IN HERE?
PAPA, IS SOMETHING WRONG? WE HEARD...LEVI
HE WAS POSING AS NAAMAH TO SCARE EVERYONE OFF. HE MIMICKED HER POWERS WITH THE SWITCHES HIDDEN IN THIS ELECTRIC MENORAH, WHICH HE OPERATED BY REMOTE CONTROL!
THE MENORAH! SUCH CHUTZPAH, LEVI! EVEN FOR AN ELECTRIC ONE!
BUT WHY?

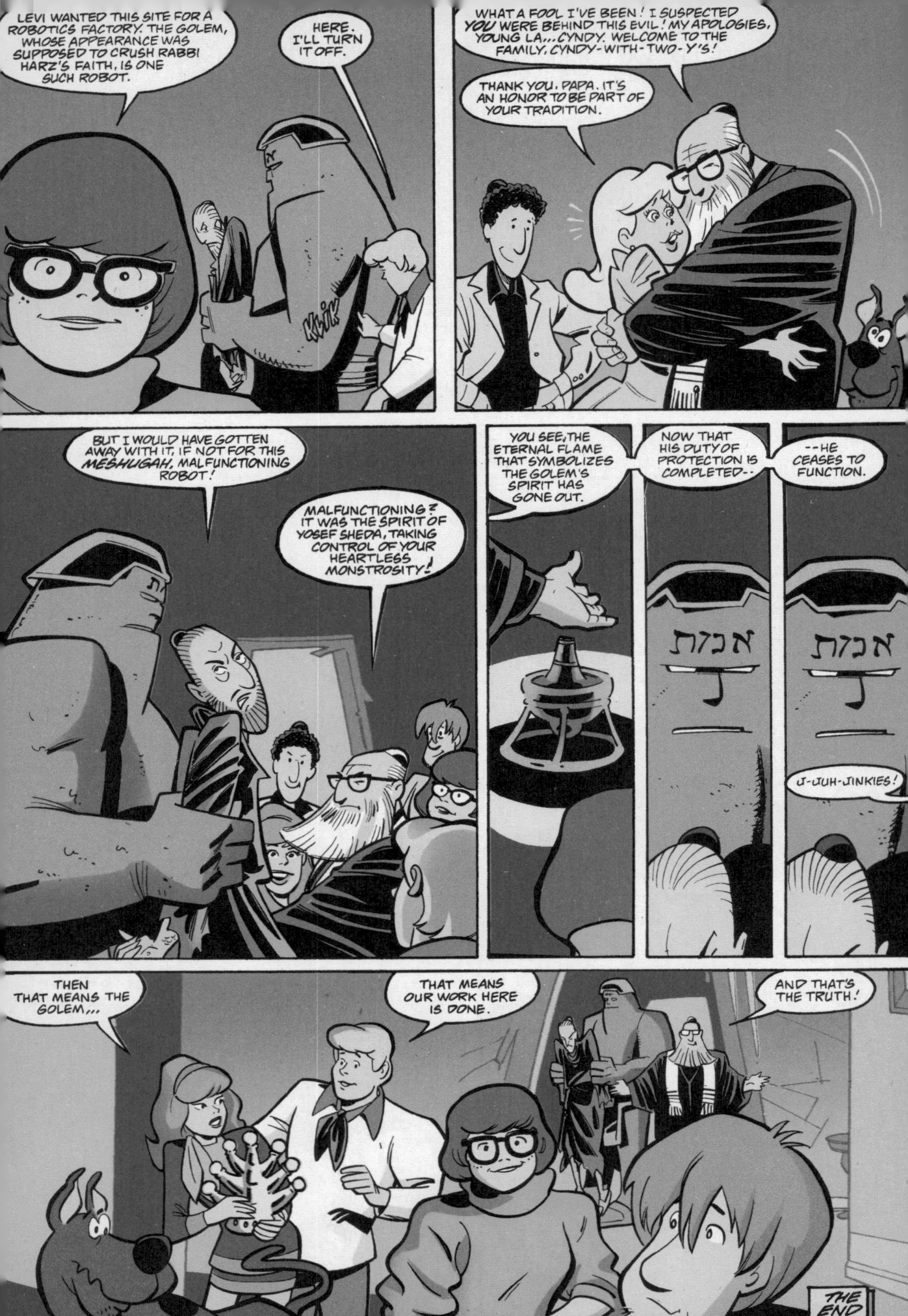
LEVI WANTED THIS SITE FOR A ROBOTICS FACTORY. THE GOLEM, WHOSE APPEARANCE WAS SUPPOSED TO CRUSH RABBI HARZ'S FAITH, IS ONE SUCH ROBOT.
HERE. I'LL TURN IT OFF.
KLIK
WHAT A FOOL I'VE BEEN! I SUSPECTED *YOU* WERE BEHIND THIS EVIL! MY APOLOGIES, YOUNG LA... CYNDY. WELCOME TO THE FAMILY, CYNDY-WITH-TWO-Y'S!
THANK YOU, PAPA. IT'S AN HONOR TO BE PART OF YOUR TRADITION.
BUT I WOULD HAVE GOTTEN AWAY WITH IT, IF NOT FOR THIS *MESHUGAH*, MALFUNCTIONING ROBOT!
MALFUNCTIONING? IT WAS THE SPIRIT OF YOSEF SHEDA, TAKING CONTROL OF YOUR HEARTLESS MONSTROSITY!
YOU SEE, THE ETERNAL FLAME THAT SYMBOLIZES THE GOLEM'S SPIRIT HAS GONE OUT.
NOW THAT HIS DUTY OF PROTECTION IS COMPLETED--
--HE CEASES TO FUNCTION.
J-JUH-JINKIES!
THEN THAT MEANS THE GOLEM...
THAT MEANS OUR WORK HERE IS DONE.
AND THAT'S THE TRUTH!
THE END

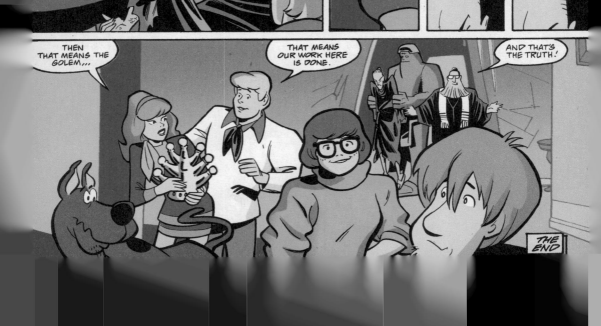

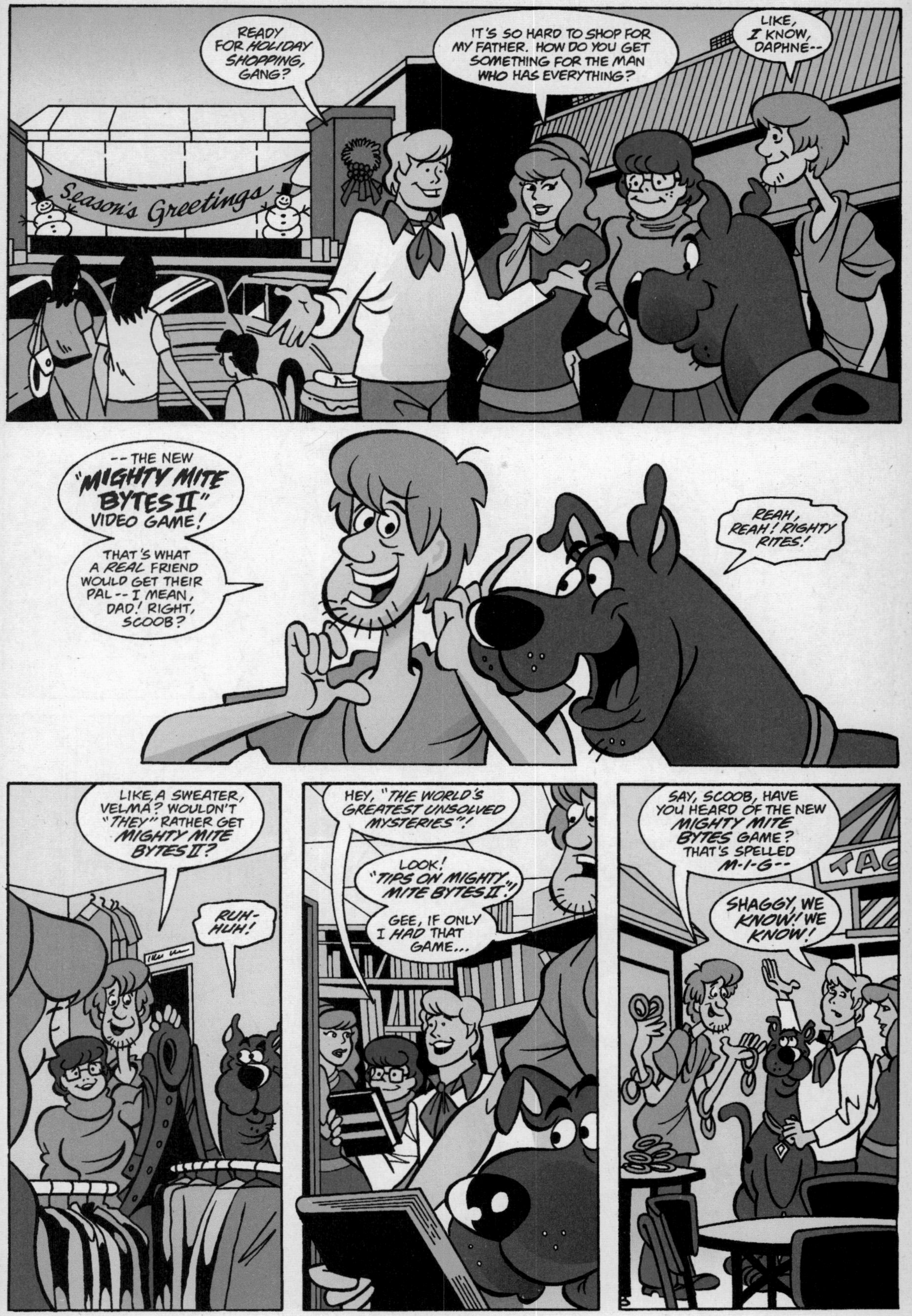
READY FOR HOLIDAY SHOPPING, GANG?
IT'S SO HARD TO SHOP FOR MY FATHER. HOW DO YOU GET SOMETHING FOR THE MAN WHO HAS EVERYTHING?
LIKE, I KNOW, DAPHNE--
Season's Greetings
--THE NEW "MIGHTY MITE BYTES II" VIDEO GAME!
THAT'S WHAT A REAL FRIEND WOULD GET THEIR PAL--I MEAN, DAD! RIGHT, SCOOB?
REAH, REAH! RIGHTY RITES!
LIKE, A SWEATER, VELMA? WOULDN'T "THEY" RATHER GET MIGHTY MITE BYTES II?
RUH-HUH!
HEY, "THE WORLD'S GREATEST UNSOLVED MYSTERIES"!
LOOK! "TIPS ON MIGHTY MITE BYTES II"!
GEE, IF ONLY I HAD THAT GAME...
SAY, SCOOB, HAVE YOU HEARD OF THE NEW MIGHTY MITE BYTES GAME? THAT'S SPELLED M-I-G--
SHAGGY, WE KNOW! WE KNOW!

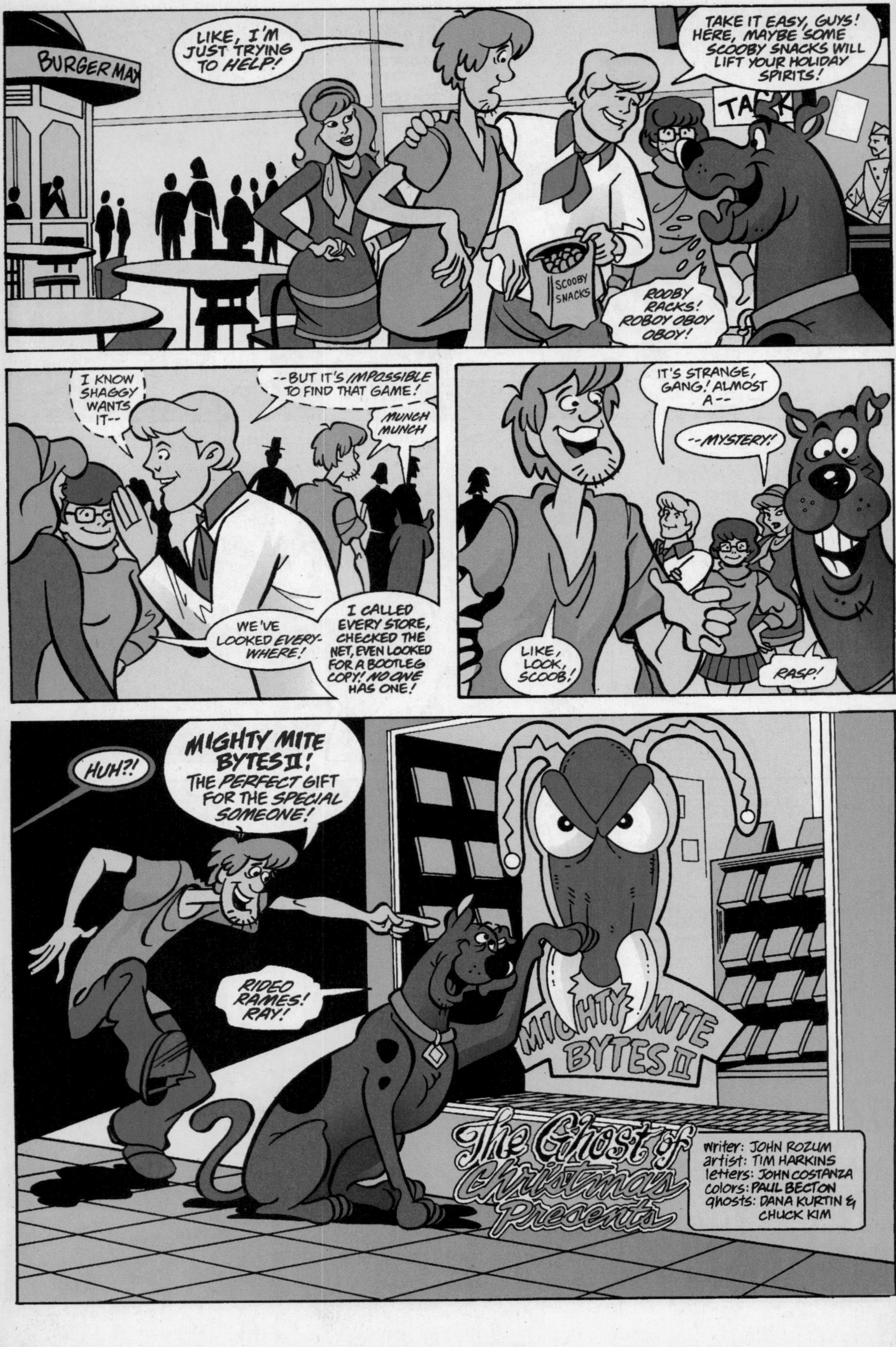
BURGER MAX
LIKE, I'M JUST TRYING TO HELP!
TAKE IT EASY, GUYS! HERE, MAYBE SOME SCOOBY SNACKS WILL LIFT YOUR HOLIDAY SPIRITS!
SCOOBY SNACKS
ROOBY RACKS! ROBOY OBOY OBOY!
I KNOW SHAGGY WANTS IT--
--BUT IT'S IMPOSSIBLE TO FIND THAT GAME!
MUNCH MUNCH
WE'VE LOOKED EVERYWHERE!
I CALLED EVERY STORE, CHECKED THE NET, EVEN LOOKED FOR A BOOTLEG COPY! NO ONE HAS ONE!
IT'S STRANGE, GANG! ALMOST A--
--MYSTERY!
LIKE, LOOK, SCOOB!
RASP!
HUH?!
MIGHTY MITE BYTES II! THE PERFECT GIFT FOR THE SPECIAL SOMEONE!
RIDEO RAMES! RAY!
MIGHTY MITE BYTES II
The Ghost of Christmas Presents
writer: JOHN ROZUM
artist: TIM HARKINS
letters: JOHN COSTANZA
colors: PAUL BECTON
ghosts: DANA KURTIN & CHUCK KIM

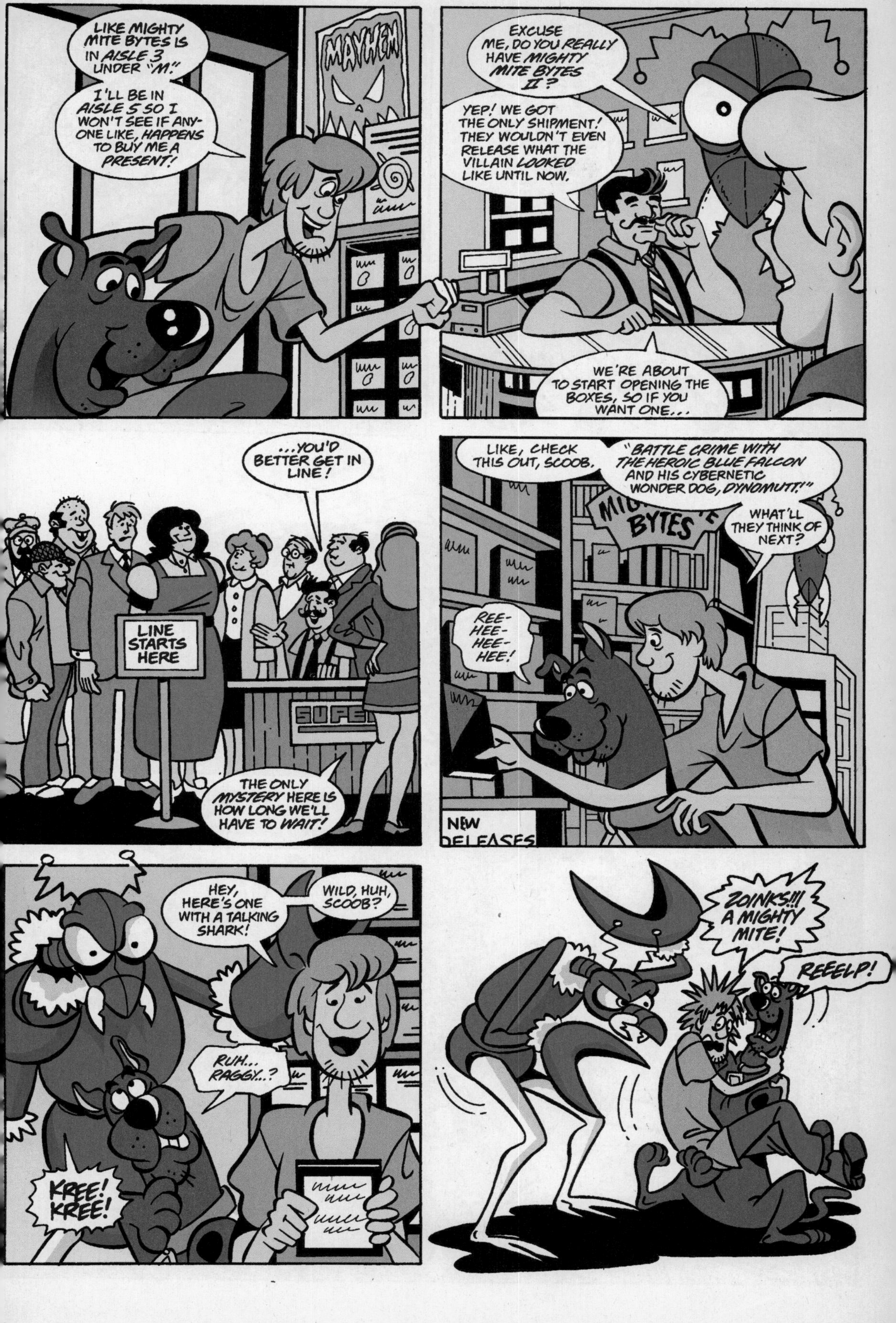
LIKE MIGHTY MITE BYTES IS IN AISLE 3 UNDER "M."
I'LL BE IN AISLE 5 SO I WON'T SEE IF ANYONE LIKE, HAPPENS TO BUY ME A PRESENT!
MAYHEM
EXCUSE ME, DO YOU REALLY HAVE MIGHTY MITE BYTES II?
YEP! WE GOT THE ONLY SHIPMENT! THEY WOULDN'T EVEN RELEASE WHAT THE VILLAIN LOOKED LIKE UNTIL NOW.
WE'RE ABOUT TO START OPENING THE BOXES, SO IF YOU WANT ONE...
...YOU'D BETTER GET IN LINE!
LINE STARTS HERE
THE ONLY MYSTERY HERE IS HOW LONG WE'LL HAVE TO WAIT!
LIKE, CHECK THIS OUT, SCOOB.
"BATTLE CRIME WITH THE HEROIC BLUE FALCON AND HIS CYBERNETIC WONDER DOG, DYNOMUTT!"
WHAT'LL THEY THINK OF NEXT?
REE-HEE-HEE-HEE!
NEW RELEASES
HEY, HERE'S ONE WITH A TALKING SHARK!
WILD, HUH, SCOOB?
RUH... RAGGY...?
KREE! KREE!
ZOINKS!!! A MIGHTY MITE!
REEELP!

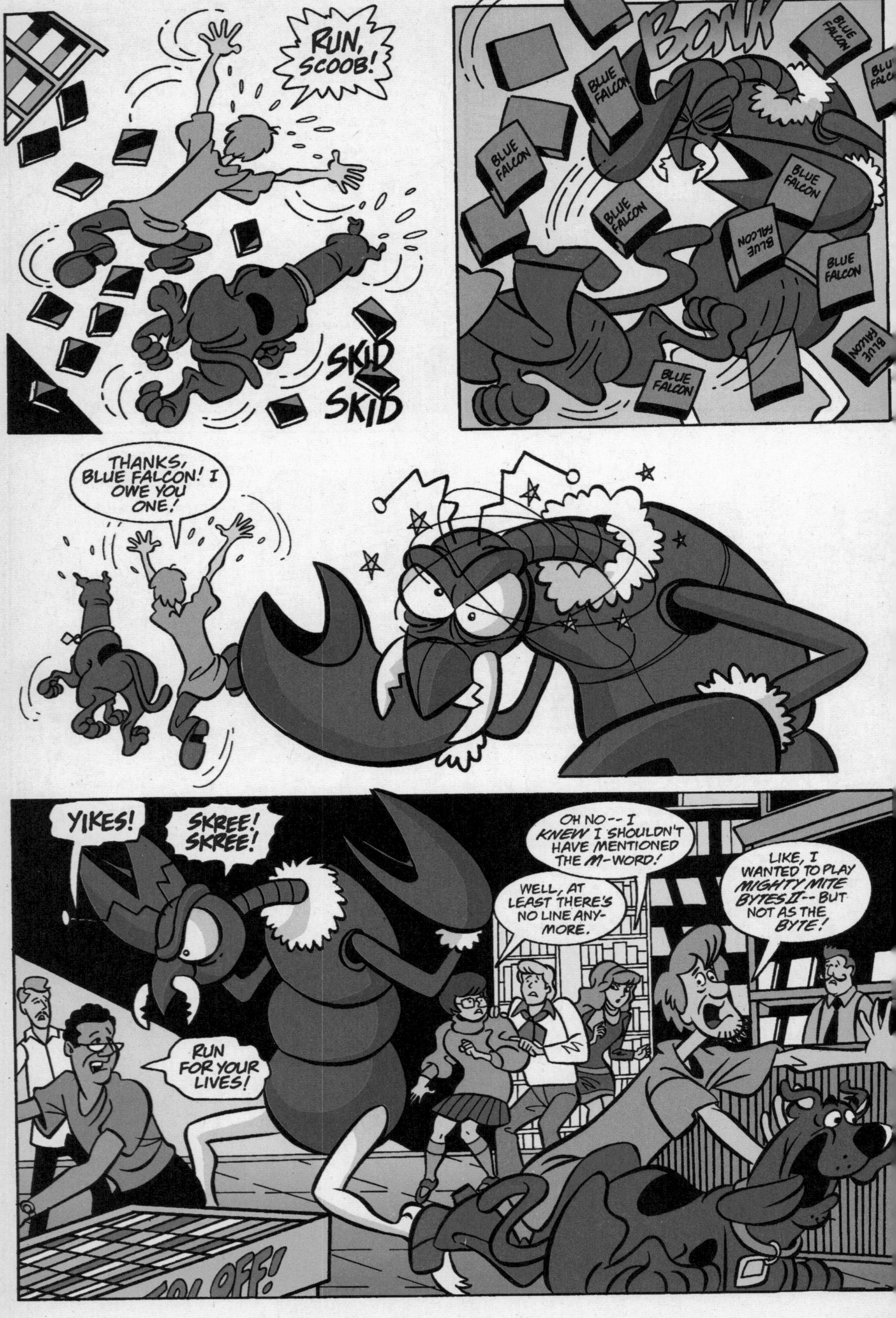
RUN, SCOOB!
SKID
SKID
BONK
BLUE FALCON
THANKS, BLUE FALCON! I OWE YOU ONE!
YIKES!
SKREE! SKREE!
RUN FOR YOUR LIVES!
OH NO-- I KNEW I SHOULDN'T HAVE MENTIONED THE M-WORD!
WELL, AT LEAST THERE'S NO LINE ANYMORE.
LIKE, I WANTED TO PLAY MIGHTY MITE BYTES II-- BUT NOT AS THE BYTE!

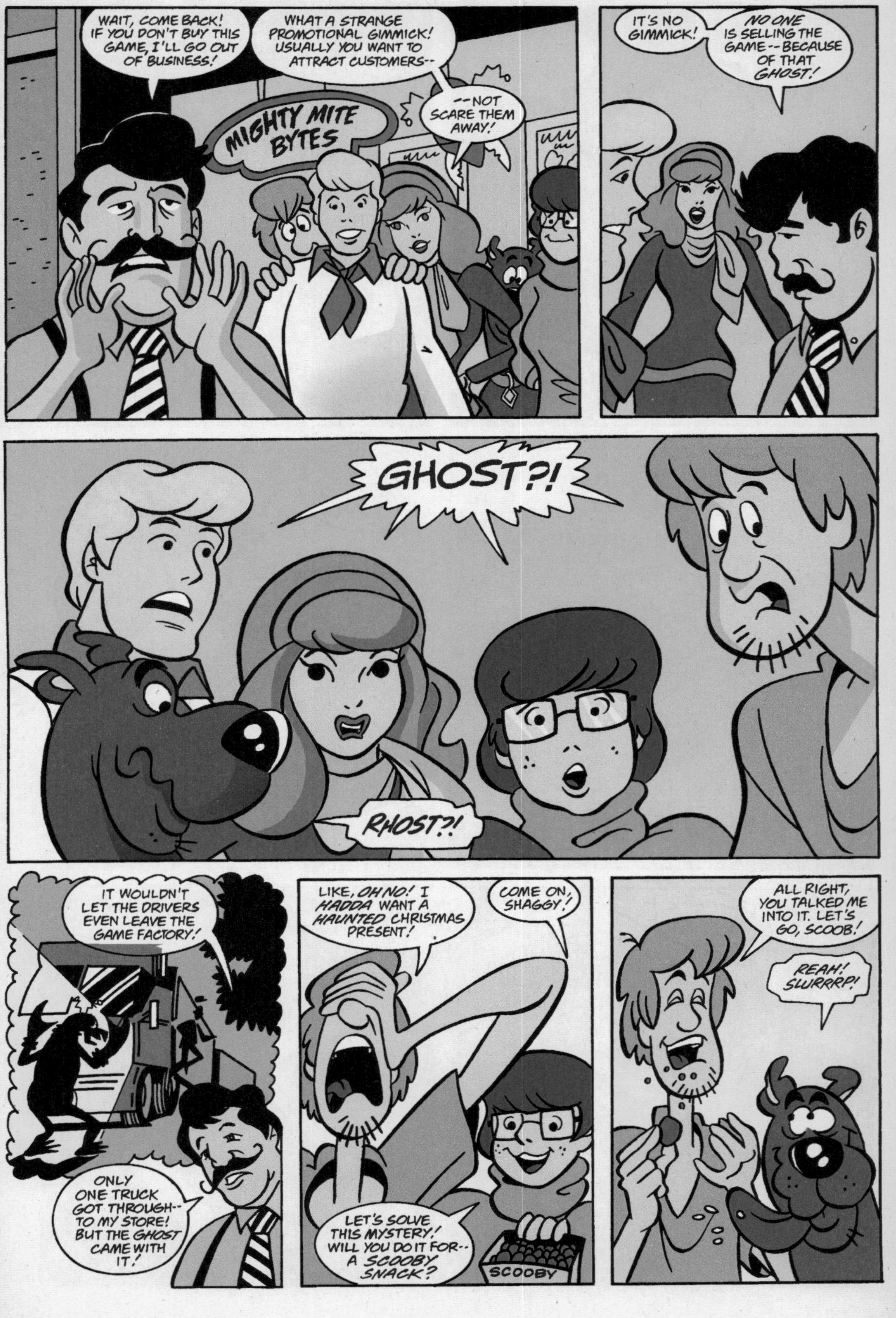
WAIT, COME BACK! IF YOU DON'T BUY THIS GAME, I'LL GO OUT OF BUSINESS!
WHAT A STRANGE PROMOTIONAL GIMMICK! USUALLY YOU WANT TO ATTRACT CUSTOMERS--
--NOT SCARE THEM AWAY!
MIGHTY MITE BYTES
IT'S NO GIMMICK!
NO ONE IS SELLING THE GAME--BECAUSE OF THAT GHOST!
GHOST?!
RHOST?!
IT WOULDN'T LET THE DRIVERS EVEN LEAVE THE GAME FACTORY!
ONLY ONE TRUCK GOT THROUGH-- TO MY STORE! BUT THE GHOST CAME WITH IT!
LIKE, OH NO! I HADDA WANT A HAUNTED CHRISTMAS PRESENT!
COME ON, SHAGGY!
LET'S SOLVE THIS MYSTERY! WILL YOU DO IT FOR-- A SCOOBY SNACK?
SCOOBY
ALL RIGHT, YOU TALKED ME INTO IT. LET'S GO, SCOOB!
REAH! SLURRRP!

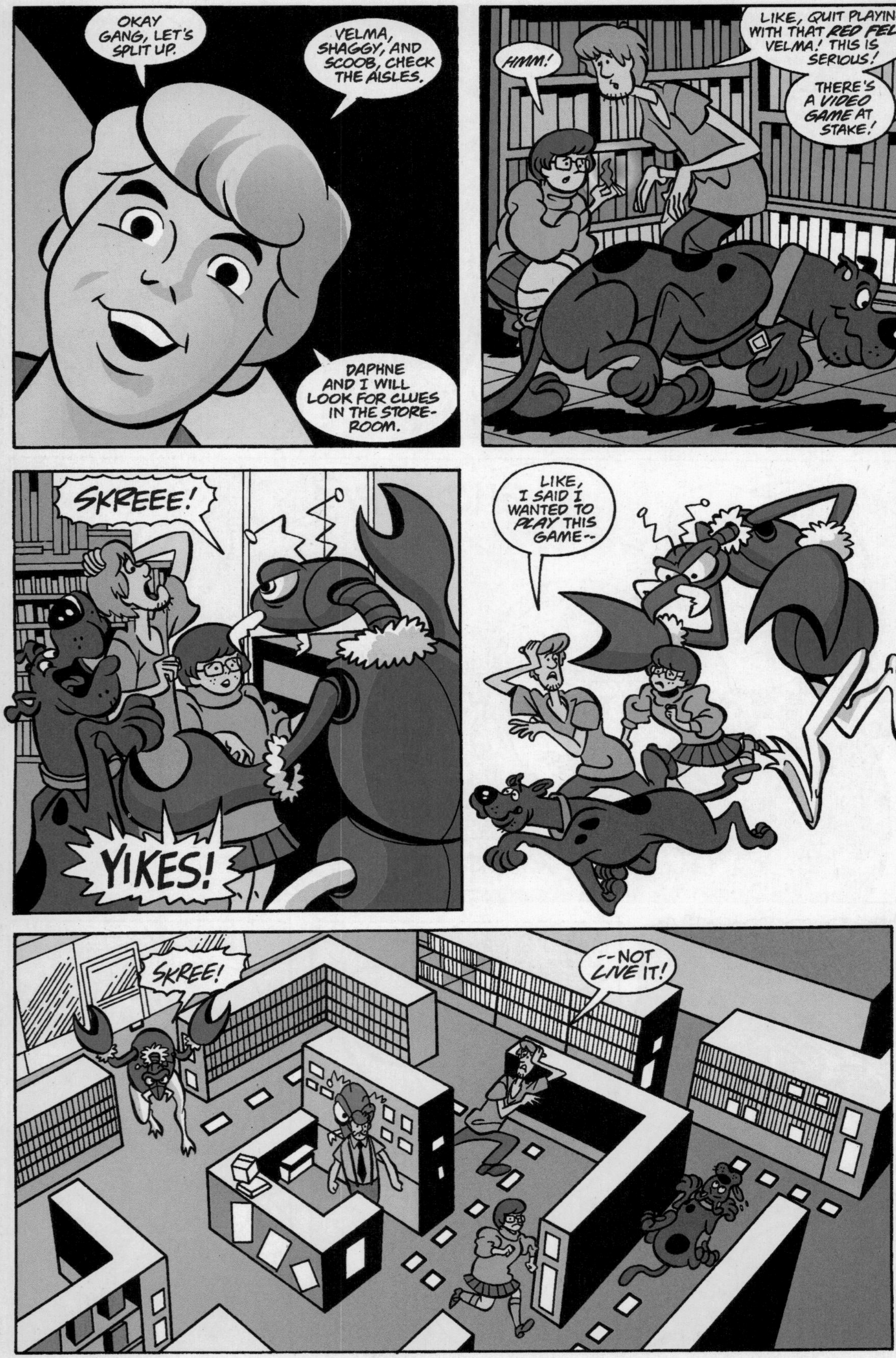

OKAY GANG, LET'S SPLIT UP.
VELMA, SHAGGY, AND SCOOB, CHECK THE AISLES.
DAPHNE AND I WILL LOOK FOR CLUES IN THE STORE-ROOM.
HMM!
LIKE, QUIT PLAYING WITH THAT RED FELT, VELMA! THIS IS SERIOUS!
THERE'S A VIDEO GAME AT STAKE!
SKREEE!
YIKES!
LIKE, I SAID I WANTED TO PLAY THIS GAME--
SKREE!
--NOT LIVE IT!

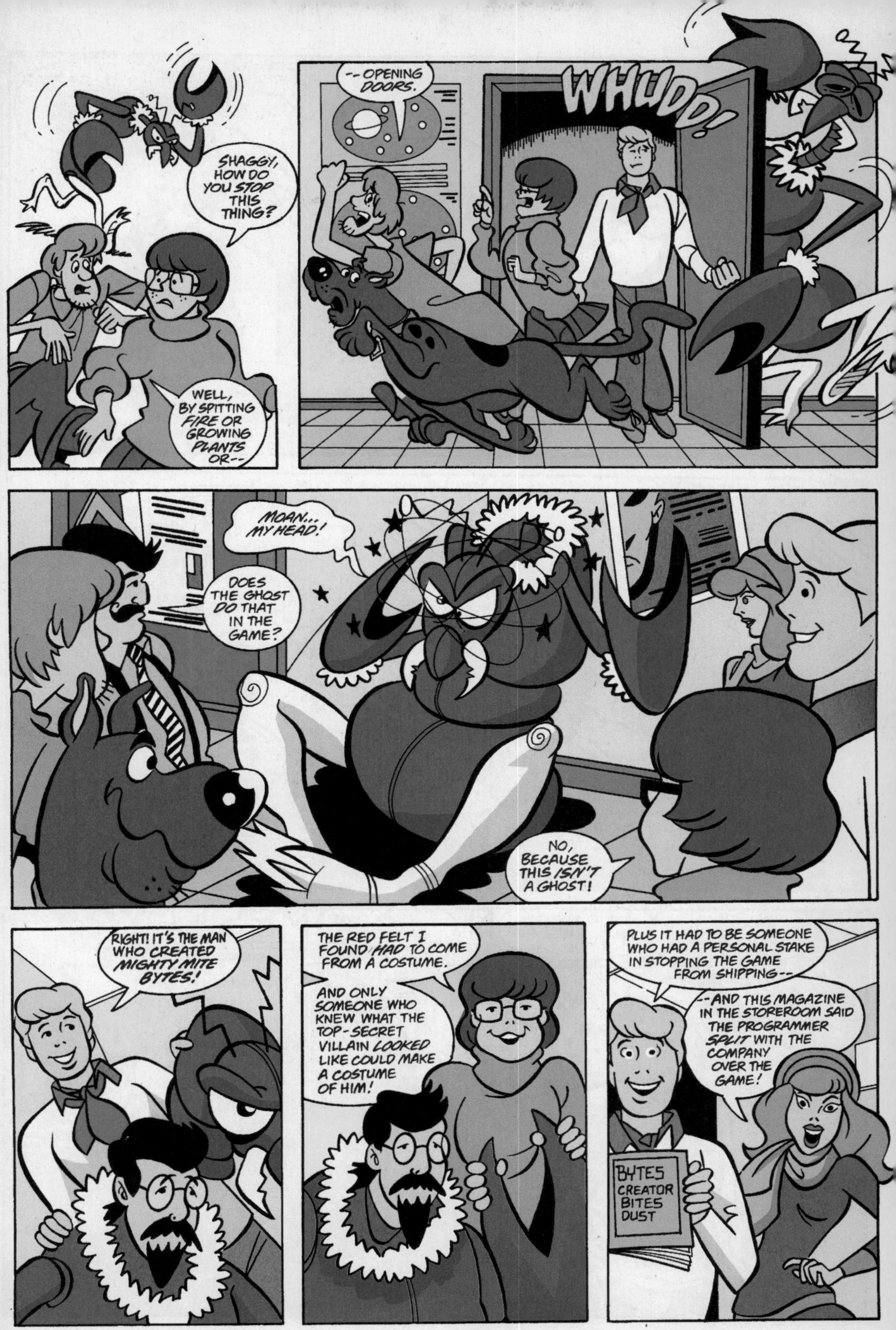
SHAGGY, HOW DO YOU STOP THIS THING?
WELL, BY SPITTING FIRE OR GROWING PLANTS OR--
--OPENING DOORS.
WHUDD!
MOAN... MY HEAD!
DOES THE GHOST DO THAT IN THE GAME?
NO, BECAUSE THIS ISN'T A GHOST!
RIGHT! IT'S THE MAN WHO CREATED MIGHTY MITE BYTES!
THE RED FELT I FOUND HAD TO COME FROM A COSTUME.
AND ONLY SOMEONE WHO KNEW WHAT THE TOP-SECRET VILLAIN LOOKED LIKE COULD MAKE A COSTUME OF HIM!
PLUS IT HAD TO BE SOMEONE WHO HAD A PERSONAL STAKE IN STOPPING THE GAME FROM SHIPPING--
--AND THIS MAGAZINE IN THE STOREROOM SAID THE PROGRAMMER SPLIT WITH THE COMPANY OVER THE GAME!
BYTES CREATOR BITES DUST

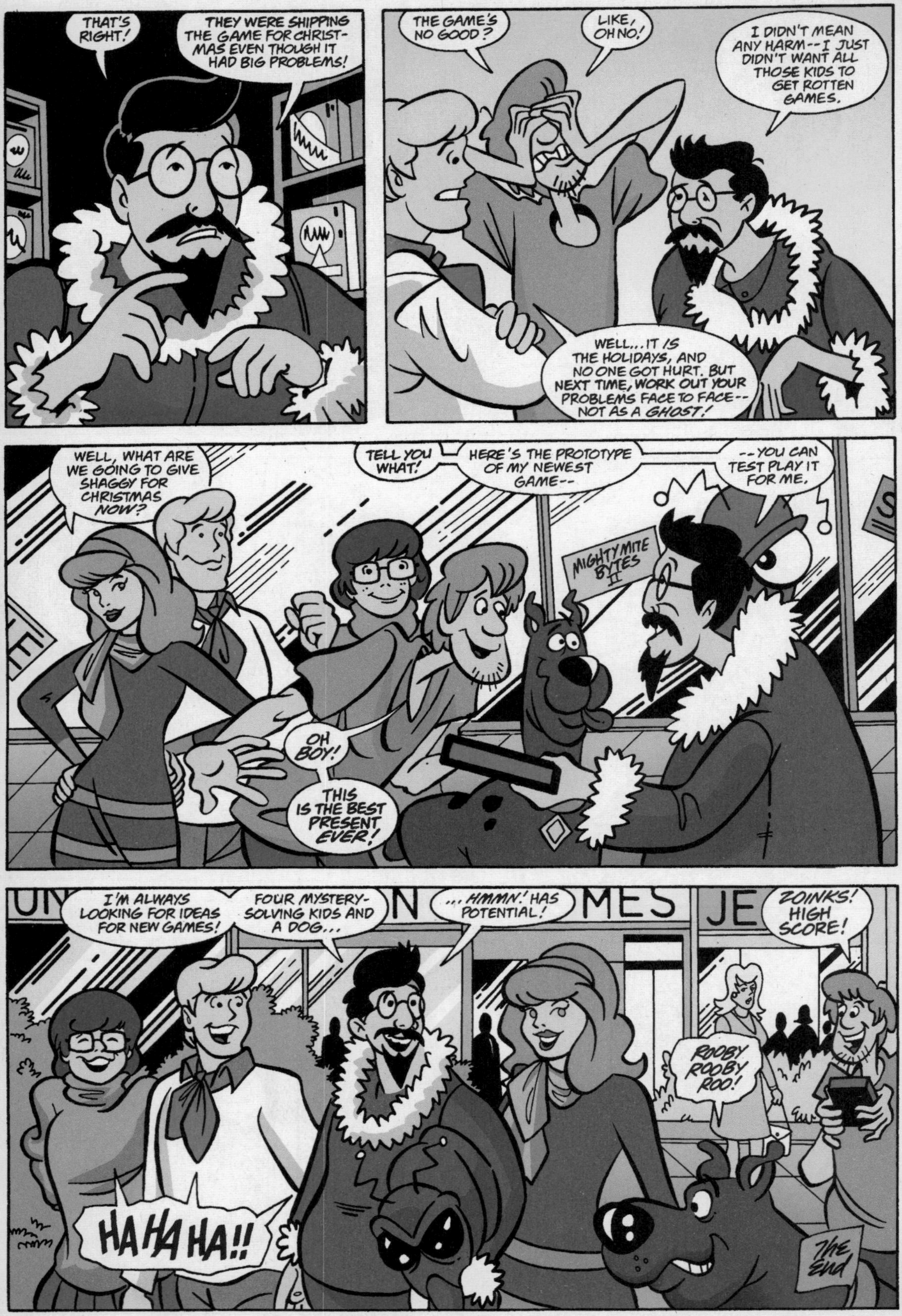
THAT'S RIGHT!
THEY WERE SHIPPING THE GAME FOR CHRIST-MAS EVEN THOUGH IT HAD BIG PROBLEMS!
THE GAME'S NO GOOD?
LIKE, OH NO!
I DIDN'T MEAN ANY HARM-- I JUST DIDN'T WANT ALL THOSE KIDS TO GET ROTTEN GAMES.
WELL... IT IS THE HOLIDAYS, AND NO ONE GOT HURT. BUT NEXT TIME, WORK OUT YOUR PROBLEMS FACE TO FACE-- NOT AS A GHOST!
WELL, WHAT ARE WE GOING TO GIVE SHAGGY FOR CHRISTMAS NOW?
TELL YOU WHAT!
HERE'S THE PROTOTYPE OF MY NEWEST GAME--
--YOU CAN TEST PLAY IT FOR ME.
MIGHTY MITE BYTES II
OH BOY!
THIS IS THE BEST PRESENT EVER!
I'M ALWAYS LOOKING FOR IDEAS FOR NEW GAMES!
FOUR MYSTERY-SOLVING KIDS AND A DOG...
...HMMN! HAS POTENTIAL!
ZOINKS! HIGH SCORE!
ROOBY ROOBY ROO!
HA HA HA!!
THE END

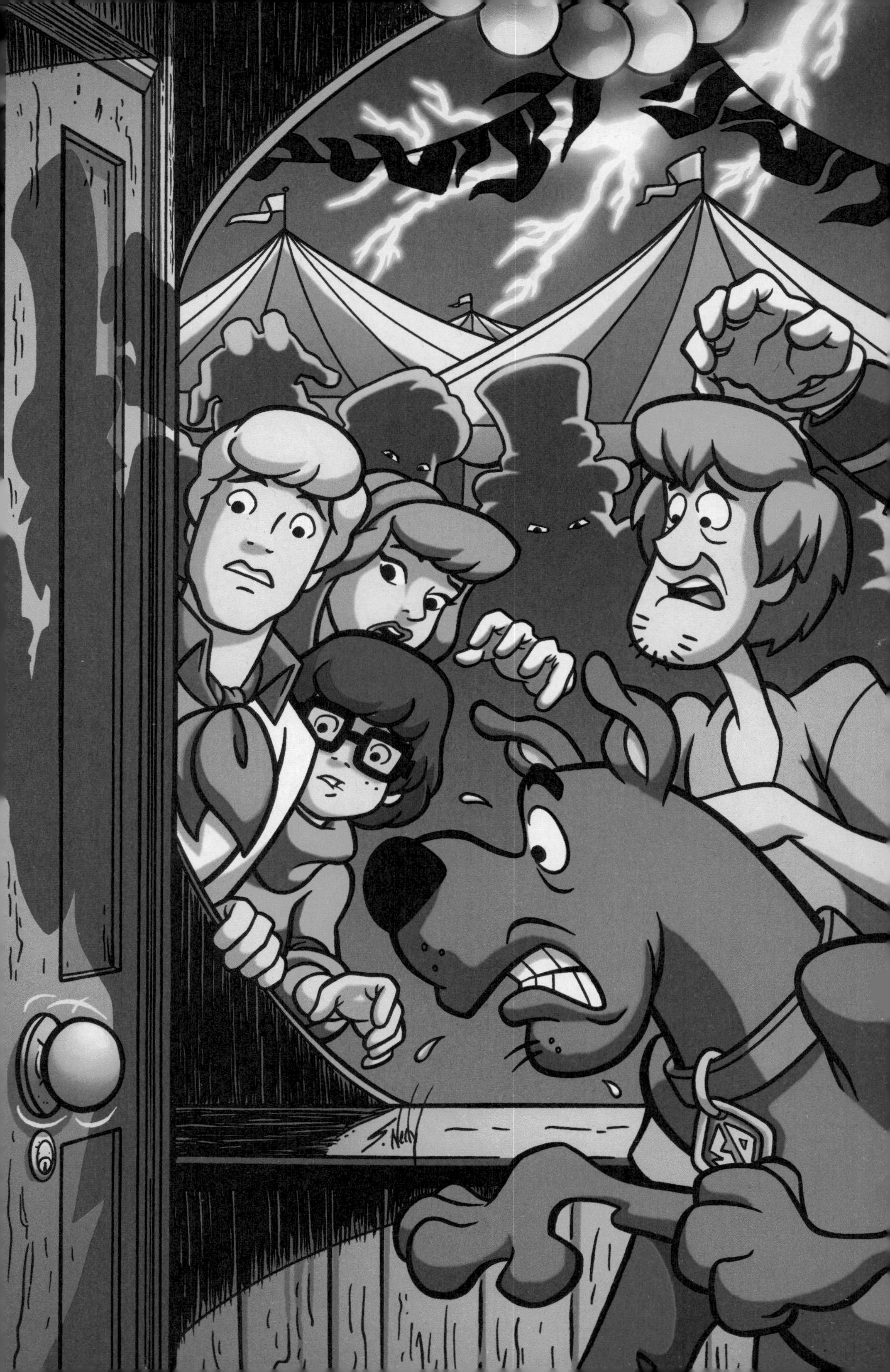

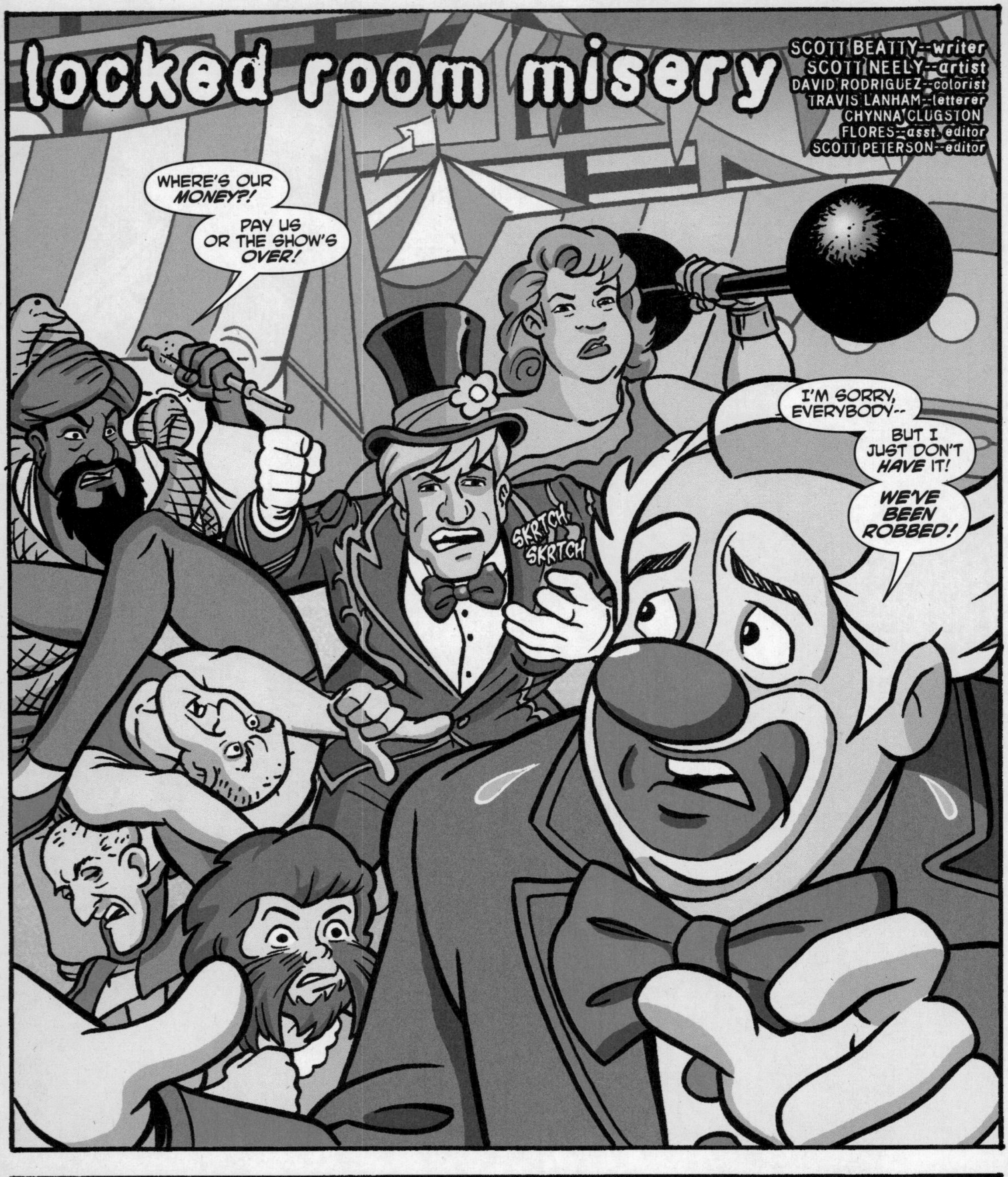
locked room misery
SCOTT BEATTY--writer
SCOTT NEELY--artist
DAVID RODRIGUEZ--colorist
TRAVIS LANHAM--letterer
CHYNNA CLUGSTON FLORES--asst. editor
SCOTT PETERSON--editor
WHERE'S OUR MONEY?!
PAY US OR THE SHOW'S OVER!
SKRTCH SKRTCH
I'M SORRY, EVERYBODY--
BUT I JUST DON'T HAVE IT!
WE'VE BEEN ROBBED!

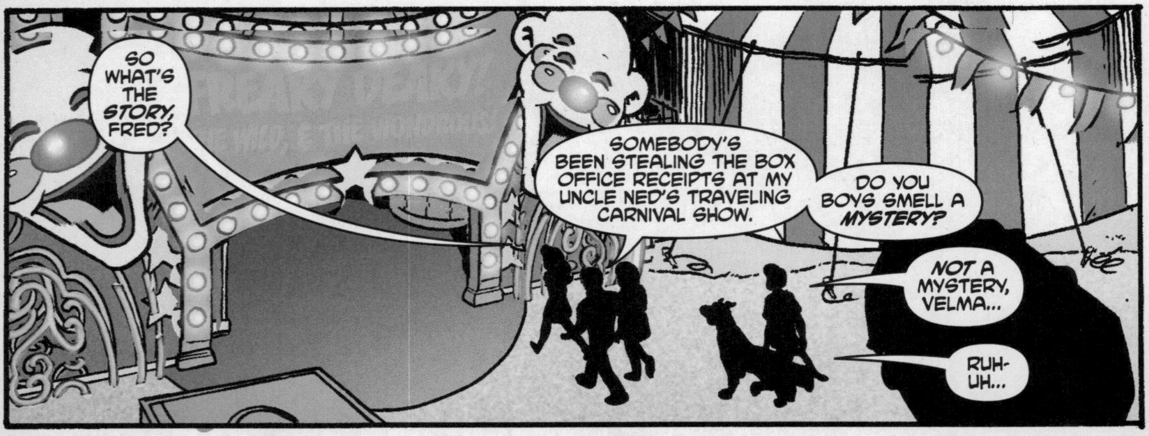
SO WHAT'S THE STORY, FRED?
SOMEBODY'S BEEN STEALING THE BOX OFFICE RECEIPTS AT MY UNCLE NED'S TRAVELING CARNIVAL SHOW.
DO YOU BOYS SMELL A MYSTERY?
NOT A MYSTERY, VELMA...
RUH-UH...

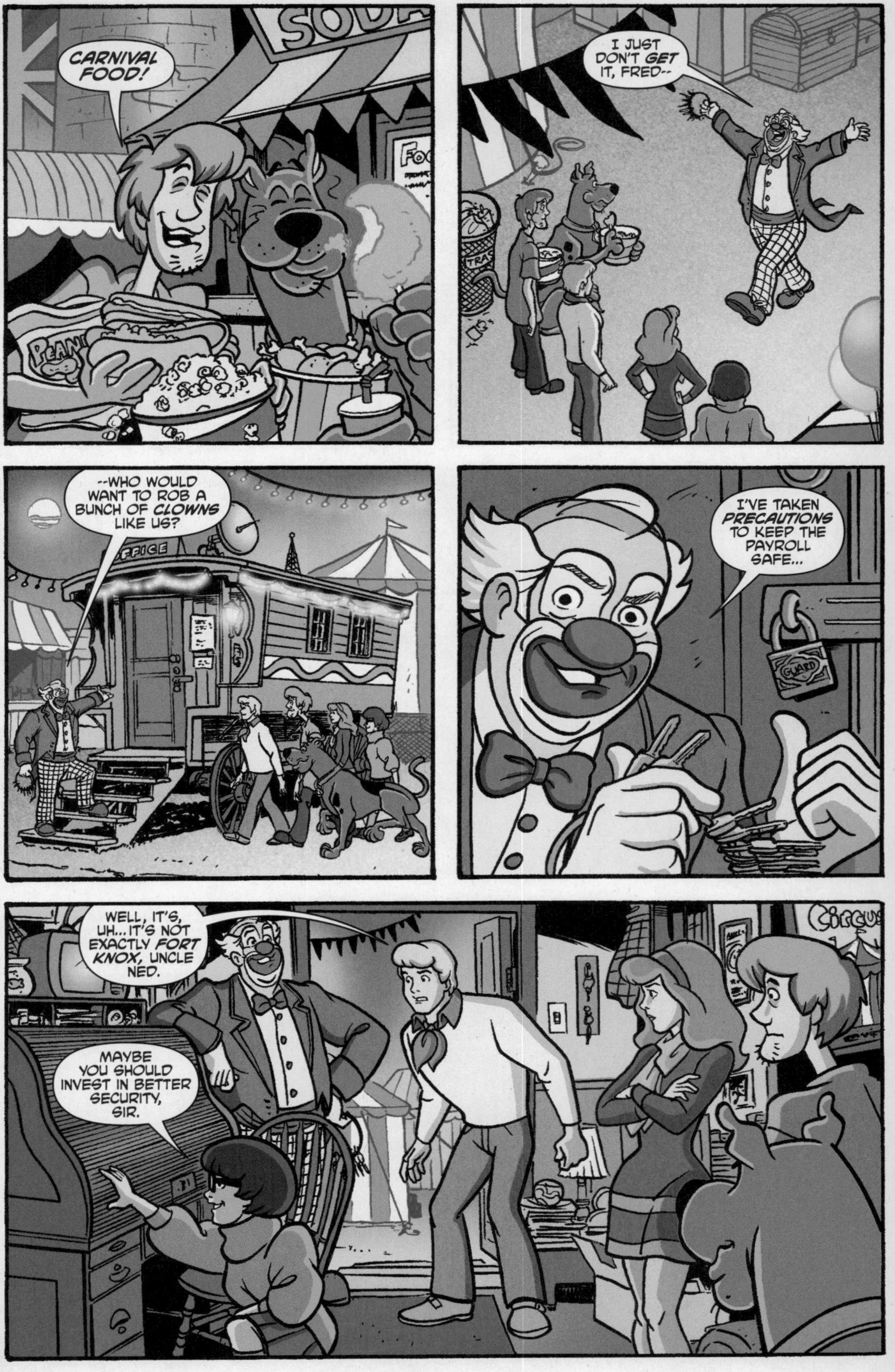
CARNIVAL FOOD!
I JUST DON'T GET IT, FRED--
--WHO WOULD WANT TO ROB A BUNCH OF CLOWNS LIKE US?
I'VE TAKEN PRECAUTIONS TO KEEP THE PAYROLL SAFE...
GUARD
WELL, IT'S, UH...IT'S NOT EXACTLY FORT KNOX, UNCLE NED.
MAYBE YOU SHOULD INVEST IN BETTER SECURITY, SIR.

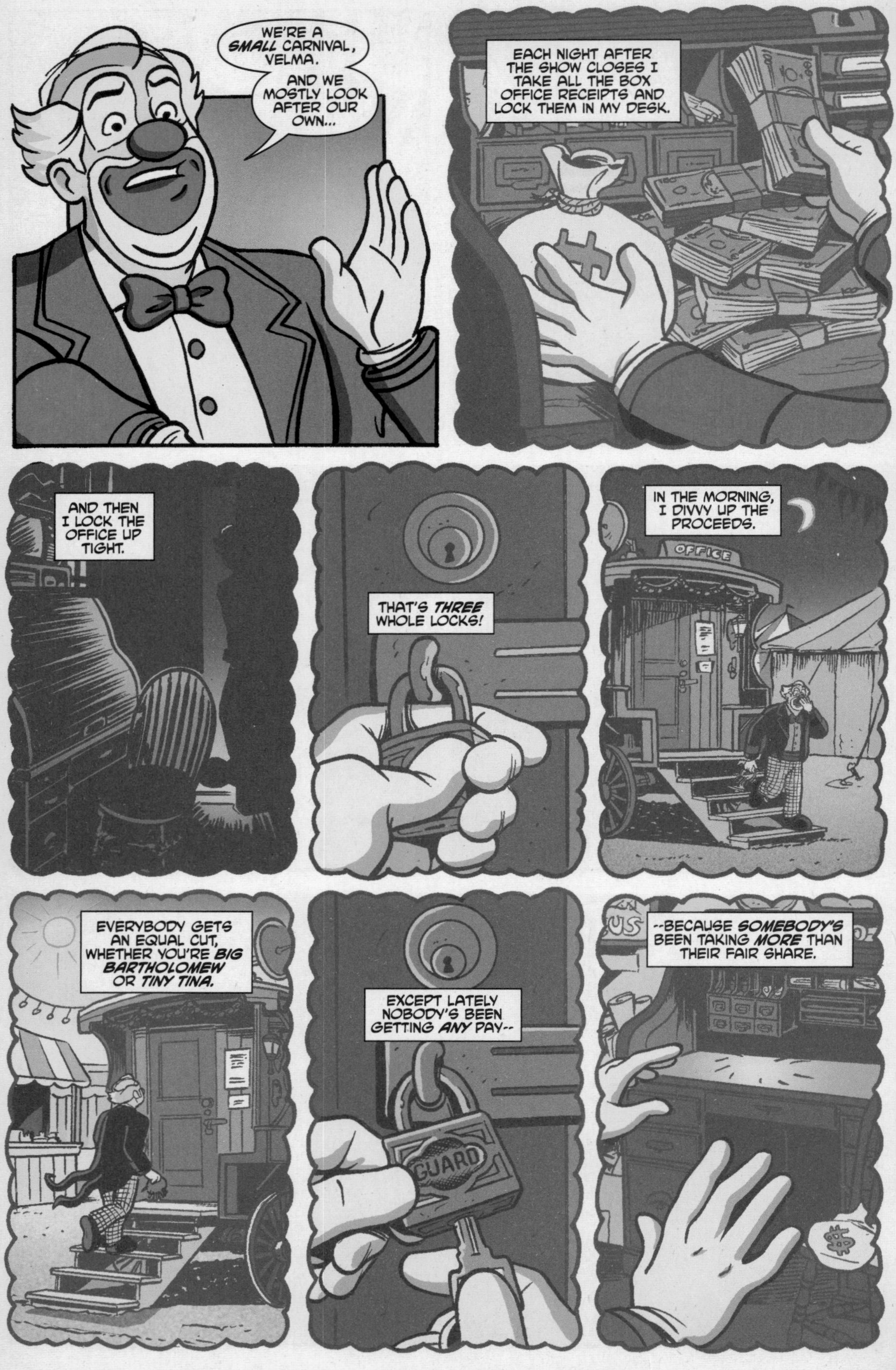
WE'RE A SMALL CARNIVAL, VELMA.
AND WE MOSTLY LOOK AFTER OUR OWN...
EACH NIGHT AFTER THE SHOW CLOSES I TAKE ALL THE BOX OFFICE RECEIPTS AND LOCK THEM IN MY DESK.
AND THEN I LOCK THE OFFICE UP TIGHT.
THAT'S THREE WHOLE LOCKS!
IN THE MORNING, I DIVVY UP THE PROCEEDS.
OFFICE
EVERYBODY GETS AN EQUAL CUT, WHETHER YOU'RE BIG BARTHOLOMEW OR TINY TINA.
EXCEPT LATELY NOBODY'S BEEN GETTING ANY PAY--
GUARD
--BECAUSE SOMEBODY'S BEEN TAKING MORE THAN THEIR FAIR SHARE.

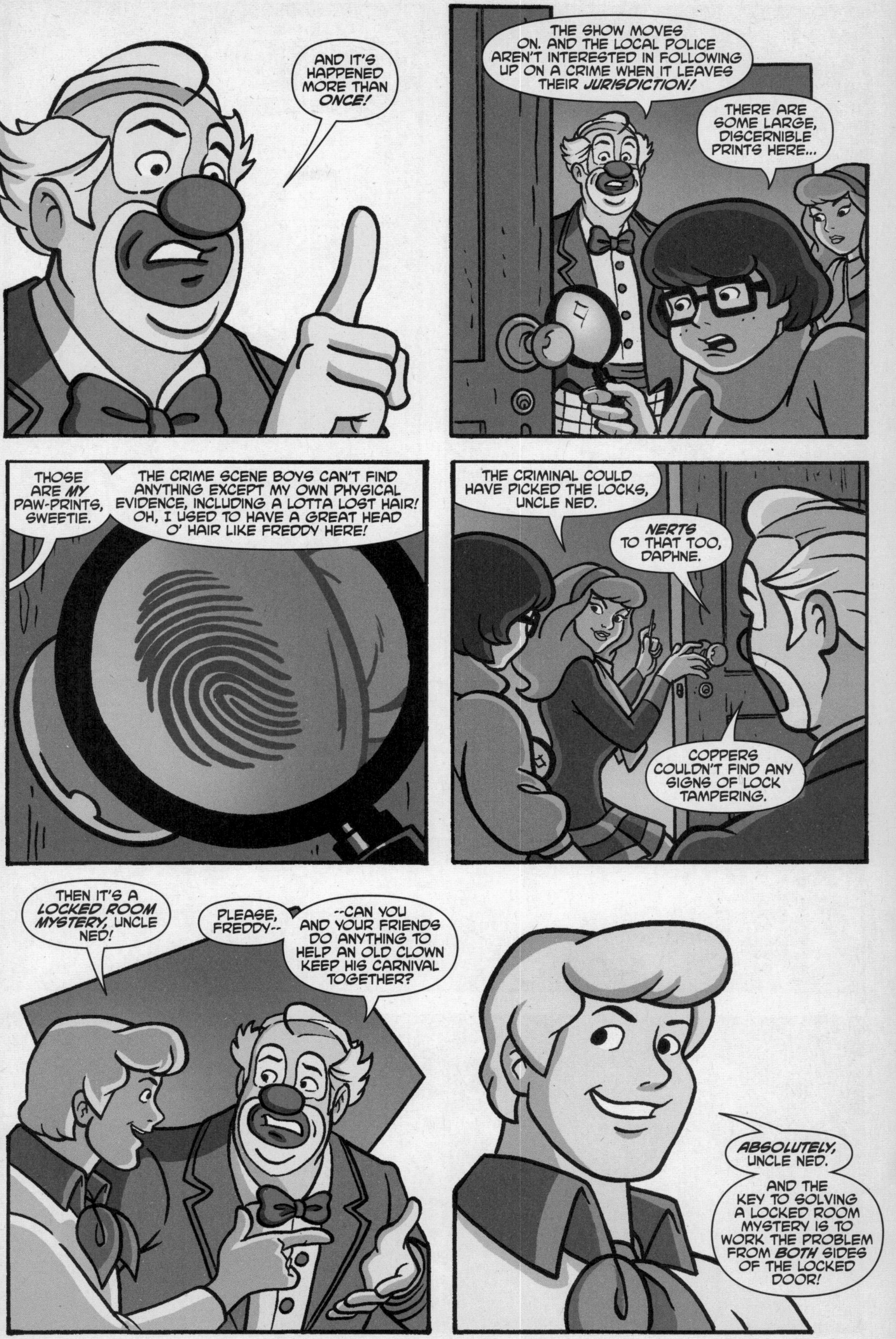
AND IT'S HAPPENED MORE THAN ONCE!
THE SHOW MOVES ON. AND THE LOCAL POLICE AREN'T INTERESTED IN FOLLOWING UP ON A CRIME WHEN IT LEAVES THEIR JURISDICTION!
THERE ARE SOME LARGE, DISCERNIBLE PRINTS HERE...
THOSE ARE MY PAW-PRINTS, SWEETIE.
THE CRIME SCENE BOYS CAN'T FIND ANYTHING EXCEPT MY OWN PHYSICAL EVIDENCE, INCLUDING A LOTTA LOST HAIR! OH, I USED TO HAVE A GREAT HEAD O' HAIR LIKE FREDDY HERE!
THE CRIMINAL COULD HAVE PICKED THE LOCKS, UNCLE NED.
NERTS TO THAT TOO, DAPHNE.
COPPERS COULDN'T FIND ANY SIGNS OF LOCK TAMPERING.
THEN IT'S A LOCKED ROOM MYSTERY, UNCLE NED!
PLEASE, FREDDY--
--CAN YOU AND YOUR FRIENDS DO ANYTHING TO HELP AN OLD CLOWN KEEP HIS CARNIVAL TOGETHER?
ABSOLUTELY, UNCLE NED.
AND THE KEY TO SOLVING A LOCKED ROOM MYSTERY IS TO WORK THE PROBLEM FROM BOTH SIDES OF THE LOCKED DOOR!

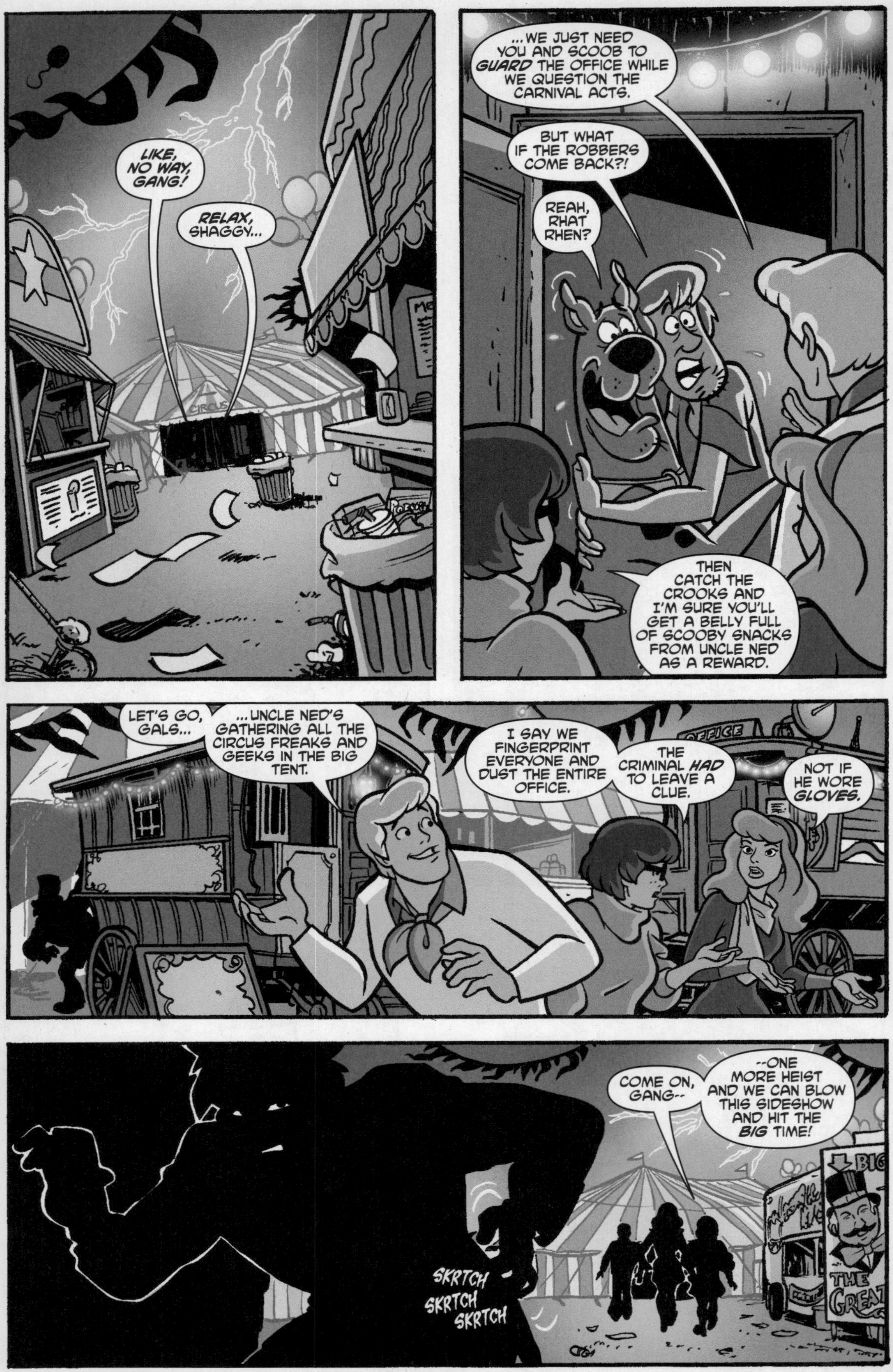
LIKE, NO WAY, GANG!
RELAX, SHAGGY...
...WE JUST NEED YOU AND SCOOB TO GUARD THE OFFICE WHILE WE QUESTION THE CARNIVAL ACTS.
BUT WHAT IF THE ROBBERS COME BACK?!
REAH, RHAT RHEN?
THEN CATCH THE CROOKS AND I'M SURE YOU'LL GET A BELLY FULL OF SCOOBY SNACKS FROM UNCLE NED AS A REWARD.
LET'S GO, GALS...
...UNCLE NED'S GATHERING ALL THE CIRCUS FREAKS AND GEEKS IN THE BIG TENT.
I SAY WE FINGERPRINT EVERYONE AND DUST THE ENTIRE OFFICE.
THE CRIMINAL HAD TO LEAVE A CLUE.
NOT IF HE WORE GLOVES.
COME ON, GANG--
--ONE MORE HEIST AND WE CAN BLOW THIS SIDESHOW AND HIT THE BIG TIME!
SKRTCH
SKRTCH
SKRTCH
THE GREAT

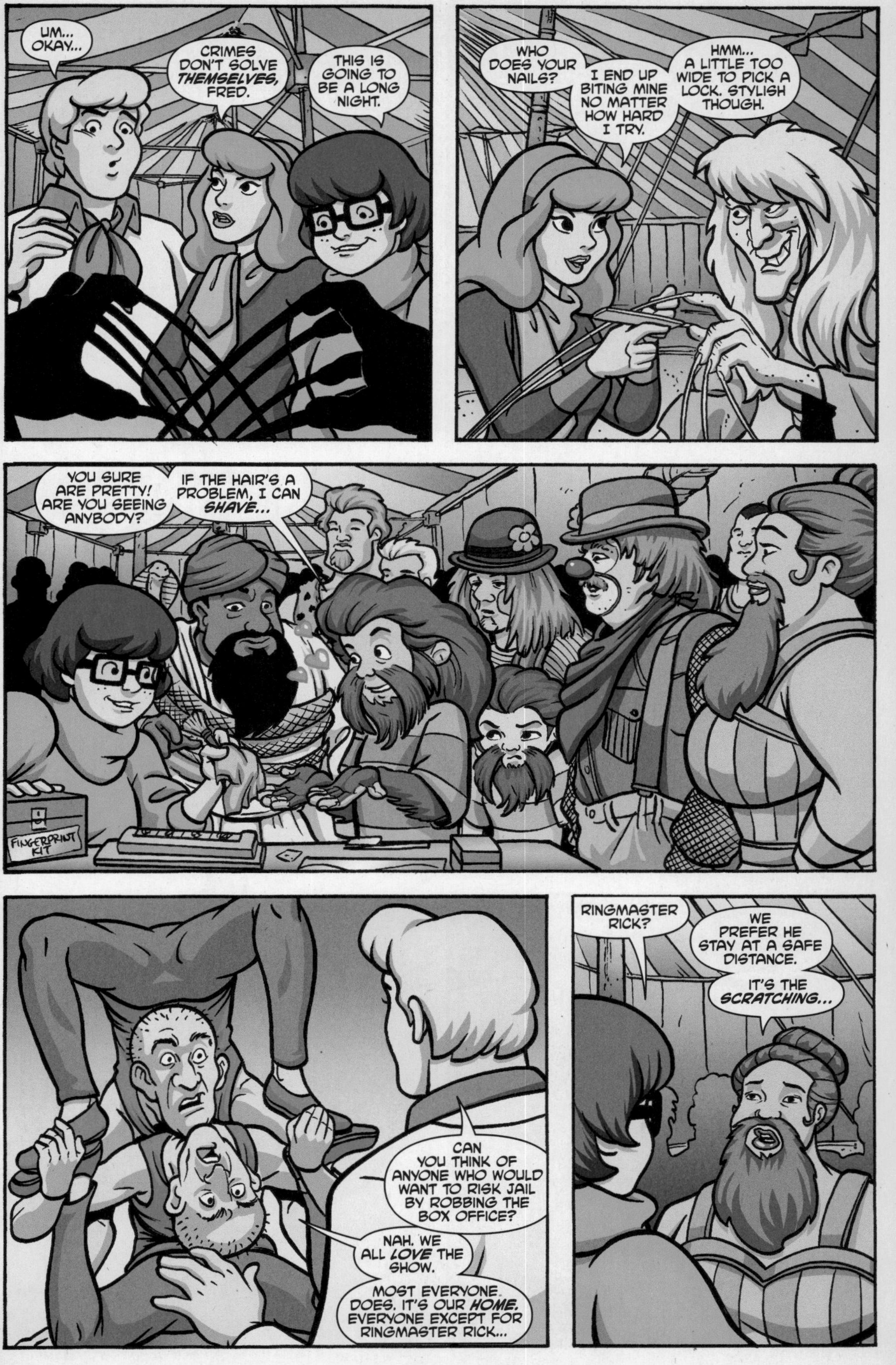
UM... OKAY...
CRIMES DON'T SOLVE *THEMSELVES,* FRED.
THIS IS GOING TO BE A LONG NIGHT.
WHO DOES YOUR NAILS?
I END UP BITING MINE NO MATTER HOW HARD I TRY.
HMM... A LITTLE TOO WIDE TO PICK A LOCK. STYLISH THOUGH.
YOU SURE ARE PRETTY! ARE YOU SEEING ANYBODY?
IF THE HAIR'S A PROBLEM, I CAN *SHAVE...*
FINGERPRINT KIT
CAN YOU THINK OF ANYONE WHO WOULD WANT TO RISK JAIL BY ROBBING THE BOX OFFICE?
NAH. WE ALL *LOVE* THE SHOW.
MOST EVERYONE DOES. IT'S OUR *HOME.* EVERYONE EXCEPT FOR RINGMASTER RICK...
RINGMASTER RICK?
WE PREFER HE STAY AT A SAFE DISTANCE.
IT'S THE *SCRATCHING...*

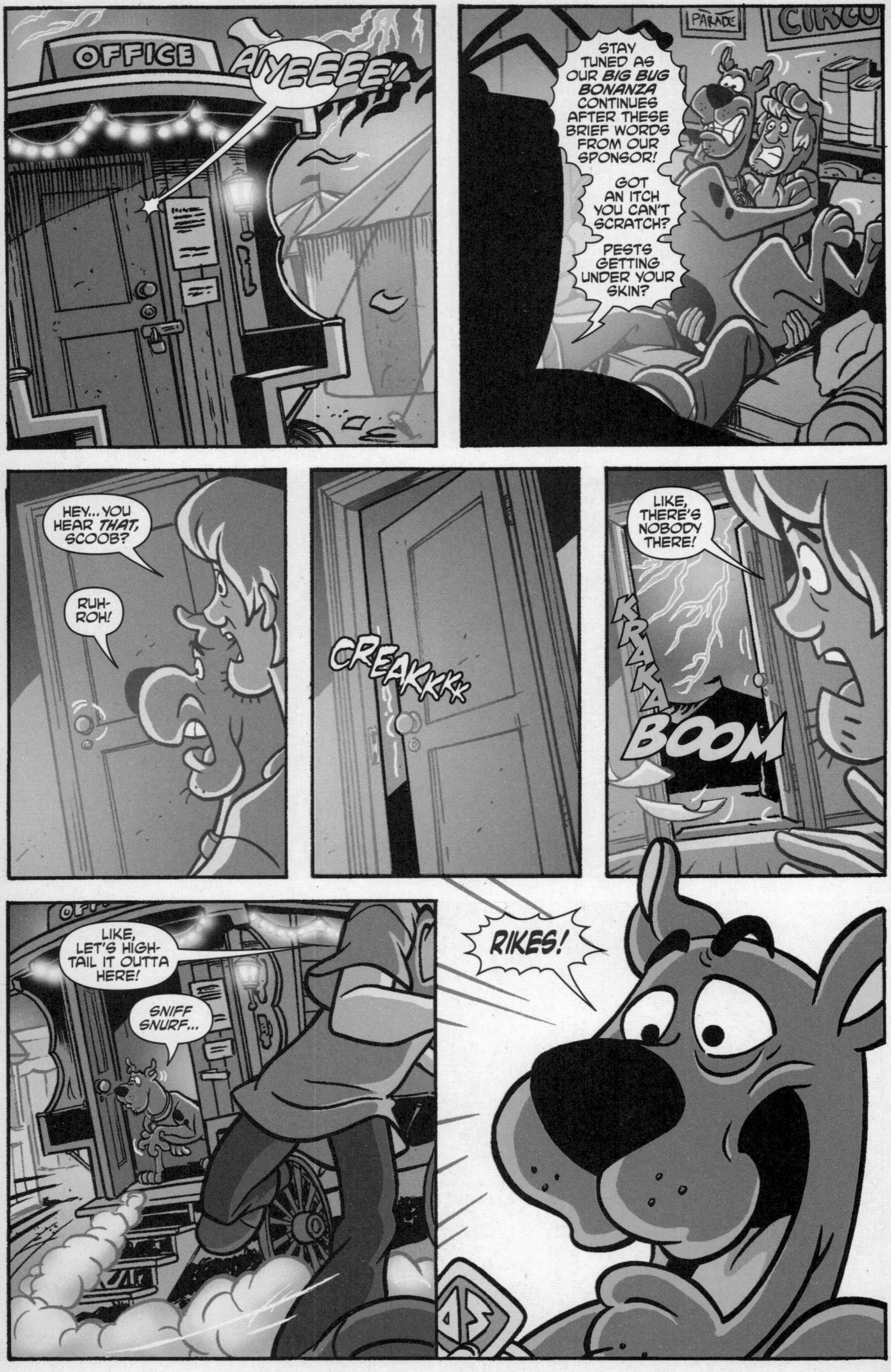
OFFICE
AIYEEEEE!
PARADE
CIRCU
STAY TUNED AS OUR BIG BUG BONANZA CONTINUES AFTER THESE BRIEF WORDS FROM OUR SPONSOR!
GOT AN ITCH YOU CAN'T SCRATCH?
PESTS GETTING UNDER YOUR SKIN?
HEY... YOU HEAR THAT, SCOOB?
RUH-ROH!
CREAKKKK
LIKE, THERE'S NOBODY THERE!
KRAKA BOOM
LIKE, LET'S HIGH-TAIL IT OUTTA HERE!
SNIFF SNURF...
RIKES!

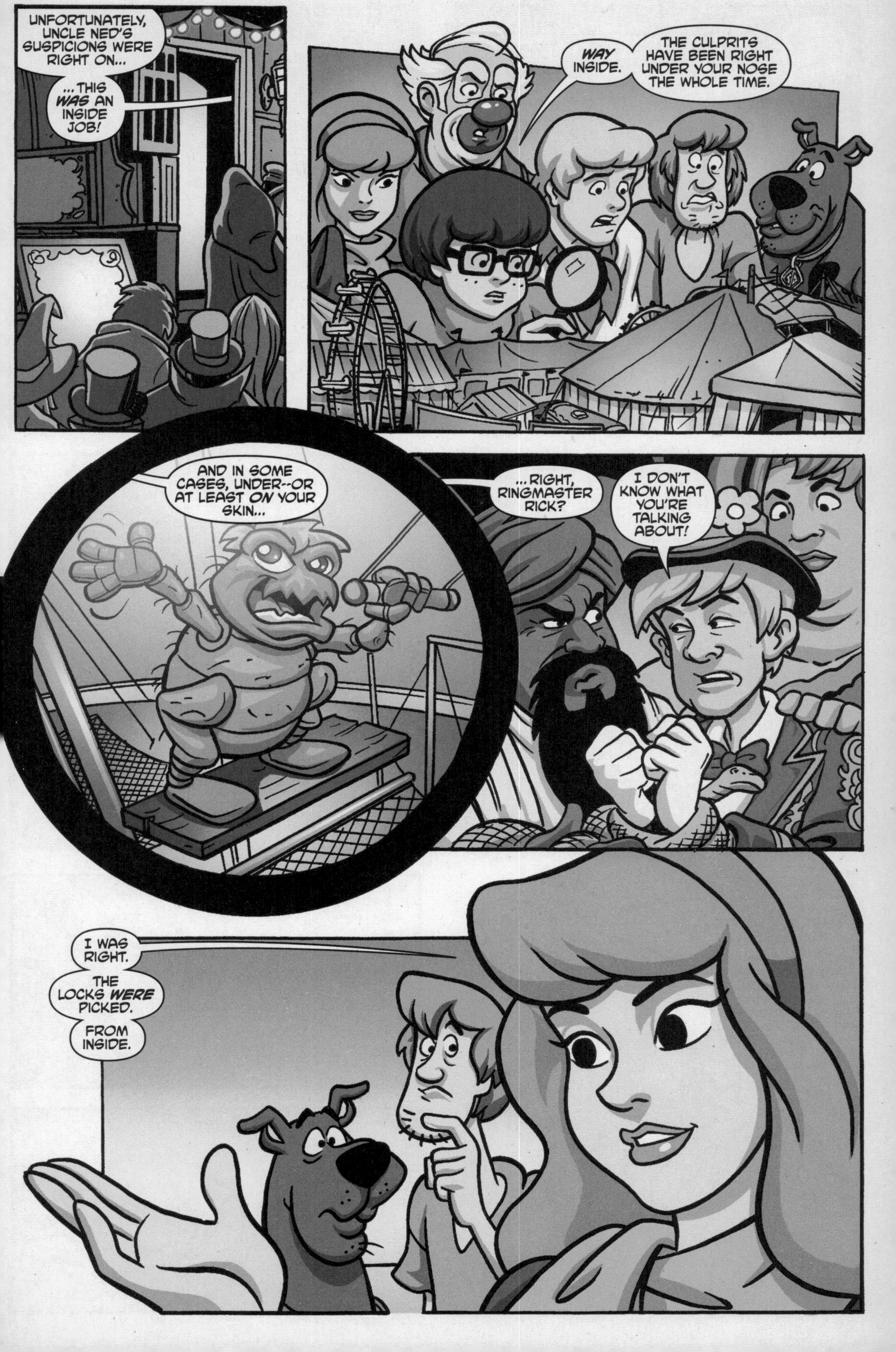
UNFORTUNATELY, UNCLE NED'S SUSPICIONS WERE RIGHT ON...
...THIS *WAS* AN INSIDE JOB!
WAY INSIDE.
THE CULPRITS HAVE BEEN RIGHT UNDER YOUR NOSE THE WHOLE TIME.
AND IN SOME CASES, UNDER--OR AT LEAST *ON* YOUR SKIN...
...RIGHT, RINGMASTER RICK?
I DON'T KNOW WHAT YOU'RE TALKING ABOUT!
I WAS RIGHT.
THE LOCKS *WERE* PICKED.
FROM INSIDE.

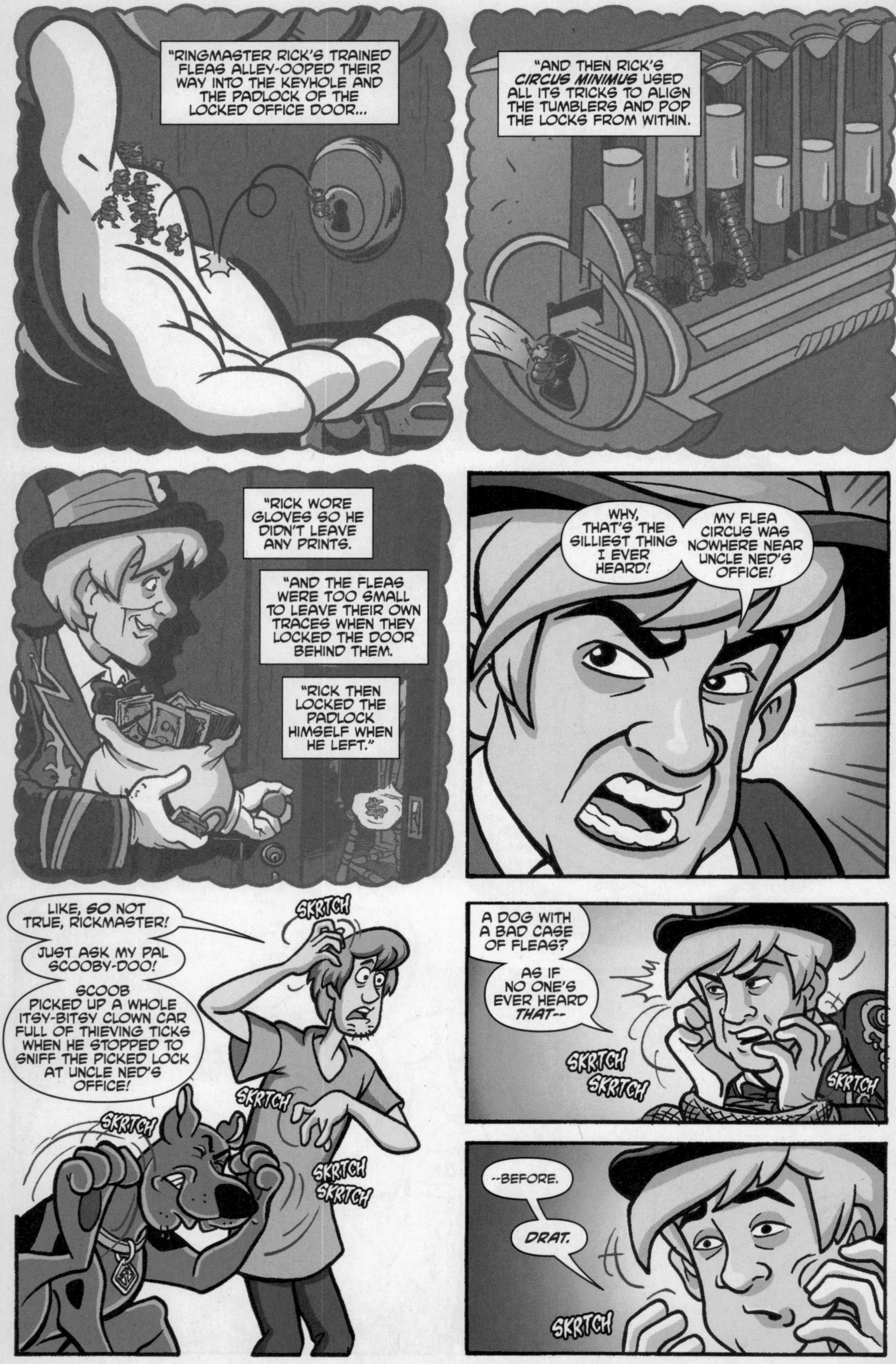
"RINGMASTER RICK'S TRAINED FLEAS ALLEY-OOPED THEIR WAY INTO THE KEYHOLE AND THE PADLOCK OF THE LOCKED OFFICE DOOR...
"AND THEN RICK'S *CIRCUS MINIMUS* USED ALL ITS TRICKS TO ALIGN THE TUMBLERS AND POP THE LOCKS FROM WITHIN.
"RICK WORE GLOVES SO HE DIDN'T LEAVE ANY PRINTS.
"AND THE FLEAS WERE TOO SMALL TO LEAVE THEIR OWN TRACES WHEN THEY LOCKED THE DOOR BEHIND THEM.
"RICK THEN LOCKED THE PADLOCK HIMSELF WHEN HE LEFT."
WHY, THAT'S THE SILLIEST THING I EVER HEARD!
MY FLEA CIRCUS WAS NOWHERE NEAR UNCLE NED'S OFFICE!
LIKE, SO NOT TRUE, RICKMASTER!
JUST ASK MY PAL SCOOBY-DOO!
SCOOB PICKED UP A WHOLE ITSY-BITSY CLOWN CAR FULL OF THIEVING TICKS WHEN HE STOPPED TO SNIFF THE PICKED LOCK AT UNCLE NED'S OFFICE!
SKRTCH
SKRTCH
SKRTCH
SKRTCH
SKRTCH
A DOG WITH A BAD CASE OF FLEAS?
AS IF NO ONE'S EVER HEARD *THAT*--
SKRTCH
SKRTCH
SKRTCH
--BEFORE.
DRAT.
SKRTCH

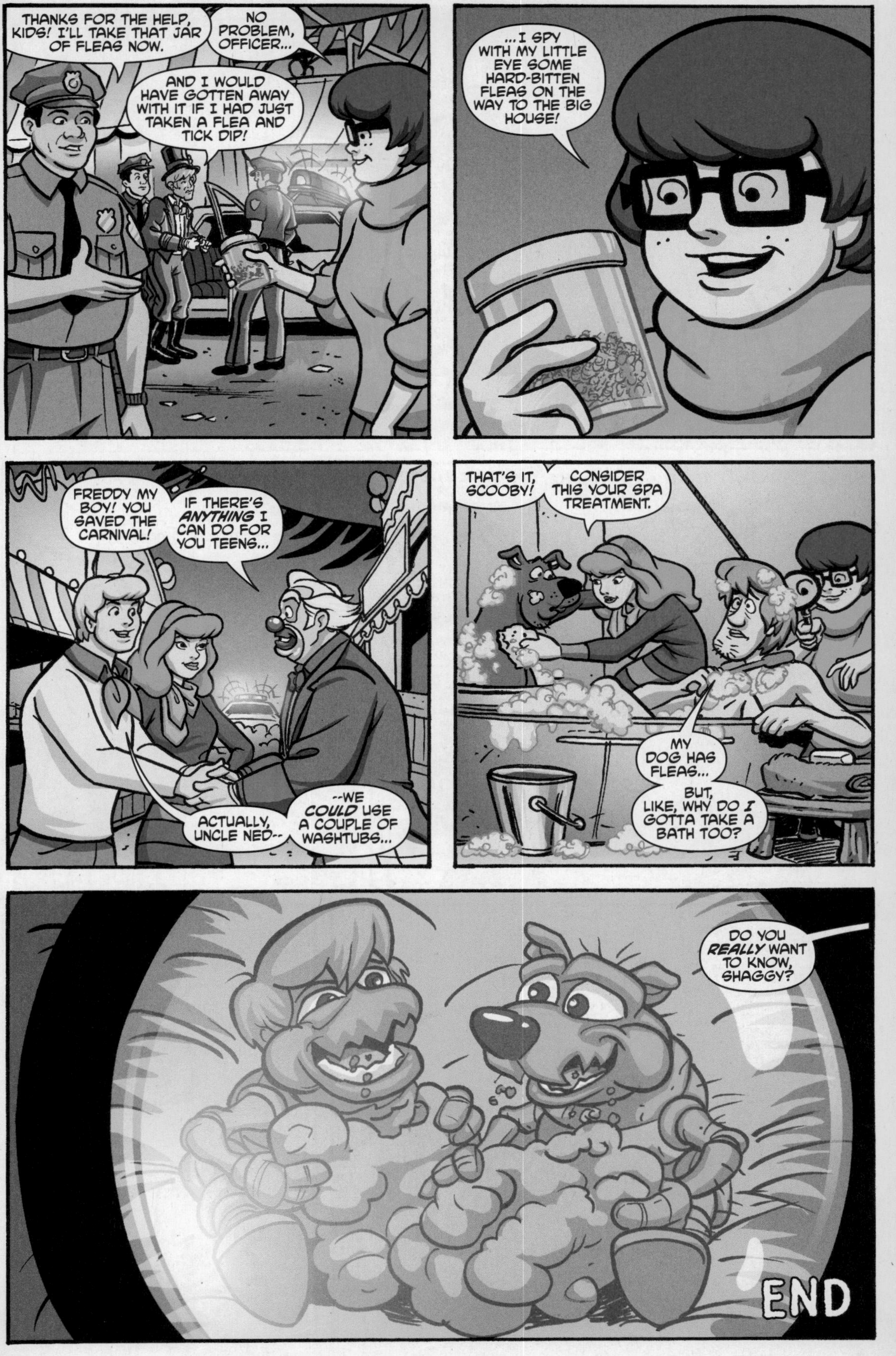
THANKS FOR THE HELP, KIDS! I'LL TAKE THAT JAR OF FLEAS NOW.
NO PROBLEM, OFFICER...
AND I WOULD HAVE GOTTEN AWAY WITH IT IF I HAD JUST TAKEN A FLEA AND TICK DIP!
...I SPY WITH MY LITTLE EYE SOME HARD-BITTEN FLEAS ON THE WAY TO THE BIG HOUSE!
FREDDY MY BOY! YOU SAVED THE CARNIVAL!
IF THERE'S *ANYTHING* I CAN DO FOR YOU TEENS...
ACTUALLY, UNCLE NED--
--WE *COULD* USE A COUPLE OF WASHTUBS...
THAT'S IT, SCOOBY!
CONSIDER THIS YOUR SPA TREATMENT.
MY DOG HAS FLEAS...
BUT, LIKE, WHY DO *I* GOTTA TAKE A BATH TOO?
DO YOU *REALLY* WANT TO KNOW, SHAGGY?
END

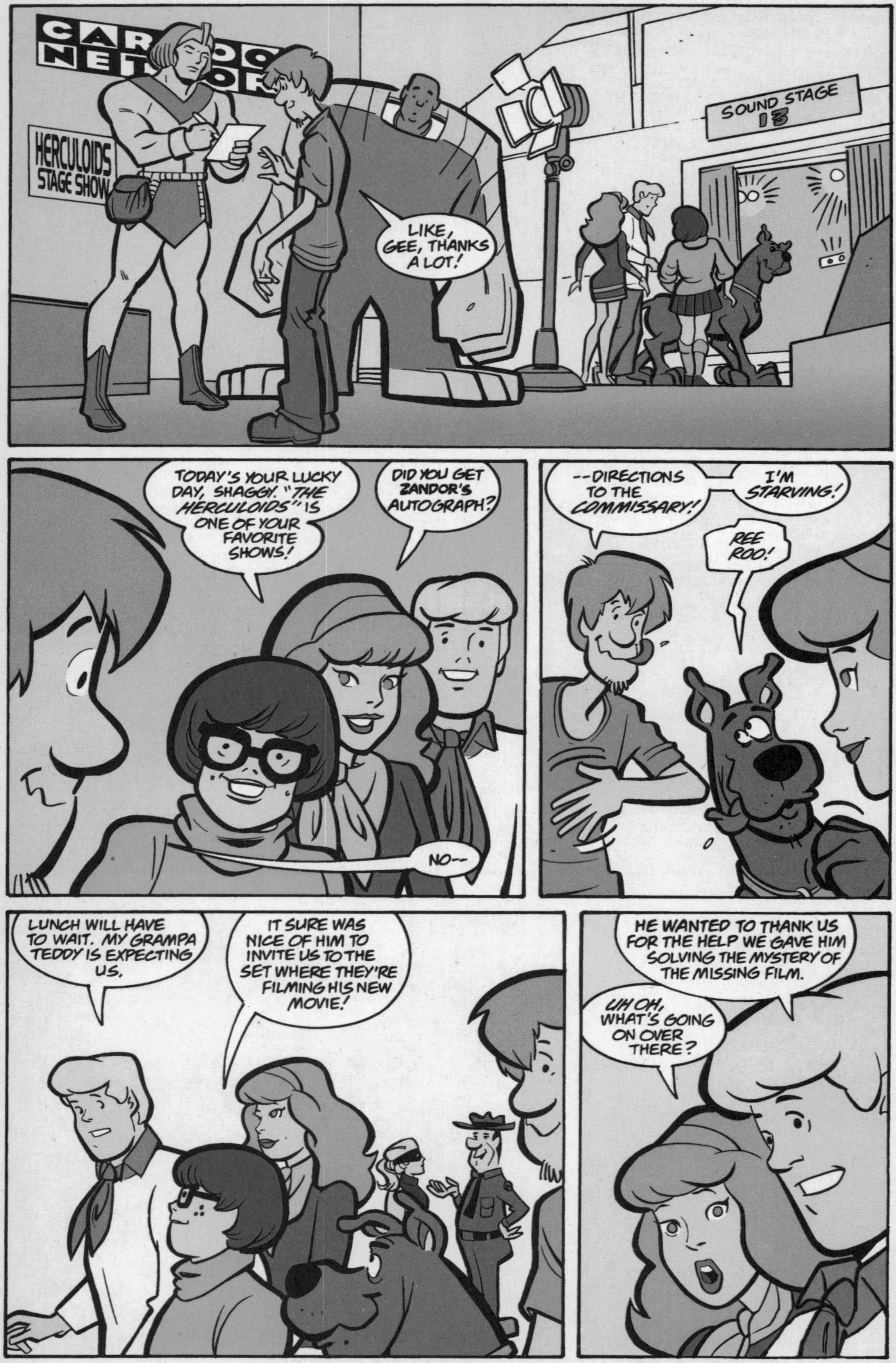
CARTOON NETWORK
HERCULOIDS STAGE SHOW
SOUND STAGE 13
LIKE, GEE, THANKS A LOT!
TODAY'S YOUR LUCKY DAY, SHAGGY. "THE HERCULOIDS" IS ONE OF YOUR FAVORITE SHOWS!
DID YOU GET ZANDOR'S AUTOGRAPH?
NO--
--DIRECTIONS TO THE COMMISSARY!
I'M STARVING!
REE ROO!
LUNCH WILL HAVE TO WAIT. MY GRAMPA TEDDY IS EXPECTING US.
IT SURE WAS NICE OF HIM TO INVITE US TO THE SET WHERE THEY'RE FILMING HIS NEW MOVIE!
HE WANTED TO THANK US FOR THE HELP WE GAVE HIM SOLVING THE MYSTERY OF THE MISSING FILM.
UH OH, WHAT'S GOING ON OVER THERE?

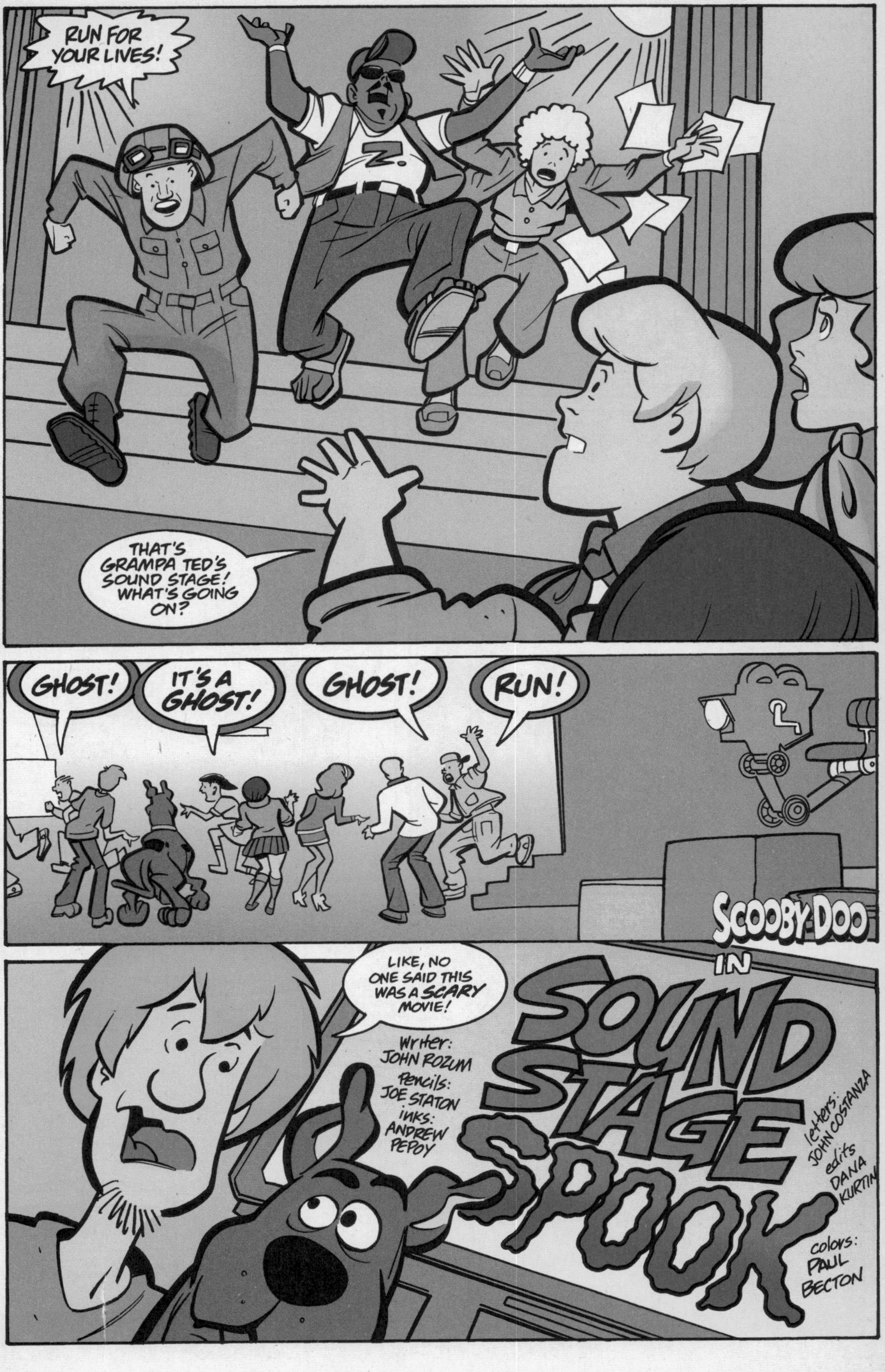
RUN FOR YOUR LIVES!
THAT'S GRAMPA TED'S SOUND STAGE! WHAT'S GOING ON?
GHOST!
IT'S A GHOST!
GHOST!
RUN!
SCOOBY-DOO
IN
SOUND STAGE SPOOK
LIKE, NO ONE SAID THIS WAS A SCARY MOVIE!
writer: JOHN ROZUM
pencils: JOE STATON
inks: ANDREW PEPOY
letters: JOHN COSTANZA
edits DANA KURTIN
colors: PAUL BECTON

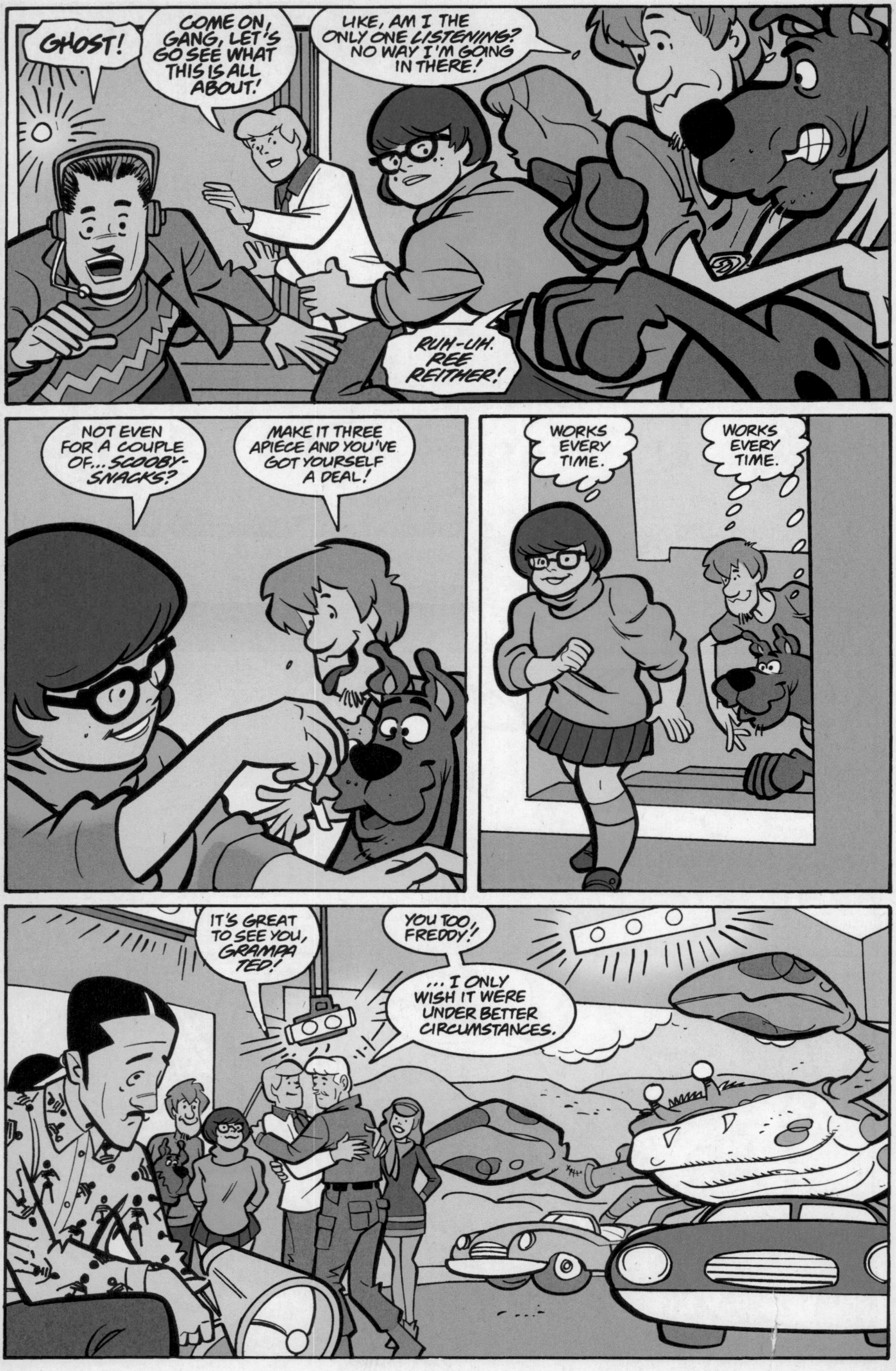
GHOST!
COME ON, GANG, LET'S GO SEE WHAT THIS IS ALL ABOUT!
LIKE, AM I THE ONLY ONE LISTENING? NO WAY I'M GOING IN THERE!
RUH-UH. REE REITHER!
NOT EVEN FOR A COUPLE OF... SCOOBY-SNACKS?
MAKE IT THREE APIECE AND YOU'VE GOT YOURSELF A DEAL!
WORKS EVERY TIME.
WORKS EVERY TIME.
IT'S GREAT TO SEE YOU, GRAMPA TED!
YOU TOO, FREDDY!
... I ONLY WISH IT WERE UNDER BETTER CIRCUMSTANCES.

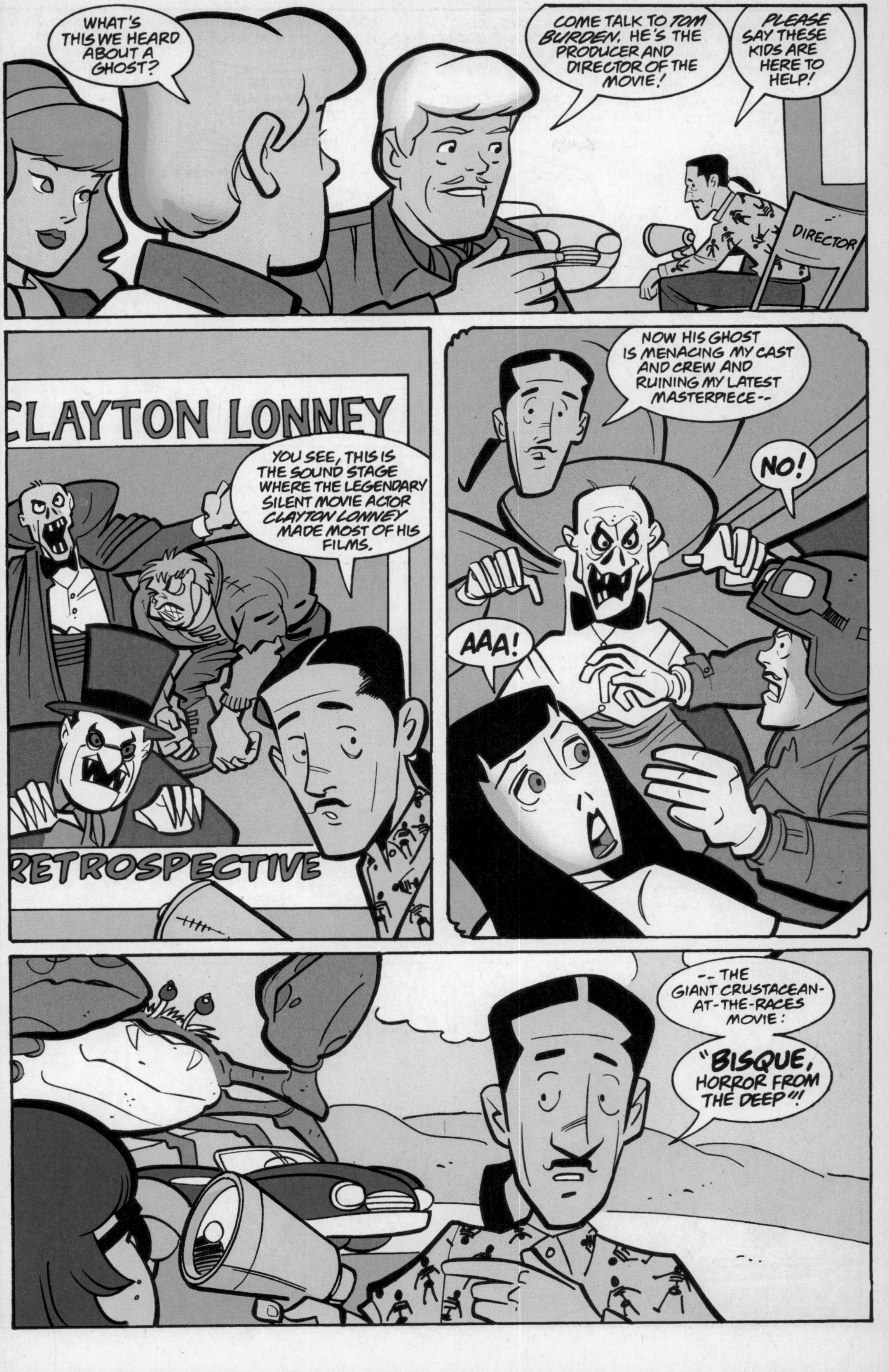
WHAT'S THIS WE HEARD ABOUT A GHOST?
COME TALK TO *TOM BURDEN*. HE'S THE PRODUCER AND DIRECTOR OF THE MOVIE!
PLEASE SAY THESE KIDS ARE HERE TO HELP!
DIRECTOR
CLAYTON LONNEY
YOU SEE, THIS IS THE SOUND STAGE WHERE THE LEGENDARY SILENT MOVIE ACTOR *CLAYTON LONNEY* MADE MOST OF HIS FILMS.
RETROSPECTIVE
NOW HIS GHOST IS MENACING MY CAST AND CREW AND RUINING MY LATEST *MASTERPIECE* --
NO!
AAA!
-- THE GIANT CRUSTACEAN-AT-THE-RACES MOVIE:
"BISQUE, HORROR FROM THE DEEP"!

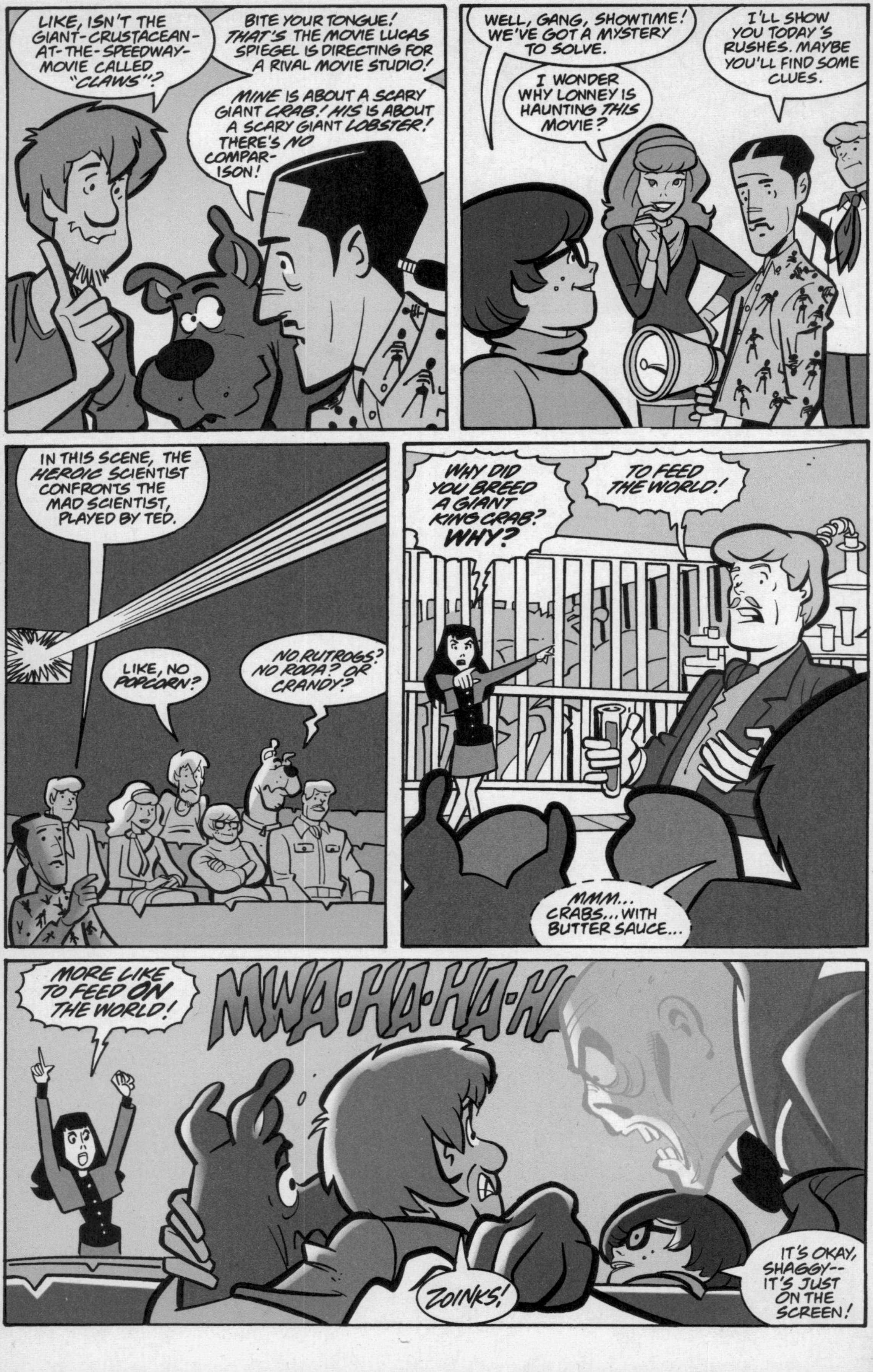
LIKE, ISN'T THE GIANT-CRUSTACEAN-AT-THE-SPEEDWAY-MOVIE CALLED "CLAWS"?
BITE YOUR TONGUE! THAT'S THE MOVIE LUCAS SPIEGEL IS DIRECTING FOR A RIVAL MOVIE STUDIO!
MINE IS ABOUT A SCARY GIANT CRAB! HIS IS ABOUT A SCARY GIANT LOBSTER! THERE'S NO COMPARISON!
WELL, GANG, SHOWTIME! WE'VE GOT A MYSTERY TO SOLVE.
I WONDER WHY LONNEY IS HAUNTING THIS MOVIE?
I'LL SHOW YOU TODAY'S RUSHES. MAYBE YOU'LL FIND SOME CLUES.
IN THIS SCENE, THE HEROIC SCIENTIST CONFRONTS THE MAD SCIENTIST, PLAYED BY TED.
LIKE, NO POPCORN?
NO RUTROGS? NO RODA? OR CRANDY?
WHY DID YOU BREED A GIANT KING CRAB? WHY?
TO FEED THE WORLD!
MMM... CRABS... WITH BUTTER SAUCE...
MORE LIKE TO FEED ON THE WORLD!
MWA-HA-HA-H
ZOINKS!
IT'S OKAY, SHAGGY-- IT'S JUST ON THE SCREEN!

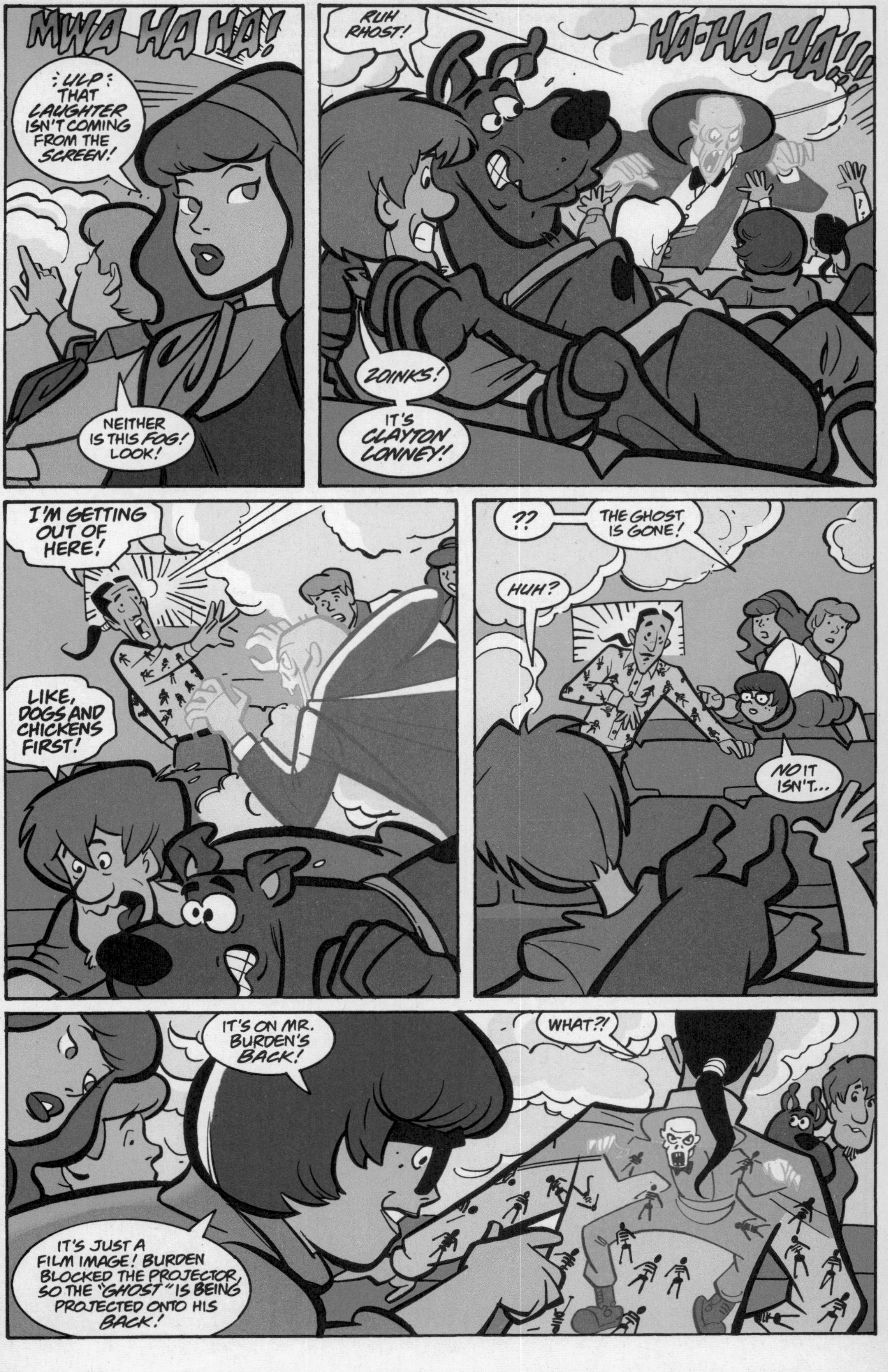
MWA HA HA!
:ULP: THAT LAUGHTER ISN'T COMING FROM THE SCREEN!
NEITHER IS THIS FOG! LOOK!
RUH RHOST!
HA-HA-HA!!!
ZOINKS!
IT'S CLAYTON LONNEY!
I'M GETTING OUT OF HERE!
LIKE, DOGS AND CHICKENS FIRST!
??
THE GHOST IS GONE!
HUH?
NO IT ISN'T...
IT'S ON MR. BURDEN'S BACK!
WHAT?!
IT'S JUST A FILM IMAGE! BURDEN BLOCKED THE PROJECTOR, SO THE "GHOST" IS BEING PROJECTED ONTO HIS BACK!

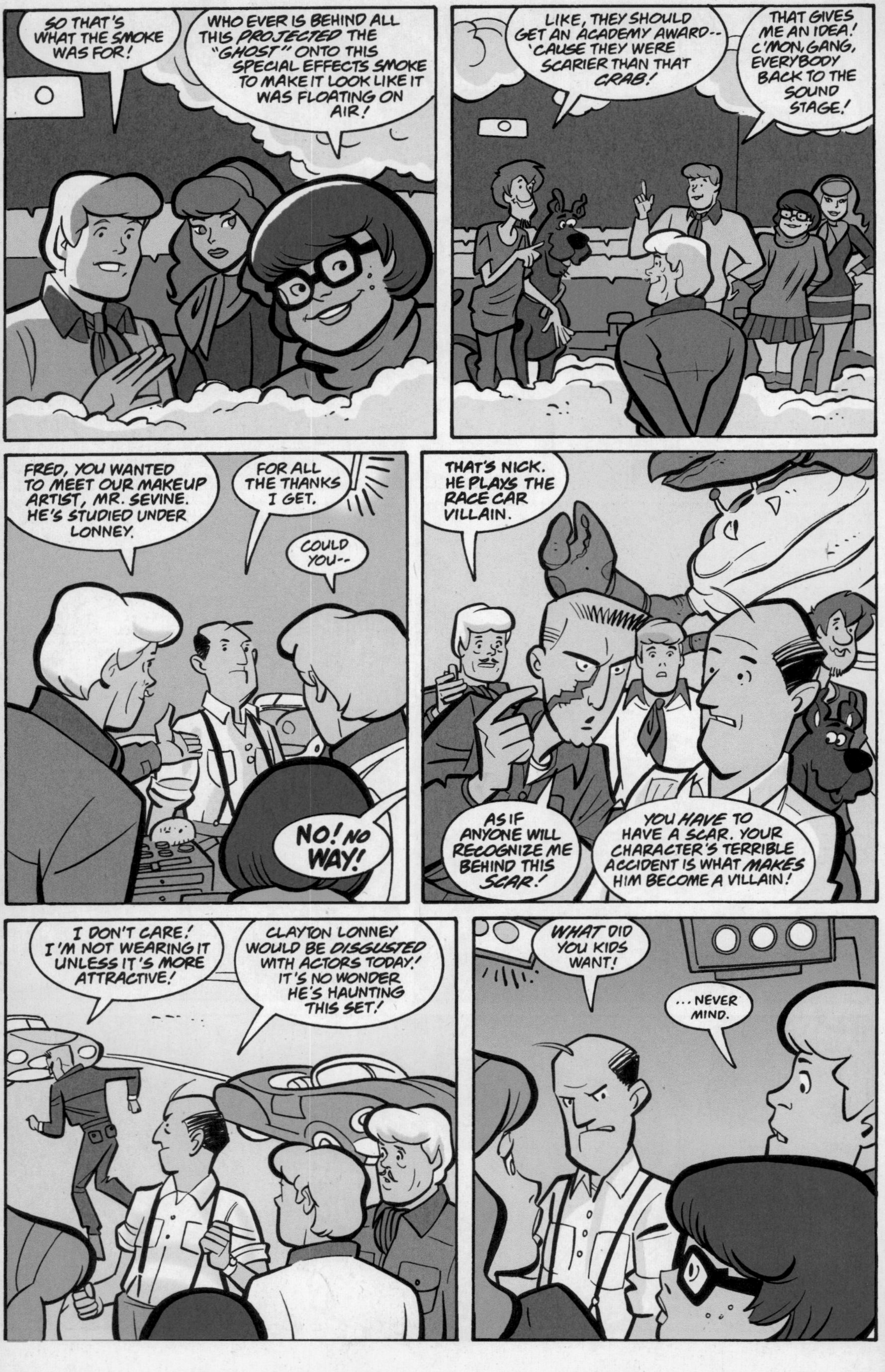

SO THAT'S WHAT THE SMOKE WAS FOR!
WHO EVER IS BEHIND ALL THIS PROJECTED THE "GHOST" ONTO THIS SPECIAL EFFECTS SMOKE TO MAKE IT LOOK LIKE IT WAS FLOATING ON AIR!
LIKE, THEY SHOULD GET AN ACADEMY AWARD-- 'CAUSE THEY WERE SCARIER THAN THAT CRAB!
THAT GIVES ME AN IDEA! C'MON, GANG, EVERYBODY BACK TO THE SOUND STAGE!
FRED, YOU WANTED TO MEET OUR MAKEUP ARTIST, MR. SEVINE. HE'S STUDIED UNDER LONNEY.
FOR ALL THE THANKS I GET.
COULD YOU--
NO! NO WAY!
THAT'S NICK. HE PLAYS THE RACE CAR VILLAIN.
AS IF ANYONE WILL RECOGNIZE ME BEHIND THIS SCAR!
YOU HAVE TO HAVE A SCAR. YOUR CHARACTER'S TERRIBLE ACCIDENT IS WHAT MAKES HIM BECOME A VILLAIN!
I DON'T CARE! I'M NOT WEARING IT UNLESS IT'S MORE ATTRACTIVE!
CLAYTON LONNEY WOULD BE DISGUSTED WITH ACTORS TODAY! IT'S NO WONDER HE'S HAUNTING THIS SET!
WHAT DID YOU KIDS WANT!
... NEVER MIND.

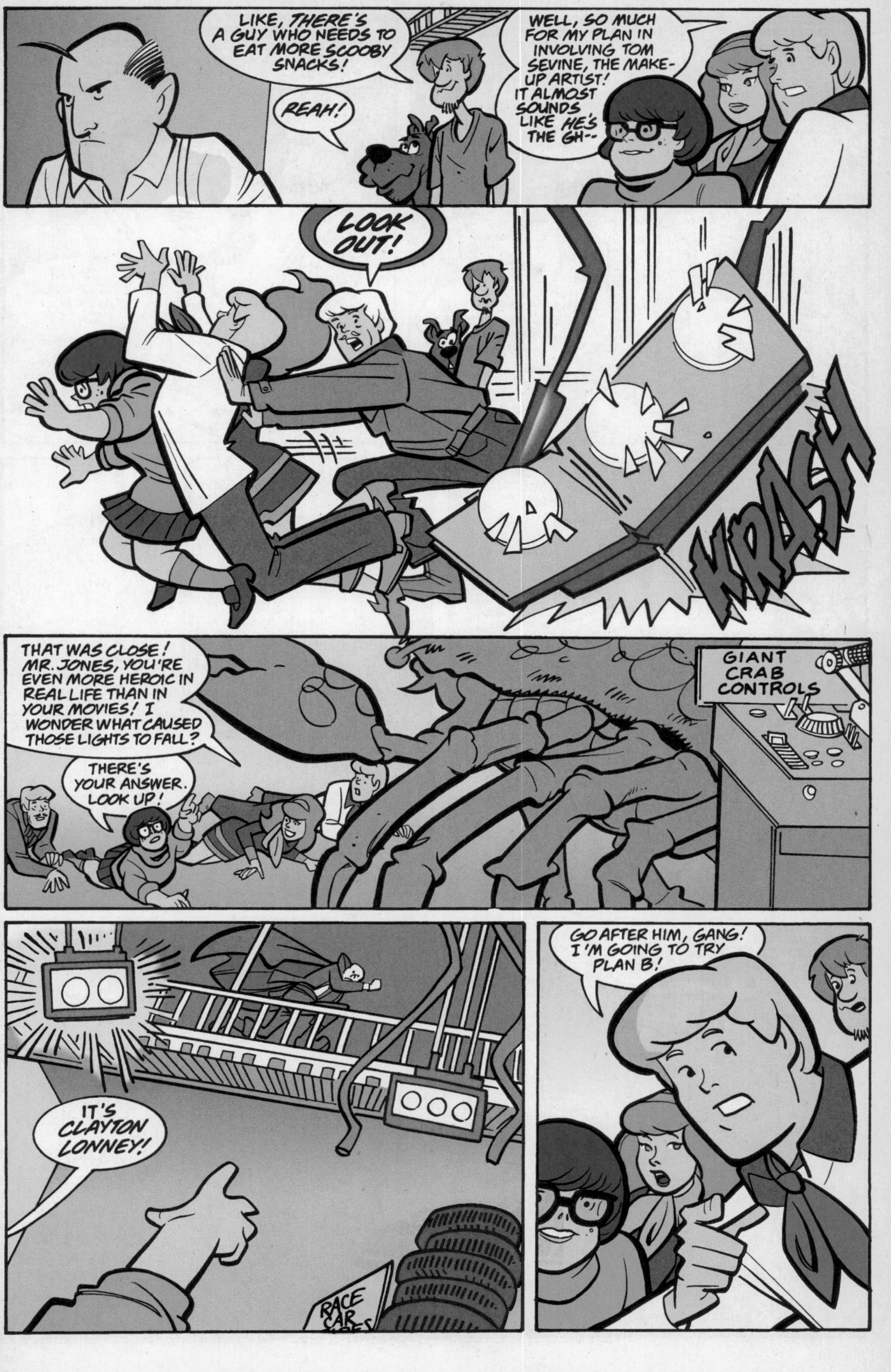
LIKE, THERE'S A GUY WHO NEEDS TO EAT MORE SCOOBY SNACKS!
REAH!
WELL, SO MUCH FOR MY PLAN IN INVOLVING TOM SEVINE, THE MAKE-UP ARTIST! IT ALMOST SOUNDS LIKE HE'S THE GH--
LOOK OUT!
KRASH
THAT WAS CLOSE! MR. JONES, YOU'RE EVEN MORE HEROIC IN REAL LIFE THAN IN YOUR MOVIES! I WONDER WHAT CAUSED THOSE LIGHTS TO FALL?
GIANT CRAB CONTROLS
THERE'S YOUR ANSWER. LOOK UP!
IT'S CLAYTON LONNEY!
GO AFTER HIM, GANG! I'M GOING TO TRY PLAN B!

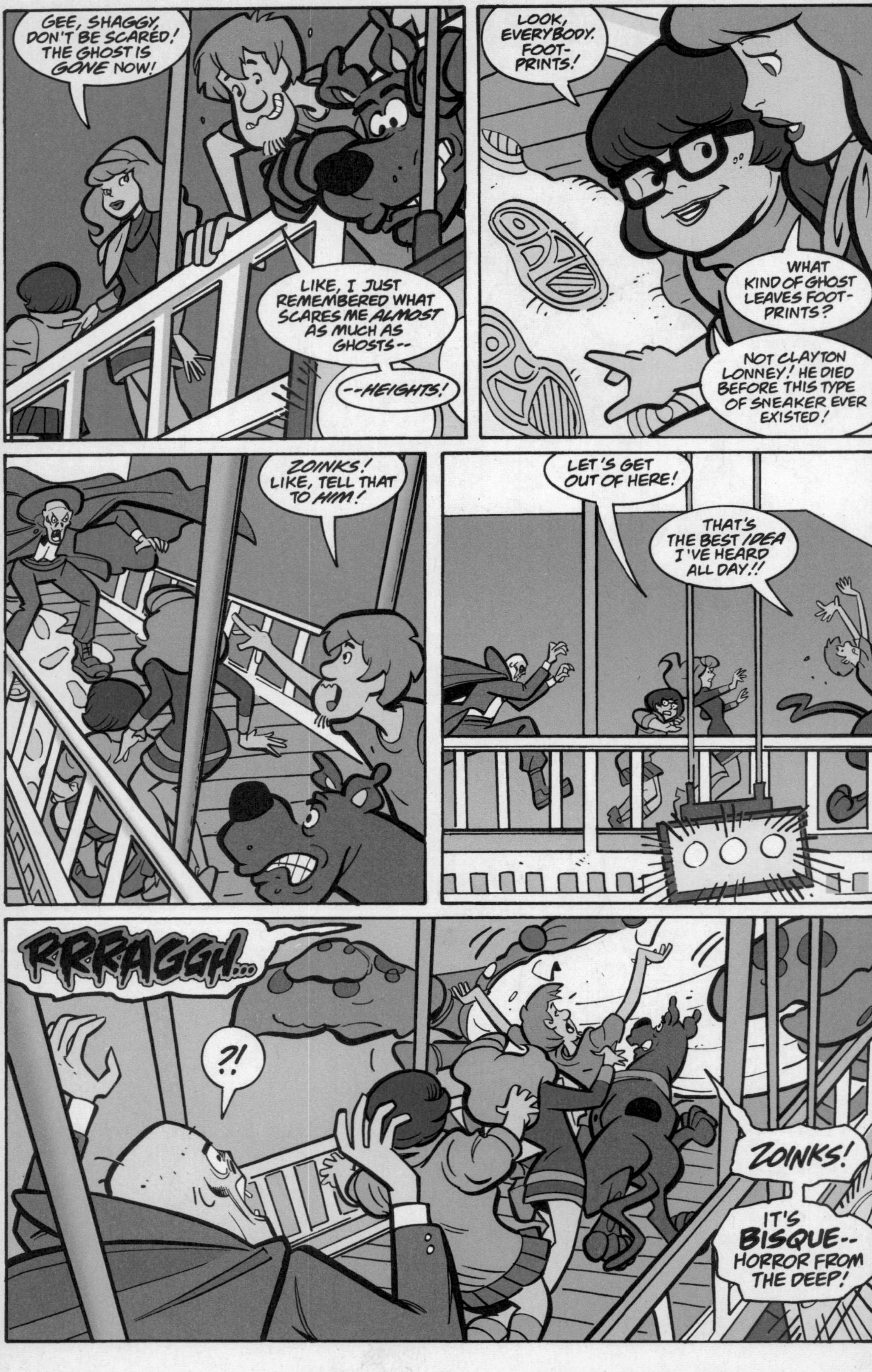
GEE, SHAGGY, DON'T BE SCARED! THE GHOST IS GONE NOW!
LIKE, I JUST REMEMBERED WHAT SCARES ME ALMOST AS MUCH AS GHOSTS--
--HEIGHTS!
LOOK, EVERYBODY. FOOT-PRINTS!
WHAT KIND OF GHOST LEAVES FOOT-PRINTS?
NOT CLAYTON LONNEY! HE DIED BEFORE THIS TYPE OF SNEAKER EVER EXISTED!
ZOINKS! LIKE, TELL THAT TO HIM!
LET'S GET OUT OF HERE!
THAT'S THE BEST IDEA I'VE HEARD ALL DAY!!
RRRAGGH...
?!
ZOINKS!
IT'S BISQUE-- HORROR FROM THE DEEP!

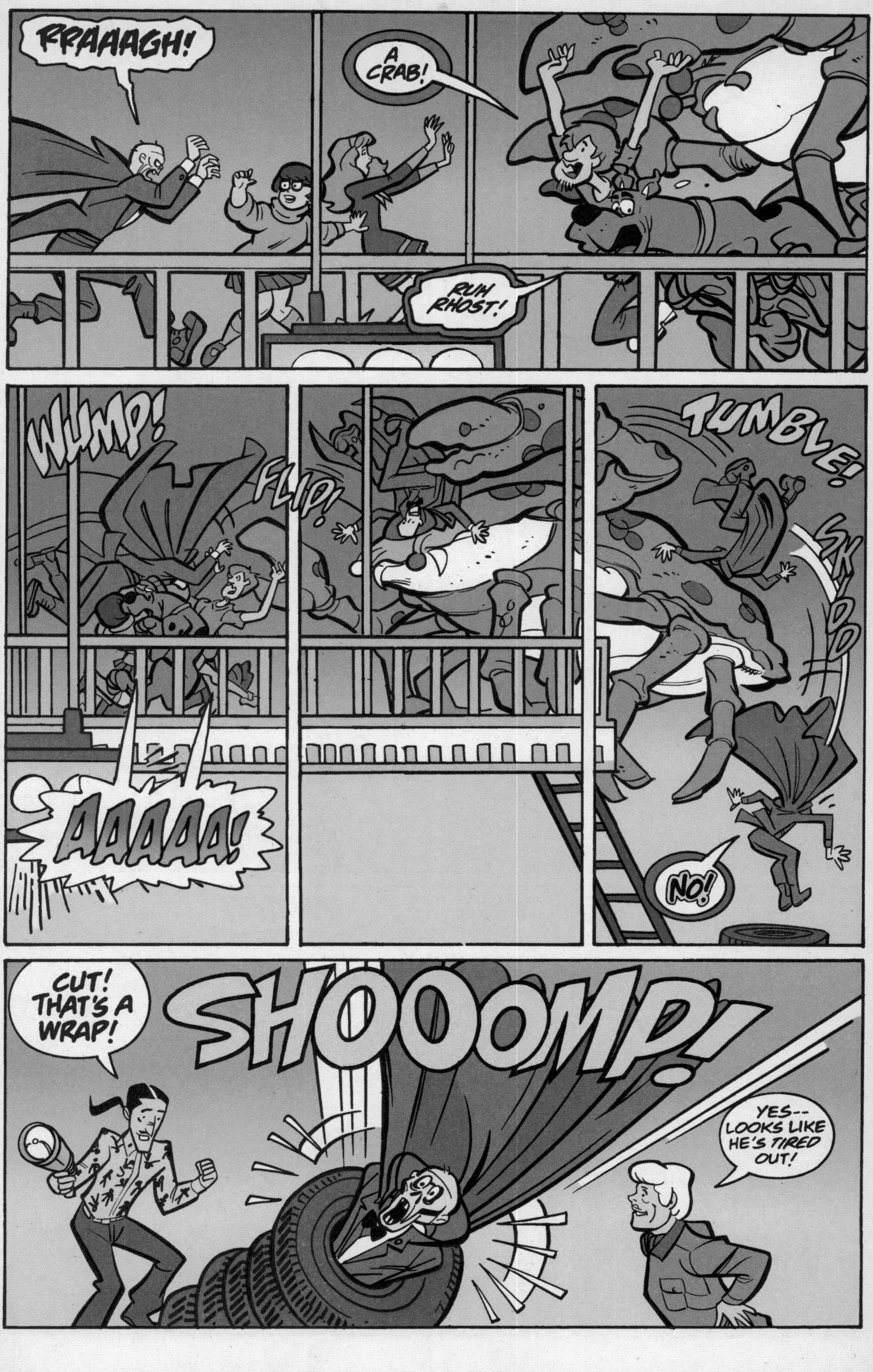
FRAAAGH!
A CRAB!
RUH RHOST!
WUMP!
FLIP!
TUMBLE!
SKIDOO
AAAAA!
NO!
CUT! THAT'S A WRAP!
SHOOOMP!
YES-- LOOKS LIKE HE'S TIRED OUT!

NICE WORK, KIDS! NOW LET'S SEE WHO THIS "GHOST" IS.

IT'S LUCAS SPIEGEL, THE DIRECTOR OF "CLAWS"!

THE OTHER GIANT CRAB MOVIE?

"LOBSTER!" IT'S A LOBSTER!

MR. SPIEGEL WAS TRYING TO STOP YOUR MOVIE SO THAT HIS WOULD MAKE IT INTO THE THEATERS FIRST!

ONLY A DIRECTOR WITH HIS SPECIAL EFFECTS KNOWHOW COULD HAVE CREATED THAT "GHOST" IN THE FOG IN THE SCREENING ROOM!

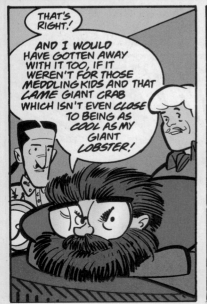

THAT'S RIGHT!

AND I WOULD HAVE GOTTEN AWAY WITH IT TOO, IF IT WEREN'T FOR THOSE MEDDLING KIDS AND THAT LAME GIANT CRAB WHICH ISN'T EVEN CLOSE TO BEING AS COOL AS MY GIANT LOBSTER!

LIKE, I'M GLAD WE SOLVED THE MYSTERY--

--BECAUSE WE'RE GONNA BE CRUSTACEAN KIBBLE!

RAAR!

ROOK ROUT!

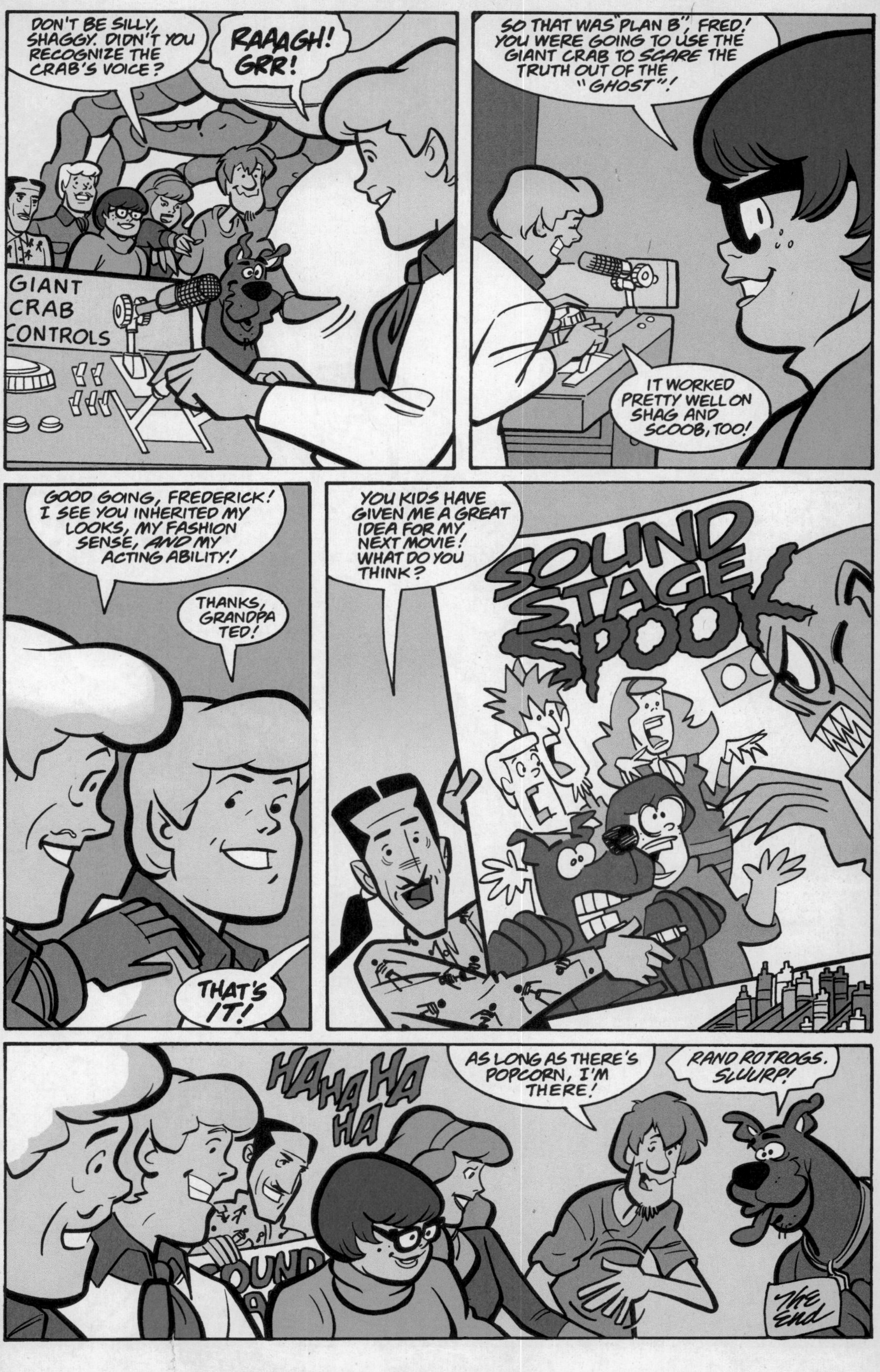
DON'T BE SILLY, SHAGGY. DIDN'T YOU RECOGNIZE THE CRAB'S VOICE?
RAAAGH! GRR!
GIANT CRAB CONTROLS
SO THAT WAS "PLAN B", FRED! YOU WERE GOING TO USE THE GIANT CRAB TO SCARE THE TRUTH OUT OF THE "GHOST"!
IT WORKED PRETTY WELL ON SHAG AND SCOOB, TOO!
GOOD GOING, FREDERICK! I SEE YOU INHERITED MY LOOKS, MY FASHION SENSE, AND MY ACTING ABILITY!
THANKS, GRANDPA TED!
THAT'S IT!
YOU KIDS HAVE GIVEN ME A GREAT IDEA FOR MY NEXT MOVIE! WHAT DO YOU THINK?
SOUND STAGE SPOOK
HA HA HA HA HA
AS LONG AS THERE'S POPCORN, I'M THERE!
RAND ROTROGS. SLUURP!
The End

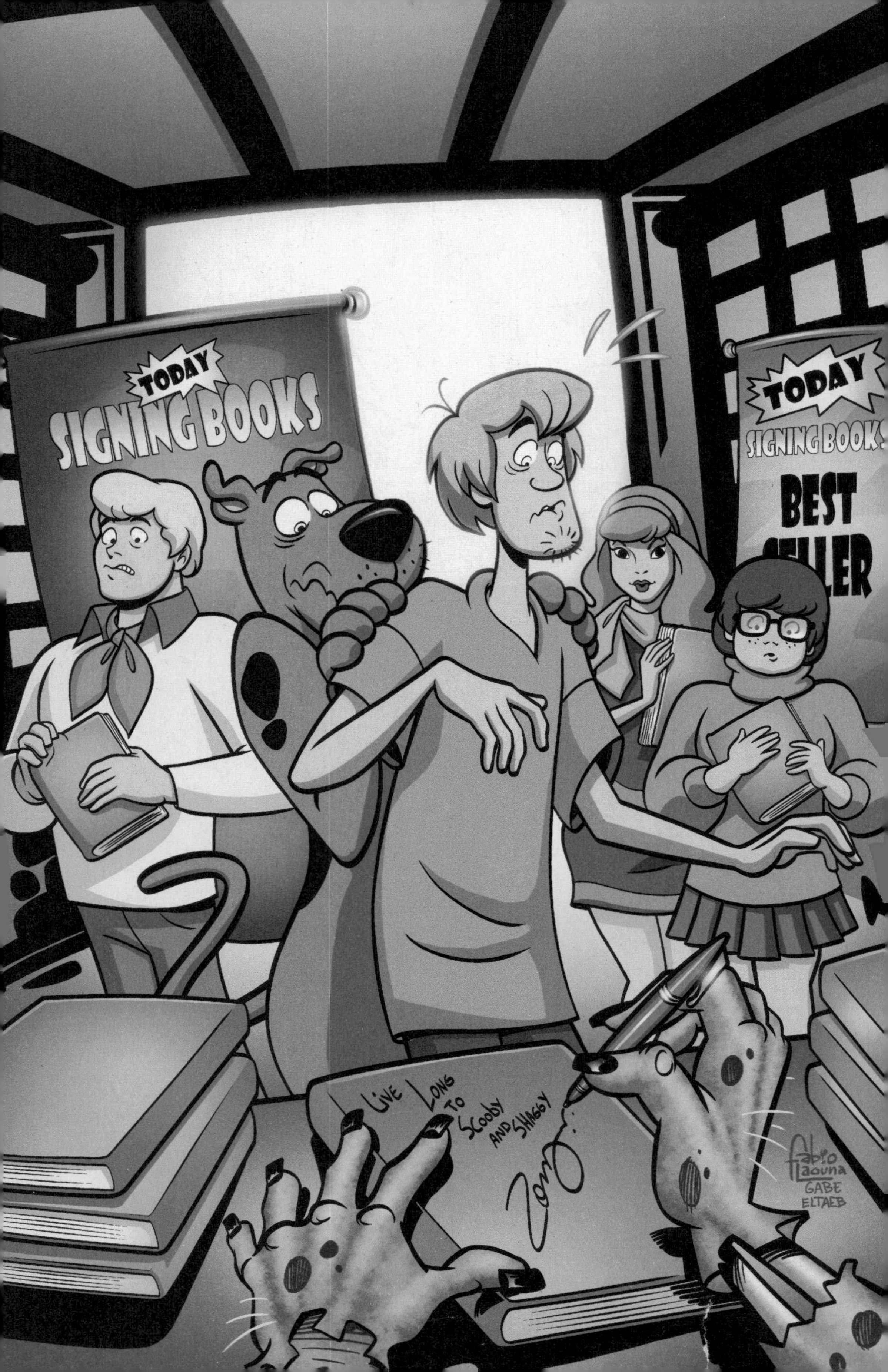
TODAY
SIGNING BOOKS
TODAY
SIGNING BOOKS
BEST
SELLER
LIVE LONG TO SCOOBY AND SHAGGY
ZOMBIE
Fabio Laguna
GABE ELTAEB

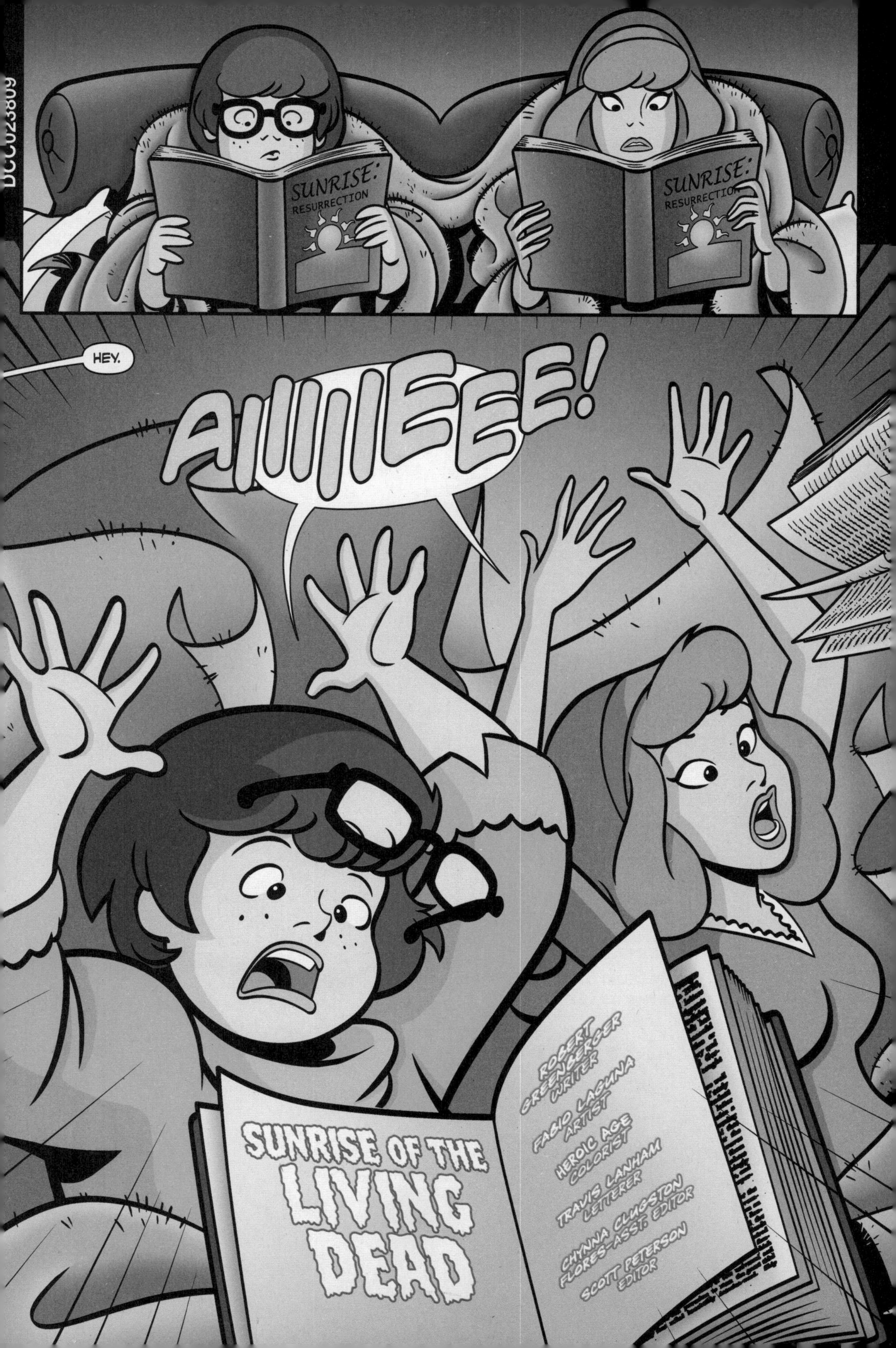
SUNRISE: RESURRECTION
SUNRISE: RESURRECTION
HEY.
AIIIIIEEE!
SUNRISE OF THE LIVING DEAD
ROBERT GREENBERGER WRITER
FABIO LAGUNA ARTIST
HEROIC AGE COLORIST
TRAVIS LANHAM LETTERER
CHYNNA CLUGSTON FLORES-ASST. EDITOR
SCOTT PETERSON EDITOR

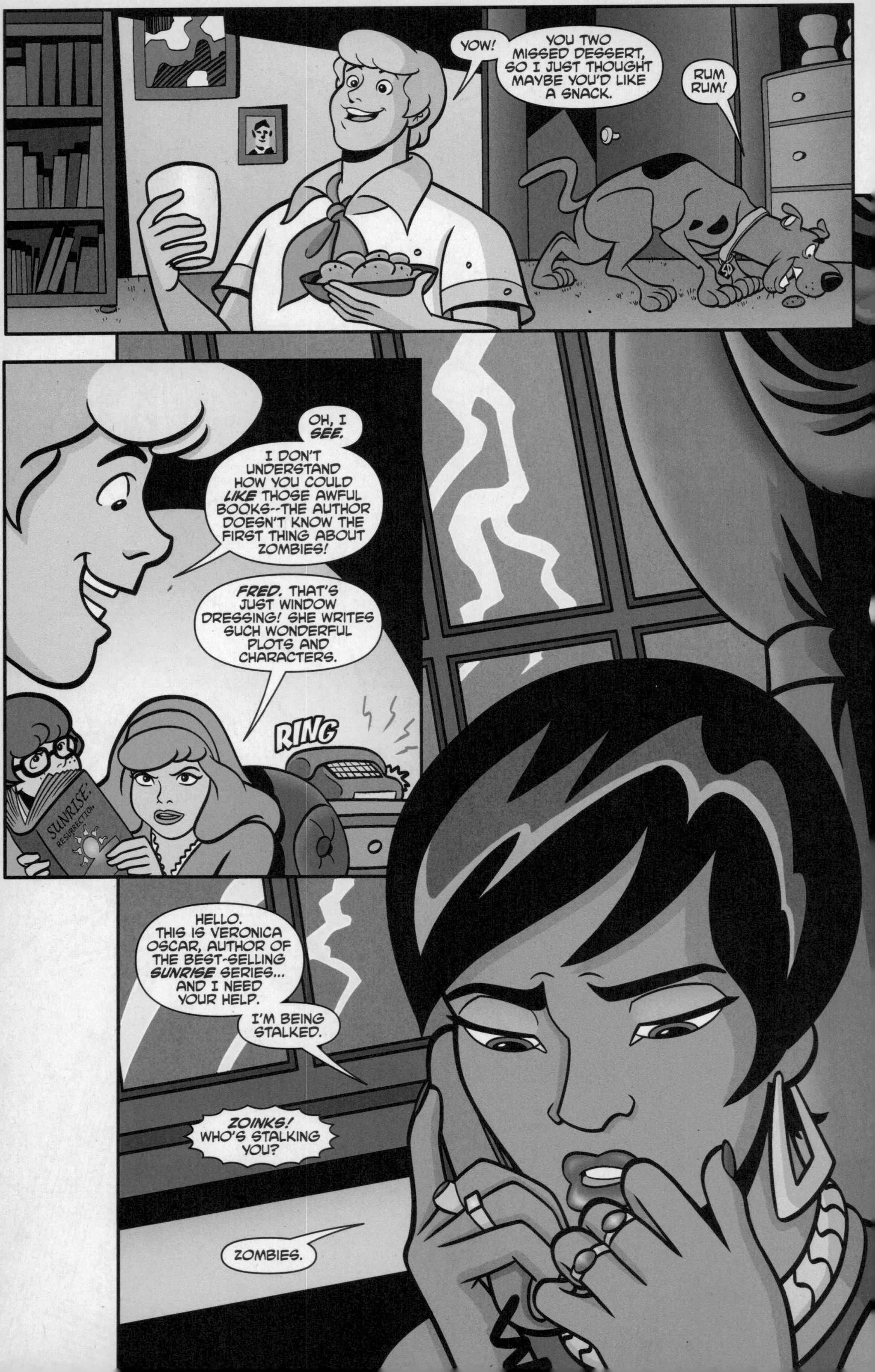
YOW!
YOU TWO MISSED DESSERT, SO I JUST THOUGHT MAYBE YOU'D LIKE A SNACK.
RUM RUM!
OH, I SEE.
I DON'T UNDERSTAND HOW YOU COULD LIKE THOSE AWFUL BOOKS--THE AUTHOR DOESN'T KNOW THE FIRST THING ABOUT ZOMBIES!
FRED. THAT'S JUST WINDOW DRESSING! SHE WRITES SUCH WONDERFUL PLOTS AND CHARACTERS.
RING
SUNRISE: RESURRECTIO
HELLO. THIS IS VERONICA OSCAR, AUTHOR OF THE BEST-SELLING SUNRISE SERIES... AND I NEED YOUR HELP.
I'M BEING STALKED.
ZOINKS! WHO'S STALKING YOU?
ZOMBIES.

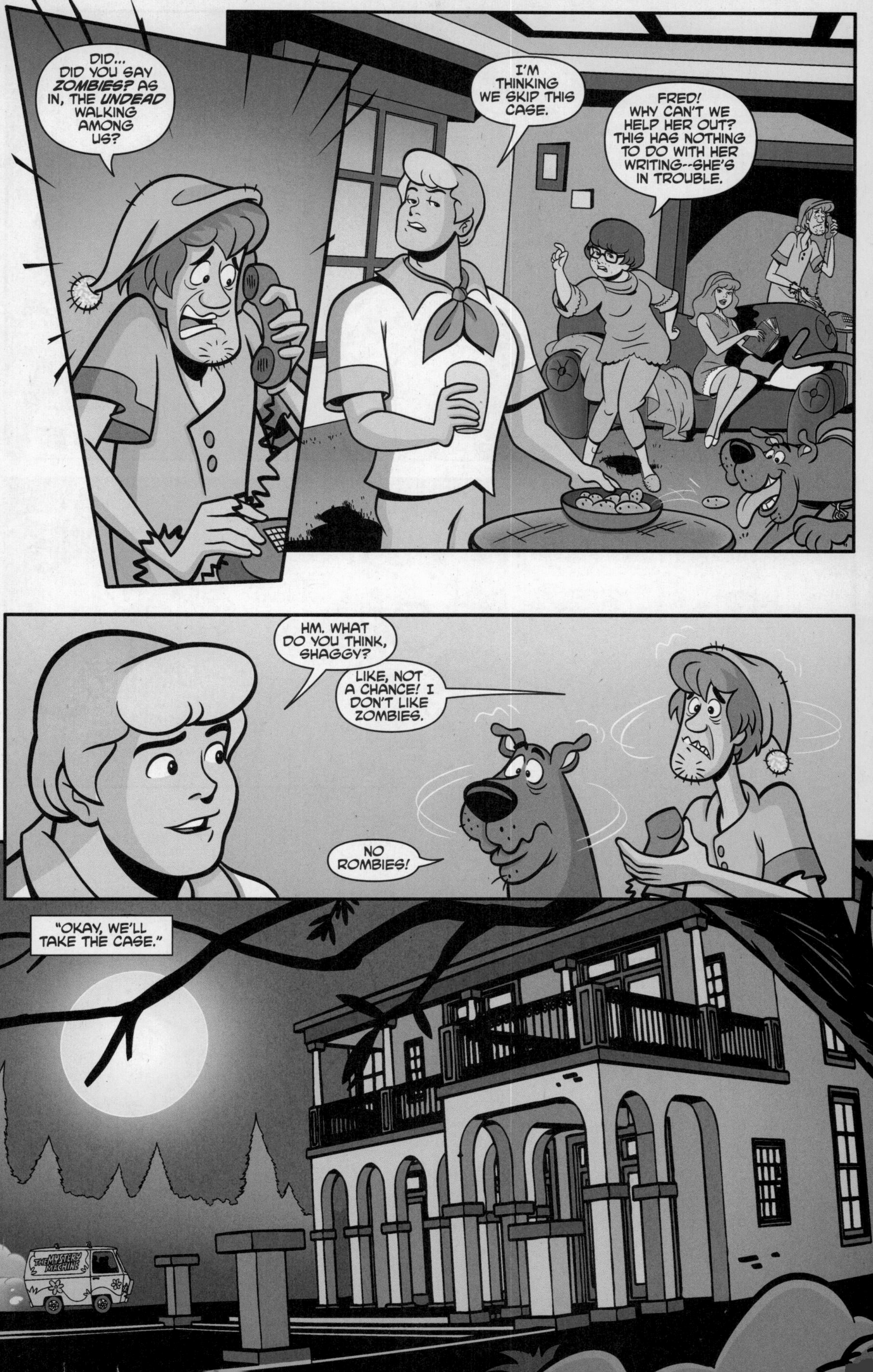
DID... DID YOU SAY ZOMBIES? AS IN, THE UNDEAD WALKING AMONG US?
I'M THINKING WE SKIP THIS CASE.
FRED! WHY CAN'T WE HELP HER OUT? THIS HAS NOTHING TO DO WITH HER WRITING--SHE'S IN TROUBLE.
HM. WHAT DO YOU THINK, SHAGGY?
LIKE, NOT A CHANCE! I DON'T LIKE ZOMBIES.
NO ROMBIES!
"OKAY, WE'LL TAKE THE CASE."
THE MYSTERY MACHINE

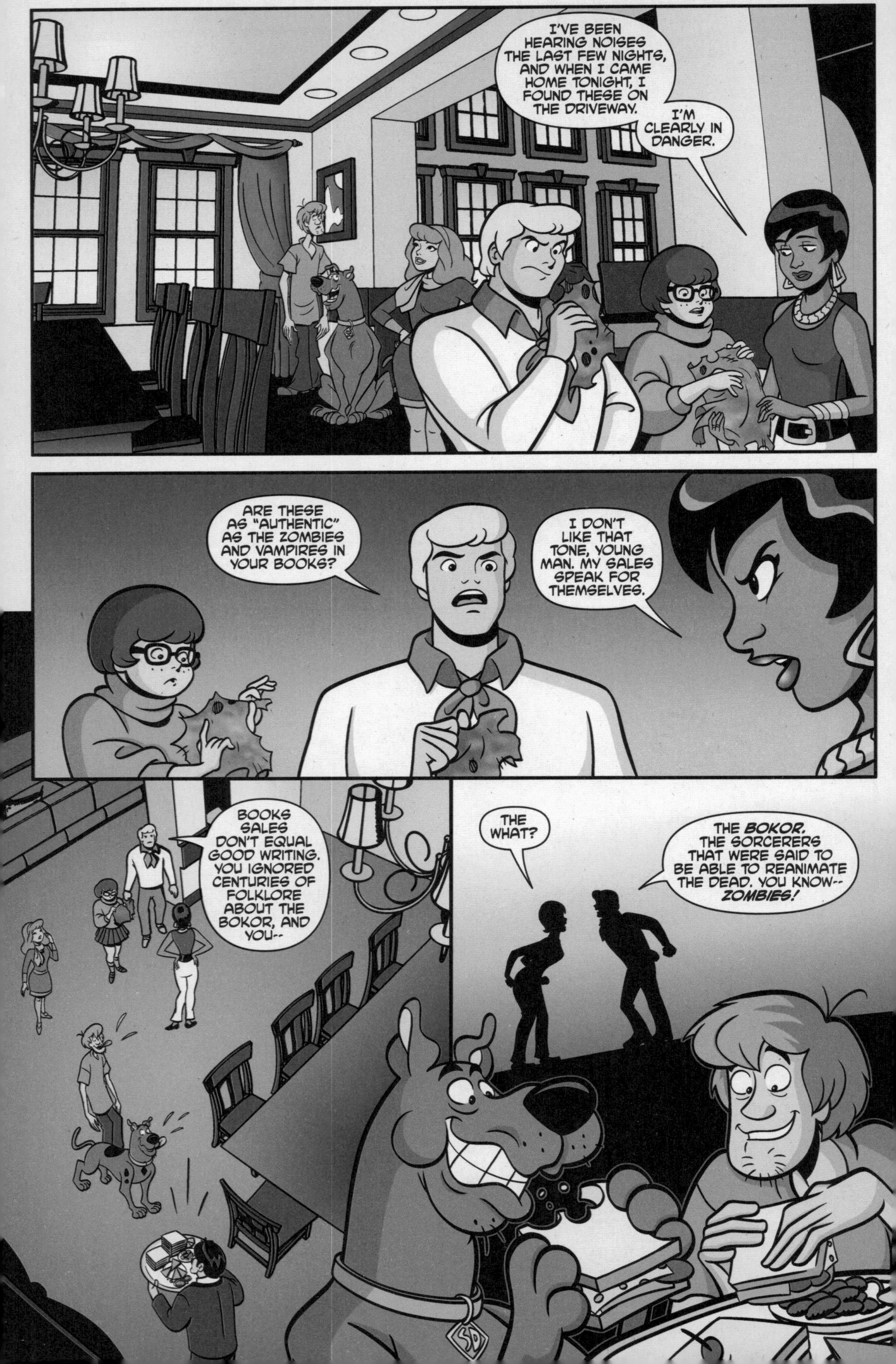
I'VE BEEN HEARING NOISES THE LAST FEW NIGHTS, AND WHEN I CAME HOME TONIGHT, I FOUND THESE ON THE DRIVEWAY.
I'M CLEARLY IN DANGER.
ARE THESE AS "AUTHENTIC" AS THE ZOMBIES AND VAMPIRES IN YOUR BOOKS?
I DON'T LIKE THAT TONE, YOUNG MAN. MY SALES SPEAK FOR THEMSELVES.
BOOKS SALES DON'T EQUAL GOOD WRITING. YOU IGNORED CENTURIES OF FOLKLORE ABOUT THE BOKOR, AND YOU--
THE WHAT?
THE *BOKOR.* THE SORCERERS THAT WERE SAID TO BE ABLE TO REANIMATE THE DEAD. YOU KNOW-- ***ZOMBIES!***

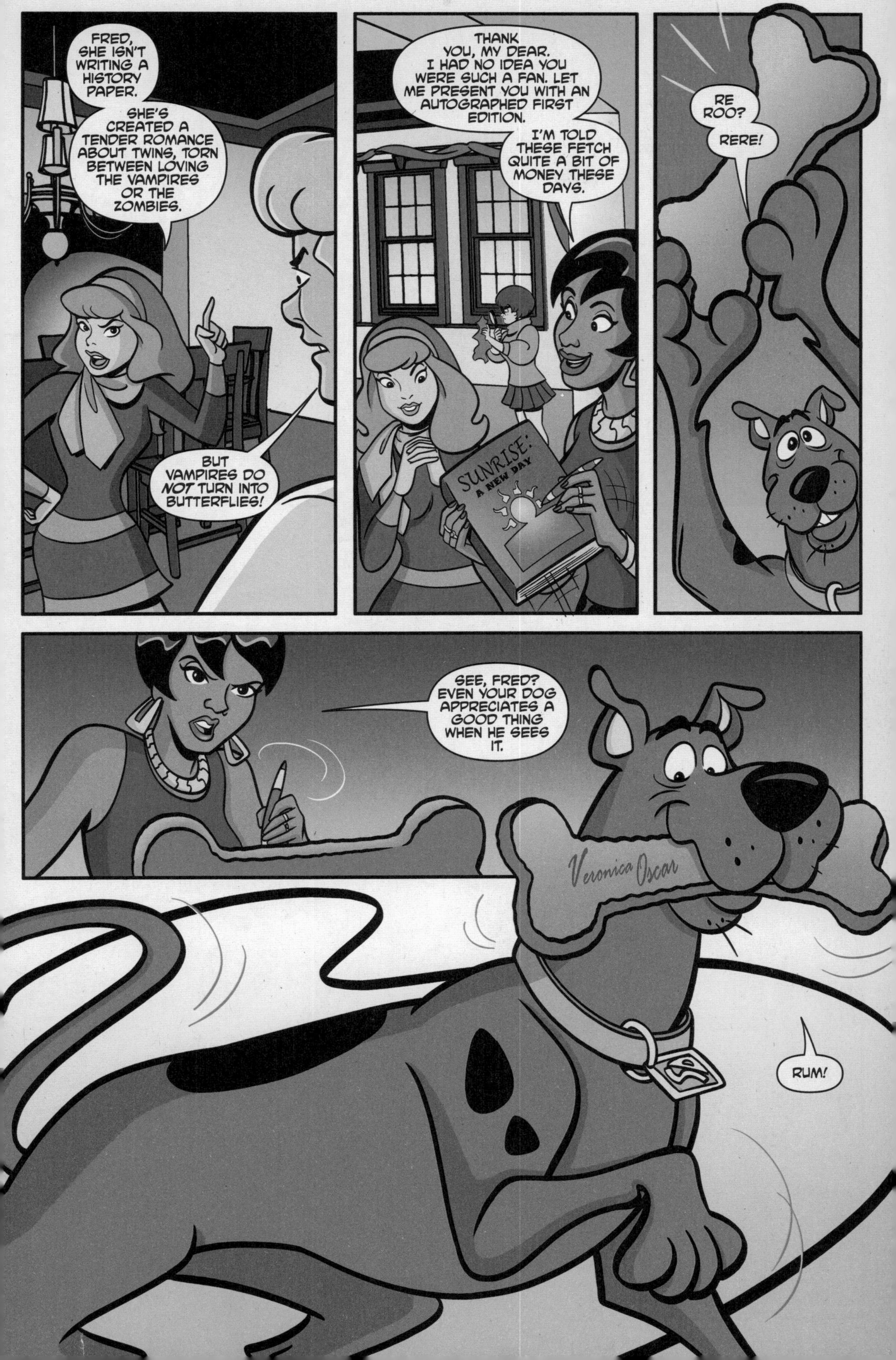
FRED, SHE ISN'T WRITING A HISTORY PAPER.
SHE'S CREATED A TENDER ROMANCE ABOUT TWINS, TORN BETWEEN LOVING THE VAMPIRES OR THE ZOMBIES.
BUT VAMPIRES DO NOT TURN INTO BUTTERFLIES!
THANK YOU, MY DEAR. I HAD NO IDEA YOU WERE SUCH A FAN. LET ME PRESENT YOU WITH AN AUTOGRAPHED FIRST EDITION.
I'M TOLD THESE FETCH QUITE A BIT OF MONEY THESE DAYS.
SUNRISE: A NEW DAY
RE ROO?
RERE!
SEE, FRED? EVEN YOUR DOG APPRECIATES A GOOD THING WHEN HE SEES IT.
Veronica Oscar
RUM!

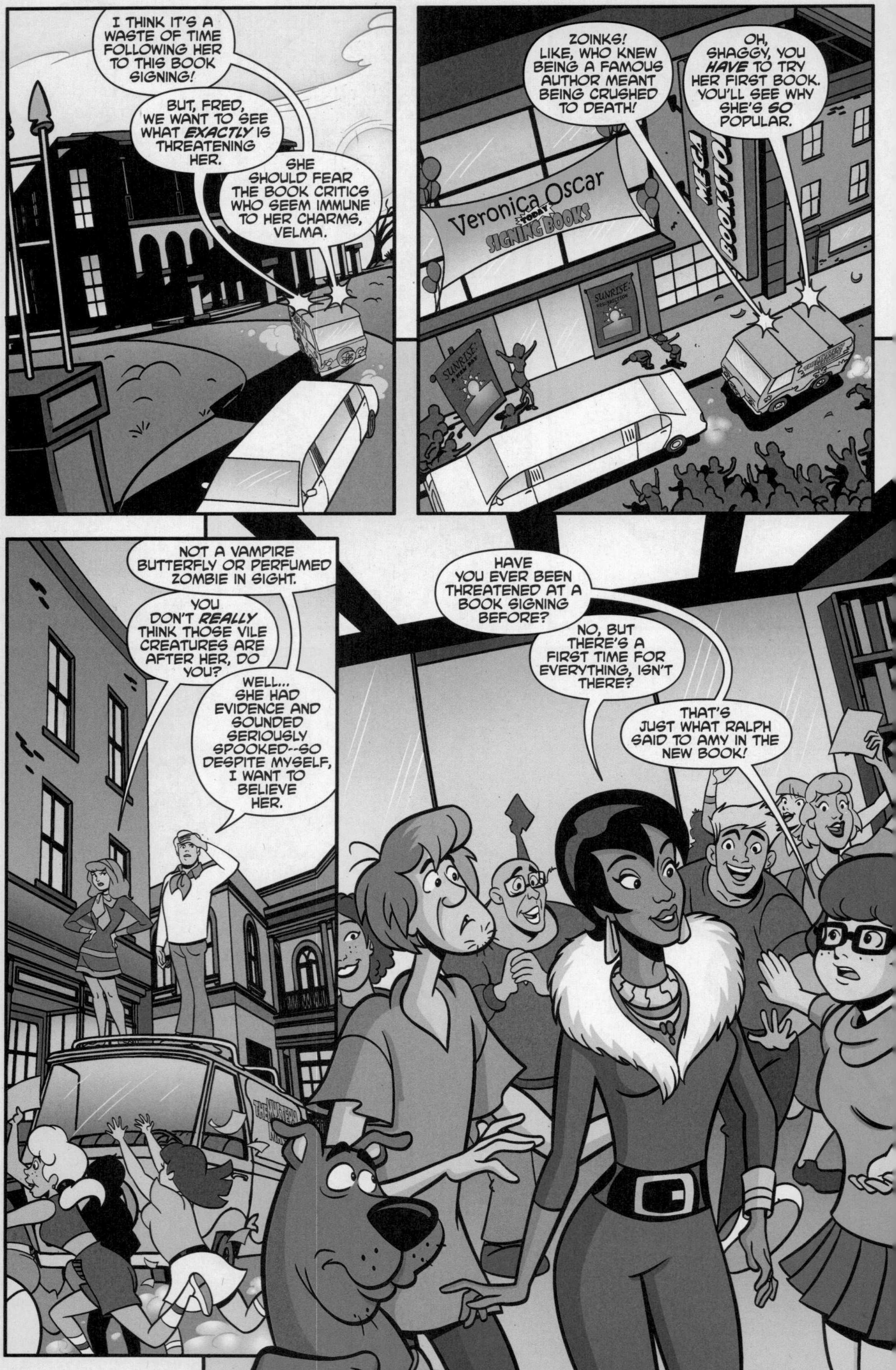
I THINK IT'S A WASTE OF TIME FOLLOWING HER TO THIS BOOK SIGNING!
BUT, FRED, WE WANT TO SEE WHAT *EXACTLY* IS THREATENING HER.
SHE SHOULD FEAR THE BOOK CRITICS WHO SEEM IMMUNE TO HER CHARMS, VELMA.
Veronica Oscar TODAY SIGNING BOOKS
MEGA
SUNRISE: RESURRECTION
SUNRISE: A NEW DAY
ZOINKS! LIKE, WHO KNEW BEING A FAMOUS AUTHOR MEANT BEING CRUSHED TO DEATH!
OH, SHAGGY, YOU *HAVE* TO TRY HER FIRST BOOK. YOU'LL SEE WHY SHE'S *SO* POPULAR.
NOT A VAMPIRE BUTTERFLY OR PERFUMED ZOMBIE IN SIGHT.
YOU DON'T *REALLY* THINK THOSE VILE CREATURES ARE AFTER HER, DO YOU?
WELL... SHE HAD EVIDENCE AND SOUNDED SERIOUSLY SPOOKED--SO DESPITE MYSELF, I WANT TO BELIEVE HER.
HAVE YOU EVER BEEN THREATENED AT A BOOK SIGNING BEFORE?
NO, BUT THERE'S A FIRST TIME FOR EVERYTHING, ISN'T THERE?
THAT'S JUST WHAT RALPH SAID TO AMY IN THE NEW BOOK!

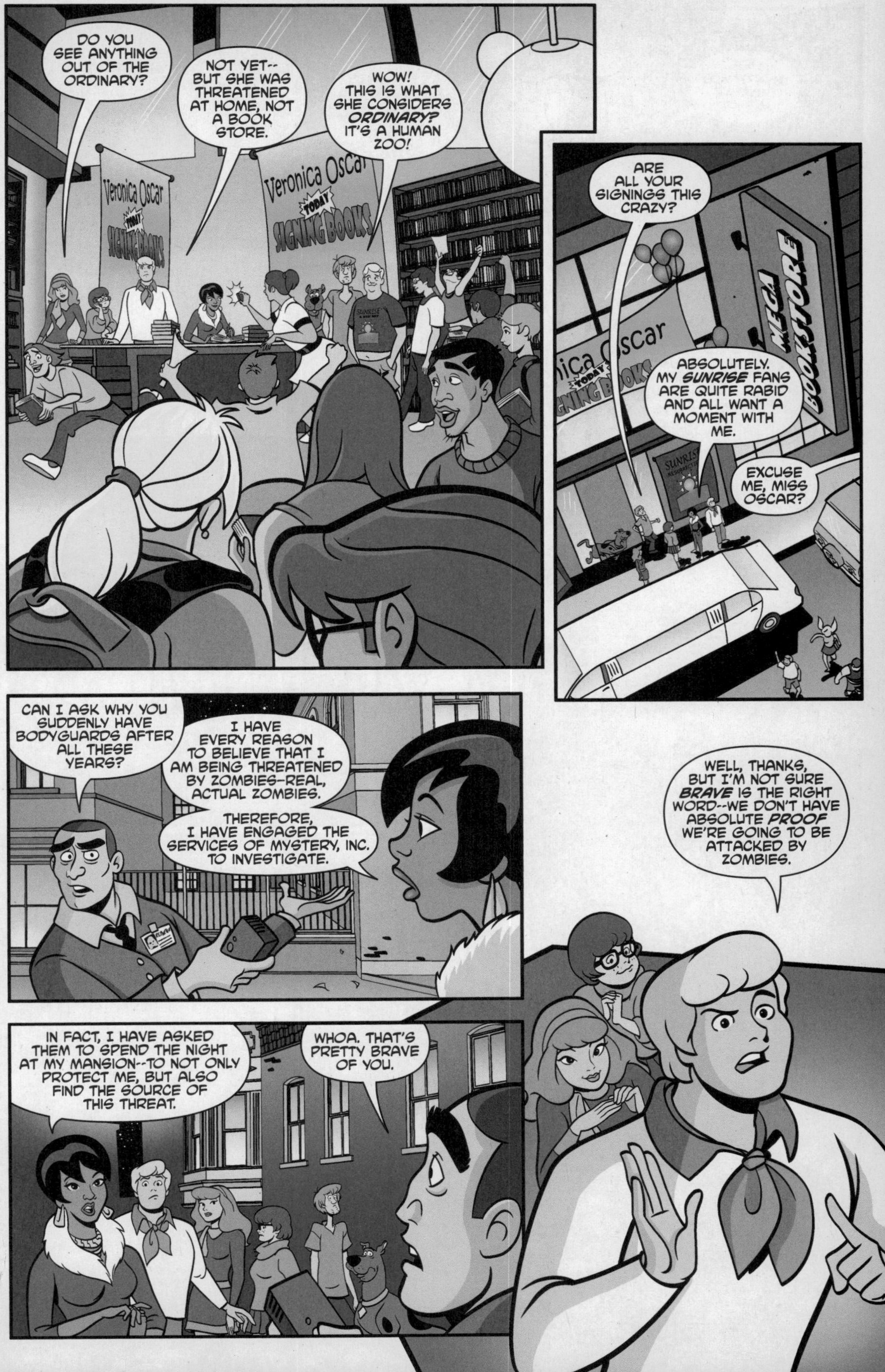
DO YOU SEE ANYTHING OUT OF THE ORDINARY?
NOT YET-- BUT SHE WAS THREATENED AT HOME, NOT A BOOK STORE.
WOW! THIS IS WHAT SHE CONSIDERS ORDINARY? IT'S A HUMAN ZOO!
Veronica Oscar TODAY SIGNING BOOKS
ARE ALL YOUR SIGNINGS THIS CRAZY?
ABSOLUTELY. MY SUNRISE FANS ARE QUITE RABID AND ALL WANT A MOMENT WITH ME.
EXCUSE ME, MISS OSCAR?
MEGA BOOKSTORE
CAN I ASK WHY YOU SUDDENLY HAVE BODYGUARDS AFTER ALL THESE YEARS?
I HAVE EVERY REASON TO BELIEVE THAT I AM BEING THREATENED BY ZOMBIES--REAL, ACTUAL ZOMBIES.
THEREFORE, I HAVE ENGAGED THE SERVICES OF MYSTERY, INC. TO INVESTIGATE.
IN FACT, I HAVE ASKED THEM TO SPEND THE NIGHT AT MY MANSION--TO NOT ONLY PROTECT ME, BUT ALSO FIND THE SOURCE OF THIS THREAT.
WHOA. THAT'S PRETTY BRAVE OF YOU.
WELL, THANKS, BUT I'M NOT SURE BRAVE IS THE RIGHT WORD--WE DON'T HAVE ABSOLUTE PROOF WE'RE GOING TO BE ATTACKED BY ZOMBIES.

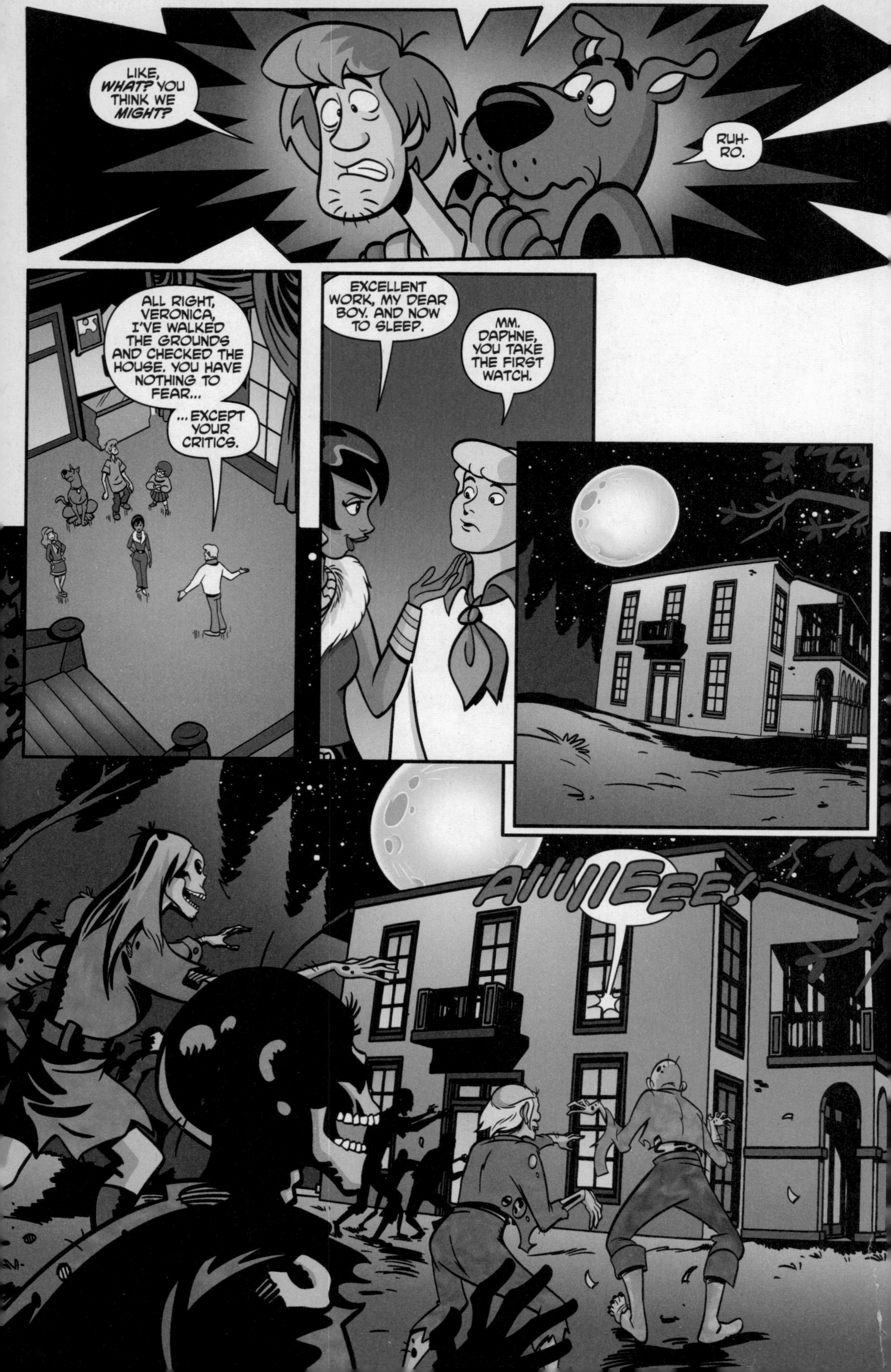
LIKE, WHAT? YOU THINK WE MIGHT?
RUH-RO.
ALL RIGHT, VERONICA, I'VE WALKED THE GROUNDS AND CHECKED THE HOUSE. YOU HAVE NOTHING TO FEAR...
...EXCEPT YOUR CRITICS.
EXCELLENT WORK, MY DEAR BOY. AND NOW TO SLEEP.
MM. DAPHNE, YOU TAKE THE FIRST WATCH.
AHHHIEEEE!

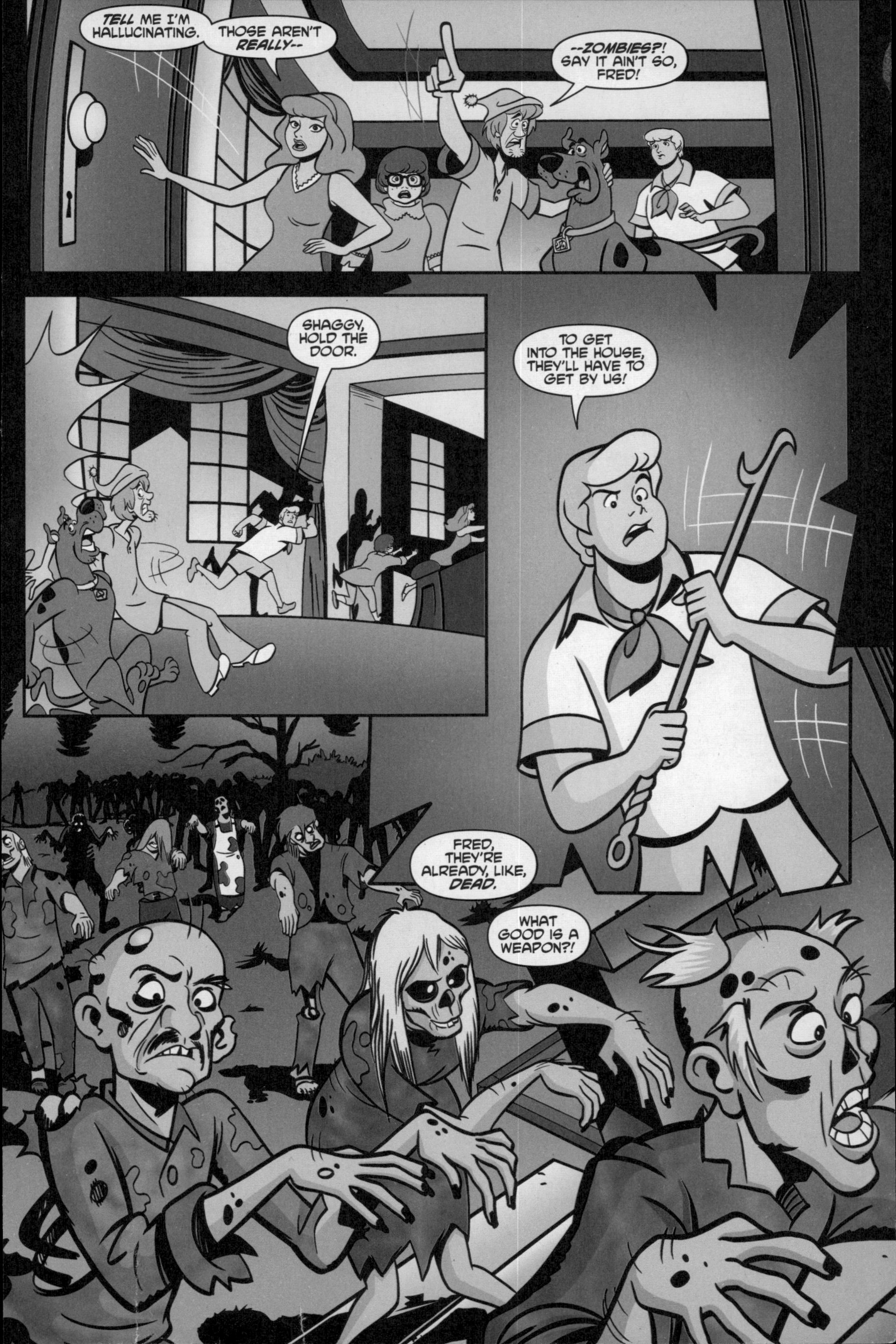
TELL ME I'M HALLUCINATING.
THOSE AREN'T REALLY--
--ZOMBIES?! SAY IT AIN'T SO, FRED!
SHAGGY, HOLD THE DOOR.
TO GET INTO THE HOUSE, THEY'LL HAVE TO GET BY US!
FRED, THEY'RE ALREADY, LIKE, DEAD.
WHAT GOOD IS A WEAPON?!

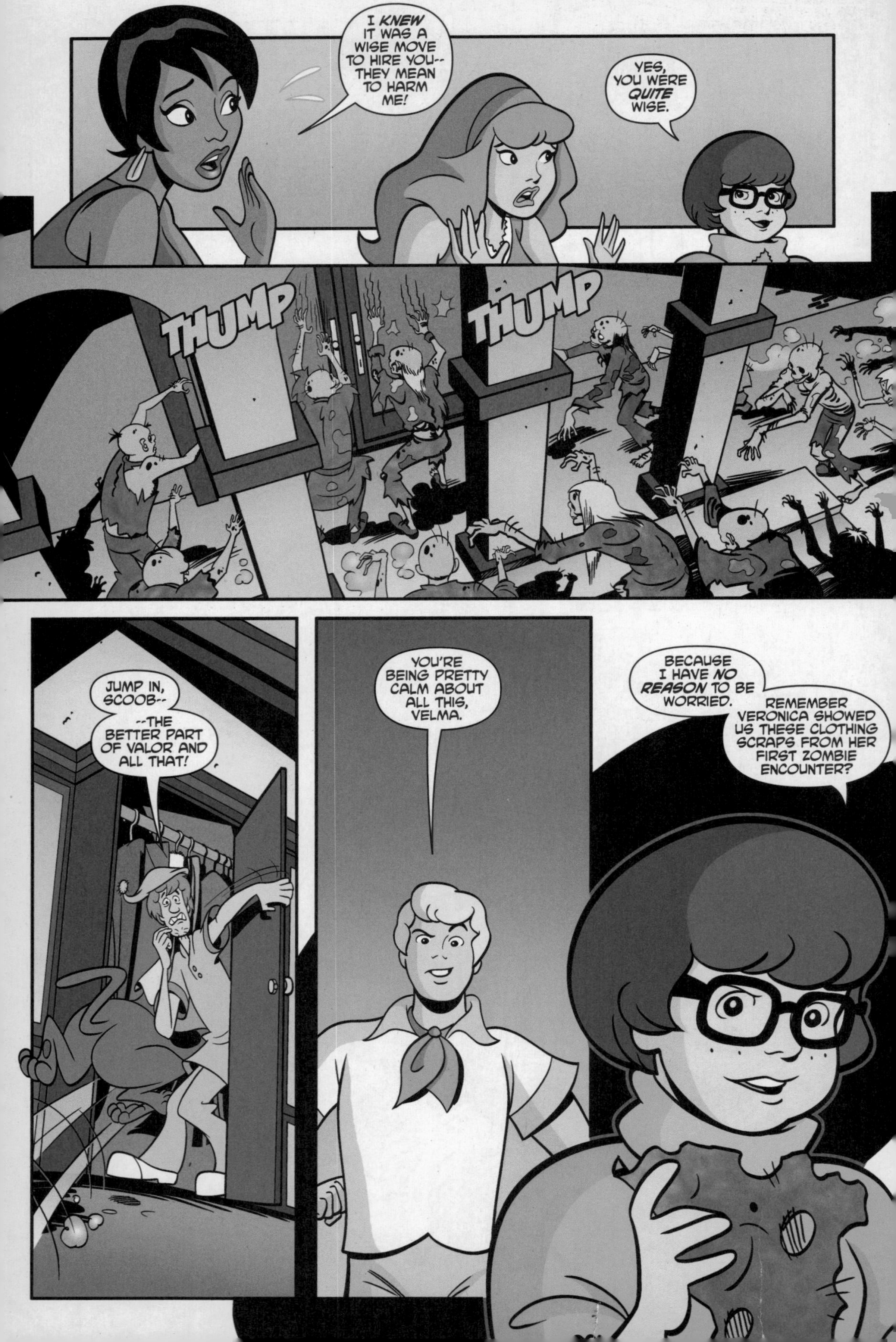

I KNEW IT WAS A WISE MOVE TO HIRE YOU-- THEY MEAN TO HARM ME!
YES, YOU WERE QUITE WISE.
THUMP
THUMP
JUMP IN, SCOOB--
--THE BETTER PART OF VALOR AND ALL THAT!
YOU'RE BEING PRETTY CALM ABOUT ALL THIS, VELMA.
BECAUSE I HAVE NO REASON TO BE WORRIED.
REMEMBER VERONICA SHOWED US THESE CLOTHING SCRAPS FROM HER FIRST ZOMBIE ENCOUNTER?

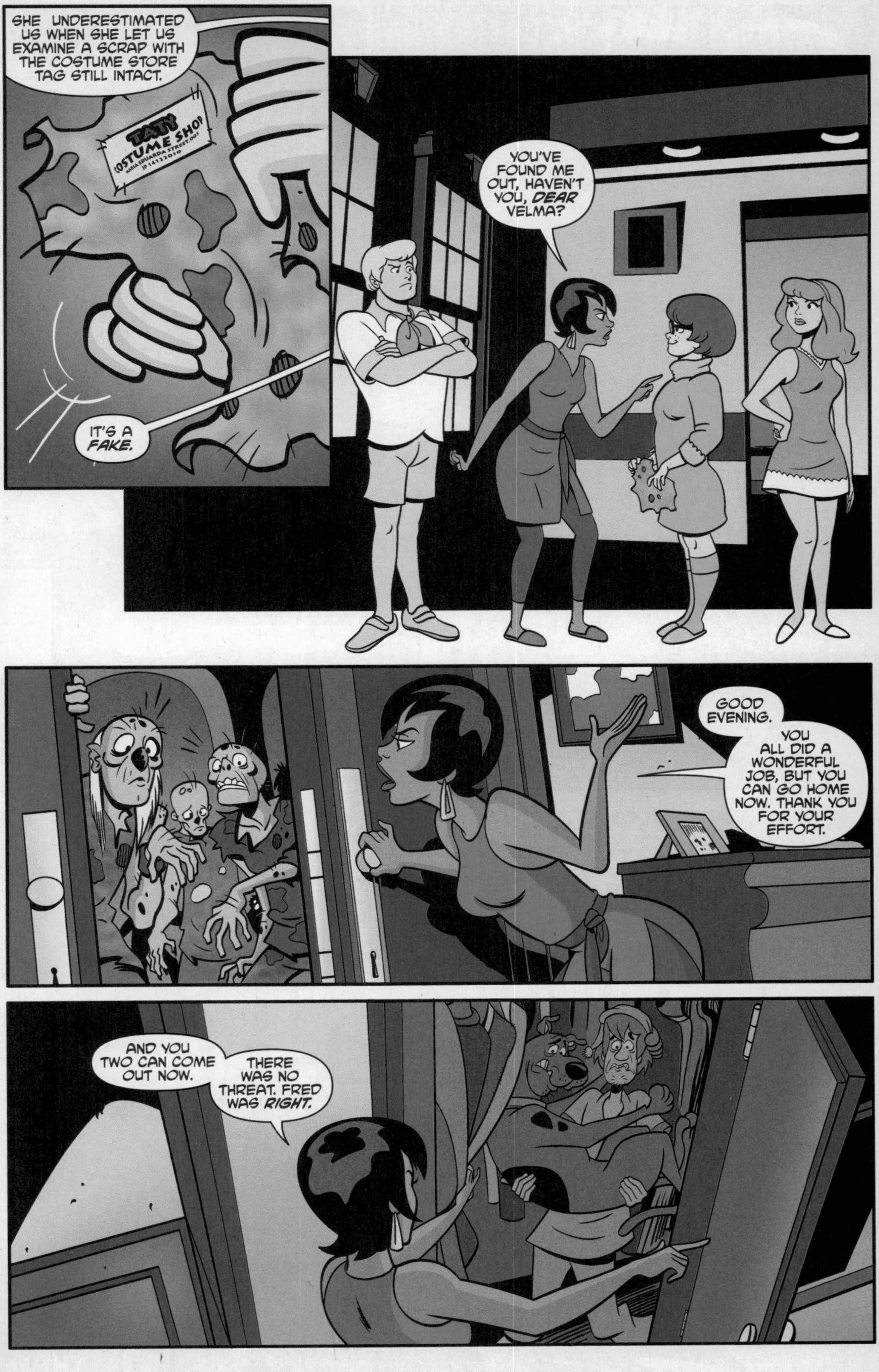
SHE UNDERESTIMATED US WHEN SHE LET US EXAMINE A SCRAP WITH THE COSTUME STORE TAG STILL INTACT.
TATY
COSTUME SHOP
IT'S A *FAKE.*
YOU'VE FOUND ME OUT, HAVEN'T YOU, *DEAR* VELMA?
GOOD EVENING.
YOU ALL DID A WONDERFUL JOB, BUT YOU CAN GO HOME NOW. THANK YOU FOR YOUR EFFORT.
AND YOU TWO CAN COME OUT NOW.
THERE WAS NO THREAT. FRED WAS *RIGHT.*

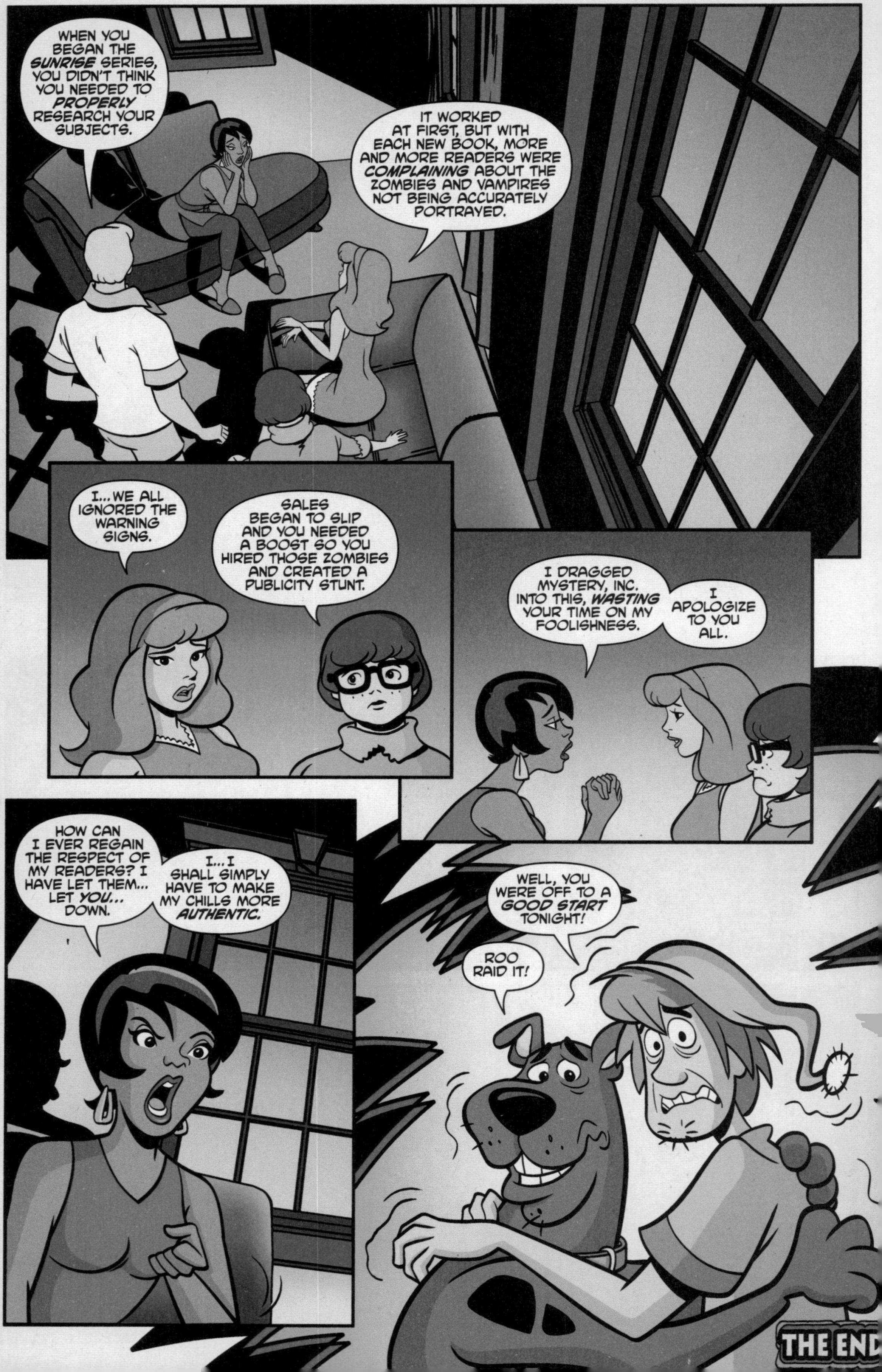
WHEN YOU BEGAN THE *SUNRISE* SERIES, YOU DIDN'T THINK YOU NEEDED TO *PROPERLY* RESEARCH YOUR SUBJECTS.
IT WORKED AT FIRST, BUT WITH EACH NEW BOOK, MORE AND MORE READERS WERE *COMPLAINING* ABOUT THE ZOMBIES AND VAMPIRES NOT BEING ACCURATELY PORTRAYED.
I...WE ALL IGNORED THE WARNING SIGNS.
SALES BEGAN TO SLIP AND YOU NEEDED A BOOST SO YOU HIRED THOSE ZOMBIES AND CREATED A PUBLICITY STUNT.
I DRAGGED MYSTERY, INC. INTO THIS, *WASTING* YOUR TIME ON MY FOOLISHNESS.
I APOLOGIZE TO YOU ALL.
HOW CAN I EVER REGAIN THE RESPECT OF MY READERS? I HAVE LET THEM... LET *YOU*... DOWN.
I...I SHALL SIMPLY HAVE TO MAKE MY CHILLS MORE *AUTHENTIC.*
WELL, YOU WERE OFF TO A *GOOD START* TONIGHT!
ROO RAID IT!
THE END

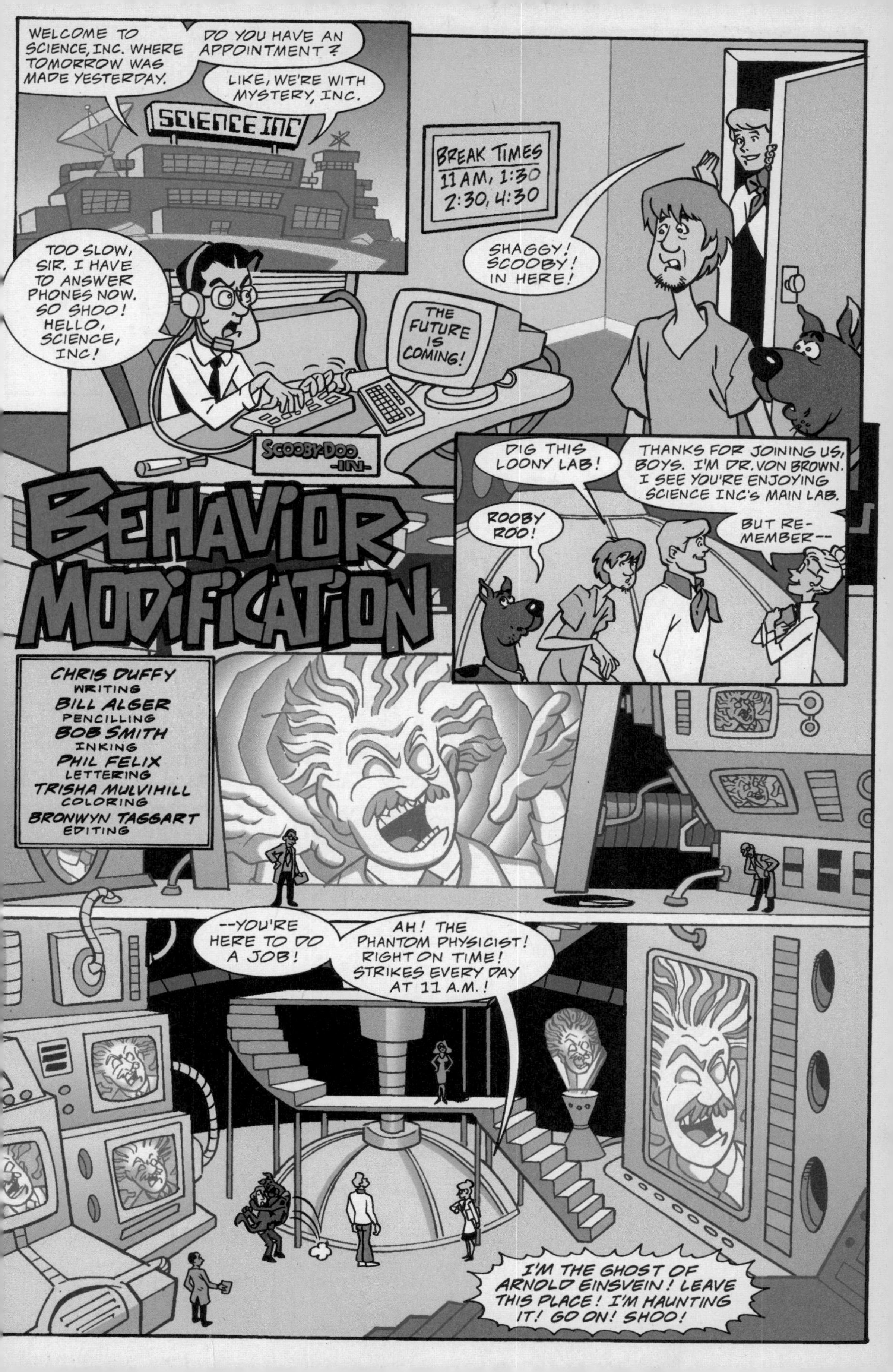
WELCOME TO SCIENCE, INC. WHERE TOMORROW WAS MADE YESTERDAY.
DO YOU HAVE AN APPOINTMENT?
LIKE, WE'RE WITH MYSTERY, INC.
SCIENCE INC
BREAK TIMES
11 AM, 1:30
2:30, 4:30
TOO SLOW, SIR. I HAVE TO ANSWER PHONES NOW. SO SHOO! HELLO, SCIENCE, INC!
THE FUTURE IS COMING!
SHAGGY! SCOOBY! IN HERE!
SCOOBY-DOO IN
BEHAVIOR MODIFICATION
DIG THIS LOONY LAB!
THANKS FOR JOINING US, BOYS. I'M DR. VON BROWN. I SEE YOU'RE ENJOYING SCIENCE INC'S MAIN LAB.
ROOBY ROO!
BUT RE-MEMBER--
CHRIS DUFFY WRITING
BILL ALGER PENCILLING
BOB SMITH INKING
PHIL FELIX LETTERING
TRISHA MULVIHILL COLORING
BRONWYN TAGGART EDITING
--YOU'RE HERE TO DO A JOB!
AH! THE PHANTOM PHYSICIST! RIGHT ON TIME! STRIKES EVERY DAY AT 11 A.M.!
I'M THE GHOST OF ARNOLD EINSVEIN! LEAVE THIS PLACE! I'M HAUNTING IT! GO ON! SHOO!

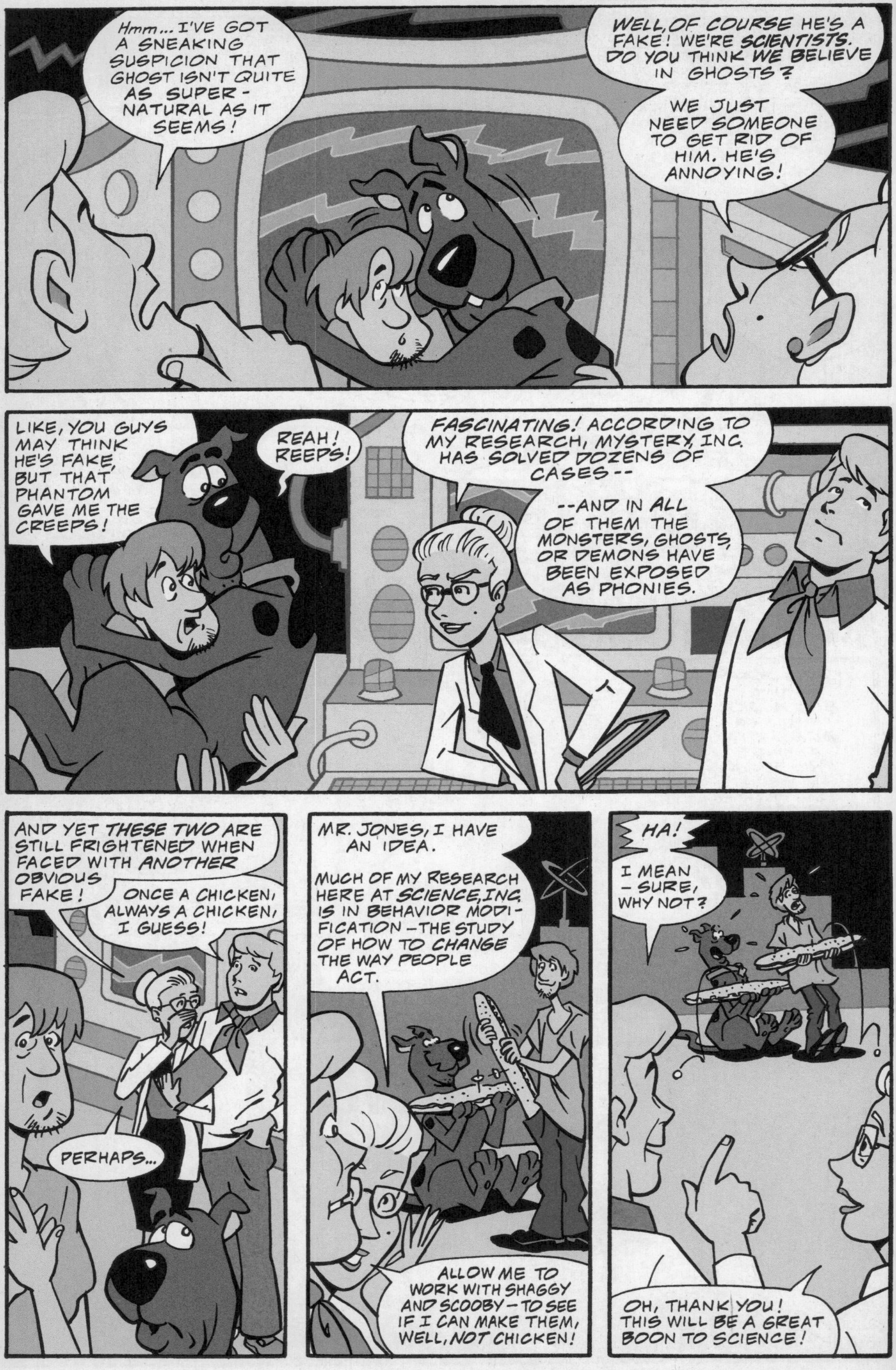
Hmm... I'VE GOT A SNEAKING SUSPICION THAT GHOST ISN'T QUITE AS SUPER-NATURAL AS IT SEEMS!
WELL, OF COURSE HE'S A FAKE! WE'RE SCIENTISTS. DO YOU THINK WE BELIEVE IN GHOSTS?
WE JUST NEED SOMEONE TO GET RID OF HIM. HE'S ANNOYING!
LIKE, YOU GUYS MAY THINK HE'S FAKE, BUT THAT PHANTOM GAVE ME THE CREEPS!
REAH! REEPS!
FASCINATING! ACCORDING TO MY RESEARCH, MYSTERY, INC. HAS SOLVED DOZENS OF CASES--
--AND IN ALL OF THEM THE MONSTERS, GHOSTS, OR DEMONS HAVE BEEN EXPOSED AS PHONIES.
AND YET THESE TWO ARE STILL FRIGHTENED WHEN FACED WITH ANOTHER OBVIOUS FAKE!
ONCE A CHICKEN, ALWAYS A CHICKEN, I GUESS!
PERHAPS...
MR. JONES, I HAVE AN IDEA.
MUCH OF MY RESEARCH HERE AT SCIENCE, INC. IS IN BEHAVIOR MODI-FICATION -- THE STUDY OF HOW TO CHANGE THE WAY PEOPLE ACT.
ALLOW ME TO WORK WITH SHAGGY AND SCOOBY -- TO SEE IF I CAN MAKE THEM, WELL, NOT CHICKEN!
HA!
I MEAN -- SURE, WHY NOT?
OH, THANK YOU! THIS WILL BE A GREAT BOON TO SCIENCE!

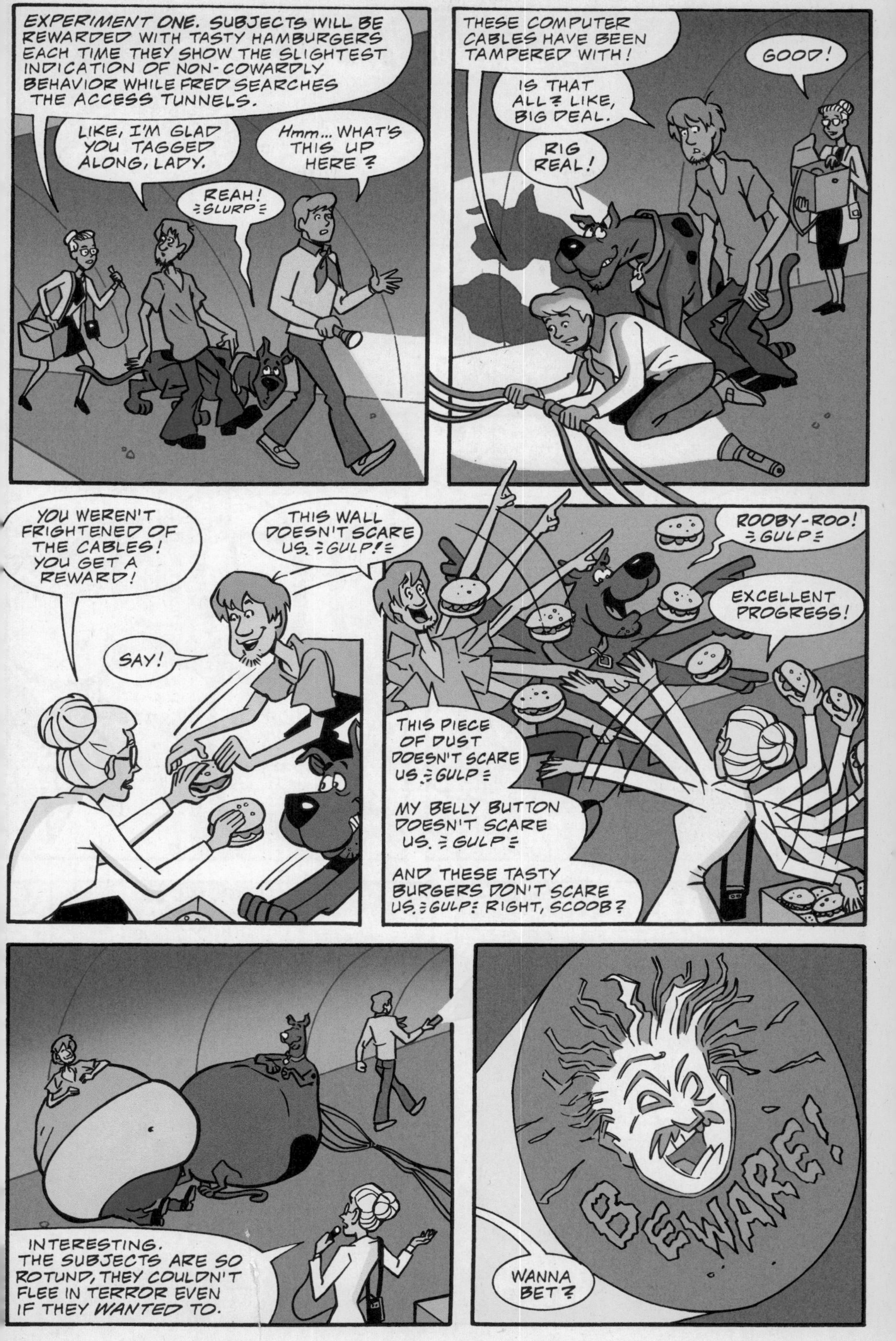
EXPERIMENT ONE. SUBJECTS WILL BE REWARDED WITH TASTY HAMBURGERS EACH TIME THEY SHOW THE SLIGHTEST INDICATION OF NON-COWARDLY BEHAVIOR WHILE FRED SEARCHES THE ACCESS TUNNELS.
LIKE, I'M GLAD YOU TAGGED ALONG, LADY.
REAH! =SLURP=
Hmm... WHAT'S THIS UP HERE?
THESE COMPUTER CABLES HAVE BEEN TAMPERED WITH!
IS THAT ALL? LIKE, BIG DEAL.
RIG REAL!
GOOD!
YOU WEREN'T FRIGHTENED OF THE CABLES! YOU GET A REWARD!
THIS WALL DOESN'T SCARE US. =GULP!=
SAY!
ROOBY-ROO! =GULP=
EXCELLENT PROGRESS!
THIS PIECE OF DUST DOESN'T SCARE US. =GULP=
MY BELLY BUTTON DOESN'T SCARE US. =GULP=
AND THESE TASTY BURGERS DON'T SCARE US. =GULP= RIGHT, SCOOB?
INTERESTING. THE SUBJECTS ARE SO ROTUND, THEY COULDN'T FLEE IN TERROR EVEN IF THEY WANTED TO.
BEWARE!
WANNA BET?

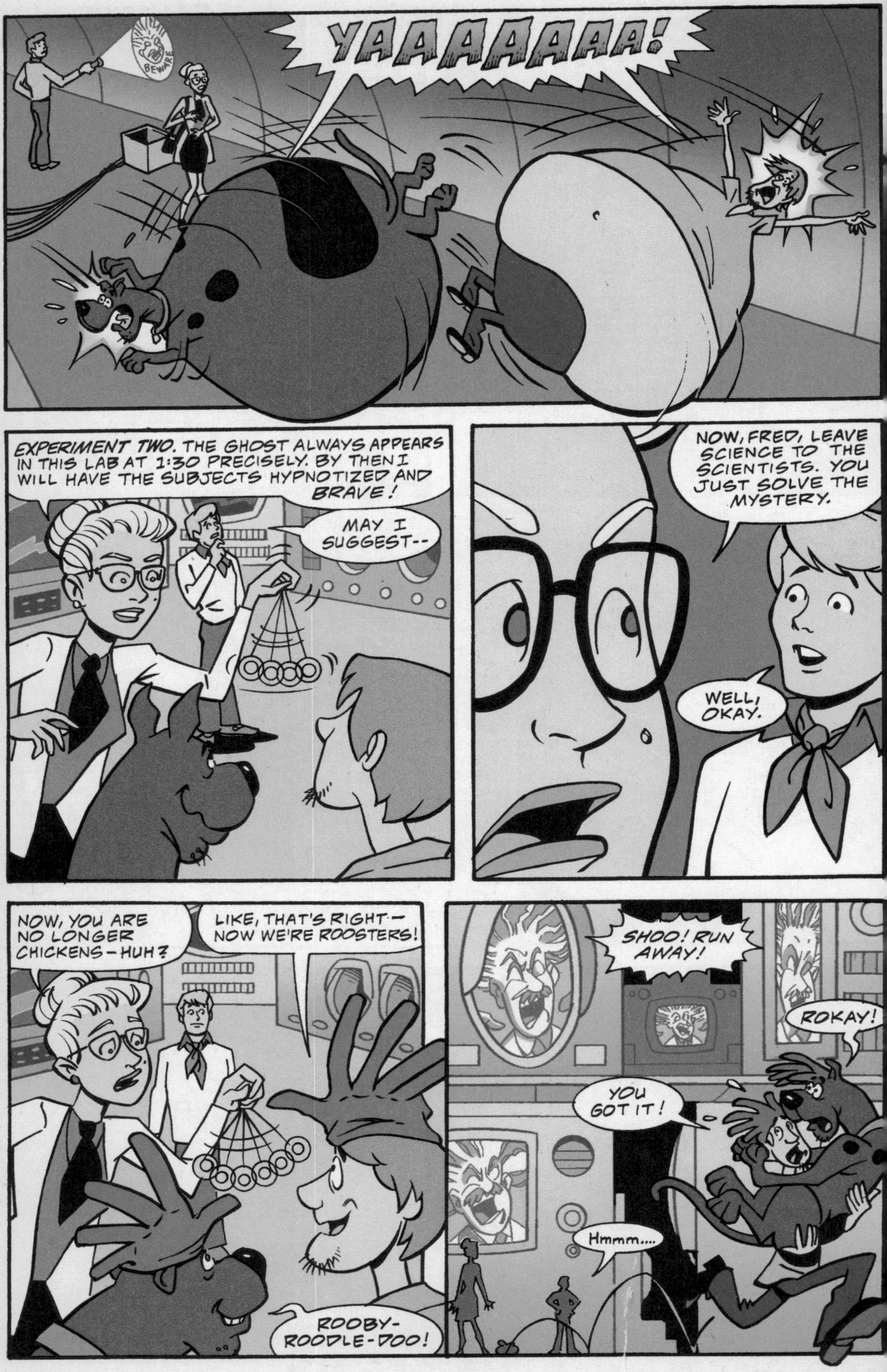
BEWARE
YAAAAAAA!
EXPERIMENT TWO. THE GHOST ALWAYS APPEARS IN THIS LAB AT 1:30 PRECISELY. BY THEN I WILL HAVE THE SUBJECTS HYPNOTIZED AND BRAVE!
MAY I SUGGEST--
NOW, FRED, LEAVE SCIENCE TO THE SCIENTISTS. YOU JUST SOLVE THE MYSTERY.
WELL, OKAY.
NOW, YOU ARE NO LONGER CHICKENS—HUH?
LIKE, THAT'S RIGHT— NOW WE'RE ROOSTERS!
ROOBY-ROODLE-DOO!
SHOO! RUN AWAY!
ROKAY!
YOU GOT IT!
Hmmm....

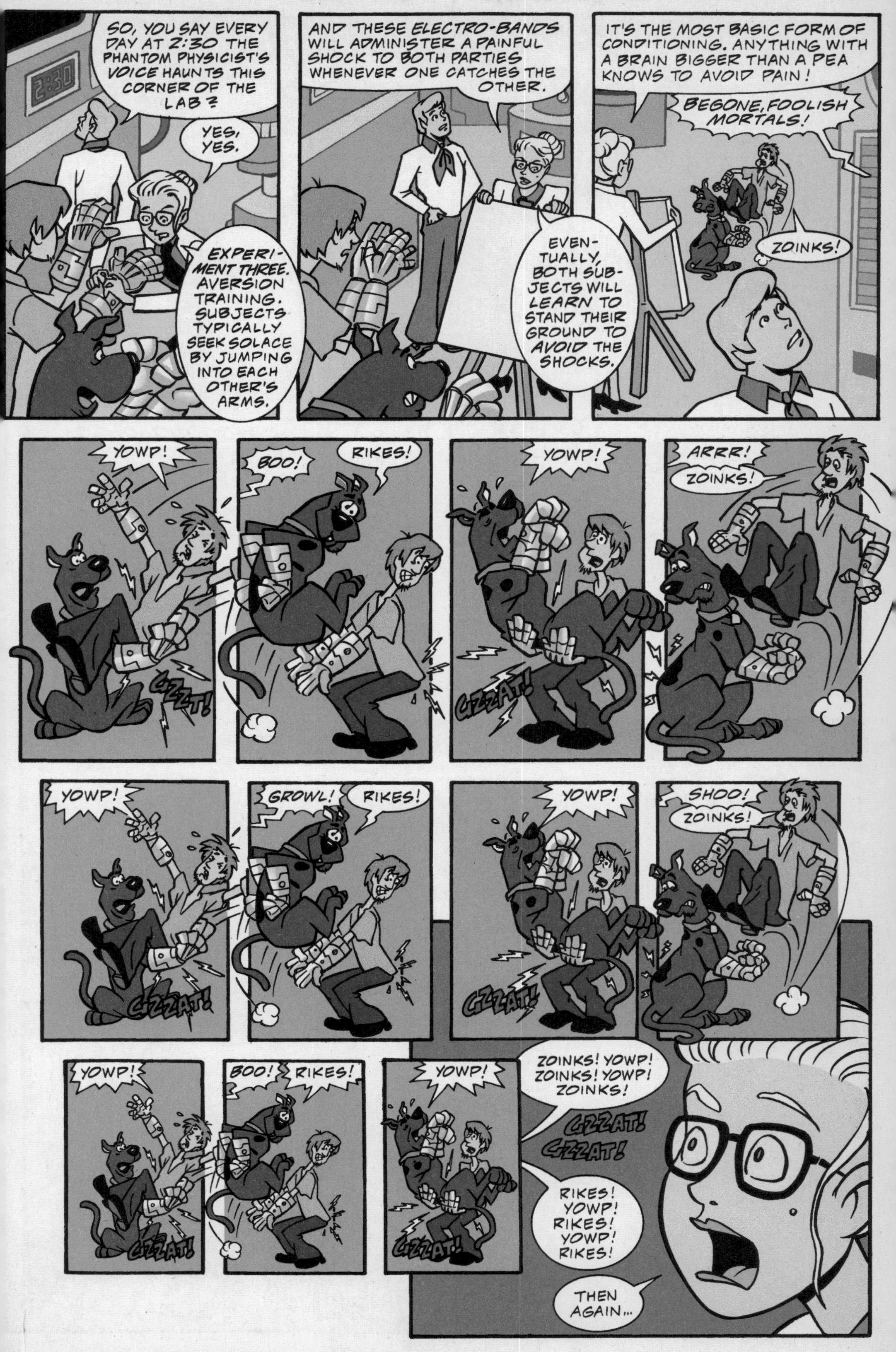

SO, YOU SAY EVERY DAY AT 2:30 THE PHANTOM PHYSICIST'S VOICE HAUNTS THIS CORNER OF THE LAB?
YES, YES.
EXPERIMENT THREE. AVERSION TRAINING. SUBJECTS TYPICALLY SEEK SOLACE BY JUMPING INTO EACH OTHER'S ARMS.
AND THESE ELECTRO-BANDS WILL ADMINISTER A PAINFUL SHOCK TO BOTH PARTIES WHENEVER ONE CATCHES THE OTHER.
EVENTUALLY, BOTH SUBJECTS WILL LEARN TO STAND THEIR GROUND TO AVOID THE SHOCKS.
IT'S THE MOST BASIC FORM OF CONDITIONING. ANYTHING WITH A BRAIN BIGGER THAN A PEA KNOWS TO AVOID PAIN!
BEGONE, FOOLISH MORTALS!
ZOINKS!
YOWP!
GZZZT!
BOO!
RIKES!
YOWP!
GZZZAT!
ARRR!
ZOINKS!
YOWP!
GZZZAT!
GROWL!
RIKES!
YOWP!
GZZZAT!
SHOO!
ZOINKS!
YOWP!
GZZZAT!
BOO!
RIKES!
YOWP!
GZZZAT!
ZOINKS! YOWP! ZOINKS! YOWP! ZOINKS!
GZZZAT! GZZZAT!
RIKES! YOWP! RIKES! YOWP! RIKES!
THEN AGAIN...

YOU SAY THE PHANTOM LEAVES A FRIGHTENING VOICE-MAIL MESSAGE ON YOUR PHONE EVERY DAY AT 4:30?

SORRY, FRED— CAN'T HEAR YOU.

MUST FINISH BUILDING RESTRAINTS!

BAM! BAM!

THERE! YOU TWO OBVIOUSLY WON'T RESPOND TO ANY CONVENTIONAL METHODS!

BUT JUST TRY TO RUN AWAY WHEN PHYSICALLY ATTACHED TO THE FLOOR!

? ?

HA!

NOW I'LL JUST ACCESS THAT VOICE-MAIL MESSAGE FROM THE PHANTOM...

BEEP-BOOP

YAAAA!

WOOOOOOOOO!

IT'S NO USE! YOU CAN'T MOVE! YOU MUST STAY AND--

K-KREAK!

--FACE YOUR FEARS.

YAAAAAAA!

CRASH! KLOMP! SMASH!

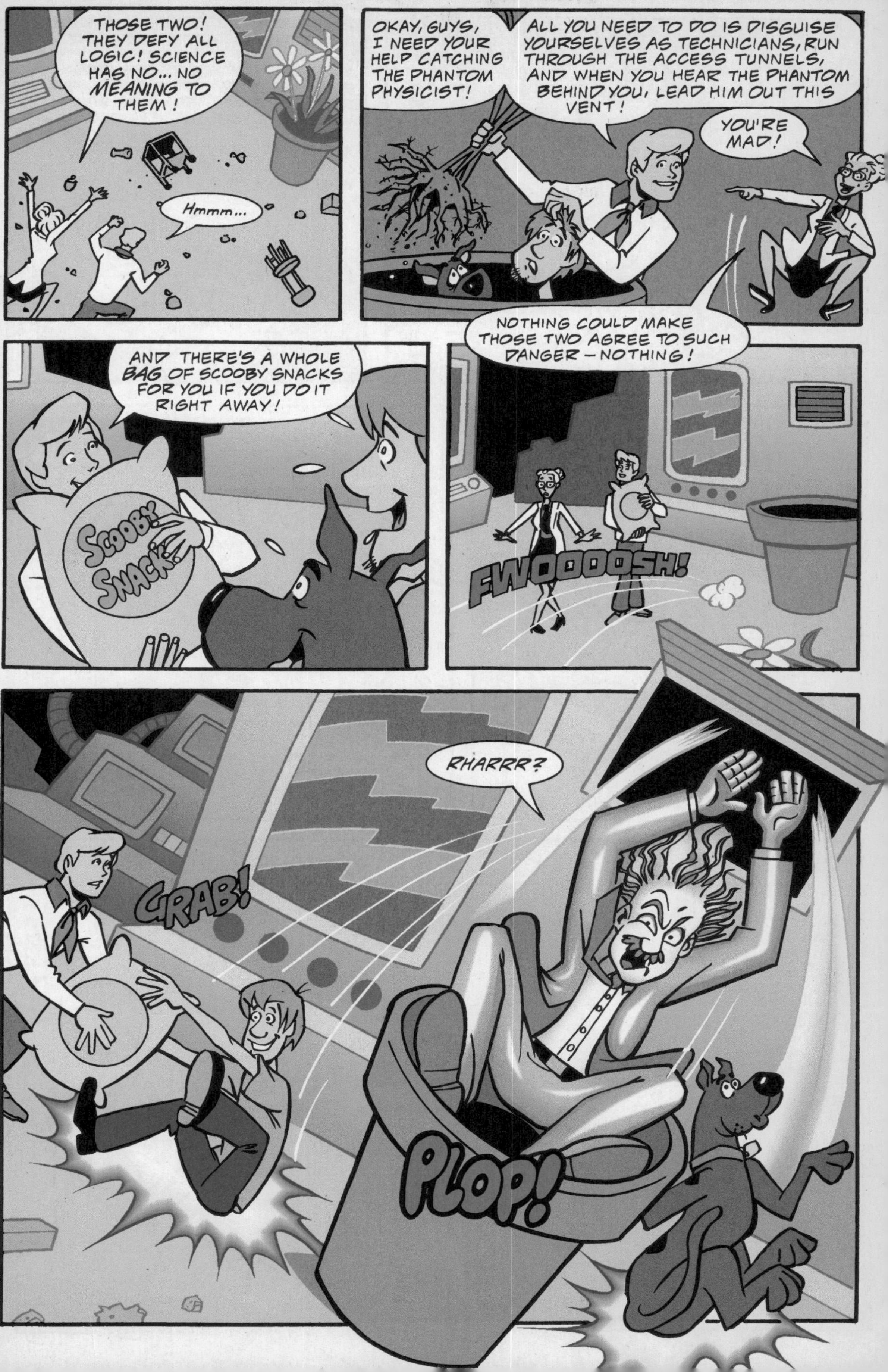
THOSE TWO! THEY DEFY ALL LOGIC! SCIENCE HAS NO... NO MEANING TO THEM!
Hmmm...
OKAY, GUYS, I NEED YOUR HELP CATCHING THE PHANTOM PHYSICIST!
ALL YOU NEED TO DO IS DISGUISE YOURSELVES AS TECHNICIANS, RUN THROUGH THE ACCESS TUNNELS, AND WHEN YOU HEAR THE PHANTOM BEHIND YOU, LEAD HIM OUT THIS VENT!
YOU'RE MAD!
AND THERE'S A WHOLE BAG OF SCOOBY SNACKS FOR YOU IF YOU DO IT RIGHT AWAY!
SCOOBY SNACKS
NOTHING COULD MAKE THOSE TWO AGREE TO SUCH DANGER — NOTHING!
FWOOOOSH!
RHARRR?
GRAB!
PLOP!

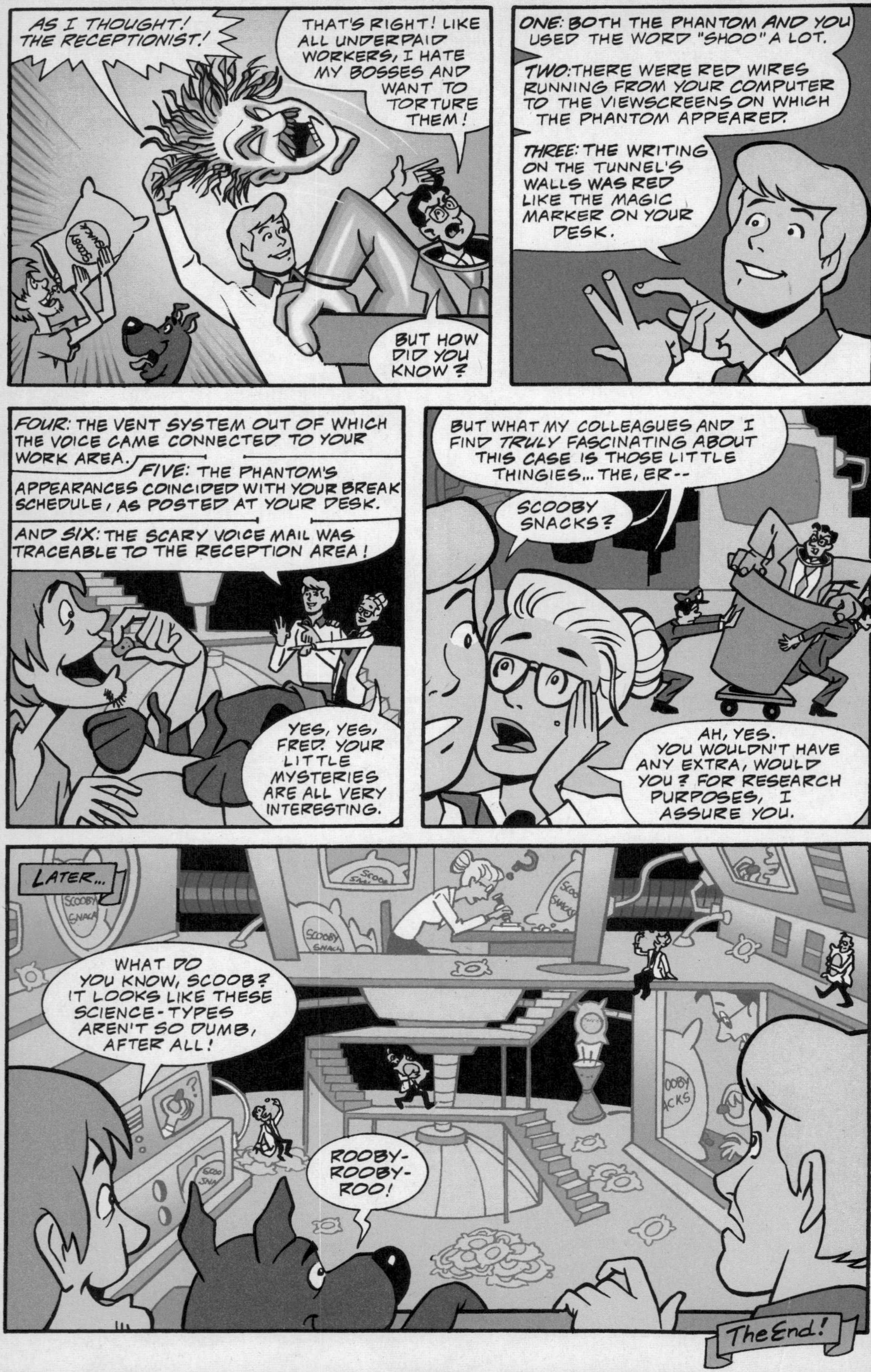
AS I THOUGHT! THE RECEPTIONIST!
THAT'S RIGHT! LIKE ALL UNDERPAID WORKERS, I HATE MY BOSSES AND WANT TO TORTURE THEM!
BUT HOW DID YOU KNOW?
ONE: BOTH THE PHANTOM AND YOU USED THE WORD "SHOO" A LOT.
TWO: THERE WERE RED WIRES RUNNING FROM YOUR COMPUTER TO THE VIEWSCREENS ON WHICH THE PHANTOM APPEARED.
THREE: THE WRITING ON THE TUNNEL'S WALLS WAS RED LIKE THE MAGIC MARKER ON YOUR DESK.
FOUR: THE VENT SYSTEM OUT OF WHICH THE VOICE CAME CONNECTED TO YOUR WORK AREA.
FIVE: THE PHANTOM'S APPEARANCES COINCIDED WITH YOUR BREAK SCHEDULE, AS POSTED AT YOUR DESK.
AND SIX: THE SCARY VOICE MAIL WAS TRACEABLE TO THE RECEPTION AREA!
YES, YES, FRED. YOUR LITTLE MYSTERIES ARE ALL VERY INTERESTING.
BUT WHAT MY COLLEAGUES AND I FIND TRULY FASCINATING ABOUT THIS CASE IS THOSE LITTLE THINGIES... THE, ER--
SCOOBY SNACKS?
AH, YES. YOU WOULDN'T HAVE ANY EXTRA, WOULD YOU? FOR RESEARCH PURPOSES, I ASSURE YOU.
LATER...
WHAT DO YOU KNOW, SCOOB? IT LOOKS LIKE THESE SCIENCE-TYPES AREN'T SO DUMB, AFTER ALL!
ROOBY-ROOBY-ROO!
The End!

WHO'S WHO?
SCOOBY-DOO

FULL NAME
SCOOBERT

AGE
7

HEIGHT
12 PAWS HIGH

LIKES
FOOD — ESPECIALLY SCOOBY SNACKS

DISLIKES
ANYTHING SCARY, HIS OWN SHADOW

THIS BIG BROWN DOG IS ONE BIG CHICKEN. JUST LIKE HIS PAL SHAGGY, HIS STOMACH IS MORE IMPORTANT TO HIM THAN CATCHING GHOSTS, BUT HE CAN ALWAYS BE TEMPTED INTO ACTION WITH THE PROMISE OF A SCOOBY SNACK.

DOGGY DISGUISES
OUR CANINE HERO IS A BRIL-LIANT MASTER OF DISGUISE. HE'S DRESSED UP AS ALL SORTS OF THINGS IN ORDER TO FOOL SOME PHANTOMS AND HE USUALLY GETS TO DRESS AS A SPOOK JUST TO FREAK OUT SHAGGY AT THE END OF AN ADVENTURE.

SCAREDY-DOG
THIS GREAT DANE IS SO COW-ARDLY, HE'S EVEN FRIGHTENED OF HIS OWN SHADOW! LUCKILY, HE'S GOT SHAGGY TO BE SCARED WITH—AND THEY USUALLY TAKE THEIR MIND OFF THINGS BY CHOWING DOWN ON SOME SNACKS.

WHO'S WHO?
DAPHNE

FULL NAME
DAPHNE BLAKE

AGE
16

HEIGHT
170 CM / 5 FT 7 IN

LIKES
SLEUTHING, BEING GLAMOROUS

DISLIKES
GETTING CAPTURED

THE DAUGHTER OF A MILLIONAIRE, REDHEAD DAPHNE IS MYSTERY INC.'S MOST GLAMOROUS MEMBER. BUT SHE'S NOT A SPOILT RICH KID, AND LOVES A GOOD MYSTERY AS MUCH AS THE REST OF THE GANG.

DAPHNE IN DANGER
IF ANYONE IS GOING TO ATTRACT TOUBLE, IT'S DAPHNE. YOU CAN BE SURE THAT SHE WILL FIND A TRAPDOOR INTO A SPOOKY DUNGEON OR FIND HERSELF KIDNAPPED BY A CREEPY VILLAIN.

GLAMOUR GIRL
HOWEVER BAD THINGS GET, DAPHNE ALWAYS MANAGES TO LOOK GREAT. IN HER FASHIONABLE PURPLE DRESS AND CLASSY LIME GREEN SCARF, SHE LOOKS LIKE SHE COULD COMBINE HER DETECTIVE WORK WITH A MODELING CAREER.

WHO'S WHO?
SHAGGY

FULL NAME
NORVILLE ROGERS

AGE
17

HEIGHT
182 CM / 6 FT

LIKES
PIZZA AND LARGE SANDWICHES

DISLIKES
SPOOKS, MONSTERS

HAIRY HIPPY SHAGGY IS A BIG COWARD. HE'S TOTALLY AFRAID OF ANYTHING SPOOKY AND WOULD RATHER BE SCARFING PIZZA THAN SOLVING MYSTERIES. NEVERTHELESS, HE'S ALWAYS THERE TO HELP HIS FRIENDS, ESPECIALLY SCOOBY.

FUNNY MAN
SHAGGY MAY BE SCARED OF EVERYTHING, BUT HE KEEPS HIMSELF HAPPY IN SCARY SITUATIONS BY TELLING SILLY JOKES. HIS RANGE OF DAFT DISGUISES ARE ALWAYS SURE TO KEEP THE REST OF THE GANG LAUGHING, TOO!

SHAGGY-SPEAK
SHAGGY HAS A WHOLE DICTIONARY FULL OF GROOVY PHRASES. HIS FAVORITE IS "ZOINKS!" HE LIKES TO SAY IT WHEN HE GETS SCARED...WHICH IS NEARLY ALL THE TIME!

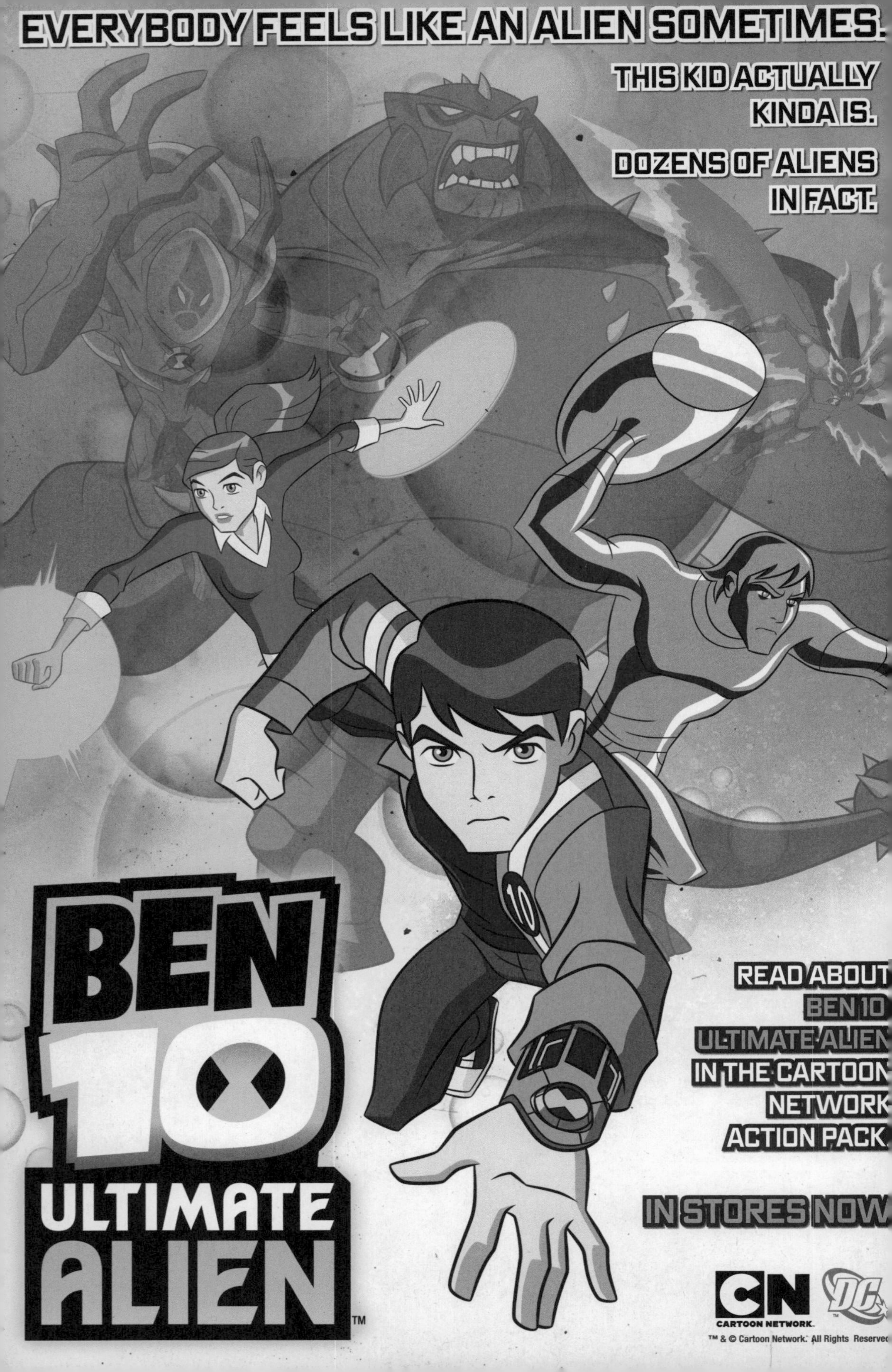
EVERYBODY FEELS LIKE AN ALIEN SOMETIMES.
THIS KID ACTUALLY KINDA IS.
DOZENS OF ALIENS IN FACT.
BEN 10 ULTIMATE ALIEN™
READ ABOUT BEN 10 ULTIMATE ALIEN IN THE CARTOON NETWORK ACTION PACK.
IN STORES NOW
CN CARTOON NETWORK.
DC
™ & © Cartoon Network. All Rights Reserved

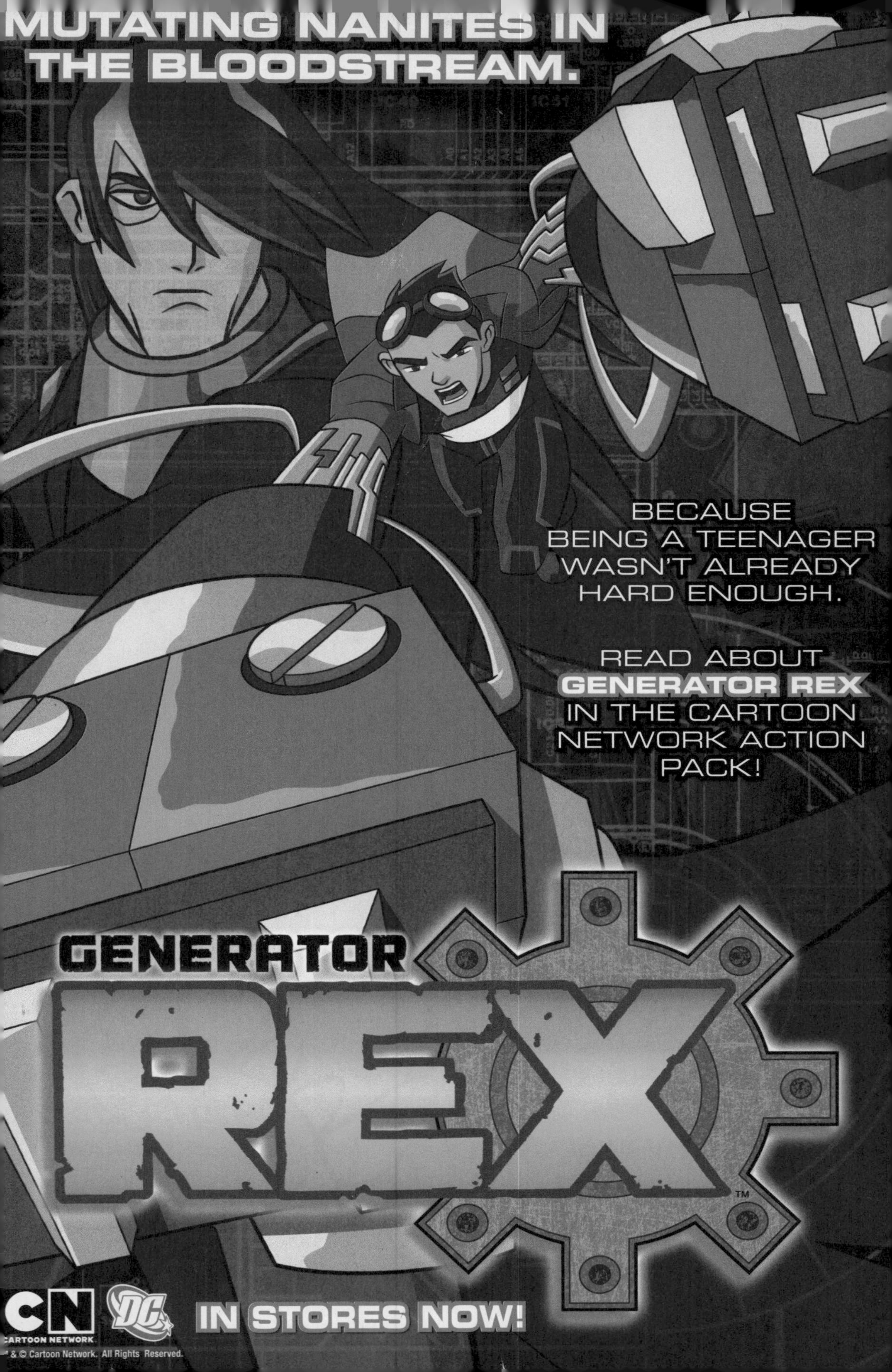
MUTATING NANITES IN THE BLOODSTREAM.
BECAUSE BEING A TEENAGER WASN'T ALREADY HARD ENOUGH.
READ ABOUT GENERATOR REX IN THE CARTOON NETWORK ACTION PACK!
GENERATOR REX™
CN CARTOON NETWORK
DC
IN STORES NOW!
™ & © Cartoon Network. All Rights Reserved.

Read the comic book based on the classic cartoons!